MARGARET ATWOOD:
WRITING AND SUBJECTIVITY

Also by Colin Nicholson

POEM, PURPOSE, PLACE: Shaping Identity in
Contemporary Scottish Verse

ALEXANDER POPE: Essays for the Tercentenary (*editor*)

CRITICAL APPROACHES TO THE FICTION OF
MARGARET LAURENCE (*editor*)

IAN CRICHTON SMITH: New Critical Essays (*editor*)

Margaret Atwood
photo credit: Graeme Gibson

Margaret Atwood: Writing and Subjectivity

New Critical Essays

Edited by

Colin Nicholson
Senior Lecturer in English
University of Edinburgh

St. Martin's Press

First published in Great Britain 1994 by
THE MACMILLAN PRESS LTD
Houndmills, Basingstoke, Hampshire RG21 2XS
and London
Companies and representatives
throughout the world

A catalogue record for this book is available
from the British Library.

ISBN 0–333–56475–8

Printed in Hong Kong

First published in the United States of America 1994 by
Scholarly and Reference Division,
ST. MARTIN'S PRESS, INC.,
175 Fifth Avenue,
New York, N.Y. 10010

ISBN 0–312–10644–0

Library of Congress Cataloging-in-Publication Data
Margaret Atwood : writing and subjectivity / edited by Colin
Nicholson.
p. cm.
Includes bibliographical references and index.
ISBN 0–312–10644–0
1. Atwood, Margaret Eleanor, 1939– —Criticism and
interpretation.   2. Subjectivity in literature.   I. Nicholson,
Colin.
PR9199.3.A8Z77 1994
818'.5409—dc20   93–6300
                                                                CIP

Contents

Acknowledgements

In a different version, Eleonora Rao's essay 'Atwood's *Lady Oracle*: Writing against Notions of Unity' first appeared in the *British Journal of Canadian Studies*, vol. 4, no. 1 (1989). W. J. Keith's essay 'Interpreting and Misinterpreting "Bluebeard's Egg": A Cautionary Tale' first appeared in *An Independent Stance: Essays on English-Canadian Criticism and Fiction* (Erin: Porcupine's Quill, 1991). Both are reprinted with permission.

The editor and publishers wish to thank Margaret Atwood for permission to reproduce the extracts from her books discussed in the following essays.

Notes on the Contributors

Isabel Carrera Suarez is a lecturer in English at the University of Oviedo, Spain. Her research interests centre on contemporary writing and literary theory, with emphasis on feminist criticism and post-colonial literatures.

Dennis Cooley is a poet who teaches at St John's College, University of Manitoba, Winnipeg. He has published several volumes of verse, including *Leaving* (1980), *Fielding* (1983), *Bloody Jack* (1984) and *Soul Searching* (1987). He edited *Draft: An Anthology of Prairie Poetry* in 1981, and in 1987 a collection of his critical essays, *The Vernacular Muse: The Eye and Ear in Contemporary Literature*, was published.

Mark Evans was a graduate student in the Department of English Literature at Edinburgh University, where he received his doctorate for a thesis on Margaret Atwood's writing.

Sherrill Grace is Professor of English at the University of British Columbia. She has published widely on twentieth-century Canadian, American and English literature, with books on Margaret Atwood and Malcolm Lowry and edited collections of essays on both writers. Her most recent book is *Regression and Apocalypse: Studies in North American Literary Expressionism* (1989). She is preparing an annotated edition of *The Collected Letters of Malcolm Lowry*.

Coral Howells is Reader in Canadian Literature at the University of Reading, and President of the British Association of Canadian Studies. Her books include *Private and Fictional Worlds: Canadian Women Novelists of the 1970s and 80s* (1987) and *Jean Rhys* (1991). In that year she co-edited *Narrative Strategies in Canadian Literature: Feminism and Postcolonialism*.

Janice Kulyk Keefer is a writer who teaches at the University of Guelph. She has published a volume of poetry, *White of the Lesser Angels* (1986), and three collections of short stories, *The Paris–Napoli Express* (1986), *Transfigurations* (1987) and *Travelling Ladies* (1991).

Her novel, *Constellations*, appeared in 1988. She has also written critical studies of maritime fiction and of Mavis Gallant.

W. J. Keith is Professor of English at the University of Toronto and a Fellow of the Royal Society of Canada. His books include *Richard Jefferies: A Critical Study* (1965), *Charles G. D. Roberts, Epic Fiction: The Art of Rudy Weibe* (1981). In 1985 his *History of Canadian Literature in English* was published.

Judith McCombs has held a Canadian Embassy Senior Fellowship and is now retired. Her *Critical Essays on Margaret Atwood* appeared in 1988, and *Margaret Atwood: A Reference Guide* which she co-authored, in 1991. As well as numerous articles on Atwood's work, she has published two books of poetry and some fiction.

Dieter Meindl is a Professor in North American Studies at the University of Erlangen-Nuremberg, Germany. Besides editing collections of critical essays, he has published monographs in German on William Faulkner (1974) and on the American novel between Naturalism and Postmodernism (1983). He has published numerous articles on American and Canadian topics and on narrative theory.

Colin Nicholson is senior lecturer in the Department of English Literature at the University of Edinburgh and editor of the *British Journal of Canadian Studies*. He has published widely on Canadian and Scottish writing, and has edited collections of critical essays on Alexander Pope (1988), Margaret Laurence (1990) and Iain Crichton Smith (1992). His book *Poem, Purpose, Place: Shaping Identity in Contemporary Scottish Poetry* was published in 1992.

Peter Quartermaine is a senior lecturer and a director of the Centre for American and Commonwealth Arts and Studies (AmCAS) at the University of Exeter. He has published widely on Commonwealth literature and arts; his most recent book is *Thomas Keneally* (1991).

Eleonora Rao studied for her doctorate on the longer prose works of Margaret Atwood at the University of Warwick. Her research interests include Virginia Woolf, Charlotte Perkins Gilman, Anna

Kavan and contemporary Canadian women writers. She is currently a research fellow in the Centre for Comparative Literature at the University of Toronto.

David Ward is senior lecturer in the School of English at the University of Dundee, and has taught in Africa, Canada and Malaysia. His books include *T. S. Eliot: Between Two Worlds* and *Chronicles of Darkness*

Introduction

COLIN NICHOLSON

Talking on BBC television about his successful film *Memphis Belle*, the producer David Puttnam described how his original intention of following the British crew of a Lancaster bomber during the Second World War had collapsed following his failure to raise sufficient funds in the UK. The story centred upon an aircraft's pilot and crew not dropping their bomb-load until they could clearly see their industrial target, located near a children's school. Since the availability of American financial backing was dependent upon American narrative contexts, the finished product consequently centred upon the youthful crew of a celebrated American B-49 Flying Fortress. British alterity was reduced to United States identity and Puttnam lamented the fact that because of this a British story could not be told in the way he had conceived it and in all probability would now never be told. In one perception this is no more than a parable of changed business priorities with Hollywood's bankers claiming the legitimate rights of those who pay the piper. A different frame of reference, though, might recognise it as another incidence of narrative expropriation in a dominant process of cultural displacement. Canadians may well be forgiven for looking on this particular example with mixed feelings.

If England, as the metropolitan centre of an erstwhile empire has to come to terms with a relative loss of control over its own story, then as Britain's last North American 'possession', Canada had already long been struggling to emerge first within and then away from British definitions and determinations. Simultaneously it was encountering the irresistible insinuations of America's commercial priorities, and became economically subordinate to the United States before it had freed itself from dominion status within Britain's imperial dispositions. Canadian history traces a transformation from one colonial mode into another. In any variety of way its ability to tell its distinctive varieties of story has always had to contend with powerful and in some mediums overwhelming discursive economies originating elsewhere. Not surprisingly, then, 'there is in the Canadian word', as Robert Kroetsch puts it, 'a concealed other experience, sometimes British, sometimes American.'[1] In such

1

circumstances the construction of authenticity in Canadian writing is problematised by the fact that centres of power located elsewhere and pursuing their own self-defined priorities authorise certain categories of experience at the expense of others. What the Nigerian writer Wole Soyinka has called the 'process of self-apprehension'[2] becomes fraught with difficulty when the structures of representation are predominantly developed and processed in and for metropolitan centres whose codes of recognition do not extend boundlessly. Over time these codes and the valorisations of experience they purvey generate a complicated dialectic of abrogation and appropriation in post-colonial writing,[3] and there now exists a considerable literary record in anglophone cultures around the world which traces these developments. As far as Canada is concerned, on another occasion Kroetsch ironically describes the narrator of T. C. Haliburton's 'The Clockmaker' (1836) as 'an early manifestation of the Canadian personality. The man who exploits social hierarchy by being falsely named into it wants also to be free of it. He wants to have a system that gives him identity and stature, but he wants to be free of that system. This man is surely ready to enter into the Canadian Federation.'[4] Codes of imperial prescription jeopardise colonial self-definition and in a complicated development from this, writing in post-colonial space then becomes a problem in and for itself. In part it became, in Dennis Lee's words, 'a search for authenticity, but all it could manage to be was a symptom of inauthenticity'.[5]

In the 20 years since 1972, when Margaret Atwood published her thematic guide, *Survival*, Canadian literary studies have come a long way. The polemic urgency of that volume, its propagandizing zeal, seems in retrospect out of key with both the nature and scope of the criticism we now read. 'I find that what I've written', Atwood remarks in a prefatory chapter, 'is ... a cross between a personal statement, which most books are, and a political manifesto, which most books also are, if only by default.'[6] She was writing to a particular context and she knew it. Her mode of direct personal address speaks a conversational intimacy with both her audience and her subject-matter, treating literary texts as ways of talking to each other and to us in a manner now disfavoured by theorising tendencies which defamiliarise and then abolish any communicative functions that might be looked for in poetry and fiction. The rhetoric of *Survival* was designed to meet particular needs. The 1960s had seen the kind of growth in Canadian writing that signified a far-reaching cultural and political change, and in response to this the country's educational curricula were being propelled into a recognition that a whole subject-area was opening up. Until that transforming decade, little had changed since Margaret Laurence's high-school days in the early 1940s when 'history was taught from the anglophone point of view . . . and . . . of course literature meant British literature'.[7] Atwood refers to the 1930s high-school teacher in Carol Bolt's play *Buffalo Jump* (1972) who requires his students to recite the names of all the wives of Henry VIII while a protest march is going past the window: 'He tells them they aren't in school to watch parades, which just about sums up the approach to Canadian history and culture that prevailed for many decades: history and culture were things that took place elsewhere, and if you saw them just outside the window you weren't supposed to look' (*S*, p. 18).

Many more people are now looking, both inside her own country and beyond, and as far as a wider world of attention is concerned, Atwood's creative output has played a significant part in stimulating contemporary interest in Canadian writing so that her own insistence in *Survival* is now being more readily acknowledged: 'The study of Canadian literature ought to be comparative, as should the study of any literature; it is by contrast that distinctive patterns show up most strongly. To know ourselves we must know our own literature; to know ourselves accurately, we need to know it as part of literature as a whole' (*S*, p. 17). Curiously, though, and then perhaps not so curiously, as Canadian writing as well as critical approaches to it have developed and widened their scope, it has become fashionable to disparage *Survival* as jejune and strategically unsound. According to Atwood writing a decade after its first appearance, this is nothing new:

> *Survival* was fun to attack. In fact it still is; most self-respecting professors of Canlit begin their courses, I'm told, with a short ritual sneer at it. It's true that it has no footnotes: the intended audience was not the footnote crowd, and it reached its intended audience, which was all those people whose highschool English teachers told them they weren't studying Canadian literature because there wasn't any.[8]

The patterns of image and response that *Survival* explores from an imaginative writer's point of view inevitably relate in part to

Atwood's poetry and fiction: 'several though by no means all of the patterns I've found myself dealing with . . . were first brought to my attention by my own work' (S, p. 14). But what then becomes interesting is the wider act of cultural construction that such a process of recovery entails; and Atwood confesses her surprise at finding 'the concerns of [*Survival*] shared by writers with whom – I found myself concluding – I seemed to participate in a cultural community that had never been defined for me' (S, p. 14). With hindsight it seems reasonable to conclude in turn that the academic sneer to which Atwood testifies might well relate to the fact that the now notorious 'basic victim positions' she proposed as typically encoded in a significant proportion of Canadian writing brought home in uncomfortably clarifying ways a set of cultural attributes and discursive predispositions that registered the shock of re-cognition in part because of the direct and uncluttered ways in which she first presented them. Arguing that 'the major profit from a colony is made in the centre of the empire', she suggests that 'of course there are cultural side-effects which are often identified as "the colonial mentality", and it is these which are examined here; but the root cause for them is economic . . . . And if you think Canada isn't a colony (or a collective victim), you'll be outraged by the reiteration of the victim theme' (S, pp. 36, 111):

Position One: To deny the fact that you are a victim.

Position Two: To acknowledge the fact that you are a victim, but to explain this as an act of Fate, the will of God, the dictates of Biology (in the case of women, for instance), the necessity decreed by History, or Economics, or the Unconscious, or any other large general powerful idea.

Position Three: To acknowledge the fact that you are a victim but to refuse to accept the assumption that the role is inevitable.

Position Four: To be a creative non-victim.   (S, pp. 36–7)

It is not difficult to see how this personalised programme would ruffle the security of prevailing complacencies, particularly within such male-dominated discourses as academic production and reproduction. Yet despite its provocative stance *Survival* was never meant to be prescriptive, still less dogmatic, but rather a preliminary exercise in identification and self-identification: 'it won't explain everything, but it may give you some points of departure' (*S*, p. 35). Looking back, what has become evident is that beyond its immediate domestic intentions *Survival* establishes parameters, in substance if not in terminology, for much of the recent theorising of post-colonial representations of literary subjectivity, whether Indian, African, Caribbean or Australian. 'If', Atwood writes, 'as has long been the case in [Canada], the viewer is given a mirror that reflects not him but somebody else, and told at the same time that the reflection he sees is himself, he will get a very distorted picture of what he is really like. He will also get a distorted idea of what other people are like' (*S*, p. 16). Generally concerned to challenge what Roland Barthes might have termed the 'myths' inscribed in literature and literary criticism emanating from imperial centres, a wide spectrum of the work that was to be carried out in the 1970s and 1980s relates in one way or another to Atwood's formulations.

But almost in contra-flow to the clear, expository style of *Survival*, Atwood's creative writing repeatedly puts in question such strategies of representation and location. As far as literary language is concerned, the oppressive relationships of imperial control mutate in post-colonial circumstances, shaping destabilising tensions between erstwhile colonisers and their linguistic centres of origin. Two years after the appearance of *Survival* Dennis Lee remarked that:

The colonial writer does not have words of his own. Is it not possible that he projects his condition of voicelessness into whatever he creates? That he articulates his own powerlessness, in the face of alien words, by seeking out fresh tales of victims? Over and above Atwood's account of it, perhaps the colonial imagination is driven to recreate, again and again, the experience of writing in colonial space . . .
Beneath the words our absentee masters have given us, there is an undermining silence. It saps our nerve. And beneath that silence there is a raw welter of cadence that tumbles and strains towards words and that makes the silence a blessing because it shushes easy speech. That cadence is home.[9]

These concerns recur in Atwood's writing. Necessarily, giving shape to Canadian cadence would involve a sustained attempt at establishing local alterity in the face of metropolitan determinations of purpose and place. 'There is', Atwood writes, 'a distinct archaeological motif in Canadian literature – unearthing the buried and forgotten past', and another of the figures she identifies as a thematic constant in her search for Canadian literary typicality is that of the explorer:

> 'Exploration' is a recurrent motif in Canadian literature, for reasons that I believe are not unconnected with the 'where is here' dilemma; that is, if a writer feels himself living in a place whose shape is unclear to him, a 'world but scarcely uttered,' to quote A. M. Klein's 'Portrait of the Poet as Landscape', one of his impulses will be to explore it, another will be to name it. (Mention of charts or maps – those direction-finding devices which attach names to place diagrams – is one clue that you're dealing with an exploration poem.) (*S*, pp. 114–15)

As she constructs her own utterance of person and place, foregrounding the intertexts she is herself negotiating, in her fiction Atwood produces patterns of textual archaeology and exploration in self-reflexive ways that connect her work to forms of attention in post-colonial – and postmodernist – writing elsewhere. But the first essay in this collection reads her earlier poetry to connect such archaeologising and explorer imagery with representations of female subjectivity within dominant cultural and social mythologies. As part of the politics of perception being examined, the map-making which several of these poems take as points of departure develops into a repudiation of the mimesis that besides providing a basis for cartographic practice, has traditionally promoted and ordered a stability of perception for the colonisers of textual space both domestically and abroad.[10] The function of mimesis in the representation of particular attitudes towards the reality being so ordered is brought into play, enabling a reading of mimetic codes as part of a signifying strategy whereby values and interests which are in fact specific to a certain place and time are projected as universal. Atwood's poetry specifies a Canadian personality and perception in invitational ways. Then, archaeologising textual production, Judith McCombs examines the ways in which *The Circle Game* (1966) selects and re-orders earlier poetry, revisiting the sites of its concern in a process of metamorphic re-vision. McCombs's detailed tracking of editorial procedures

exposes a series of paired and mirroring feminine iden
not all of which survive in the book's final form. Chance a
play their different parts as we watch *The Circle Ga*
towards publication.

Differently emphasised, Dennis Cooley's essay appropriat
of the idiomatic and colloquial modes of address that char
Survival to focus upon the role of voice in Atwood's poetic per
These sometimes querulous, sometimes fearful speakers str
control their narratives in contexts of evasion, fragment
or disguise. *Power Politics* (1973) is the volume mainly ur
consideration here, as Cooley traces an 'I' under siege and quest
for more secure locations in space. Uneasy correlations betwe
identity and place compose a continuing motif as the first-persc
pronoun encounters, at first gingerly – even caustically – but the
with increasing confidence, a recurrently masculine 'you' held in
nervy counterpoint. And these frontiers or boundaries are spatial
and as well as linguistic, as David Ward's account of the early novel
Surfacing (1972) makes clear. Mapping is both ontological and
topographical, making an approach to the text through Arnold van
Gennep's classic in comparative ethnography, *Les Rites de passage*
(1909) peculiarly resonant. Van Gennep's three moments, of
territorial separation, transition and incorporation, broadly coincide
with the novel's tripartite structure, and as his analysis proceeds,
Ward incorporates in turn Kristeva's work in semiotics to expose
strategies of becoming through myth and ritual. These processes of
self-construction connect with Peter Quartermain's reading of the
same novel's images of place and landscape as an attempt to locate
and identify a sense of self at once personal and cultural. Tracing
the tense-shift from present to past, the narrator's own past is seen
as surfacing through a time-loop of discovery. Memory is duplicitous, and an unstable sense of personal past contrasts with an
ability to 'place' others in the narrative. *Surfacing* operates
successfully as both mirror and map. Its sharp reflection of national
mythologies in the text's unfolding yields a teasing combination of
complex narrative and vivid regional locales.

In post-colonial experience the concept of an autonomous,
self-determining subjectivity, and more emphatically of female
subjectivity, is additionally problematised by the diversity
and volume of role-constructions, and particularly of gender-
constructions, inscribed in writing from the 'home' country. For a
country whose constitution was repatriated (the term itself

maintaining a whole set of subordinating assumptions) as recently as 1982, these pressures can assume defining significance, and literary form can itself encode a prescriptive writ constraining and containing attempts at differential composition. *Lady Oracle* (1976) plays intertextual games with Gothic forms and the expectations of popular romantic fiction in an effective challenge to generic and other hierarchies. Eleanora Rao's essay reads the novel as a comic deconstruction of codes of reading as well as of writing. Atwood's protagonist Joan Foster is a divided self, publishing under a pseudonym and presented in a narrative that separates her cheerful public voice from a silent one that is itself double-edged, being both discontented and desiring. Rao concedes that Atwood habitually involves her fiction in aspects and elements from other genres, other modes, and in that sense *Lady Oracle* is characteristic. But the novel which followed it, *Life Before Man* (1979), is not, and this prompts Janice Kulyk Keefer to consider why a story of deracinated, lower-middle-class urbanites, isolated and miserably pressured by the mundane, should also have proved so remarkably popular with a reading public.

Keefer brings a writer's attention to bear upon what she terms the 'minimalist form of naturalism' of *Life Before Man*, as well as its adoption of multiple forms of consciousness – male and female – 'to register overlapping and often contradictory perceptions of a rigidly controlled number of perceptions'. Locating the novel in the field of Atwood's fiction, Keefer discriminates its peculiar and compelling qualities. But different *Life Before Man* certainly is, not least for Atwood's temporary abandonment of her customary concerns with prior systems of signification. By contrast, *The Handmaid's Tale* (1985) composes Puritan New England mores into a disturbing precursor for its oppressive dystopia, and the text's ancestral voices are exposed by Mark Evans to a historicist reading of some of those seventeenth-century actualities signalled by Atwood's named dedicatees for this novel. Sources in the past for *The Handmaid's Tale*'s unnerving descent into a present thinly veiled as future are brought to light. Recursive structures differently conceived are the subject of Sherrill Grace's inventive treatment of Atwood's recurrent use of an autobiographical 'I'. Grace's reconsideration of what constitutes feminist autobiography focuses upon *Lady Oracle*, *The Handmaid's Tale* (1985) and *Cat's Eye* (1988) to test our gendered assumptions concerning identity. Identifying the traditional autobiography as a central object of parody in *Lady*

Oracle, Grace contrasts Joan Foster's story-telling as that of a born escape-artist with the more fundamental existential challenge faced by Offred in *The Handmaid's Tale*. In both novels life-stories confirm being, make real to themselves their speaking subjects even as they provide avenues of escape from oppressive predefinitions. But Offred's voice is textually appropriated by Professor Pieixoto's concluding 'Historical Notes on The Handmaid's Tale' in a narrative tactic which radically questions any notion of predetermined genre. Male recuperation of female textuality perpetuates strategies of reading as modes of domination.

From comic deconstructions of traditional assumptions about autobiography in *Lady Oracle* to a questioning of the very possibility of self-construction in *The Handmaid's Tale*, Grace sees *Cat's Eye* as a recapitulation of the tactics of representation in those earlier texts but shaped, now, into 'a new, complex and deeply satisfying image of the female self'. Joan Foster's apologetic self-questioning and Offred's fragmented stammering is resolved into Elaine Risley's confident reflections, and a formative development in Atwood's fiction is manifest in an emerging autobiographical 'I' that is textually secure and self-aware. Extending Grace's treatment in a different direction, Coral Howells pursues the theme of feminine life-writing in *Cat's Eye* through the novel's combination of discursive memoir and the 'figural' versions of subjectivity presented through Elaine Risley's paintings: a double figuration of the self. 'While Elaine's discursive narrative remains incomplete, ... her paintings [act] as a kind of corrective to the distortions and suppressions of memory and [offer] the possibility of theoretical solutions.' Howells tracks Atwood's paradoxical exposure of the limits of autobiography and its artifice of reconstruction.

The last three essays in this collection turn their attentions to Atwood's short fiction, with *Dancing Girls* (1977) and *Bluebeard's Egg* (1983) forming the basis of Dieter Meindl's consideration of the gender and narrative perspectives they encode. Hingeing narrative perspective between authorial and figural frames of reference, Meindl groups the tales into themes of non-communication and victimisation. Together with an examination of such techniques as tense-use and first-person narration, modernist and post-modernist elements are exposed, to determine that the prototypical Atwood story is a dual or polar affair in being both woman-derived and man-focused. But in a different consideration of *Dancing Girls, Bluebeard's Egg* and also including *Wilderness Tips*

(1991), Isabel Carrera Suarez detects a shift in emphasis from individual soul-searching subjectivities in the first of these to more expansive treatments in the two subsequent collections. This correlates with a shift from an earlier deterministic view of the limits of language to a critique of its use as an instrument of power and towards the possibility of a feminist expropriation of its instrumentality. Carrera Suarez describes an affirmative drift in the range of fictions she discusses. Finally, in a cautionary tale for all of us, W. J. Keith closes the volume with an account of the pitfalls that can be encountered when an ideologically committed reading of a single Atwood story substitutes for the words on the page its own predetermined expectations.

Notes

1. Robert Kroetsch, 'Unhiding the Hidden: Recent Canadian Fiction', *Open Letter*, Fifth Series, vol. 4 (1983) p. 17.
2. Wole Soyinka, *Myth, Literature and the African World* (Cambridge, 1976) p. xi.
3. See Bill Ashcroft, Gareth Griffiths and Helen Tiffin, *The Empire Writes Back: Theory and Practice in Post-colonial Literatures* (London, 1989) p. 38ff.
4. Robert Kroetsch, 'Canadian Writing: No Name Is My Name,' in David Staines (ed.), *The Forty-Ninth and Other Parallels: Contemporary Canadian Perspectives* (Amherst, Mass., 1986) p. 118.
5. Dennis Lee, 'Cadence, Country, Silence: Writing in Colonial Space', *Boundary*, vol. 2, no. 3 (Fall, 1977) p. 1.
6. Margaret Atwood, *Survival: A Thematic Guide to Canadian Literature* (Toronto, 1972) p. 17. Subsequent citations will be marked *S* and page-numbers given parenthetically.
7. Margaret Laurence, *Dance on the Earth: A Memoir* (Toronto, 1989) p. 77.
8. Margaret Atwood, *Second Words: Selected Critical Prose* (Toronto, 1982) pp. 105–6.
9. Lee, 'Cadence, Country, Silence', pp. 162, 165.
10. See Graham Huggan, 'Decolonizing the Map: Post-colonialism, Post-structuralism and the Cartographic Connection' in *Past the Last Post: Theorizing Post-colonialism and Post-modernism* (Brighton, 1991) pp. 125–38.

1

Living on the Edges: Constructions of Post-Colonial Subjectivity in Atwood's Early Poetry

COLIN NICHOLSON

In an article called 'Permanently Canadian' Al Purdy tempers impatience with irony as he returns to the difficult assumptions involved in debates about nationalism and individuality: 'Certainty of nationality and personality is an illusion, since there is no permanence in anything, anything at all. And yet we cling to this shifting and uncertain self, this rag of ageing bone, this handful of dust to which we've given a loved name.'[1] Purdy's protest at the coercive unification implicit in the notion of a self-conscious, self-identifying subject connects with one of the central themes of post-structuralism, and in such contexts Margaret Atwood's poetry gathers to itself the defining attributes of a Canadian paradigm. Her elaborate constructions of a post-colonial subjectivity encode a running parallel between the conditioning of Canada as a nation-state and the positioning of women within it, and then by extension the positioning of women within any governing patriarchy. It has already been argued that the circumference of Atwood's imagination is often contained by Canada's national and literary boundaries: 'it is almost as if she consciously sets herself down, right in the middle of the Canadian literary landscape, and tries to orient herself by filtering Canadian experience through archetypes of her poetic sensibility.'[2] Geographical locations and the figuring of selfhood form a continuing motif of uncertainty and anxiety, as words come into conflict with a seemingly recalcitrant environment. But Atwood as often interrogates any notion of a subject, expressing a meaning, through which the world is presented to that subject.

Insofar as it is held to be a founding intervention in the creation of the (male, white) humanist subject, the Cartesian ego that thought and therefore was is destabilised in Atwood's poetry: the principles of subjectivity and its prevalent forms of representation are themselves at issue, and Atwood speaks to reading subjects beyond her domestic, Canadian parameters.

The celebrated opening poem of *The Circle Game* (1966), 'This is a Photograph of Me', springs the same kind of surprise as does Magritte's caption for his painting of a tobacco-smoker's implement: 'This is not a pipe'. But the poem sets itself up as an invitational speech act, in which an assumed relationship between the speaking subject and any reader is implicitly accepted, only to be explicitly disconcerted. One result is that the dividing line between speech and its objects is blurred, as is our understanding of the subject implied by that speech. By using metaphors of self-representation to start a pattern of drowning imagery which then constantly recurs, a position of indeterminacy is conjured which paradoxically becomes a defining characteristic when it acknowledges that both the speaker's location and her dimensions are hardly to be detected: 'It is difficult to say where / precisely, or to say / how large or small I am.'³ 'Who and where am I?' asks the poem, 'and where do you the reader come from?' In compensation, 'This is a Photograph of Me' opens up dialogic space with the addressee, and ends by promising satisfaction if the desiring gaze perseveres in intersubjective exploration.

> the effect of water
> on light is a distortion
>
> but if you look long enough,
> eventually
> you will be able to see me.
>   (CG, p. 11)

What is occurring is a foregrounding of the *direction* of the gaze, in a calculated disruption of assumptions about the subject as self-grounding and self-transparent, since the evidences a perceiving subject has open to it are merely evidences and not the states of affairs themselves, of which they are only the evidence. The poem sets up a field of tension between an identity that cannot be represented and a representation which is not easily acceptable as that of identity. The positioning of any witnessing public outside the ontology of a speaking subject becomes, in turn, a subject of Atwood's writing. A questioning of accepted boundaries between representational practices and disciplines is common to both feminism and post-structuralism, and the word which turns our attention from a photographically visual form of referentiality to another linguistic-poetic form is 'scan' in the poem's sixth line: 'then, as you scan / it, you see in the left-hand corner / a thing that is like a branch' (*CG*, p. 11). The terms of similitude are themselves at question here, as a remarkable poem opens for consideration the possibility that a perceiving subject including and centring upon woman, is not so much exterior to the system of representation as reduced to invisibility within it, subordinated to a system hitherto controlled from elsewhere: both the snapshot and the language which describes it are forms of containment. Atwood thus explores conceptions of a unified subject as well as the givenness of a unified subject's perceptions, in a process which inevitably entails a readerly participation towards differential reassembly. Elsewhere, while representation is preserved as a system through which meaning, a specifying world of landscape, and the possibility of subjectivity itself is produced, she will question continuous temporal process as she formulates an ontology of Canadian actuality which in the dominant codes of representation is, like women in a broader spectrum of attention, at one and the same time in history and not in history.

'After the Flood, We' extends water imagery and introduces other specifying patterns of imagery – a post-apocalyptic mode of survival in the company of a human other who remains protectively enclosed and refusing participation in the difficult tasks of negotiated perception. Not knowing, not hearing, not seeing anything apart from surface structures, this other abandons the possibility of communication between the human and the specular world. Also triggered in this poem and subsequently to recur, is an equally difficult emergence of human form, often facially presented, from rock: 'the almost-human / brutal faces forming / (slowly) / out of stone' (*SP*, p. 10). A fondness for bizarre images sometimes incorporating hazard and menace further contextualises a marginalised yet expansive consciousness struggling towards a firmer purchase on identity. This voice earns the right to claim representative status on behalf of all experience relegated to peripheral status:

> I move
> and live on the edges
> (what edges)
> I live
> on all the edges there are.
>
> (*CG*, p. 16)

In a movement beyond that marginalised perspective, 'A Messenger' figures a male from a world of signification which excludes the perceiving subject – a woman – from his codes of identity. The poem as a whole, though, refuses that position and instead proposes the feminine as elaborating, alternative processes of self-constitution which transcend the male's, leaving him:

> shouting at me
> (specific) me
> desperate messages with his
> obliterated mouth
>
> in a silent language.
>
> (*CG* p. 14)

Masculine dominance over colonised space – 'forcing her universe to his / geography' (*CG*, p. 18) – is experienced by a younger sister in 'An Attempted Solution for Chess Problems' before ambiguities in the poem's conclusion expose the threat of male coercive power to the possibility that the sister might assume his garments of aggression:

> In her cellar the mailed
> costumes rustle
> waiting to be put on.
>
> (*CG*, p. 18)

Appropriating as female this geography of contestation, and reading into its space male cycles of innocence and predation, 'In My Ravines' inscribes woman in the construction of representation. As the poem moves towards a striking image of cyclically recurrent masculine violence to younger selves, the present tense of 'small boys climbing' transforms into the past of 'young boys climbed' and the word 'eyelid' inserts the blink of a gaze which sees no escape for them in the self-enclosing progressions of boyhood to violent maturity:

> while the young boys
> climbed and swung
> above them wildly
> in the leafless eyelid
> veins and branches
> of a bloodred night
> falling, bursting purple
> as ancient rage
> (*CG*, p. 19)

Initially sustaining distances between inner and outer realms of experience are collapsed when 'A Descent Through the Carpet' shifts into an area that will increasingly occupy Atwood's attention, her fascinated representations of feral existence and experience. Ironising a developing pattern of submersion the poem brings to the surface conjunctions of autobiographical data (Atwood was born in 1939 on the eve of the Second World War), parameters of geological time, and threatened senses of survival: 'here / to be aware is / to know total / fear' (*CG*, p. 22). Beyond a patterned domesticity the poem disrupts inherited notions of continuous time to drift backward through a paradisal state 'overfilled / with giving' and into a hostile temporality. The economy of desire glimpsed here gives way to an unfulfilled economy of need where human succour finds no response in the world where the teeth of savage competition – 'the cold jewelled symmetries' – emphasise that survival of the fittest promises no continuity since 'the voracious eaten' and 'the voracious eater' cannot be discriminated. In these contexts, 'here' is where we all are. Few writers have inscribed the body so insistently at the centre of her work, and Atwood's poetics of desire combines with her continually historicising consciousness to connect an imagery of human anatomy, in this instance her infant self, with predecessors beyond conventional time-frames and back along the evolutionary chain:

> my fisted
> hand
>   my skin
> holds

remnants of ancestors

fossil bones and fangs

(*CG*, p. 23)

Typically, the poem extends an image already deployed in 'After the Flood, We', where a speaker 'walk[s] across the bridge' over engulfing waters: 'gathering the sunken / bones of the drowned mothers / (hard and round in my hands)' (*CG*, p. 12). Thus retrieved, the human body, and particularly for Atwood the female body, constitutes a ground of possibility for the construction of identity, as the creative aspect of the feminine, its capacity to resist the destructive orderings of a masculine identity, are flexed and developed. Prior to being satirised in 'The City Planners', a masculine pragmatism blindly asserting its 'efficient' powers in prolonging a technological (and destructive) dominance over nature is sardonically exposed in 'Man with a Hook'. At its root, such male rationalisation can be read as a psychoanalytic category defined by Laplanche and Pontalis as a 'procedure whereby the subject attempts to present an explanation that is either logically consistent or ethically acceptable for attitudes, ideas, feelings, etc., whose true motives are not perceived.'[4] In language that drily accepts technological mastery as in some ways superior to human aptitudes, Atwood presents her male figure as blind not only to his own motivation but necessarily refusing to interrogate those attitudes to the natural world which produced his maimed state.

Unassumingly epic in scope and often ironically self-deprecating, Atwood's writing project both embodies and resists inherited definitions and determinations. As part of her strategy of contesting discursive priorities which effectively colonise the scripted space available for self-definition, she develops an archaeologising imagery in a process of cultural retrieval and differentiation. That strategy foregrounds writing itself, scrutinising the act of textual clarification, and establishing it as the necessary site of reorganised power-relationships: and her foregrounding opens a space in which reifying and disintegrative pressures might be reformulated beyond 'scraps glued together / waiting for a chance / to come to life' (*CG*, p. 30). Recognising that an important concern of modernism focuses upon the attempted retrieval of classical ideals in a form compatible with contemporary conditions, Atwood engages in her own reinventions of the past. In so far as they serve to stabilise hierarchies of power, the possession and control of myths and of mythic structures becomes part of a pattern of literary contestation. Responding to such previously hegemonic interpretations and their cultural function of securing prevailing dispositions, Atwood flexes her own shape-changing capacities, displacing Homer's shape-changer Proteus by a containing and controlling female power:

> I held you
> through all your shifts
> of structure: while your bones turned
> from caved rock back to marrow
> (*CG*, p. 12)

What then complicates Atwood's response is a returning feminine complicity in male power-relations even when his narrative supremacy has been effectively dislodged:

> your flesh has no more stories
> or surprises;
>
> my face flinches
> under the sarcastic
> tongues of your estranging
> fingers,
> the caustic remark of your kiss.
> (*CG*, p. 32)

The equation of speech and story with bodily process in 'Eventual Proteus' also establishes a continuing form of attention in Atwood's verse. If the limit of her words is the limit of her world then she will constantly test how extensible those limits are. As part of her engagement with physical contours of subjectivity, language itself encodes the difficulties of self-definition in what is always a definingly prior system of signification. As she develops her production of meaning and identity, contesting masculine positions of assertion and innovation, patterns of complicity and differentiation in male/female coalitions both determine and are determined by linguistic constructions of identity and relationship extending from intimate to national and on to transnational spheres of experience. It has been part of Atwood's particular achievement in the postwar world of anglophone writing to co-ordinate the position of woman writing in a male-dominated world of discourse with newly emergent post-colonial structures of consciousness.[5] Ontological figures of possession and repudiation speak political dimensions, as seeing and being in the personal realm articulate being and seeing on the plane of cultural self-recognition. 'The early / languages are obsolete', claims 'Eventual Proteus', and continuing cross-pollinations of gender-formation in the social construction of reality come to suggest alternative possibilities. As a case in point, a western consumption ethic and the codes of propriety it engenders are foregrounded in 'A Meal', and subversively reconstituted to include 'the necessary cockroach / in the flesh / that nests in dust' (*CG*, p. 33). The conquering of revulsion encodes an extension of sympathy in a gesture of self-control explicitly challenging male self-mastery.

Watching children at play leads to a series of meditations in the title-sequence of Atwood's first volume which explore further some of these concerns. The sequence breaks into Romantic idylls of childhood innocence to read them instead as paradigms of mindless pleasure in which a surrounding ecology is ignored, and where maladjusted rhythms of movement displace responsive con-sciousness. An opening section reconstructs this tranced dancing as a North American parable of unconcern, a motion without direction which disguises isolation as a spurious collectivity and masks alienation in a display of togetherness. Deriving from this childhood, the adults in the second movement of the sequence contend with consequent problems of subjectivity and perception. If subjectivity presupposes reflection, a representation of experience as that of an experiencing subject, then intersubjectivity is problematised, and the fluidity of intuition jeopardised:

> Being with you
> here, in this room
>
> is like groping through a mirror
> whose glass has melted
> to the consistency
> of gelatin
>
> (*CG*, p. 26)

Metaphors of mirroring in 'The Circle Game' inventively propose the impossibility of pure self-presence:

You refuse to be
(and I)
an exact reflection, yet
will not walk from the glass,
be separate.

(*CG*, p. 36)

This house of mirrors '(chipped, hung crooked)' suggests the problematic construction of a Canadian subjectivity and the difficult location of its appropriate linguistic home. At the level of perception and self-perception the silent question 'who are we?' merges into the equally unspoken enquiry 'where is here?' And these complications are directly linked to the distracting proximity of an unknown neighbour occupying part of the same house:

There is someone in the next room

There is always

(your face
remote, listening)

someone in the next room.

(*CG*, p. 37)

What then happens is that the opening poem of the sequence is revisited and re-read as a mechanism of defence against a history of violence and threat. Ironically chiding the 'garrison mentality' of an earlier Canadian paradigm, water returns to obliterate the children's sand trenches 'fortified with pointed sticks'. The pathos of their 'last attempt' to make 'maybe, a refuge human / and secure' is again underlined by the threatening presence of 'whatever walks along / (sword hearted) / these night beaches'. Hesitancy and indeterminacy convey a sense of fragility and impermanence, and a corresponding nervousness permeates the 'calculated ploys / of the body, the witticisms of touch' by which the adult male and female encounter and avoid each other. This fourth section, having returned to adult enclosure, then dissects a male appropriation of language and space; an appropriation that is also read as a defensive attempt: 'to keep me / at a certain distance / and (at length) avoid / admitting I am here' (*CG*, p. 39). Watching male gender-

constructions in operation, the female voice makes explicit those
patterns of correspondence which have hitherto been intimated: the
mapping of the body and the designation of the body politic become
discernible as cognate activities. These are fraught activities for the
feminine. Like the younger sister in the chess game, the speaker here
also confronts a masculine control of recall and a male coloniser of
discursive space who is:

> a memorizer
> of names (to hold
> these places
> in their proper places)

With woman thus reduced to the status of a signified in someone
else's signifying practice, the poem structures a rival process of
identity and recall by invoking as intertext the silenced other in
John Donne's American 'new-found-land', where woman is figured
as a 'kingdome, safeliest when with one man mann'd',[6] mapped
and exposed as a construct of male desire. Atwood gives this
colonised woman voice:

> and I am fixed, stuck
> down on the outspread map
> of this room, of your mind's continent.
>   (*CG*, p. 40)

   The childhood idyll put at question in the sequence's opening is
revealed as generating male dreams of possession and control
which the fifth movement traces in turn to a mystification of history
and the historical identity thereby produced. Canadian paradigms
of the fortress mentality, and the ontologies they have shaped,
create the conditions for a role-playing subjectivity in which the
speaker acknowledges partial complicity and which is more a
strategy of evasion than of interpersonal commitment. Through a
masculine inheritance of codes of perception, Romantic archetypes
of childhood and the art and ritual they inspired link an adult
world to ways of being and seeing that divide and separate: for the
male other as for the children, 'there is no joy in it'. Atwood's title-
sequence looks for nothing less than an abolition of the
competences and assumptions implicit in the paradigms she
exposes. So when we read 'as we lie / arm in arm, neither / joined

nor separate', we encounter an image of the personal which reverberates with complicating North American relationships, adding further political resonances to the female's understanding of the ways in which the male's construction and location of her identity seeks to transform her into 'a spineless woman in / a cage of bones, obsolete fort / pulled inside out'.

First appearing in this title-sequence and to recur in her writing, the idea of the trace both as recorded surface detail and as marking a survival into the present of earlier significations gives another insight into Atwood's technique. As she constructs and positions a personal response to Canada's circumstance in relation to a colonial past, an American-dominated present and on-going constitutional per-plexities of national self-definition, she engages in a cartography of the imagination at once deconstructive and reconstructive. Since the dominant culture within and against which Canadian artists operate is self-evidently that of the United States, it becomes germane to Atwood's developing design that a tracing of Canadian difference should form a constant attraction. As a creative preliminary, 'The Circle Game' sequence ends with a voiced desire to 'erase all maps' and to disrupt a trancing encirclement: 'I want the circle broken'. It is an example of Atwood bringing into deconstructive play the assumption that subjectivity is something self-contained, isolated from and standing over against an other that is the object of knowledge. Her poetry habitually returns to the pathos of a self, as often as not male, confined within the circles of its own constructed perceptions and unable to make contact with anything external which does not turn out to be simply the activity of 'watching / your own reflection somewhere / behind my head' (*CG*, p. 37). If 'This is a Photograph of Me' took codes of representation as its topic, then 'Camera' speaks directly to an omnipresent construction of perception which reduces alterity to its own determinations of containment. 'You want this instant' goes the poem's opening line and the dominance of this perceiving ego is denounced as an arbitrary coercion. In the compulsive identifying of the photographer we encounter a willed sacrifice of future becomings to a moment's control. The mastery of nature for an organised instant is repudiated as a stasis against which the poem mobilises natural energies of change and flux while comically transforming the feminine subject into a vanishing point of invisibility.

Such propositions of a world of feminine alterity discompose the male attempt to lay static systems over it, and these tensions at the heart of subjectivity form another continuing motif. 'Spring in the Igloo' composes a compelling image of domestic entrapment arising from a coercive centring of subjectivity: 'We who thought we were living / in the center of a vast night' are decentred by developing human awareness of an earth which 'turns for its own reasons / ignoring mine, and these human miscalculations'. But continued enclosure within that garrison mentality which once secured a European colonisation of the wilderness now finds difficulty in breaking out into the thawing perceptions of modernity. The poem takes its place in a wider construction of change as a function of continuity, and rehearses a moment from *Circle Games* where locations for a constructed subjectivity – 'where you could be / if only by comparison, a / substitute for sun' – are themselves subjected to change and flux, from a cosmic (in this case heliotropic) centring to shifting and less controllable developments. So change entails indeterminacy as an inevitable consequence, and given an environment of fearful potential, whether encoded externally as hostile climate or internally as frozen presuppositions, a thawing of fixity brings dangerous uncertainties: 'with ice the only thing / between us and disaster' (*CG*, p. 48). Such pressures and indeterminacies create conditions for despair as the schizophrenic self-image of 'A Sibyl' makes clear, and Atwood's conjuration of the figure of death strikes a disconcerting familiarity:

> time runs out
> in the ticking hips of the
> man whose twitching skull
> jerks on loose
> vertebrae in my kitchen
> (*CG*, p. 50)

But what is also in process of construction is an aesthetic of cognitive mapping[7] in which Canadian prehistory will be imagistically recalled to install a sense of discrimination-in-similarity from dominant United States literary practice. North American palaeontology elides national boundaries, but in her persistent inscription of the prehistorical record Atwood registers a distinctive approach to the task and possibility of cultural retrieval. Gambling that the way forward is the way back, 'Migration: C.P.R.' (*CG*, pp. 52–6) will help to reinstate alternative systems of signification. Welcomed by a Canadian reader as 'one of the best individual poems in the collection', and one in which the speaker and her companion are 'trapped ... in the nets of ancestors and language',[8] its return to 'not-quite- / forgotten histories' charts a possible escape from 'allegories / in the misty east, where inherited events / barnacle on the mind' through a westward journey away from oppressive ideologies of the past. The poem interrogates positions of uncertain enclosure – 'facing / neither sea- / wards nor inland' – and dramatises an acknowledgement that entrapping modes of thought must be untangled, and that the language which reproduces those positions becomes a system of authority to be reorganised. The desire for 'a place of absolute / unformed beginning' proves delusive, since travellers always carry with them 'too much of ancient oceans / first flood': unformed beginnings are always already inscribed with earlier experience, which in turn pre-scribes perception. 'Even the mountains' are read as allegories of subjective response in which language shapes and determines:

> (tents
> in the desert? triangular
> ships? towers? breasts?
> words)
>
> (CG, p. 53)

Although these colonising travellers jettison emotional freight during their developing encounter with geographical reality, and step 'unbound' and with 'faces scraped as blank / as we could wish them' into different space, residual structures of feeling survive with them, and acceptance that 'many / have passed the same way / some time before / this' attaches them to a history which precedes European incomers. The recovery and deciphering of this earlier story and history are characteristically registered parenthe-tically (to suggest, perhaps, the tenuousness of the venture), but none the less produced for inspection: '(like an inscribed shard, broken bowl / dug at a desert level, where they thought / no man had been / or a burned bone)'. As the poem shores these fragments against the ever-pending ruin of an historical community, early traces connect inscription here with '(hieroglyphics / carved in the bark)' a little later, and Atwood's interest in perceptual con-structions of the world we move through is given different emphasis when a 'Journey to the Interior', as ontological as it is geographical, foregrounds the subjective construal of similitude:

> There are similarities
> I notice: that the hills
> which the eyes make flat as a wall, welded
> together, open as I move
> to let me through
>
> (*CG*, p. 57)

Against masculine codes of subordination and control, the poem sets a mapping of the self in a world of words which will always privilege transformation. Seeing and being are intimately compromised in contexts of a permanently shifting chiaroscuro where:

> travel is not the easy going
> from point to point, a dotted
> line on a map, location
> plotted on a square surface
> but that I move surrounded by a tangle
> of branches, a net of air and alternate
> light and dark, at all times;
> that there are no destinations
> apart from this.
>
> (*SP*, p. 30[9])

And while 'Journey to the Interior' suggests the self-consciousness and difficulty of this alternative mapping of cultural identity, it also implies the inadequacies of language, voiced or written, in Canadian space: 'Words here are as pointless / as calling in a vacant / wilderness', where neither maps nor language serve an easily apprehended deictic function. An ever-present threat of disintegration is emphasised in the poem's closing recognition that: 'it is easier for me to lose my way / forever here, than in other landscapes'.

In different ways, 'Some Objects of Wood and Stone' continues the trace of Canadian archaeology in terms which extend the search for an appropriate language. An identification with the totems of native North American culture is as intense and immediate as it is unspoken, and there is, too, a clear awareness of native spirituality lending a depth and resonance to experience that is now felt as an absence. The difficulty of shaping a language responsive to this psycho-territorial complexity is broached. 'Pre-Amphibian'

assumes female control over the mapping of another self's contours. Construction of the subject requires a calculation 'according
to solidities' but orgasm suggests an ontological merging into the
evolutionary chain to project a unifying paradigm and an image of
renewal:

> but here I blur
> into you   our breathing sinking
> to green milleniums
> and   sluggish   in our blood
> all ancestors
> are warm fish moving.
>
> (*CG*, p. 63)

Metaphors of fixity contending with motion reappear in 'Against
Still Life' where transformation in a renewal of uttered story
positions woman as coaxing this response from the male in a process of continual becoming. That recovery and renewal ironically
reconstructs the closing moment of 'This is a Photograph of Me' but
now with woman eliciting a truth-telling: 'If I watch / quietly
enough / and long enough // at last, you will say // . . . all I need
to know' (*CG*, pp. 66–7). 'The Islands' represents another taking to
task of the assumption that subjectivity is self-defining and
standing separate from the world it perceives, while 'Letters,
Towards and Away' explores the difficult demands of love-
relationships in a continuing sway between power and independence, response and subordination, and between self-determination
and libidinal need for a human other.

But in 'A Place: Fragments', the very title of which registers
characteristic concerns, we watch a development from periphera-
lising imagery jeopardised but persistent at the poem's opening to a
geological metaphor where: 'The land flows like a / sluggish
current. / The mountains eddy slowly towards the sea' (*CG*, p. 74).
Setting that kind of timescale renders manageable the sense of loss
and uncertainty which the poem explores. This poem is a
significant document in Atwood's elaboration of post-colonial
alterity, and one which brings into focus both the problematised
subjectivity characteristic of postmodernist writing and the post-
colonial desire to move from positions of marginalisation, not to
opposing versions of falsely centred subjectivity but towards an
acceptance of identity defined in and through relationships that are

themselves shifting, specular and permanently in process of construction. Visiting an old woman of Scottish descent triggers reflection upon the fragility of cultural ordering in Canadian space. From the peripheral perspective of an isolated house in 'a little-visited province', an urban pedestrian is seen walking a brittle surface over 'vegetable decay / or crust of ice that / might easily break and / slush or water under / suck him down'. A favoured metaphor relocates specific subjectivity in geological formations over aeons of time which then creates destabilising conditions of fluidity in the human realm. But for a subject-position 'cringing / under the cracked whip of winter', the prospect of sensuous engagement in a 'patch / of lichen / and in love, tangle of limbs and fingers' is not always an option. Accordingly, the final movement of the poem registers a sense of loss related to apprehensions that appropriate cultural inscription is either 'locked against us' or 'just not found yet'. The quest for that language is the stuff of Atwood's writing and 'A Place: Fragments' closes on a wager that linguistic processes of archaeological retrieval might yet discover a fit speech:

> that informs, holds together
> this confusion, this largeness
> and dissolving:
>
> not above or behind
> or within it, but one
> with it: an
>
> identity:
> something too huge and simple
> for us to see.
>
> (CG, p. 76)

The two poems which close this collection seems to be paired in a discordant kind of way, one constructing a posture of negative irony towards survival and the other opening into more-promising possibilities. In 'The Explorers', the island image recurs in a structure of parenthesis which repeats a hesitant, self-deprecatory stance towards the narrative being presented. A tone of wry satire looks back upon the progress of the male and female figures who have become the space upon which many of the volume's tensions are inscribed, in a re-processing of material that is to characterise a good deal of Atwood's output. But now the discoverers will arrive too late, and only cannibalised skeletons remain to be deciphered; bones which thereby join those that have formed part of the collection's archaeologising mode. There is a mordantly self-reflexive edge to the irony here, as some of the poetic strategies earlier deployed take their own place in a too-long-delayed act of textual excavation and recovery. History, though, will always decentre earlier subjectivities, and 'The Settlers' who close the volume open another epoch. In ironic reprise of the image of the human emerging from rock in the book's second poem, centuries after 'The Explorers' arrived 'several minutes' too late, these new settlers 'dug us down / into the solid granite / where our bones grew flesh again, / came up trees and / grass' (*CG*, p. 79). Though calcified, the human bodies which have been the site of various circle games still sustain the life-cycle and lend it historical resonance, even if an ignorance of their existence continues to be a condition of youthful Canadian perception:

> Now horses graze
> inside this fence of ribs, and
>
> children run, with green
> smiles, (not knowing
> where) across
> the fields of our open hands.
>   (*CG*, p. 80)

With the appearance of *The Animals in That Country*[10] in 1968 it became clear that Atwood's concern with establishing differential positions for a Canadian culture still defensively fragile in the face of invasive United States valorisations had deepened and broadened. As the participating interdependence which she speaks and represents reinvents its origins, she identifies the play of power structures in often disconcerting ways. Responding to experience becomes something of a metaphor in itself as she revisits earlier scenes in her writing, refashioning images from earlier poems, reconstituting alternative rhythms of perception. At a linguistic level she continues to rehearse strategies of retrieval in which she is attentive to Canadian perception of event, and there is dry humour in her self-parody of this compulsive activity in the open poem 'Provisions' with its figure of urban researchers exposed 'on the disastrous ice' and armed only with a wealth of as yet unassimilated facts.

This repeated, ill-prepared journeying into a hostile climate sets an appropriate ambience for the volume's concerns, as the title poem returns to feral associations of masculinity, and in particular man's addictive mastering and slaying of animals that turn out to be images of himself. 'The Animals in That Country' then specifically sets the protective assimilations of sentimental anthropomorphism which facilitates animal slaughter against a domestic tradition of representation where animal difference resists such easy enclosure and where, in the unyielding actuality of a surviving wilderness, they remain uncompromisingly Other. As if in recognition of Walter Benjamin's difficult assertion that 'there has never been a document of culture which was not at one and the same time a document of barbarism',[11] Atwood deciphers flora and fauna as well as traces of the past in relation to particular human depredations. Ecological spoliation by 'The Surveyors' calls back into play an imagery of mapping which now conceals from sight the environment it subordinates. But in the geological time-frame which the poem projects, these contemporary figures merge into a genocidal history to take their place alongside earlier occupants of the territory they now abuse; to become in turn 'red vestiges of an erased / people, a broken / line' (*AC*, p. 4). An organising metaphor here as elsewhere in Atwood's poetry encodes writing as imposed signification upon an alien facticity, where the gap between signifier and signified is itself an index of the distance separating person from place. Language and perception, as well as language and act can bifurcate as often as they coincide in this work. 'Painted assertions' achieve only temporary signification and a recurrent perplexity Atwood exposes is a sense that the language she is given to use functions as often as a barrier to integration as a means to its achievement. The pebbles which are 'sea-smoothed, sea-completed' in 'Some Objects of Wood and Stone' are perceived as 'shapes / as random and necessary / as the shapes of words', and when they are flung into the sky these same pebbles become a 'flight of words' (*CG*, pp. 32–3).

Humans are animal in duplicitous ways and in 'A Foundling' the figure of an expanding male dependency upon the female while the male continues to claim territorial and experiential superiority is given comic treatment. 'Part of a Day' begins with physical separation after lovemaking and watches figures moving through an emotionally unsustaining environment which yet sustains them physically. 'The despair of the separate object' is very much a concern of Atwood's writing, as recurrent a theme as the male desire to intervene in female consciousness and colonise its space:

> if he could cram his mind
> into my body
> and make it stay there,
> he would be happy.
> (*AC*, p. 6)

Not surprisingly, 'The Shadow Voice' questions continuing desire for the male but seems to acknowledge the insufficiency of articulacy in the absence of love. Then a male fear of connecting is graphically illustrated in 'Attitudes Towards the Mainland', and an unsettling image of humans drowning while 'their eyes' quick pictures' conjure visions of harmonious nature is enclosed in a male perception of death in a pervasively hostile climate. 'Notes From Various Pasts', seemingly written from a submerged position but interested in what might be recovered from even greater depths, not only tracks confounding mutations of meaning as it trawls the seas of prehistory for 'messages from a harsher level', it also registers the mismatch between human forms of coding and those systems of communication and relationship which connect and identify worlds beyond our words. Ultimately one signifying system comes into conflict with another. Crustacean forms 'all / sheathed in an armoured skin / that is a language' signal their alien otherness and the marginalisation that might otherwise be construed as only a post-colonial self-perception is transformed into a wider human condition:

> The words lie washed ashore
> on the margins, mangled
> by the journey upwards to the bluegrey
> surface, the transition:
>
> these once-living
> and phosphorescent meanings

>fading in my hands
>
>I try to but can't decipher
>
> (AC, p. 11)

The lair of 'The Landlady' is experienced as inhospitable in several ways. Her ownership of all available space, even generating 'the light for eyestrain', is an oppression of the spirit for the tenant who escapes in dreams to walk 'always over a vast face / which is the landlady's'. Codes of possession create conditions of dispossession where the act of seeing clearly is itself compromised: 'my senses / are cluttered by perception / and can't see through her', even though she is 'a slab / of what is real, // solid as bacon' (*AC*, p. 15). And technological enclosures of the self create different alienations in 'A Fortification' which produces an interiorised self-referential look back down the evolutionary chain to:

>catch sight of the other creature,
>the one that has real skin, real hair,
>vanishing down the line of cells
>back to the lost forest of being vulnerable
> (AC, p. 16)

In response to such linguistic displacements of the female as are routinely encoded in phrases like 'the animal kingdom', Atwood convincingly repossesses the territory. The animals of her poetry are various and distinctive, and in 'The Festival', male hunters with their ritual self-justifications are held up to a peculiarly withering contempt. A human ecology forgetful of its wider responsibilities is guilty of a wanton self-diminishing, as 'The Totems' makes clear, and by borrowing a metaphor from the wave theory of light to invite a readerly participation in the process of image-construction, Atwood generates an appropriately apocalyptic note in 'Elegy for the Giant Tortoises'. For these genetically damaged creatures it is indeed the last day.

Two poems which cross-fertilise each other to bring comic deciphering to a poetic voice that insistently thematises a problematic identity in uncertain location are 'At the Tourist Centre in Boston' and 'A Night in the Royal Ontario Museum', the first of which makes sport of the ways in which perceptions too attentive to American requirements reduce to invisibility the actualities of

Canadian context. Once again prescriptive mapping elides actuality and once again assertive signification displaces candour. In mild but meaningful parody a 'dream' of American provenance produces 'a manufactured / hallucination, a cynical fiction, a lure / for export only'. What is left of a domestically constructed subjectivity must then be nothing more than a 'mirage' that will safely 'evaporate' upon the speaker's return home. Once home, however, accidental entrapment in a national museum reveals bemusement and disarray in a multicultural bazaar. Domestically mapped and directed now in overdetermining ways, the speaker is paradoxically mazed in the enclosing space of cultural fragmentation. She reveals too an ironic awareness of the ways in which this present situation parodies her previous textual excavations: 'I say I am far / enough, stop here please / no more' – until her voice faints away 'in the stellar / fluorescent-lighted / wastes of geology' (*AC*, p. 21).

But as 'The Progressive Insanities of a Pioneer' indicates, Atwood's fascination with all aspects of Canadian experience, and in particular its derivations within a history also young enough to be part of active memory, proves an irresistible textual lure. Anthropocentric delusions are the subject here, together with a comic recognition of the ways in which human insistence upon the supremacy of its own signifying systems leads to mental entrapment within an environment always defiantly beyond male efforts to control and subordinate it. Perhaps with more than a glance at United States paradigms, the 'great vision' that refuses to form at this pioneer's bidding is itself exposed as a strategy of misplaced desire. In terror at the prospect of human life as random contingency in a wilderness resistant to patterns of imposed order and unable to accept that wilderness as 'an ordered absence', the male figure is overwhelmed. Such too, though given different emphasis, is the fate outlined for Mary Shelley's notorious protagonist in 'Speeches for Dr Frankenstein'. A pervasive Gothic element in Atwood's verse thematises both the discursive pressures of British literary antecedent upon post-colonial self-definition, and a Canadian attitude of 'deep terror in regard to nature' noticed by Northrop Fyre. 'It is not a terror of the dangers or discomforts or even of mysteries of nature', says Fyre, 'but a terror of the soul at something that these things manifest.'[12] Turning the Arctic opening of Mary Shelley's narrative to Canadian account, Atwood's favoured topic of the construction of subjectivity is given memorable airing. Deriving as it does from prior textuality, the poem foregrounds linguistic assembly as the site of experiment and establishes artistic complicity in the violence of a created world. As Judith McCombs points out, 'Atwood's creating *I* is author-victim to her lover-Other':[13]

> Blood of my brain,
> it is you who have killed these people.
>   (*AC*, p. 45)

'Speeches' gives iconic form to feral existence in the Canadian wilderness:

> The sparkling monster
> gambols ahead,
> his mane electric:
> this is his true place.
>
> He dances in spirals on the ice,
> his clawed feet
> Kindling shaggy fires
>   (*AC*, p. 46)

before the independence of created construct speaks its own separating identity: 'I will not come when you call' (*AC*, p. 47).

Increasingly, one of the ways in which Atwood creates imaginative space for her own devising is by embracing aspects of native cosmology. In the animism of Indian and Inuit approaches to the world of experience she could find possibilities for a more responsive articulation of her local orientations. The gods her poetry conjures relate as much to that ancestry as they do to Graeco-Roman iconographies,[14] and Sherrill Grace reminds us that 'Ojibway and North coast Indian mythology, both based upon fundamental homologies that facilitate transformation, have an important place in Atwood's work'.[15] The 'Totems' section of 'Some Objects of Wood and Stone' regrets that as 'tourists of another kind / there is nothing for us to worship' (*CG*, p. 59), and the traces of earlier civilisations which her poems often retrieve are further evidence of desired identifications. 'The Totems' (*AC*, p. 22) takes inspiration from Indian mask and ritual, and with equal specificity 'The Gods Avoid Revealing Themselves' evokes spirit figures:

green in the torchfire, standing
on grave colossal feet
with metal feathers and hooked
oracular beaks and human bodies
polished, reflecting but also
giving out their own light.

(*AC*, p. 24)

But the poem ends with invisibility, with a male unwillingness to open to this kind of perception, and if Indian cosmology can inspire metaphors of merging union with a surrounding landscape – 'More and more frequently the edges / of me dissolve and I become / a wish to assimilate the world' – Atwood will as frequently create verbal representations of dissolution. Fluid annihilation is already a favoured figure and, as becomes evident in the later poetry, an absence of defining borders becomes an ontological problem as much as it disturbs processes of cultural self-definition. In the meantime Atwood contends with the most powerful imperialising culture the world has yet sustained.

Intimate with the United States' market economy and yet seeking to preserve cultural distance from it: intricately and inseparably involved in linguistic similitudes with a globally determining neighbour while constructing patterns of representation which formulate dissimilarity and variation, the political inheritance Atwood invests in her writing bequeaths a complication of response which generates distinctively violent dualities,[16] sometimes apocalyptic, often self-destructive. An acutely compromised textuality, self-conscious of its ensnared situation, produces a frequently disturbing resonance. From a childhood contemporary with Nazi death-camps, 'It is Dangerous to Read Newspapers' centres upon image-representation and Atwood's own scripted performance to bring into focus the barbarism which underpins cultural production. In its powerful indictment of America's assault upon Vietnam the poem remains alert to its own complicities. For a citizen in North America's second liberal democracy to produce any other response could be seen as callow and self-serving: but there were clearly issues of simulation, replication and resemblance to be addressed, and in very different mood but to pointed effect 'Backdrop Addresses Cowboy' shifts focus from journalism to film to explore some of them. The positioning of the poem's voice is a first marker of resistance: the mute setting whose sole purpose is to present a hero demonstrably unaware of its existence is here articulate. As a parody of the relationships between centre and periphery the poem makes some headway and as a satire on the values implicit in Hollywood's banal but lethal ideology of gunslinger as lawmaker it has continuing relevance. The self-righteous assumption of exclusive virtue and consequent construction of any opposing Other as vice is neatly conveyed in the misprision of 'laconic / trigger-fingers / peopl[ing] the streets with villains'. Over many poems Atwood has refined her own understated, succinct and self-deprecatory irony which fuses different levels of response and makes all the more effective the break in 'Backdrop' when the stage-setting shifts to speak from a different positioning, that of the Canadian viewer subjected to a steady stream of colonising imagery:

> What about the I
> confronting you on that border
> you are always trying to cross?

Environmental disregard here produces detritus in the vandalised mental landscape of a spirit of place not acknowledged or recognised by the semiotic invader: 'I am the space you desecrate / as you pass through' (*AC*, p. 50).

As provocatively, and still concerned to vocalise a response to American master-narratives, the echo from Walt Whitman's *Leaves of Grass* which opens 'A Voice' identifies the poem's articulation with one of the great nineteenth-century documents of United States self-definition. Given that 'small' is repeated twice, the brevity of Atwood's utterance contributes to the political and cultural suggestions she is making:

> A voice from the other country
> stood on the grass. He became
> part of the grass.
>
> (*AC*, p. 58)

But to respond appropriately to these suggestions it might be worthwhile pausing to consider the possibilities open to a Canadian women in the embrace of the greatest American lover of them all. As Whitman's nineteenth-century ego expanded to fill North American space and beyond, he tempered his possessive transcendence with a universal benevolence. Decades before the Statue of Liberty was inscribed with a call to those whose aspirations he sought to embody, Whitman was riding the crest of an irresistibly attractive democratic optimism, while his generosity of spirit translated the gospel of sovereign individualism into a cosmic communion of the free. In *Leaves of Grass* America's manifest destiny is written harmoniously large to become one of the most compelling invitations ever penned.

For Atwood writing from Toronto more than a century later the party has somewhat palled and Whitman's benevolent inscription has come to seem an engulfing textuality. 'Starting from Paumanok' sends out its 'exulting words, word's to Democracy's lands' and these include 'land of Ontario'.[17] Whitman's discursive invasion is only benignly aware of a dialectic of textual possession and embrace:

> Yet sailing to other shores to annex the same, yet welcoming every new brother,
> Hereby applying these leaves to the new ones from the hour they unite with the old ones,
> Coming among the new ones myself to be their companion and equal, coming personally to you now,
> Enjoining you to acts, characters, spectacles, with me.
>
> (p. 60)

That 'enjoining' carries its own determinations, and within the empire of his text Whitman's leaves unite with others in overwhelming ways. 'I know perfectly well my own egotism', he writes, 'know my omnivorous lines and must not write any less, / And would fetch you whoever you are flush with myself' (p. 112). But it is his privileged present tense that most successfully embalms any possible dissent: the now of his unfolding charms resistance into corporation. And in that respect Atwood's recourse to history finds appropriate justification. Nothing could more concretely specify their rival claims on our attention than the ways in which Atwood's 'Surveyors' contrasts with 'Starting from Paumanok'. As the characters in Atwood's poem clear 'their trail of single reason' they are themselves relocated in a time-frame which associates colonisers with colonised across time. Incoming surveyors are joined to native North Americans by a historical process transcending them both. An ambiguous pattern of identifications is subtly registered, from 'red paint' to 'red arrows'

and 'faint ritual markings', and it is a barely seen but displaced
Indian culture that is significantly memorialised when the poem's
closing gesture connects surveyors with the 'red vestiges of an
erased / people' (*AC*, p. 4). By their 'numbers and brash letters'
European incomers impose their signifying systems upon a
territory that none the less outlasts them.

Whitman's speech-act by contrast turns from his hymning of
present and future in a self-conscious pause: 'Still the present I raise
aloft, still the future of the States I harbinge glad and sublime, /
And for the past I pronounce what the air holds of the red
aborigines.' What the air holds, we note, and not the territory in
their erstwhile possession. Since the Whitmanian persona is at once
past and present rolling logocentrically towards a triumphantly self-
legitimising future, his act of present-tense pronunciation becomes
one of possession and displacement: Anglo-American cadence
incorporates a thereby dispossessed Indian speech-register of place:

> The red aborigines,
> Leaving natural breaths, sounds of rain and winds, calls as of
>   birds and animals in the woods, syllabled to us for names,
>   . . .
> Leaving such to the States they melt, they depart, charging the
>   water and the land with names.

It is a moving conjuration of human evanescence over geographical
permanence which the poem's succeeding section immediately
translates into the energetic speed of present and future
expectations:

> A new race dominating previous ones and grander far, with new
>   contests,
> New politics, new literatures and religions, new inventions and
>   arts.
> These my voice announcing . . .

> (p. 61)

So when the bard of United States promise turned to his 'Song of
Myself', his prescriptive invitation: 'I celebrate myself, and sing
myself, / And what I assume you shall assume, / For every atom
belonging to me as good belongs to you' – could hardly help but
echo not as promise but rather as a threat of dissolution to a

postmodern Canadian recipient. That at any rate is the tenor of Atwood's reaction, for whom Whitman's: 'I loafe and invite my soul, / I lean and loafe at my ease observing a spear of summer grass' (p. 63) becomes a distinctly more sinister 'The sun shone / greenly on the blades of his hands' (*AC*, p. 58). And to Whitman's all-encompassing confidence: 'At home on Kanadian snow-shoes or up in the bush, or / with fishermen off Newfoundland' (p. 79), Atwood's poem posits a different and more diminutive kind of domesticating detail: 'you / in your blue sweater . . . My skirt was yellow' (*AC*, p. 58). 'A Voice' quietly acknowledges the positioning which is involved in this intertextual transaction:

> He could see that
> we did not occupy
> the space, as he did. We
> were merely in it.

Transcendent possession inevitably entails material displacement, with Whitman's visionary power blinding to his pervasive presence the figures it incorporates: 'We moved along / the grass, through / the air that was inside / his head. We did not see him.' Thus incorporated and displaced, Canadian figuration disappears as 'his brain grew over / the places we had been'. Always already a construct in someone else's conception, Atwood's figures, unseeing and now unseen, become vanished possibilities for an idealism that allows no scope for differentiation. Alterity can only be countenanced as a transient vagary in the mental construction 'from the other country'. The expansionist politics which *Leaves of Grass* aestheticises as a poetics of personal possibility is momentarily bemused by, but then narcissistically dismissive of, an alternative awareness of space:

> He sat. He was curious
> about himself. He wondered
> how he had managed to think us.
> (*AC*, p. 59)

It is perhaps the defining paradox of Whitman's all-inclusive textuality that, as its syncretising voice proceeds, amalgamating into the flow of its own utterance the multiplicity of North American abundance, difference is obliterated:

And these tend inward to me, and I tend outward to them,
And such as it is to be of these more or less I am,
And of these one and all I weave the song of myself.

(p. 79)

But alterity is precisely the imaginative terrain which Atwood composes and in the problematic Canadianisation of the English personality of Susanna Moodie (1803–85), she found an answerable nineteenth-century context and persona which enabled her to pursue her theme of a constructed subjectivity in greater detail. *The Journals of Susanna Moodie* (1970)[18], constituting 'Atwood's major poetic achievement to date',[19] records both a journey in post-colonial exploration and a meditation on alienating systems of signification in which space, place and language play a disconcerting role. A specifically European identity struggles towards Canadian recognition and self-recognition in ways that foreground both the confusions of immigrant consciousness and the indeterminacies generated by conflict between inherited and indigenous codes of perception. 'This space cannot hear', cries the opening poem as a middle-class sensibility comes into contact with an unprepossessing and alien Quebecois Other, and envy for contemporary optimism south of the border in the United States is registered: 'The others leap, shout // Freedom!' In a recalcitrant environment, the persona Moodie's initial loss of identity is mirrored in several ways, including a sense of strangeness in linguistic orientation:

> The moving water will not show me
> my reflection.
>
> The rocks ignore.
>
> I am a word in a foreign language.

(*JSM*, p. 11)

As she weaves in and out of image and event deriving from the life of a pioneer woman in the Canadian backwoods, Atwood's textual contrast with Whitman's North American panegyric is immediate, sustained and deepened throughout the volume. Her song of a reconstructed self comes up against history and precedence in the third poem 'First Neighbours':

The people I live among, unforgivingly
previous to me, grudging
the way I breathe their
property, the air,
speaking a twisted dialect to my differently-
shaped ears.

(JSM, p. 14)

Rather than a transcendent self subordinating an Other to its own priorities and designs Atwood's relocated 'I' is itself subjected to shaping influences in ways that encode a very different kind of sensibility. The Indian who is submerged within the imperatives of Whitman's textual locomotion, traced as memory and figured as historically superseded, enters here as a surviving marker of difference from, and cultural confusion for, the newly arrived European:

(asked the Indian
about the squat thing on a stick
drying by the fire: is that a toad?
Annoyed, he said No no,
deer liver, very good)

These early encounters produce ontological reformations in which speech, climate and mapping combine to image a redefining of contours for the perceiving self:

Finally I grew a chapped tarpaulin
skin; I negotiated the drizzle
of strange meaning, set it
down to just the latitude:
something to be endured
but not surprised by.

(JSM, p. 15)

A resilient uncertainty is being elaborated for which a resolve to be 'both sensitive and hard to startle' is appropriate, and where imported linguistic constructions are at best a dubious premise for accurate knowledge of what is to come: 'in this area where my damaged / knowing of the language means / prediction is forever impossible' (*JSM*, p. 15). The pioneer becoming progressively insane who 'imposed himself with shovels' and 'asserted / into the furrows, I / am not random' (p. 36), is imagistically related to

Moodie's husband who with others sows the same wilderness. But the female consciousness which presents 'The Planters' now acknowledges the spectral phantasm of beckoning dissolution which encircles and jeopardises their labours. They:

> pretend this dirt is the future.
> And they are right. If they let go
> of that illusion solid to them as a shovel,
>
> open their eyes even for a moment
> to these trees, to this particular sun
> they would be surrounded, stormed, broken
>
> in upon by branches, roots, tendrils, the dark
> side of light
> as I am.
>
> (*JSM*, p. 17)

Though their setting is far from the most hostile that Canada has to offer, these are lines which none the less call to mind the words of the historian W. L. Morton, words which also help to contextualise many of the feelings of anxiety and insecurity which characterise the *Journals*:

> The heartland of the United States is one of the earth's most fertile regions, that of Canada one of the earth's most ancient wildernesses and one of nature's grimmest challenges to man and all his works. No Canadian has found it necessary to revise Cartier's spontaneous comment as he gazed on the Labrador coast of the Shield. It was, he said in awe, 'the land that God gave Cain'. The main task of Canadian life has been to make something of this heritage.[20]

In Atwood's 1970 reconstructions, the heritage Morton identifies, is in significant ways experienced as Susanna Moodie's daily existence. In 'The Wereman' a Protean wilderness transforms the perceiving subject and 'Paths and Thingscape' deepens a sense of angst-ridden ontology: 'I am watched like an invader / who knows hostility but not where'. That ruptured syntax, creating an air of unknown connections, generates a concluding metaphor that finely catches the persona's alienation from context. All that can be hoped for here is a dream of postponed possibility:

> When will be
> that union and each
> thing (bits
> of surface broken by my foot
> step) will without moving move
> around me
> into its place
>
> *(JSM, p. 21)*

In the course of an essay identifying technical recurrences in Atwood's poetic politics Eli Mandel remarks: 'it is the mirror poems that suggest, more pointedly than usual in her work, questions about duplicity and reflexiveness and techniques of demystification'.[21] 'Looking in a Mirror' ambiguates this suggestion, exposing as it does the persona's mystified perplexity concerning who or what she is. Also ambiguating a favoured Atwood image, the human here transforms into the botanic: 'my skin thickened / with bark and the white hairs of roots ... fingers / brittle as twigs', before a striking geological comparison is produced: 'the mouth cracking / open like a rock in fire / trying to say // What is this' *(JSM*, p. 25). At the poem's conclusion, developing patterns of syntactic incompletion and parenthetical utterance combine to reinforce a perplexed loss of identity. The idea of the body as unmapped space, of animal existence as invasively metamorphosing into human form and of a more general registration of the uncertainty of Euro-Canadian experience come together in 'Departure from the Bush': 'There was something they almost taught me / I came away not having learned' *(JSM*, p. 27). That perplexity is as finely caught in 'The Immigrants' which brings into inventive conjunction image-patterns of time, cartography and ontology that are already established as characteristic:

> my mind is a wide pink map
> across which move year after year
> arrows and dotted lines.
>
> *(JSM, p. 33)*

Living along all the edges there are, Atwood's persona has dreams of violence which turn Canada's bush garden to surreal, apocalyptic effect; where ontological instability is the substance of recall; where the juice of strawberries metamorphoses into the blood of pioneers and where the failed suicide 'Brian the Still-Hunter' returns to haunt Moodie from beyond the grave with his account of how at the moment of shooting he felt himself changing into the animals who were his prey. In 'Dream 3: Night Bear Which Frightened Cattle', nightmare becomes a waking condition of tenuous displacement as if Moodie, the immigrant who had known existential displacement and transformation, were able to convert it backwards and forwards in time. A radical instability of perception defines her continuing reality:

> I lean with my feet grown intangible
> because I am not there
> watching the bear I didn't see condense
> itself among the trees, an outline
> tenuous as an echo
>
> (*JSM*, pp. 38–9)

And the poem which follows this, 'The Deaths of the Other Children', reflectively links property values to self-as-mother in metaphoric conjuring of disintegration and damaged survival:

> Did I spend all those years
> building up this edifice
> my composite
>   self, this crumbling hovel?
>
> (*JSM*, p. 41)

So 'The Double Voice' registers more than simply a bourgeois sensibility in conflict with recalcitrant realities that compose its surface tensions. In context, these apparently rival vocalisations of perception merge to produce a convergence which eschews any idealising aesthetic. The poem's conclusion brings into focus an organic transcendence of human life in the forms of cyclical regeneration, and this too is a recurrent image. As 'Resurrection' puts it with pragmatic accuracy: 'at the last / judgement we will all be trees' (*JSM*, p. 59).

It seems, then, a natural exfoliation of Atwood's art and craft that *The Journals of Susanna Moodie* should end with the spectral transmigration of a nineteenth-century persona into a twentieth-century Toronto winter landscape: a trans-historical relocation of a soul entirely in keeping with Atwood's shamanistic predilections.

An urban wilderness is a wilderness of sorts, and modern hubris towards individual transience is hubris after all. An antagonistic climate persists and the seemingly harmless old lady who is the figure of transmogrified sensibility is far from being the domestically passive perceiving subject she might at first appear. Atwood's calculated mapping of Canada's geological continuities prepares us for, but does not lessen the impact of, the *trompe l'oeuil* of the volume's quietly apocalyptic conclusion:

> Turn, look down:
> there is no city;
> this is the centre of a forest
>
> your place is empty
> (*JSM*, p. 61)

By refracting her voice through someone else's, Atwood emphasises the relation established between speaking subjects, her own and Susanna Moodie's. What becomes important in this endeavour is the restoration of the past not merely as an affective reanimation but as a reconstruction. The process is not merely a remembering but a rewriting of history, and as such it is a reshaping of present possibilities. Since the effectivity of the past, like that of any present event in the experiencing subject's perception, is determined by the manner of its interpretation, the way in which the past is understood has profound effects upon the way history is in turn seen as shaping subjectivity. History, Lacan reminds us, is 'that present synthesis of the past' which forms 'the centre of gravity of the subject',[22] by which means historical knowledge is simultaneously a process of self-discovery and self-comprehension. Accordingly, Atwood's archaeologising mode contextualises a contemporary politics.

But politics as a present synthesis of the past is problematised in particular ways by the fact that Canada occupies a difficult position as subordinate to United States economic priorities at the same time as it governs its own increasingly fractious body politic. Its post-colonial tensions are not unknown in other erstwhile imperial territories struggling to survive in changing circumstance. Canada's Prime Minister Brian Mulroney gained much of his experience as a labour-relations negotiator for an American-owned company in Quebec, and as far as Quebec is concerned, an anglophone dominance is seen as oppressive and subordinating. What then makes Canadian experience as relevant to a newly transforming Soviet Union as to a Europe embarked upon uncertain processes of closer integration is that its political and constitutional evolutions and deliberations bring into the open issues and difficulties being encountered elsewhere. Michael Ignatieff reminds us that 'something large is at stake in the Canadian crisis, and it is this: if one of the top five developed nations on earth can't make a federal, multi-ethnic state work, who else can?':

> The central incompatibility ... is between English and French Canada, but it is no longer the only strain on the fabric. The Western provinces resent the domination of Central Canada; the Atlantic provinces fear, as the poorest region, that the richer ones will no longer give them a helping hand; and most important of all, the native peoples of Canada have risen up with claims for self-government and self-determination in large areas of resource-rich Northland.

And Ignatieff's subsequent remarks bring home the political urgency of the problems facing Canada:

> What all Canadians are discovering, with varying degrees of horror, is that when you add up all these claims on the federation: native self-determination, recognition of Quebec as a distinct society, enlarged powers of economic development for the West and Atlantic Canada, the centre simply cannot hold. Something will have to give, in what is already the most decentralised federation on earth.[23]

Canadian intersections of the personal and the political were brought into greater public prominence when the country's ethnic heterogeneity received constitutional sanctity in the Charter of Rights and Freedoms enshrined in the Canada Act of 1982. According to the political scientist Alan Cairns, there has been in consequence 'a fundamental change in Canadian constitutional culture' which has 'changed the nature of the constitution and its relation to Canadian society' and provided a serious challenge to federalism which 'in relative terms has lost status as a constitutional organising principle'.[24] But poetry speaks politics as personal perception, and four years before the Canada Act the title-sequence from Atwood's 1978 collection *Two-Headed Poems* focused upon political divisions between francophone Quebec and the rest of Canada's anglophone provinces, bringing into play themes of separation, resentment and potential disintegration. We can assess some of the correlations between these poems and Canada's constitutional dilemmas by noting a speech given by Brian Mulroney in Calgary, Alberta, in 1990:

> Canada is being torn apart by myths created by anger and zeal and encouraged by indifference ... The first myth is that Canada does not work any more. The second is that the status quo is adequate to meet the challenges of the twenty-first century. The third myth is that, instead of trying to resolve our problems, we should prepare to negotiate separation. And the fourth is that our country can be split apart with few or no consequences.[25]

One way of registering the cross-cultural value of what Atwood has to say might be to imagine a group of conservative Soviet politicians sitting in the audience alongside their post-Meech Lake Canadian counterparts and listening to the first of the 'Two-Headed Poems':

> Well, we felt
> we were almost getting somewhere
> though how that place would differ
> from where we've always been, we
> couldn't tell you
>
> and then this happened,
> this joke or major quake, a rift
> in the earth, now falling south
> into the dark pit left by Cincinnatti
> after it crumbled

As always with Atwood, fears of a total assumption into United States power and priorities is never far distant, and domestic disintegrations bring the unwelcome prospect nearer. 'This rubble is the future', the poem continues, 'our fragments made us'. Cold war iconographies are appropriately encoded:

> What will happen to the children,
> not to mention the words

> we've been stockpiling for ten years now,
> defining them, freezing them, storing
> them in the cellar.
> Anyone asked us who were, we said
> just look down there.

But it is such assumed senses of identity that are jeopardised by transforming political evolution. Then, Atwood turns the poem at its close to register a more profound terror at the closing off of hitherto shared assumptions of social being and political citizenry; a closing off which leaves experiencing subjects without a common discourse to inhabit, nakedly exposed and without a political environment to protect their sense of self:

> But we weren't expecting this,
> the death of shoes, fingers
> dissolving from our hands,
> atrophy of the tongue,
> the empty mirror,
> the sudden change,
> from ice to thin air.
> (*THP*, pp. 60–126)

The second poem of the sequence turns its attention to a perceived threat implicit in United States attitudes to Canada's constitutional perplexities. An economy of conspicuous consumption generates linguistic profligacy in signifying systems that threaten to overwhelm and thus form a continuing danger:

> Those south of us are lavish
> with their syllables. They scatter, we
> hoard.

Direct reference to the notorious US–Canadian free-trade agreement, which is in effect an ill-concealed contract for American dominance, acknowledges the contempt with which economic power constructs perceptions in the lesser partner: 'Sneering is good for you / when someone else has corned / the tree market.'

Taking its inspiration from a case of Siamese twins 'joined head to head, and still alive', the 'Two-Headed Poems' sequence is designed, as an initial note informs us, for the heads to speak 'sometimes singly, sometimes together, sometimes alternately within a poem. Like all Siamese twins, they dream of separation' (*THP*, p. 59). It is a compelling metaphor of survivability together, since in such a case the dream of separation can never be actualised:

> but we are not foreigners
> to each other; we are the pressure
> on the inside of the skull, the struggle
> among the rocks for more room,
> the shove and giveway, the grudging love,
> the old hatreds.
>
> (*THP*, p. 70)

Within that controlling metaphor, and doubtless owing something to her alertness concerning the invasive infiltrations of American practice and valorisation, Atwood is able to manifest some empathy for a Quebec subjected to the overwhelming discourse of English-speaking Canada. Her version of Susanna Moodie had moved in Canada's francophone province feeling alien; unknown and unknowing. Now, in Quebec's cultural encirclement Atwood could not help but see a version of Canada's relationship to the discourses of imperialism, and she complicates an allusion to Yeats's rough beast, moving its slow thighs towards apocalypse, with an image of infesting birds in large flocks:

> To save this language
> we needed echoes,
> we needed to push back
> the other words, the coarse ones
> spreading themselves everywhere
> like thighs or starlings.
>
> (*THP*, p. 65)

There is also, though, an uncompromising awareness of the violent extremism nurtured within the self-seeking blandishments of party political overtures:

> these hearts, like yours,
> hold snipers.
>
> A tiny sniper, one in each heart,

> curled like a maggot, pallid
> homunculus, pinhead, glass-eyed fanatic,
> waiting to be given life.
>
> (*THP*, p. 72)

In social conflict of this kind, Atwood becomes strategically two-headed herself, as when the deliverer of a calculated and stinging insult is effectively diminished by monetary associations:

> Surely in your language
> no one can sing, he said, one hand
> in the small-change pocket.

But this eleventh and final poem includes a metaphor of geese being force-fed to produce a gastronomic delicacy associated with French values. A violent and unpleasant process is turned against its practitioners in an uncomfortable transformation of cultural victim into victimiser. It is an image which expands to incorporate any and all efforts by a dominant discursive economy to instill its linguistic practices into those who are imprisoned in a subordinate position:

> In these cages, barred crates,
> feet nailed to the floor, soft
> funnel down the throat,
> we are forced with nouns, nouns,
> till our tongues are sullen and rubbery.
> We see this language always
> and merely as a disease
> of the mouth.

In the elaborate dialectic of political subordination and cultural survival any effective political programme must involve a necessary buying off of dissent, a provision of policies for social amelioration with which the dominant power seeks to neutralise resistance and to secure its acceptance by those it colonises. What makes a dominant ideology powerful, after all, is in part its ability to intervene in the consciousness of those it subjects, appropriating and reinflecting their experience, and also, in the process, answering real needs. Any language thus forcefully intruded as a set of signifying practices which constitute the subject in her or his subordination is consequently seen: 'Also / as the hospital that will cure us, / distasteful but necessary' (*THP*, p. 74).

But Atwood would not be Atwood if the sequence did not close on a colder recognition of the nature of ethnic disputes: 'Dreams are not bargains, / they settle nothing' (*THP*, p. 75). Characteristically, the final lines of the sequence, lines that have achieved a certain provenance as descriptive of Canada's domestic crisis, resonate beyond that to touch upon polarisations between centres and peripheries which aspire to become rival centres, wherever opposing ethnic and cultural identifications contend for effective power:

> This is not a debate
> but a duet
> with two deaf singers.

Notes

1. Quoted in Linda Hutcheon, *As Canadian as ... Possible ... under the Circumstances!* (Toronto, 1990) p. 22.
2. Sandra Djwa, 'The Where of Here: Margaret Atwood and a Canadian Tradition', in A. E. and C. N. Davidson (eds), *The Art of Margaret Atwood* (Toronto, 1981) pp. 15–34.
3. Margaret Atwood, *The Circle Game* (Toronto, 1966) p. 11. Subsequent quotations will be marked *CG* and page references given parenthetically.
4. J. Laplanche and J. B. Pontalis, *The Language of Psycho-analysis* (London, 1980) p. 375.
5. In 'The Pronunciation of Flesh: a Feminist Reading of Atwood's Poetry', Barbara Blakely persuasively associates the politics of dominance with the mutual construction of self and other in Atwood's verse. 'Dominant within her work [are] paradigms of woman and man, their identity, interaction and mutual construction' (p. 38); in Sherrill Grace and Lorraine Weir (eds), *Margaret Atwood: Language, Text and System* (Vancouver, 1983) pp. 33–51.
6. 'To His Mistris Going to Bed', in *John Donne*, ed. John Hayward (Harmondsworth, 1950) p. 89.
7. The phrase is Frederic Jameson's, from *Postmodernism, or, The Cultural Logic of Late Capitalism* (Verso, 1991) p. 51.
8. Sherrill Grace, *Violent Dualities* (Montreal, 1980) p. 16.
9. Margaret Atwood, *Selected Poems* (Toronto, 1976) pp. 29–30. Subsequent quotations will be marked *SP* and page references given parenthetically in the text.
10. Margaret Atwood, *The Animals in that Country* (Toronto, 1968).

Subsequent quotations will be marked *AC* and page references given parenthetically.

11. Walter Benjamin, 'Theses on the Philosophy of History', VII, in *Illuminations*, ed. Hannah Arendt (New York: Schocken Books, 1988) p. 256.

12. Northrop Frye, 'Conclusion', in Carl F. Klink (ed.), *Literary History of Canada*, 2nd edn, vol. 2 (Toronto, 1976) p. 342.

13. Judith McCombs, 'Atwood's Haunted Sequences: *The Circle Game, The Journal of Susanna Moodie*, and *Power Politics*', in Davidson (eds), *The Art of Margaret Atwood*, p. 37.

14. In a reading of a single novel, Marie-Françoise Guedon usefully examines the Indian theme and the shamanic tradition in '*Surfacing*: Amerindian Themes and Shamanism', in Grace and Weir (eds), *Margaret Atwood: Language, Text and System*, pp. 9–111.

15. Sherrill Grace, 'The Poetics of Duplicity', in Davidson (eds), *The Art of Margaret Atwood*, p. 57.

16. Sherill Grace's *Violent Dualities* argues that polarity, not duality, is destructive and suggests that Atwood's concern is with a freedom that comes from accepting the duplicity we share with all living things.

17. Walt Whitman, *Leaves of Grass* (Harmondsworth, 1975) p. 59.

18. Margaret Atwood, *The Journals of Susanna Moodie* (Toronto, 1970). Subsequent quotations will be marked *JSM* and page references given parenthetically.

19. Grace, *Violent Dualities*, p. 33.

20. W. L. Morton, *The Canadian Identity*, 2nd edn (Toronto, 1972) pp. 4–5.

21. Eli Mandel, 'Atwood's Poetic Politics', in Grace and Weir (eds), *Margaret Atwood: Language, Text and System*, p. 54.

22. Jacques Lacan, *Le Seminaire*. Book 1: *Les Écrits techniques de Freud* (Paris, 1975) p. 46.

23. In *The Observer*, 9 June 1991.

24. A. C. Cairns, 'Citizens (Outsiders) and Governments (Insiders) in Constitution-making: the Case of Meech Lake', *Canadian Public Policy*, IX, special issue (September 1988) pp. 124–8.

25. The official text of this speech was reproduced by the Press Office of the Canadian High Commission in London.

26. Margaret Atwood, *Two-headed Poems* (Toronto, 1978) pp. 60–1. Subsequent quotations will be marked '*THP*' and page references given parenthetically in the text.

2

From 'Places, Migrations' to *The Circle Game*: Atwood's Canadian and Female Metamorphoses

JUDITH McCOMBS

Margaret Atwood's first real book, *The Circle Game* (1966) is not what is usually meant by a first book. *Circle* is not imitative, derivative or of beginner quality; nor is it an early achievement that later works have left behind. On the contrary: *The Circle Game* is a major and mature poetic structure, enclosing a number of Atwood's best poems: 'This is a Photograph of Me', 'A Descent Through the Carpet', and 'Camera', to name a few. And *Circle* is the metamorphic source-book for Atwood's Stage I, the Closed World, 1966–77; from *The Edible Woman* on through *Dancing Girls*, *Circle's* surfaces and archetypal depths reform and reoccur.[1]

In the poetry, *Circle's* vision of the Canadian land as unpeopled flux and its human constructions as temporary, becomes in *The Journals of Susanna Moodie* (1970) the invading wilderness, the fragile lighted cabin and the city's temporary bulldozers. *Circle's* female vs. male tensions, costumes and doubles are reincarnated in *Power Politics* (1971) and *You Are Happy* (1974). In criticism, *Circle's* freezing Nature and passive victims recur in *Survival's* (1972) germinal guide to Canadian literature. In fiction, *Circle's* camera-eye man and orphan-waif man become camera-wielding Peter and hapless, foetal Duncan of *The Edible Woman* (1969). The camera man and the drowned 'Photograph' seer become in *Surfacing* (1972) the fraudulent film-maker David and the drowned father, whose body drifts under the lake, prevented from surfacing by his camera's weight. *Circle's* 'Descent Through the Carpet' – which is so far the best of Atwood's many descent poems – metamorphoses as the *Surfacing* dive, where, as in *Circle*, the questing female *I* descends to

51

prehistoric depths whose frigid waters are the source of death and of ancestral life.

The Circle Game is not, of course, the first book Atwood wrote: ten years of chapbooks, sequences, one short novel, a number of stories and several poetry book typescripts precede *Circle*. The last of those, 'Places, Migrations', a finished typescript of 42 poems, might have been Atwood's first real book: if Ryerson of Toronto had not rejected it, with regrets, at the beginning of 1965.[2]

'Places, Migrations' appears a predictable first book for a young, intelligent, consciously Canadian poet of the 1960s to write. It shows Atwood's increasing skill and control as a poet; and it shows a writer determined to speak not individually but for the educated young Canadians of the 1960s – those who would claim and affirm (albeit ironically and provisionally) their identity as Canadians. The Ryerson editor's 'Notes' accurately commend the talent and examining intelligence; find the calm control surprising and perhaps too detached; find missing a power, a voice, the thrill that spears the reader (Earle Toppings to Margaret Atwood, 2 January 1965).

Addressed to Northrop Frye's famous question of Canadian identity 'where is here?' (*The Bush Garden*, p. 220), 'Places, Migrations' answers with a collection of sites inhabited and journeys made by a generic young Canadian couple who are conscientiously trying to claim their land, and through it, their own identity. Mostly the migrations are positive; mostly the couple is positive; and the book is structured to move, in loosely linear fashion, towards the paired ending poems of the longest, westernmost journey ('Migrations: C.P.R.') and the hardest, northernmost journey ('A Place: Fragments').

This linear structure makes 'Places, Migrations' a daylit book, from the upper world of the living and their surface journeys. It does not seem probable that a book so structured would become a book of *Circle's* archetypal depths. But 'Places' did, literally, turn into *Circle:* and hindsight sees how fortunate it is that this metamorphosis was not interrupted – or prevented – by 'Places' being accepted for publication.

Metamorphosis, as Atwood has helpfully said, means that things 'go through some mysterious process and emerge as something else' (Sandler, p. 14). This paper will trace, in some detail, the two metamorphoses that occurred from 'Places' to the final *Circle*, by pointing to what emerged when, and by speculating a little on how.

The process can be followed in the five surviving 'Orders' – tables of contents – in the Atwood and Contact Press Papers at the University of Toronto. What these show is a major metamorphosis of theme and image, wherein the surface, rational structure of 'Places, Migrations' is overwhelmed by poems from the negative, irrational, menacing depths. The depth poems came in two metamorphic surges, during the fall of 1964 and then during the first half of 1965, intruding into the 'Places, Migrations' structure that at first absorbed them and then gave way.

In creative terms, Atwood was by 17 October 1964 conscious of being on a writing streak; new and better poems kept coming as she sat down to type the old ones; the expressed wish to turn it off was not totally a joke (letter to Charles Pachter). Of the 42 'Places' poems submitted to Ryerson by 17 December 1964, 26 are marked as new ones in Atwood's holograph on Order One. (There is an error: one so marked is old.)[3]

I would speculate that the change in working habits, from conscientiously revising and retyping old poems to accepting the new ones that kept coming, was a change from the letter to the spirit: perhaps something in the older poem led not to revision but re-vision, another poem. And that metamorphic flow broke an opening, wore down a channel, so that the first surge was not the last – not for *Circle*, nor Stage I, nor Atwood.

Measuring by the final *Circle's* 28 poems, this first surge of 25 amounts to a book's worth; as in *Circle*, the poems are long, and five are sequences. Taken as a group, all 25 are in Atwood's mature Stage I style: narrow vertical lines rather than horizontal ones, unrhymed colloquial language, minimal capitalisation and punctuation. Imitative echoes have all but vanished; myth and tradition now feed into what are recognisably Atwood poems, though, as Ryerson notes, many of them are too prosy. But the voice *is* recognisably Atwood: the ironic, detached, controlled intelligence that leads us into danger.

This first metamorphic surge is no sudden change in quality: though none of these 25 matches the best of the 12 *Circle* poems written earlier – which include 'This is a Photograph of Me', 'After the Flood', 'The Circle Game' sequence, and 'Migrations: C.P.R.' – few are so slight as 'The Islands'; none so imitative as 'In My Ravines', to name the weakest *Circle* poems of Order One. The best of the new ones, the female-identified 'Prehistoric Effigy' and several sections of the 'We (and the Voices behind Us) Ascending' sequence, are better than many of the final *Circle* poems.

Taken as a group, pulled out of the misleadingly positive structure of the 'Places, Migrations' that Ryerson saw, these are death poems and fear poems; only four of the 25 definitely do *not* have death and/or fear in them. Deaths caused by, or threatened by, generic civilised Man, acting as farmer, criminal, doctor, dentist, scientist. Deaths suffered by humans (both genders); almost as often by animals and birds (the identification with victims crosses species lines); occasionally by the land, trees, gods. The dominant emotion is fear, of death by violence, by civilisation, by entrapment. The dominant effect of the Stage I, vertical-line, colloquial style – speed – intensifies the fear.

Though deaths by far outnumber depths in this first metamorphic group, depths are implicitly there; and *Circle's* fusion of deaths and depths has tentatively begun. 'Maps Are Traps', for example, the new poem that comes second in 'Places, Migrations', has its generic *we* craving three-dimensional freedom, but caged, perhaps fatally, inside the mapmaker's depthless vision. But that the upper world is not the only world can, in the first two Orders which are 'Places, Migrations', scarcely be recognised, because the positive land-journey structure surrounds and minimises deaths and depths.

Among the 12 'Places' poems that are to survive in *Circle*, few and scattered hints of the real depths exist – the parenthetical 'lake ignored' (p. 35) in the 'Circle' sequence, the seaweed like 'small drowned hands' in 'Migration: C.P.R.' (p. 55). Of the 12, only two clearly reveal archetypal depths: and these two, 'After the Flood' and 'This Is a Photograph of Me', are so placed, as first and fifth poems, that 'Flood' becomes a more-hopeful-than-not beginning of a new couple in a new world, and the depths of 'Photograph' seem an odd aberration.

After deaths and hints of depths, one other dominant characteristic of this first metamorphosis must be considered: these are female poems. Of these 25 new ones, some dozen are – in 1964 – openly female-identified: women are central characters, have power over others, are allied with primitive or with Edenic natural powers, are fertility goddess, harpy, Euridice, seer. About half a dozen others of this first group are covertly female-identified, as are so many of the final *Circle*: that is, these covertly female poems side with an I who is at least implicitly a female and who is at least intellectually opposed to an other who is at least implicitly male.

About half of the first metamorphosis, then, was overtly female-identified; about 60 per cent of it was overtly and covertly female.

In 1964 such female identification was a prophetic voice in the wilderness (as was the female-identified *Edible Woman* that Atwood wrote in 1965).

For the 16 older poems in the 'Places, Migrations' typescript, the proportion is far less female: only seven are overtly female-identified ('After the Flood' and 'The Circle Game', for example), and of those seven only two would be female-empowered. Of the older 16, two would be covertly female-identified ('This Is a Photograph of Me' and 'A Meal', for example); the remaining six either avoid gender ('The Islands') or have the unidentified I watching both female and male (as in 'Evening Trainstation', where gender must be one of the edges the edgy *I* inhabits).

The second metamorphosis, of poems *and* structure, begins at the bottom of the first Order of 'Places', where *Circle's* new, paired and mirroring end poems, of the castaway, drowned and buried couples of 'Explorers' and 'Settlers', appear in Atwood's holograph as inserts dividing – and thereby undercutting – the positively paired land-journey ending poems of 'Migrations' and 'A Place'. (Atwood remembers very definitely that 'Explorers' and 'Settlers' *had* to be new-created in that first Order ([personal interview, 6 August 1983]; the typescripts corroborate this.)

These paired and mirroring 'Explorers' and 'Settlers' are a darker version of Canadian history, as depths and deaths; here inhabiting the land means not a journey but drownings and burials. In contrast to Robert Frost's poem of national identity, 'The Gift Outright', these heroes are in death the land's, before the land is theirs.[4] These paired depth poems are also a grisly closing version of the opening 'After the Flood' couple: they turn cannibal, they drown and die, the only children produced will sprout, in an unspecified future, from their buried hands. And these final, drowning couples are a grisly version of the inset 'Circle Game's sterile couple and unclaimed circling children.

But that 'Places' had begun to metamorphose into *Circle* was still, in the finished typescript of Order Two, scarcely discernible. Only the two historic depth poems have appeared, dislocating the earlier manuscript's progressive westernmost and northernmost journeys. The only other drowning poem, 'Photograph' is still surrounded by surface poems of maps, gardens and trainstation, that go no further down than depthless vision and deep trenches. The chief change seems to be that ten (mostly inferior) poems from the first metamorphosis have been cut, in Atwood's holograph, from Order One.

In the third Order, of June 1965, *Circle* has metamorphosed, and 'Places' gone under. All *Circle*'s drowned world poems are suddenly there, in *Circle*'s consecutive order, and much of *Circle*'s final structure suddenly exists. What had happened? The second metamorphosis, of 28 new and better poems – a second book's-worth – that is the definitive breakthrough of Atwood's Stage I, mythic Drowned World.

These 28 bring major poems from the archetypal depths: their general quality is much higher than in the first metamorphosis; and their best are still, over 20 years and 20 books later, among Atwood's best. In contrast to the first surge, here depths overwhelm mere surface deaths: of the 11 most powerful, nine fuse depths and deaths, as in 'A Descent through the Carpet', 'Camera', 'Explorers' and so on; the other two, 'Journey to the Interior' and 'Pre-Amphibian', descend into more shallow depths. Compare the first surge's 'depthless' vision and high (22 of 25) death ratio: here death occurs in 13 of the 28.

All the 11 most powerful are, like 'Explorers' and 'Settlers', paired and mirroring, rather than solitary poems: 'A Messenger' reflects 'A Sibyl', 'Camera' reflects the earlier 'Photograph'; 'Winter Sleepers' reflects 'Spring in the Igloo'; and, mirror of mirrors of mirror, 'A Descent through the Carpet' reflects 'Journey to the Interior' / 'Pre-Amphibian' and the unpublished 'Tsonoqua: Someone Else'. Together these eleven mirroring depth poems form the boundaries, threshold clusters and internal descents that structure Order Three – and the final *Circle Game*.[5]

This second metamorphosis must be the reason why every remaining first metamorphosis poem, including some of value, has disappeared in Order Three: swept away, gone under, along with the 'Places' linear structure and 'depthless' surface vision. But re-embodied: eight of these abandoned first surge poems appear, metamorphosed, in Order Three's new poems. And 11 of these abandoned first surge poems will appear, metamorphosed, in six yet-unwritten books: *The Edible Woman, The Animals in That Country, Procedures for Underground, Power Politics, Surfacing, You Are Happy*. Though one regrets the valuable poems here abandoned, one must approve the overriding metamorphic principle.

The second metamorphic surge apparently occurred between January and 24 June 1965: on which date Atwood submitted Order Three, the then-untitled *Circle Game* typescript, to Raymond Souster of Contact Press, Toronto. Of its 43 poems, 28 counting 'Explorers' and 'Settlers', were new. Of those 28, 15 were final *Circle* poems; only one last *Circle* poem, 'Some Objects of Wood and Stone', did not emerge in this second metamorphosis. Atwood's 24 June submission letter indicates that the typescript had been put together practically the previous day, written mostly in Vancouver, and most of the Vancouver ones since January 1965.

Atwood has talked, in the 1977 Sandler 'Interview' (Sandler, p. 19), of the way poems, once written, can attract other, kindred poems: evidently the new depths of 'Explorers' and 'Settlers', allied with the original depths of 'Photograph' and 'Flood', begin to call forth more of their kind. For, in the third Order, the depth poems move into positions that structure the entire book: *Circle* now opens with 'Photograph' and 'Flood' and closes with 'Explorers' and 'Settlers'. The land-journey poems have been further separated, and thereby further weakened: 'Migrations' has been moved well forward from the end, and 'A Place: Fragments' to third from the end, so that its icy northern muskegs now precede the drowned end poems. This Order is a Drowned World, opening and closing with death by water: and the entire book may, in fact, be spoken from the depths, by the invisible, drowned seer of 'This is a Photograph of Me'.

And, in the third Order, after 'The Circle Game' sequence, a new, second opening has emerged, with a new 'Camera' poem that obviously re-enacts the initial drowning 'Photograph', and with the paired, drowning 'Winter Sleepers' and 'Spring in the Igloo' poems, which obviously re-enact both 'After the Flood' and the final 'Explorers' and 'Settlers' drowning couples. Now the unnamed *Circle* has its outer boundaries, of deaths by water, plus its second opening, of camera and deaths by freezing water. I think of this second, inner structure as a smaller loop or threshold within the encircling Drowned World poems.

Opening and second opening now further mirror one another in the new, complementary poems, 'A Messenger' and 'A Sibyl'. The first, 'A Messenger', comes immediately after 'Flood'; he is a myth-swallowing Hanged Man, disintegrating outside the modern *I* narrator's window glass, shouting silent messages. The second poem, 'A Sibyl', comes immediately after the drowning

'Winter' and 'Spring' poems, in the book's second opening, and portrays an abortive female god in a glass jar, preaching fertility and death, ignored by the modern *I* narrator. Both the Hanged Man and the Sibyl should be sacred: in *Circle*'s Drowned World, they are freaks, glassed out or glassed in, ignored, unable to reach the modern *I*.

In this second metamorphosis, then, Atwood reverses, transforms and incorporates into a Canadian Drowned and Freezing World a number of the myths and images T. S. Eliot uses for his 'Wasteland': Death by Water, the Hanged Man, the sibyl, sterility, regeneration, the voices of the children. This Eliot material can probably be traced back to the beginning of the second metamorphosis, with those two new poems of the faceless, failed 'Explorers' and the drowned, buried 'Settlers' who will somehow sprout children. Probably those 'Settlers' invoke Eliot's corpse planted in the garden – 'Has it begun to sprout?' (p. 39) – and certainly both poems reverse the 'Wasteland's' European overload of history to Atwood's Canadian absence of history. Probably the most important example of reversal and metamorphosis would be Atwood's mythic Drowning and Freezing Waters. In Eliot's arid 'Wasteland' the flowing waters are, as Frye noted, 'the containing form of the poem'; and the mythic Freeing of the Waters in the spring rains regenerates the land, as Frye also noted (*Anatomy*, p. 323, *T. S. Eliot*, p. 66). But in Atwood's Canadian Drowned Land, the Freeing *and* the Freezing of the Waters threaten, imprison, kill.

Atwood was, of course, a member of the T. S. Eliot generation of aspiring poets, and had studied him at the University of Toronto (where an undergraduate essay on Eliot's archetypal water symbolism is preserved in the Atwood Papers).[6] Before the two *Circle* metamorphoses, Atwood had incorporated Prufrock's fear of 'the eyes that fix you in a formulated phrase' (5) into the centre image of the 'Circle' sequence, where the *I* is 'transfixed / by your eyes' / cold blue thumbtacks' (40). During the two metamorphoses of fall 1964 and spring 1965, Atwood had included T. S. Eliot in a University of British Columbia survey course. It is possible, therefore, that the myths Eliot used, now re-read by Atwood, somehow triggered the second *Circle* metamorphosis. It is equally possible that these myths, being convenient to the writer's Muse, got incorporated into metamorphoses that were already under way. Atwood has, in the retrospective Margaret Atwood review ('*Second Words*', *Globe and Mail*, 20 November 1982, L2) accused her

Muse of behaving like a caddis-fly larva, sticking anything handy on to whatever structure she's creating.

The real question, with this (or any) writing streak that suddenly produces a powerful bookful, may be not what triggers or feeds the breakthrough, but rather what had been holding it back. For it is not logical to think that such a powerful surge could just happen all at once, unless it had been stacked up and waiting to happen; in which case something must have been holding it back. Nor, in the case of Atwood's obviously self-contagious second metamorphosis, is it logical to think that there *had* to be almost a year elapsing between, say, 'After the Flood', which Milton Wilson accepted for *Canadian Forum* of 18 April 1964, and the corresponding 'Explorers' and 'Settlers' of early 1965. Either the writer's energies were wholly preempted by other work, and/or the writer was distracted by other claims. In this case, the deceptive structuring and depthless contents of the two 'Places' Orders argue that it was Atwood's conscious quest for surface affirmations which covered over the depths.

Whatever its genesis, the second metamorphosis of Order Three establishes the then-untitled *Circle Game* as Atwood's 'Wasteland', a Canadian Drowned and Frozen Land. And, in the second metamorphosis, three descent poems – all of which re-enact Great Mother myths – suddenly appear. The first, 'A Descent Through the Carpet', has reversed and metamorphosed from an almost totally different poem of family 'Descents' in Order One, which *ascends* the evolutionary ladder from grandfather's apple farms to father's brambly acres to the uncertain modern *I* (*English*, 15 (1965): 216–17). In 'A Descent Through the Carpet', which *descends* Darwin's ladder, these kindly human ancestors have been replaced by prehistoric undersea bones and fangs, and the narrator's claiming of kinship has become a Perilous Undersea Journey to the frigid evolutionary depths of the Great Mother.

The new 'Descent Through the Carpet' has metamorphosed also from an Order One sequence, 'We (and the Voices behind us) Ascending', which goes *up* the ladder; the other two new descents, 'Journey to the Interior' and 'Pre-Amphibian', also metamorphosed from that 'Ascending'. 'Journey' and 'Pre-Amphibian' obviously mirror parts of 'Descent Through the Carpet': all three are mythic dives or descents, exploring the depths of the unconscious and of the Great Mother; the first is deeper and colder; the latter two explore territories that are shallower, warmer, belonging to the land and to mammals (Neumann, pp. 177, 260–1).

Boundaries and threshold clusters were created by the depths–deaths poems; what these three Great Mother descents create is the internal centres before and after the 'Circle' sequence. In the first two 'Places' Orders, the pastoral 'Descents' and the 'Ascending' sequence were placed exactly or almost exactly at the midpoint between 'Circle' and the beginning or end of the book. Here, in the third Order, their two reversed and metamorphosed descendants, 'Through the Carpet' and 'to the Interior' are placed almost exactly at the midpoint between the 'Circle' sequence and the beginning or end of the book. ('Interior' begins a depths cluster of itself, 'Tsonoqua: Someone Else', and the third descendant, 'Pre-Amphibian'.) Apparently Order Three, like the 'Places' Orders, has two internally almost-centred parts, separated by the still nowhere-near-centred 'Circle' sequence. And, from the third Order on, the second part, with its camera and multiple drownings, freezings, gods and descents, elaborately re-enacts and remirrors the first part. The effect, for me, is that of a mirror chamber within the Drowned World boundaries of the whole.

The second metamorphosis is, far more than the first, a break through of female-identified and female-empowered poems. Of its 28 poems, 26, including all 11 from the depths, and all but two rather awkward surface poems, are female-identified. In 20 the female identification is overt, as in 'Playing Cards'; in six more it is covert, determined by context, as in 'Explorers'. Of these 26, 17 are overtly female-empowered dissents: that is, the poem sides with an overtly female *I* against a losing or wrong male; in most of these dissents the female has the active power, to win, to metamorphose him, to defy him, to heal him, to survive him. In a few, such as 'Messenger', she is merely a seer; in three ('Camera', 'Winter' and 'Spring') she is an endangered victim. To these 17 overtly female-empowered dissents should be added four that are covertly female-empowered: one awkward 'Skier in a Cage', and the three great descents, 'Through the Carpet', 'to the Interior', and 'Pre-Amphibian', where the poem's power comes from female-imaged ideas or beliefs.

The second metamorphosis, then, was almost totally female-identified, and that mostly overtly; 75 per cent of it was female-empowered and sexually polarised dissents, most of them overt. Obviously female energies, from the surfaces and from the depths, fuelled this creative breakthrough; the older 'Places' and first metamorphosis poems had more often used an unsexed *I*, or a coupled, agreeing, or traditional female *I*.

The best of the non-victim, actively female-empowered poems is 'The Fate of the Symbolic Man', which is the most clever, cruel and arrogant of the several Circe poems here, and the serious Canadian Indian goddess poem, 'Tsonoqua: Someone Else', which is the centre depths–deaths poem between 'Journey to the Interior' and 'Pre-Amphibian' in Order Three. Tsonoqua is a cannibal Earth Mother, more savage and more powerful than the educated female *I*, who is both repelled and humbled by Tsonoqua's sacred power. Ironically, Tsonoqua has been invoked by the male, who projects her raw femaleness onto the modern *I*; but as the poem progresses Tsonoqua's powers take over, and the modern *I* becomes, in contrast, a silenced head without a body. In Gilbert and Gubar's 1979 terms, Tsonoqua is a Canadian goddess *Madwoman in the Attic*; in contemporary feminist terms, the alienated and disempowered *I* is a perfect example of the male-educated female, cut off from her own body, voice and goddesses.

What happened to 'Tsonoqua' and almost all the rest of these 1965 actively female-empowered poems? Why is the female *I* in the final *Circle* confined to seer, victim and lover roles *vis-à-vis* the male – that is, either agreeing or a silent dissenter? What happened to the several Circe poems, and why is the only metamorphosing *Circle* poem, 'Eventual Proteus', the only one where he does the metamorphosing, while she merely holds him?

The answer can be traced in the Atwood and Contact Press Papers. Between Atwood's 24 June submission and receipt of the 29 September 1965 acceptance letter from Contact, she made several alterations in the untitled Order Three, creating a fourth Order. The new and last *Circle* poem, the westernmost 'Some Objects of Wood and Stone', was centred exactly between the 'Circle' sequence and the book's end. (This balanced journeys and depths: the overland 'Migration: C.P.R.', the inland journey-depths 'to the Interior', and the westernmost journey's end 'Objects' were followed by two Great Mother depth poems, the dangerous, prehistoric, Indian 'Tsonoqua' and the warm, sexual, Darwinian 'Pre-Amphibian'.) 'A Descent Through the Carpet' was placed exactly at the midpoint before 'Circle', while two poems on each side of it were cut, and one slight poem added. Two other poems, 'Playing Cards' and 'A Meal', were revised, for the better.

In Order Four the 'Circle' sequence was still nowhere near centred, and the book's two parts nowhere near symmetric in size. Apparently Atwood was unable, at this point, to see *Circle*'s final structure; or to name the book, which had been submitted untitled: 'Winter Sleepers' and 'Journey to the Interior' were suggested as possibilities but not endorsed.

One speculates that the inability to name and edit completely was a side-effect of the radical creative breakthroughs. Those 1964–5 metamorphoses had demanded openness to taboo depths and female powers, to generation and abandonment. By 7 October 1965 Atwood was involved with a new group of poems and a Harvard doctorate, and had removed from the site of the metamorphoses: a high, 180-degree open view of Vancouver (see 'A Descent Through the Carpet').[7]

On 29 September 1965 Peter Miller officially accepted Atwood's book for Contact Press, subject to the major cuts (17 of 43) by which were excluded every overt, actively female-empowered dissenting poem; but which had the covertly female-empowered 'Carpet' and 'Pre-Amphibian' internally centred, with 'The Circle Game' as thirteenth of 26, all but centred, and which proposed the final title.

Miller's lengthy, two-page, single-spaced letter explains the omissions neutrally: they were being done for critical reasons and for Contact's usual size; but his cautionary paragraphs about communicability, humanisation, and (again) communicating something the reader can share, all convey his uneasiness with Atwood's content.

Contact Press had no strong record of being open to female work; of the 53 books it published from 1952 to 1967, only four, counting *Circle*, were by women. Correspondence between the editors makes explicit their suspicions of women poets; the senior editor, Louis Dudek, was most negative; Peter Miller, the junior editor, was Dudek's literary protégé. Contact's internal correspondence on *The Circle Game* shows explicit distrust and rejection of the female-empowered poems; in fact the book could have been rejected as private, queer, neurotic, had not Raymond Souster's indignant eloquence saved it. Atwood's earlier typescript, 'The Journey (Maybe)', had previously been accepted by Contact Press. It was then rejected for its alleged queerness when the senior editor reversed his acceptance and the junior followed; on 14 December 1963 Souster had reluctantly notified Atwood. But Atwood felt that Contact Press, except possibly Ryerson, was the only Canadian press doing first books of poetry; and Atwood felt strongly that Canadian poetry belonged in Canada.[8]

On 7 October 1965 Atwood agreed to all but two of the Contact Press cuts, and accepted their offer. Atwood's Order Five (which is a clear typescript of her amended Order Four) is now marked in Atwood's holograph in accord with all Contact cuts; and Miller's list of 'Poems for Inclusion' is amended, in Atwood's holograph, to reinstate 'A Messenger' and the revised 'Playing Cards', and to delete the inferior 'Invader'. (Atwood's letter offers to trade 'Invader' for 'A Messenger'.) Atwood also added the new group, 'Some Objects of Wood and Stone', and offered tentatively, in brackets, a deletable older poem called 'Hunting: Observations'. She also accepted the title which two Contact editors (Souster and Miller) proposed: *The Circle Game.*

Now *Circle*'s final mirroring, symmetric structure exists: its 28 poems are four groups of seven, with the seven-part, self-centred 'Circle' sequence at the centre, as a fifth group of seven, from whose sterile couplings and eyes and eyers the drowned and sterile world of *Circle* radiates. Seven is, of course, a magic, centred number; many of *Circle*'s poems, from 'Photograph' on, are seven-part structures. And it should be noted that *Circle*'s northernmost 'A Place: Fragments', which was the concluding poem of 'Places, Migrations', is a seven-part sequence which follows, in its quest for identity, the Canadian nationalist painters called the Group of Seven.

Circle's two now-equal parts have as outer boundaries the three sets of paired Death by Water poems: 'Photograph' and 'Flood', 'Winter' and 'Spring' and the final 'Explorers' and 'Settlers'. Opening and second opening, after 'Circle', have the mirroring thresholds of camera, flood and glass-exiled gods. Now, at precisely seven, and imprecisely 20 and 22, the undrowned descent poems, 'Through the Carpet', 'to the Interior', and 'Pre-Amphibian', provide *Circle*'s mythic and fertile alternatives to death by water. (The new 'Objects', at precisely 21, is a group of three whose centre water poem attempts the visionary.)

Such mirroring symmetries, now structured in the book as earlier in many of its sequences and poems, are not coincidental. Such symmetries confine, focus, remirror and refract *Circle*'s powers. That is why, as Miller noted, *Circle* gets better upon re-reading. Without these final, seven-part mirroring symmetries, *Circle*'s powers would be, as in the earlier Orders, diffused.

Who structured *Circle* finally? Atwood's Order Four and uncorrected Order Five make no attempt at the final centring or halving. But incredibly, Contact did *not* perceive that its list halved the book, all but centred 'Circle', and exactly centred the descents 'Through the Carpet' and 'Pre-Amphibian' before and after 'Circle': Miller's 29 September letter refers to a second half starting with 'On the Streets', which had been twenty-fourth of 43 in the submitted Order Three, but which was now, in Contact's list, tenth of 26, a place of no significance. Incredibly, at no point in the extensive Contact Papers is there any reference whatsoever to 'Circle's centring, or *Circle's* halves or boundaries, thresholds or descents.

Atwood's precise changes of 7 October would indicate that the Contact cuts suddenly made visible *Circle's* symmetry – were it not for that bracketed 'Hunting' poem, which Atwood added as deletable, and which Miller, happily, deleted. A distraction technique? That seems far-fetched. Or an elegant and demanding seven-part structure created now unconsciously, or with conscious confusion, by a writer who had been making seven-part, centred poems and sequences for years?[9] Atwood, in an interview (6 August 1983), does not remember who made what. Do strange things happen when one centres magic numbers?

However *Circle's* structure came, it came. Compared to Atwood's Orders, clearly Contact's exclusions revealed, and almost made, the structure that *Circle* needed to concentrate its powers: clearly Atwood saw, and made, or all but made, that final centring and mirroring. But compared to Atwood's Orders, clearly Contact's list excluded Atwood's overt and actively female-empowered poems. In the same exclusions. Which Atwood accepted. Which heighten *Circle's* fears: for the female *I* is silent, victim, witness, caught in statically circling the male. Had those female-empowered poems not been cut, *Circle* (1966) would have been far closer to the sexual realism of *Power Politics* (1971) and the 'Circe/Mud' metamorphic powers of *You Are Happy* (1974); many of *Circle's* excluded poems did metamorphose into those two books. Were the genders here reversed, one could borrow the idea that Contact used explicitly in 1966, when the senior and junior editors agreed not to cut poems from a man's book, because that would be castrating the writer. But English has no word that means gutting a woman's work of its female-empowered parts.

From 'Places, Migrations' to the final *Circle Game*, the stories that the Orders tell are several: the story of Atwood's two creative metamorphoses, the first generated and abandoned, but feeding into the second and into six future Stage I books; the second the breakthrough of the overwhelming, irrational depths that made *Circle* Atwood's Drowned and Freezing Canadian 'Wasteland', and first revealed Atwood's Stage I. These Orders also tell the story of female-identified and female-empowered poems, which in both metamorphoses broke through and blossomed, but which were refused by Contact's editors and abandoned by the writer. And last, these Orders tell the story of a powerfully centred, symmetric, mirroring structure, essential to the final *Circle*'s powers, which can*not* be by chance or coincidence, and yet which happened by zigzag and, at the end, by what looks almost like coincidence, almost like chance.

Notes

A shorter form of this paper was given at 'Cultural Metamorphosis in Margaret Atwood's Work', Popular Culture Association Convention, Toronto, 1 April 1984.

1. Stage I and Stage II are drawn from my book in progress on Atwood's creative metamorphoses. I am grateful to Margaret Atwood, Richard Landon and Katharine Martyn for their help with the Atwood Papers; to the National Endowment for the Humanities for a Fellowship for College Teachers; and to the Canadian Embassy for Faculty Research and Senior Fellowship grants which have supported this paper.

2. Earle Toppings (Ryerson), 'General Notes' on 'Places, Migrations' to Margaret Atwood, 2 January 1965 (Box 1, Atwood Papers). Two TS Orders – tables of contents – for 'Places, Migrations' are in Box 10, Atwood Papers; only the earlier, of 42 poems, has 'The Brothers', which Toppings criticised.

    In early 1965 the senior poet Al Purdy apparently recommended and sent to McClelland & Stewart of Toronto a 'Places, Migrations' – probably the second Order, of 37 poems including 'Explorers' and 'Settlers'. But nothing came of Purdy's try: on 5 March 1965 McClelland rejected the book after mixed reports, which they withheld (Box 1, Atwood Papers).

3. Apparently Atwood has made one error: 'A Detective Story', the fourteenth of the 26 marked new ones, is identical to the old 'A Detective Story', twenty-eight of the 40-poem TS, 'The Journey (Maybe)' in Atwood's Box 10; the Contact Press Papers show that 'Journey' was submitted to them before 1 November 1963. I have followed the physical, textual and contextual evidence to number

and date the manuscript 'Orders'.

4. 'The land was ours before we were the land's' is the first line of 'The Gift Outright', which Frost read in 1961 at President John F. Kennedy's Inauguration.

5. Atwood's pre-Order Three holograph worksheet shows the breaking-up of the 'Places' Order Two; the pairing of 'Photograph' and 'Camera', 'Messenger' and 'Sibyl', 'Igloo' and 'Winter Sleepers', 'Explorers' and 'Settlers'; and the questioning of 'Migrations'. 'Someone Else', also questioned, is tentatively to follow 'Interior'. Apparently 'A Descent Through the Carpet' is the only one of the 11 structuring depth poems that has not been written: but room has perhaps been cleared for it; and its antecedent 'Descents' is off in left-hand marginal exile; 'Pre-Amphibian', unpaired, is standing nearby, among the poems that come before 'Circle'. 'Circle' is at the centre of the worksheet, marked '(7)' for its parts, about half a year before 'Circle' would be centred among groups of seven in the final *Circle* structure.

6. Cf. James Reaney, 'Editorial', *Alphabet*, vol. 8 (1964), quoted as preface to Atwood's retrospective 'Eleven Years of *Alphabet*', *Canadian Literature*, vol. 49 (1971) p. 60; rpt. in Atwood's *Second Words*, p. 90:

    > Now the young intellectual living in this country, having gone perhaps to a Wordsworth high school and a T. S. Eliot College, quite often ends up thinking he lives in a waste of surplus USA technology, a muskeg of indifference spotted with colonies of inherited, somehow stale, tradition. What our poets should be doing is to show us how to *identify* our society out of this depressing situation.

    One can glimpse *Circle*'s waters where the undergraduate essay, 'Water Symbolism in *The Dry Salvages*', for Dr [Peter] Buitenhuis, traces the static circling, and the divine and daemonic aspects of Eliot's archetypal waters (Box 3, Atwood Papers, TS 2–3). An awful undergraduate 'Spratire' on 'The Wasteland' and 'Prufrock' was concocted by Atwood and Dennis Lee, alias Shakesbeat Latweed, for Victoria College's *Acta Victoriana*, vol. 83, no. 2 (1958) p. 22.

7. Margaret Atwood, letter to Peter Miller, 7 October [1965], Contact Press Papers; personal interview with Margaret Atwood, 14 December 1982.

8. Personal interview with Margaret Atwood, 14 December 1982; Margaret Atwood, letter to Peter Miller, [early] January 1966, Contact Press Papers.

9. For example, 'The Seven Wonders', *Acta Victoriana*, vol. 84, no. 2 (March 1960) pp. 10–13; rpt. *Canadian Forum*, August 1960, pp. 14–15; 'Avalon Revisited', *Fiddlehead*, vol. 55 (Winter 1963): pp. 10–13; and 'Fall and All', *Fiddlehead*, vol. 59 (Winter 1964): pp. 58–63.

References

Atwood, Margaret, *The Animals in that Country* (Toronto: Oxford University Press, 1968).
——, Atwood Papers, Boxes 1, 10, 54, TSS and MSS. Fisher Rare Book Library, University of Toronto.
——, *The Circle Game* (Toronto: Anansi, 1966).
——, *Dancing Girls* (Toronto: McClelland & Stewart, 1977).
——, *The Edible Woman* (Toronto: McClelland & Stewart, 1969).
——, *The Journals of Susanna Moodie* (Toronto: Oxford University Press, 1970).
——, *Lady Oracle* (Toronto: McClelland & Stewart, 1976).
——, *Power Politics* (Toronto: Anansi, 1971).
——, *Procedures for Underground* (Toronto: Oxford University Press, 1970).
——, *Second Words: Selected Critical Prose* (Toronto: Anansi, 1982).
——, *Selected Poems* (Toronto: Oxford University Press, 1976).
——, *Surfacing* (Toronto: McClelland & Stewart, 1972).
——, *Survival: A Thematic Guide to Canadian Literature* (Toronto: Anansi, 1972).
——, *You Are Happy* (Toronto: Oxford University Press, 1974).
Contact Press Papers, TSS and MSS. Fisher Rare Book Library, University of Toronto.
Eliot, T. S., *The Complete Poems and Plays 1909–1950* (New York: Harcourt, Brace, 1952).
Frost, Robert, *Complete Poems of Robert Frost* (New York: Holt, Rinehart & Winston, 1949).
Frye, Northrop, *Anatomy of Criticism: Four Essays* (Princeton, NJ: Princeton University Press, 1957).
——, *The Bush Garden: Essays on the Canadian Imagination* (Toronto: Anansi, 1971).
——, *T. S. Eliot: An Introduction* (Chicago: University of Chicago Press, 1963).
Gilbert, Sandra M. and Gubar, Susan, *The Madwoman in the Attic: The Woman Writer and the Nineteenth-Century Literary Imagination* (New Haven, Conn.: Yale University Press, 1979).
Neumann, Erich, *The Great Mother: An Analysis of the Archetype*, trans. Ralph Manheim (Princeton, NJ: Princeton University Press, 1955).
Sandler, Linda, 'Interview with Margaret Atwood', *Malahat Review: Margaret Atwood: A Symposium*, 41 (1977): 7–27.

3

Nearer by Far: The Upset 'I' in Margaret Atwood's Poetry

DENNIS COOLEY

The extent to which Margaret Atwood's poetry involves hurtful connections between people and their environment is evident to anyone who has read her books. The theme figures prominently from the outset, in *The Circle Game* (1966), *The Animals in That Country* (1968), *The Journals of Susanna Moodie* (1970), and *Procedures for Underground* (1970). Atwood's attention to 'nature' soon extends dramatically to spiky relationships between the sexes in *Power Politics* (1971). The book set off such shock waves in Canada that to this day literary folk will readily invoke the first poem: 'you fit into me / like a hook into an eye // a fish hook / an open eye' (1).[1] Yet the speaker who presides over the rest of the book is, I eventually will argue, neither so ferocious nor so beleaguered as the quotation or some readers would have us believe.[2]

I shall be doing this mainly by showing how in style and grammar – how in varying and in telling strategies – the speakers situate themselves by virtue of supervising their own narratives.[3] As a consequence I shall not concern myself with whether or not the speakers' fears are justified, nor shall I consider whether they are able to alter the conditions of their external worlds. Such questions are important but perhaps not easily answered. In so far as the speakers' acts of verbal power are internal to them, so are their accounts of exterior (male) threat. If it is important to observe that the protagonists' actions are confined to their mental processes and that they perhaps do not involve active intercession in their environment, we might note that much the same holds for the antagonists – that they operate only within the minds of the speakers and the speaker's prerogatives – and that in an important sense their behaviour is no more overt or public than are the narrators' thoughts.

Though *Power Politics* shook readers – pleased some, offended others[4] – when it appeared, we can easily trace its origins in earlier books. Certainly, readers with Gary Geddes's two Oxford anthologies of poetry[5] daily before them will attest to a view of Atwood's poetry as centred on figures in threat and crisis. As often as not they are in pain – aggressive, isolated, suspicious, hostile, fearful. They retract or lash out, work the edges of paranoia. They speak characteristically of shocking experience in taut lines and impersonal language. What represents perhaps a bigger break in Atwood's poetry comes actually three years later with her next book of poems, *You Are Happy* (1974). What I want to do is to locate the early poems (most specifically those in *Power Politics*) as they can be identified in a certain kind of speaker, then briefly to locate some of the later poems in quite another speaker.

Situate is not such a bad word when it comes to Atwood. She has long been possessed by space and means of location. Along with Northrop Frye she has long asked, in search of herself, her Canadian self: where is here?[6] Her poetry is populated with maps and photographs and scrolls and pages. It is full of explorers and settlers and pioneers and visitors to museums – all kinds of lost arrivals – who need to know where here is. That many of her characters haven't an inkling where they are merely confirms what in Atwood's cartographical imagination is crucial to human habitation and sense of self.

I shall be exploring this mainly by showing how in style and grammar – how in varying and in telling strategies – the speakers situate themselves by virtue of supervising their own narratives. As a consequence I shall not concern myself with whether or not the speakers' fears are justified, nor shall I consider whether they are able to alter the conditions of their external worlds. Such questions are important but perhaps not easily answered. In so far as the speakers' acts of verbal power are internal to them, so are their accounts of exterior (male) threat. If it is important to observe that the protagonists' actions are confined to their mental processes, we might note that the same can be said for the antagonists and that in an important sense their behaviour is no more overt or public than are the narrators' thoughts.

We could take as representative of this obsession the very first poem in *The Circle Game*, one which, when it first appeared, caught readers' attention and regularly has occasioned comment – 'This is a Photograph of Me' (p. 11). The photograph it describes, 'this' photograph, is close to the speaker, brought close to us, for intense scrutiny. It matters that much to her. In the second stanza we discover

> then, as you scan
> it, you see in the left-hand corner
> a thing that is like a branch: part of a tree
> (balsam or spruce) emerging
> and, to the right, halfway up

there is a house. Left, right – these words define space as it relates to the speaker's body: *her* left, *her* right (our left and right, too, as we are invited to share her perspective). We learn that 'In the background there is a lake, / and beyond that, some low hills.' One of the most remarkable things about what the speaker chooses to dwell on is a painstaking sense of where everything and everybody is to be found. Granted the choice of subject, the photograph itself, legitimises this attention, but the choice in itself is indicative.

The speaker scans space with remarkable care. There are left corners, parts of images, acts of emerging (moving or potential moving through space), visual configurations, which she notices halfway up the scene. There are backgrounds and still more distant loci for attention. How spatial this world is, how given to the eye. We go on to discover, surprisingly, that the speaker is not sure exactly where she is: 'It is difficult to say where / precisely, or to say / how large or small I am.' That she is unsure of herself in no way diminishes the point. On the contrary, in groping toward some spot she is trying to situate and to define herself by means of what Eli Mandel has called 'that precise meticulous speech' (p. 170). It is noteworthy that her definitions of self reside in those very markers of location, as if they were spoors staking out her territory.

We can in several ways place the speakers in Atwood's poems. I intend to proceed in a fairly loose way, concentrating on what we might call deictics or proxemics – those words that serve to locate us in space or time. They include prepositions and adverbs, certainly, but in one way or another they involve many parts of speech – verbs and pronouns most conspicuous among them.

We can ease our way into the topic by describing a typical or a composite speaker in Atwood's early poetry.[7] This persona is under the gun, wary as badger, and so perhaps beneficiary of the reader's sympathy, at least in so far as the point of view invites shared understanding. The narrator is not without her resources (I say 'she', though the gender is not certain in every case). Not by a long shot. Readers will recognise this figure from almost any of the early Atwood poems they know. She is distant, distinct, this figure, given to holding off overtures and to forestalling contact. To my reading she is a long way from the persona, 'mocking . . . the man's spatial assumptions', which Frank Davey purports to find in *Power Politics* (p. 27)[8] and much closer to the 'cold, controlled, anaesthetized' speaker Sherrill Grace speaks of (p. 54). Her vocabulary is thick as porridge with talk of war and conflict, goes steely-eyed with suspicion. At times the scenes she recounts are shocking and bizarre, bordering on dream or the surreal. The speaker is watchful to the point of catatonia, and yet she breaks out in sarcastic wit, relishing comical incongruities. She likes scoring points, sometimes scathingly, off her unnamed 'partner'. She seems genuinely to take off when she steps into breezy vernacular. Listen to her throughout *The Circle Game*, where the sardonic voice throws everything on to the table – this, those, these. Take that, it says, there's more where that came from. It is in a way a gesture of throwaway bravado, amused derision. It is this voice Tom Marshall is thinking of when he describes *Power Politics* as 'an account of grim sexual warfare with all the Atwood bite and mordant humour' (pp. 91–2). Irony governs her voice so strongly that it is easy to forget or to overlook its other registers. It is not easy, however, to overlook in these poems the voice which, even as it is confined to the page or to the speaker's mind, loves to direct and to inform. For all the speaker's love of startling metaphor and brisk speech, her language moves often into discursive formations, close to bald statement in fact.

The effect of the voice finds reinforcement in Atwood's lineation. The guiding voice – anxious for all its smart-ass moments – now and then breaks across poetic lines in such a way that the line resists grammar. The grammar asserts itself across lines, in a larger trajectory, yet the line asserts its own integrity and fights a larger arc which the syntax follows. The result is a series of halts, hops, uncertainties, interruptions – made all the more acute by the incisive punctuation which Atwood inserts within the line. The poems at times will move within a series of tight spasms and ticks, rhythms we may choose to assign expressively to the speaker. We can hear them as signs of tight-lipped anxiety from which she delivers in inspired moments enough sardonic jabs to keep off her fears for a little while.

What can be said and what has been said about Atwood's early speakers – they are 'matter-of-fact' (Geddes, 'Now You See', p. 6), 'spare, laconic' and 'clinical' (Colombo), that they observe a 'neat, economical style' and 'dispassionate statement' (MacCallum, p. 359)[9] – holds true for the most part. We can refine those observations, however, and extend them into more minute analyses of the poems. I take it as a given, then, that the early personae are under siege and act as though they are under siege. I am after a more minute look at how they are figured grammatically and deictically.

The speakers in *Power Politics* (I am treating, perhaps recklessly, the speakers in each poem as instances of the same speaker) conform to this rough construction – a speaker insisting – anxiously, facetiously – on orientating herself. Her persistent efforts to establish herself in a place, and to maintain herself there, can of course be read within any number of interpretative schemes. Feminism offers perhaps the most obvious and the most inviting strategy these days,[10] but it is not one I intend directly to enter. I am going to work my way sketchily through a series of determinants. Most of them will be grammatical or linguistic. Each serves to reinforce how concerned the speaker is with defining and maintaining her own space.

It is not perverse in reading *Power Politics* to remind ourselves of a long poetic tradition within which it is written and within which it can be received. These are – for all their quirkiness and contrariness – love poems. As Gloria Onley tells us, they operate within an 'ironic inversion of courtly love' (p. 21). Allowing for considerable range in these matters, we might remind ourselves of that in appreciating how Atwood has positioned her lovers. One convention of the love poem has become so standard as to have turned virtually transparent on us – the prominence and interplay of the two pronouns 'I' and 'you' (the 'you' figuring overwhelmingly to a point of exclusivity in the singular). If I were to hazard a few other wild generalisations I would add that the love poem as we have received it largely is centred *in* the 'I' and anchored *by* the 'I'. (The same can be said for many other poems, I know, above all those derived from Romantic precept and example.) We can say more. This 'I', the 'I' in love poems is not only sensitive to experience (as is the 'I' in the larger category of 'Romantic' form), this 'I' is usually solicitous of the 'you' and commonly will define itself in painful remission from a 'you'. Lamenting the absence of 'you', meditating on the 'you', wanting to bring 'you' into its presence (at least in rhetoric: I say nothing of 'fact'), into the intimacy of 'thou' – the 'I' in love will forever unearth emblems of that absence. Everywhere the 'I' will find consonance between inner self and outer world – the earth will blow a thousand blizzards if need be, if only the speaker might speak of his/her love. 'I' in this sort of love poem (how soon Cooley begins to hedge) will be a humble figure in a condition of abjection, possibly, but so defined that s/he lacks power, often, and seeks somehow to gain it, if only to meet the beloved 'you', in mind if not in body. Such an 'I' is tender, considerate, honouring, self-abnegating even. This 'I' is known for authenticity and is in all things, in all love at least, sincere. That this 'I' derives from centuries-old conventions and participates, arguably, in modern versions of courtly love is something we might remind ourselves of too.

We know, too, of comical inversions to the tradition, all those poems, John Donne's, say, which work – in reverse, in irreverence, in parody – in opposition to the type I have summarised. Such parodies, no less that 'serious' poems, take their life from the conventions. In certain ways the strategy lies behind Atwood's cycle of poems in *Power Politics*, though she works a feminist wrinkle on them, inserts something blacker in her denial of solicitous or desiring lover. Her speakers characteristically announce themselves as refusers of love or at least as nay-sayers to certain definitions of love whose terms they do not happily accept. It can be illuminating therefore to think of Atwood's 'I''s within these conventions.

To begin, we can say this 'I' is not powerless, not by any stretch of the imagination. For starters she lays out the four corners of the universe, takes their measures, tape in hand, compass ready. At times her situation would appear to be precarious, as so visibly it seems in the first poem. There it is, you can see for yourself. (Its topography reinforces our reading): small poem, bottom right corner, the enormous weight of the open page above it, its lop-sided disproportion nearly pushing the words off the page or under it. The empty page feels heavy upon us. The huge silence of all the white would hint of pressure in, what? – disapproval? bruise of the withheld voice? This is no discrete reticence, no gentle pause; we can see that. The enormity of the silence is great enough apparently to imperil the small brief utterance. It would crush it perhaps if we didn't have the hit of the words themselves, their shock, to counterbalance the page, to give it ballast: 'you fit into me / like a hook into an eye // a fish hook / an open eye' (p. 1).[11]

From the outset the speaker anchors herself as the one who does all the thinking, the one who is in charge. She forever defines others (more often the *other*) in proximity to herself: the other is beside her or approaching her or (more characteristically) far from her, right where she wants him. The other in tentative rhythms comes toward her and – reprimanded? spurned? – moves away from her without uttering a word. The speaker doesn't say much either, and seems to assume without explanation or apology an intimate past from which she has expelled a baffled auditor who floats now and then on to the edges of her domain as ineffectual supplicant. From time to time the speaker mentions indices of travel – suitcases, trains, doors. Typically 'I' acts, if only in her mind, to prohibit or sabotage movement through the world, particularly as it involves any approaches 'you' might make toward her.

Yet it is striking how little detail of place we find. Even as Atwood's personae persist in their spatial identities and seek to hold on to their positions, however precarious or provisional they may be, they take no particular hold on the minutiae of place. Despite a splatter of deictics, the vocabulary in fact remains at some 'remove' from specifics we might weigh on our skin or test on our tongues. We move, instead, into lexia that are almost generic. We read of birds, trees, water, for example, but the vocabulary seldom falls into more specific species or occasions, never enters the domain of the proper noun (north of Belleville, on 4th Street, whatever) which might locate the drama demographically, say. The speakers survey their world – survey is the word, so visual and therefore so distanced are they – at some midpoint in the landscape (p. 26). The poems operate, in other words, at a level of the allegorical that exempts them from the demands of a 'reality' effect. Space, then, is symbolic space.

'I' also likes to parcel up the human body into parts – partly in mockery of romantic love and its conventions – into hands and eyes and hearts and faces. We find in *Power Politics* what we find in so many Atwood books of the 1970s especially (I include the novels): namely, a division of head and body at the neck. The neck figures as pinched conduit between faculties (mind/body) whose schism is disastrous. The sense of space this body-sectioning establishes is striking. I would assume that the partial view which these perceptions imply is something we can take as sign of the speaker's divided psyche. But what? Her inability or unwillingness to see anything more than the provenance of mind would permit? Probably. It is convincing to argue also that the scattered body participates in a pattern of the broken body we connect with vegetation deities and the crucifixion (poems on pp. 12, 20, 35, 6, 42, for example), the references also participate in a larger fearfulness which leads into many evasions and suppressions. That they should centre on hands and faces – two of the most expressive parts of the body, where (emblems of self, synecdoche of desire) supposedly we are most realised and most recognisable – cannot be incidental.

The speaker's continual concern for place is evident at every turn, as in the following lines from an untitled poem in *Power Politics*: 'Because you are never here / but always there, I forget / not you but what you look like' (p. 14). We discern another dimension to her stance too. She loves to proceed through structures of logic or apparent logic. Time and again her words are hinged on a vocabulary or argument: because, but, not [this] but [that]. There are many markers of logic in these poems, many resorts to 'or' and 'but'. On one page, after we read that the speaker can do such-and-such, we find in subsequent stanzas, one option per stanza, that alternatively she can do other things: 'or', 'or better', 'or one twist further' (p. 4). The sequence clearly articulates structures of choosing and of thinking one's way through options, even if, as is the case here, the options are themselves facetious and inventive.

The same holds for a conjuction of logic and dispute we run across in a hilarious poem about dining lovers: 'though the real question is / whether or not', 'only I / can do it and so', and 'but you were always ambitious'. In this poem we find a syntax of deliberation in parallel structures: 'some with awe, some only with boredom' (p. 5). On another page we read 'not the shore but an aquarium' (p. 12). The lines practise a modulated knowing, a controlled thinking. The parallel structures set into opposition – not this but that – and so show how solidly placed the speaker is or wishes to be. The migration toward logic is so compelling that a cerebral voice breaks out again and again in these poems. Take the construction 'and you conversely / on whom' (p. 32), where the adverb and the subordinate conjunction register an 'I' so aware that in spite of her emotion – we remind ourselves that these poems bristle with resentment and fear – she still can put cooly into place premeditated patterns. At times the logic takes the form of developed structure. In one case the speaker runs us through a series of options (p. 22). In 'They are hostile nations' the anonymous speaker (she is always anonymous) says, as if writing an elegant essay,

> *In view of* the fading animals
> the proliferation of sewers and fears
> the sea clogging, the air
> nearing extinction
>
> *we should* be kind, *we should*
> take warning, *we should* forgive each other
>
> *Instead* we are opposite, we
> touch as though attacking,
>   (p. 37; my italics)

The structure here proceeds as if advancing an argument: here is the evidence we must weigh, this is what we should do; instead we err, we do not do as we ought. The logical structure often takes on a tone of persuasion in *Power Politics*, the speaker being more than a little inclined to direct her analyses into anxious injunctions.

'They are hostile' observes another sign of calculated control which operates throughout the collection. The sustained metaphor, which Atwood so likes, shows up in many of these pieces. The 'aquarium' poem uses an aquarium as guiding metaphor for its entire length. The human body in its division finds informing and sustained metaphor of water and buoyancy in another part of the book (p. 9). Global disaster provides thematic centre at another point (p. 23). In one of the well-known poems from the collection 'I' defines her relationship with 'you' by means of a subsuming metaphor of the movies (p. 3). The trappings of chivalric romance govern yet another poem from start to finish (p. 7).

If such terms seem inappropriate to this discussion it would be well to remind ourselves of how much Atwood's speakers turn to language of statement and generality. Two would-be lovers go out for supper, discuss various topics; though, as the woman wittily admonishes the man, 'the real question is / whether or not I will make you immortal' (p. 5). One poem ends with these highly discursive lines:

> growing older, of course you'll
>
> die but not yet, you'll outlive
> even my distortions of you
>
> and there isn't anything
> I want to do about the fact
> that you are unhappy & sick
>
> you aren't sick & unhappy
> only alive & stuck with it
> (p. 16)

The lines show verve, true, but little sign of image or trope that often we hope to catch glimpses of in poetry. The words operate, rather, as something approaching simple assertion. There can be no question that on other occasions they baldly assert: 'it is no longer possible / to be both human and alive' (p. 30). Sometimes they are latinate and polysyllabic, close to jaw-wrenching lectures:

> our bodies
> are populated with billions
> of soft pink numbers
> multiplying and analyzing
> themselves, perfecting
> their own demands, no trouble to anyone
> (p. 9)

Wry, yes, it is that, but it announces – as so many features in *Power Politics* announce – towards a language that controls the world and centres that control in the speaking 'I'.

This is a speaker who can self-assuredly say 'This is the way it is' (p. 9). She is into defining in a big way. There are all those copulas to begin with, the way she throws them around the page, the numerous uses of 'there is' and 'there are'. One of the most notable pursuits of a syntax of definition comes in the poem 'He Is a Strange Biological Phenomenon' (p. 8). The title itself establishes the pattern – a state of being verb followed by a noun. In the poem itself we read 'You are widespread / and bad', 'Your flesh ... / is pure protein', 'You are sinuous and without'. The same poem advances a clutch of other definitions, each under aegis of another verb: 'you feed / only on dead meat', 'Your tongue leaves', 'You thrive on', 'you have / no chlorophyll', 'you move / from place to place', and 'you live in'. In another poem, which lampoons romantic love, the speaker proceeds in much the same way: 'You take', 'it goes', 'We waltz', 'we meet', 'you climb', 'I ... stay', 'I paid', 'I have to peel', 'the smell ... lingers' (p. 3). These expressions would seem to avoid the structures of definition and as 'active' verbs to open some kind of movement. In effect they do no such thing. They, too, contribute to the speaker's confident assigning of roles and realities. The verbs are as much part of definition as the copula verbs, for they lay out what are habitual and therefore defining actions, seldom if ever transforming. Know what you are? the lines ask. You are a feeder on dead meat, is what. You're one of those guys who thrive on whatever. This is what you *do*, this is what we *do*, this is what we *are*. The figures are contained within representative behaviour which by its very nature is unchanging.

'I' is the one who gets to do all the defining, though; she holds the dictionary, right there in her hand, subjects those she meets – most commonly 'you' – to the lexical privilege she exercises. She points, she names. This 'I' is pedagogical, sardonic, open-eyed apparently, by her style committed to hard truths – often for other people's benefit, most often for them. You can tell her heart is in all this directing and instructing, she can work up some real fervour for that.

She does something more than identify figures within her own taxonomies. Invariably the names she confers or the definitions she derives reflect unflatteringly on 'you'. The process of disparaging by merely identifying emerges in the narrator's appositives and nouns of address: 'General, you' (p. 7) 'Scavenger, you' (p. 8), 'Imperialist' (p. 15). Here the names stand in full accusation, the pattern of double subject serving to show that the subject is already known and hence already named, and, further, to drive the point home as intensifier. 'You did it / it was you who . . .' the speaker cries out in one poem, 'and it was you whose skin / fell off', 'and you also who laughed'. It was you it was you it was you – accusation rides anaphorically, almost (to my ear) petulantly, through the chant. And then in full flourish of discourse, derision snorting through the polysyllables like a tractor under heavy load, 'I' sums up the man's sins: 'You attempt merely power / you accomplish merely suffering' (p. 32). A more facetious version of this grammar of condemnation enters the speaker's put-down where she says, peremptorily, 'but you were always ambitious' (p. 5). Bad enough to be ambitious, but to be *always* ambitious, there's unremitting, irredeemable, out-and-out evil for you. The grammar – snappy with aphorism – shows how full of presumption the speaker is. It is enough, evidently, to identify the villain, that alone slanders him, puts him in his place. 'I' points the finger – it was you – and that's it, the jig is up, the verdict is in. She puts the finger on him. Judgement by naming, vilification by vocative. She fingers the rascal in her definitions, definitely. She finds power in a fancy kind of name-calling, perfectly in keeping with the prominence she assumes throughout the first part of *Power Politics*.

Her propensity to judge is evident in a preponderance of value-laden terms. 'It would be so good if you'd' (p. 21) she says. 'After all', 'quite ordinary', 'a reasonable body', 'a few / eccentricities, a few honesties / but not too many, too many', 'of course' – all these expressions she arrays in one poem (p. 16). Slightly dismissive, somewhat self-congratulatory, she glosses her superiority with a shower of judgements. Her flourishes establish a tone of slight boredom and dismissal. This, alongside the flippant, easily derisive way she loves to talk.

This same 'I' speaks a language of obligation and compulsion, of 'should's, and 'must's, and 'have-to's. Largely they are directed against the distanced 'you', as are a scurry of imperatives. At one point she turns on him in admonishment, tells him 'you have to admit' (p. 21); at another time tells an 'Imperialist' to 'keep off' (p. 15); on still another occasion scolds 'you' about the nature of the universe and admonishes him to 'get used to it' (p. 9). Even what seems to be formulated as a request takes the form of disguised command: 'Please die I said / so I can write about it' (p 10). Though the two lines are couched within the conventions of courtesy – 'Please die' – they point in quite another direction.

Apparently petition, they turn to command. Such structures often do. The lines certainly express a wish that something should happen and in that way they prove to be less solicitous than at first blush they might appear to be. The imperative is a grammatical form, and a social form, within which this narrator finds herself perfectly comfortable.

She is rather fond, too, of active and transitive verbs. But only under proper conditions. She's a doer, this one. She badgers some figure: 'if you'd / only stay up there / where I put you' (p. 21). Granted her language here is playful and parodic, as it is so often and so attractively throughout the collection, the work jumping with smart-alecky irony. Nevertheless the central figure does preside over verbs whose grammar confers upon her not only power, not only power to do things, but power to do things to other people, notably to govern 'you'. You in such constructions is construed as recipient of action, and more often than not he heels hard as object to the transitive verbs which hold sway over him. That is why she can write with perfect aplomb 'I locate you' (p. 26). Isn't she cartographer of love, map-maker of romance?

Doesn't she get to ask all the questions? And isn't that a lot of fun? Social protocol, in the larger cultural formations within which Atwood's poems participate, requires that we answer questions, it is only decent that we do. We are virtually obliged to respond. The rules of social discourse, more specifically conventions of courtesy, empower the interrogative mode with enormous privilege. Atwood's speaker knows the rules rather well and is quick to exercise every prerogative within its permissions. In her inner fantasies at least she asks, he should answer, he has to. The linguistic relationship which she formulates is asymmetrical in her favour. (Again, my point is not that such a relationship holds in the 'actual' world between the two, merely that within the terms the book offers us, the speakers get to call most of the shots.)

A question can be, of course, sign of openness and searching, even of confusion and vulnerability (it becomes so by the end of the book). More often than not, however, the question for our narrator provides excuse to hector and bully. Take the following lines: 'What do you expect after this? / Applause? Your name on stone?' Clearly, these words are not meant to elicit information nor are they designed to register doubt. On the contrary, they expect no reply, the answers presumably already having come in.

Even allowing for its witticism, this construction is out-and-out tongue-lashing. It is meant to say virtually the opposite of what on the grammatical surface it would seem to be saying. The listener is required to orientate himself within a language created by the speaker. Much of the same holds for the rhetorical question with which the speaker whips the cowed and silenced 'you': 'Do you want to be illiterate?'(p. 9). No, of course not, you're no fool, are you?, not a total fool, shame on you, shape up. Do as you're told and listen for a change, why don't you? The question comes as such questions do, not in solicitation but in exacting instruction. The persona scolds the erring object of her lesson, holds him up to ridicule – it's for his own good – even as she is perhaps teasing, jocular, parodic. 'When will you learn ... ?', 'How long will you demand ... ?' (pp. 32–3), the speaker berates, implies in her kind of questions that these ain't no questions she a-askin', ain't no sense disputin' with her, answerin' back. No question about it.

Pedagogue of the question, governor of the transitive, ruler with irony, namer of all blames, parodist of all folly – the character who presides in the first batch of *Power Politics* poems is a shaker and a maker. Her patterns of definition, of imperative and interrogative, suppose that understanding precedes experience, and that instances follow categories which she has already formulated. She loves as part of her command to pull the rug out from under us. In many poems she introduces a possibility, often what could be construed as a positive one, and will sometimes amplify the hope – then yank away everything she has offered. The take-away structure informs a poem which flirts with the edges (and the clichés) of romantic love. It then speaks of taking the 'beloved' home to – to what? what do we expect? love? sex? Nope, this is Atwood. 'I' takes him home to throw up in the bathtub (p. 6). In the banality, she throws away all romantic possibilities, violates the cultural codes. She shoves disparate codes against one another for sardonic effect. Similarly, another poem teases out some trope on the city as emblem of 'you', moves to what sounds like tender memories, then turns to gruesome end (p. 13) – joke ends, we hit violence, the jolt of that. Another breezes through a crazy parody of history, parodies gestures of male adventure and male supremacy, then comes crashing down into sober horrors in the imminent future (pp. 28–9). Still another opens some sympathy for 'you', and offers telling details about his misery and exhaustion, only to undermine that empathy by turning him into a category of the inept and unglamorous (p. 12).

My favourite example of the give-and-take strategy occurs in 'Small Tactics' (pp. 17–20) whose first two sections I want to spend some time on. The poem opens with compelling signs of human suffering, offered without the corrosion of Atwood's habitual irony. The speaker for once presents herself in so understated and vulnerable a fashion that we are apt to take her language as confession. Her voice takes on a pleading tone: 'Let's go back please / to the games, they were / more fun and less painful.' She admits too to the needs and pain of the other, the recognition culminating in two compelling stanzas:

> in the half light
> your body stutters against
> me, tentative as moths, your
> skin is nervous

> I touch
> your mouth, I don't
> want to hurt
> you any more
> now than I have to
>
> (p. 17)

Here 'you' is allowed some presence, is permitted to come out of his abeyance and to enter gentle moments, coded in references to his eyelashes, the half-light. His overtures bring him into recognition. The painful attempts to 'speak' his fragility find expression in the stutter, in all its metalingual poignancy. The metaphor draws out the effort of speech, the reality of its difficulty. The speech of his body is inadequate, unavailable. Even the mention of 'half' light accentuates the moment of uncertainty, in completion verging on something more (something more than 'half'), some index of romantic setting. The first few stanzas articulate the most lyric poem to this point in the book, in the trembling desire – a stuttering that finds reinforcement in the spasmodic lines – to speak out and to reach across gaps.

That's not what it remains. The poem has opened with confession, apparently naked confession, of the speaker's pain, then assured us of her sensitivity to her lover, of his sensitivity, has brought us to breathless expectancy. There is her poignant response, her moving to tenderness, the moving moment: 'I touch / your mouth, I don't / want to hurt / you any more'. We seem brought here to confession, to apology, to reconciliation even. But then, we hit that last line: 'I don't / want to hurt / you any more / now than I have to.' The counter of that, it stops us in our tracks. The lines at first betray us into belief, finding, just this once, the tenderness we have come to expect in love poetry – an emotional poignancy we so often want. She will not hurt the beloved 'any more'. That's it, it's all over, no longer will they fight, the line closes with that promise, closes on it.

And then the reversal. No, the completion is not there, after 'any more', the line is not over. The adverb detaches from the reassurance, reattaches in a new syntax, enters in the subsequent line a qualification so shocking it comes as threat. There is no absolution. Now we read that 'I' will not hurt 'you' any longer (any more), 'I' will not hurt 'you' more greatly (any more) than 'I' has to. But hurt 'you' 'I' will. 'I' has to. The whole structure of promise and denial pivots on the adverb. One arm (the entire poem up to the penultimate line) takes us in with its simple monosyllabic words which we receive as promise of sincerity, guarantee of romantic love. It wraps us into itself by virtue of the lines' weight, the voice's consistency. In our first reading of the adverb 'any more' the apparently intact line would seem to guarantee that knowledge. Another arm, that single last line, takes its duration from another understanding, wrenches the adverb into a new knowing, and drops us once again into failed romance.[12]

The final line of part 2 then reopens our earlier reading and sends us back where we came from. What looked only a moment ago so positive, so tender, takes on other and bleaker meanings. How about the lines now as they stand on their own, and as they stand under this new awareness, stained in retrospect? How about 'your mouth, I don't'? Is there a *refusal* we now can see if we read the line as self-contained, in the negation of your mouth? In this trajectory 'I' doesn't want 'you's mouth at all, much less does she want to touch or kiss it. When we tip over into the next line this reading finds even more confirmation: 'your mouth, I don't / want'. How about 'I don't / want to hurt', if we were for the moment to suspend ourselves there, as the lines both permit and invite us to do? The words would then not tell us of the speaker's tenderness toward her lover, they would express her desire to avoid pain to herself and would centre not on him but on her.

The speaker in *Power Politics* can scarcely fathom, in her grammatical projections, a world which she does not centre or a world which she does not control. She constantly raises the spectre of a dissolving or prismatic self (pp. 3, 4, 5, 8, 16, 22, for example), an outcome she is resolved throughout the first part of the book to forestall. Above all else, she is determined to keep herself intact and to repel any encroachments on her space or her personal integrity. One of the most dramatic forms of control she exercises is metalingual, language and art being the arena in which the self is tested and defined. We have seen how important it is to the persona to name and to assess the world, to set it in proper directions and categories. It is just as important for her that she be the one who constitutes her world and who serves as creator of it. Quarrelling in a restaurant the speaker sardonically announces 'the real question is / whether or not I will make you immortal' (p. 5). We read elsewhere of her views: 'Please die I said / so I can write about it' (p. 10). It's striking that his death should enable her writing. Write she does, and she talks about it. 'Should I make you a mirage?' (p. 43). 'Because we have no history / I construct one for you' (p. 26). And then, late in the book, even when she comes to reassessment of herself and to personal change, she still thinks of herself as creator, however mistaken now: 'Why did I create you' (p. 47).

It seems safe to say, then, that the first-person pronoun is remarkably pronounced in *Power Politics*. Cool, distant, deprecatory, opinionated, the protagonist anchors herself with wit and seeming certitude. She stabilises herself in spaces which threaten to throw her into vertigo, by pinning herself at the beginnings and endings of lines in self-assertion. The following lines from 'They Eat Out' are typical of the way she locates herself at those points within the line that bear special stress: 'At the moment only **I** / can do it and so // **I** raise the magic fork' (p. 5, my stress). Here she is – bearing witness to herself in a wonderfully sarcastic poem that mocks romantic movies and the clichés which seize the would-be lovers: 'Other people are leaving / but I always stay till the end / I paid my money, I / want to see what happens' (p. 3). In 'She Considers Evading Him' she writes 'I can change **my-** / **self** more easily / than I can change you // I could grow bark' (p. 4, my emphasis), and manages further to foreground herself by multiplying through the breaking of 'myself' into two words 'my' and 'self'. Typically 'I' starts lines and ends lines, finds those moments when the reader's eye and ear will emphasise her naming.

Because hers is an egotism that will not allow 'you' into presence, she never accords him speech nor ever admits him to escape from silence into the independence of dialogue where he could be supposedly self-commissioned (not once does 'you' talk). Her determination to speak of him and for him, and to permit no voices but her own, is something we could name productively within linguistic terms.[13] As 'you' remains always subject to 'I's constitution, he is never allowed to move from her diegesis into his own mimesis, where he would be immune, presumably, from her conceptions of him. It is evident that in her diegetic zeal she has seized the floor and taken over the discourse. Through command and interrogation she is resolved to keep him in his place.

She never permits him to escape from anonymity either, to enter a proper noun in which he may become a particular person with awkward claims on life or embarrassing nearness to her. The distant and would-be lover she conveniently contains in nameless nonentity from which he cannot rise into selfhood and acquire personal substance. A name would perhaps allow him to slide past her deliberate unknowing into the scandal of nearness and the possible terror of agency as someone who might figure as subject of active or (worse) transitive verbs. The 'you' is held – everyone is held for that matter – within the anonymity of pronoun. Certainly the pattern follows a common practice in love poetry (the beloved as pronoun, the lover as pronoun) but in love poems the 'you' is granted exemptions, allowed to appear in glimpses of intimacy, in something other than ironical displays of failure or in generic displays of a totally other. 'I' in Atwood's love poems spurns the beloved's approaches, is something more and something other than Petrarchan lady when she ridicules his vulnerability and his reaching out.[14] Atwood's 'I' conspicuously rejects his 'hand' and its offers of contact and openness.

In refusal, sometimes in reprisal, she slaps it away: 'You asked for love / I gave you only descriptions' (p. 10). The spurning is part of a grammatical strategy we have identified: the personae stick to verbs of definition and command and how, though they are tempted, they refuse predicates of transformation. They also go for the adjective, and for much the same reason. Long stretches of the poems fill up with adjectives and participial phrases – elaborating attitudes, adding up properties (p. 6). At one point the speaker mentions 'what I have to do / in order to stay alive, / I take stock' (p. 23). I take the words to refer more to her lists of qualities than to her lists of nouns. Other entries would encourage that reading. Take the words that reveal the dissolution of self which begins to occur some way into the book. We read that 'the adjectives / fall away from me' (p. 22) and that the speaker must work her way painfully back to more adequate speech. The adjective serves to deliver the narrators into a stasis that they want as counter to a world of change which would go beyond their jurisdiction. The transforming verb would put an end to the anxious hold they have and would eject them from uneventful conditions into a world of narrative shifts. It is precisely such change that the personae's initial strategies are designed to prevent. Until late in the sequence the 'I' goes into a holding pattern, which is visible in every tic of her style and grammar.

Virtually everything I have said applies less well to the last part of *Power Politics*. I have ignored those poems until now because some of them lead us in another direction. In what I say about them lead us in another direction. In what I say about them I disagree with Sherrill Grace who, though she sees signs that the speaker is coming in the end to some understanding (p. 58), argues there is no discernible development in the sequence (p. 55) and that the figures remain locked in 'continued winter and death' (p. 60). I would argue that there is movement toward growth and reconciliation which remarkably resembles the narrative in *The Journals of Susanna Moodie*. Several pieces bring the 'I' of *Power Politics* into openness and acceptance and into greater symmetry of power in her relationship with the shadowy 'you'. She begins to change, as figures in Atwood's book generally change towards the end. Many of the qualities we have identified disappear as the 'I' starts to dissolve into flow and fusion, learns to risk tenderness, comes to notice the pain with which 'you' experiences the world and her own role in it. The book works its way towards the breakthrough and renewal Atwood perennially builds into her narratives. Without any total or irrevocable alteration, the 'I' now comes to enter the world and to immerse herself in it – 'I bend and enter' (p. 52) – she who in the past (if we choose to read the sequence in *Power Politics* as narrative) held off the world and held herself back from it. To cite one instance of the change, we can see how, even though she continues to ask questions, they no longer serve to bully or to reprimand. Now the questions encode uncertainty: 'Should I help you? / Should I make you a mirage?' (p. 43) and 'Should we go into it / together' (p. 29). The speaker now shows hesitation in her speech, moves in thoughtful stops, gentler meditations, opens provisional starts. The rhythms are more and more expressive of humility instead of tension or self-assertion. In further surrender of power she even allows 'you' access to future tense and to the possibilities it permits – if, wish, speculation – she who previously has confined him to past tense, scarcely let him into the present, never mind the future.

By the time we hit *You Are Happy* (1974) Atwood presents different speakers, some of whom are more confident, less self-concerned and ironical. Their world is still often bulging with violence and trauma, perhaps even more so as the poetry comes in later volumes to address the atrocities of terrorist politics and the most brutal misogyny. Still, the poetry titles from then on – *Two-Headed Poems* (1978), *True Stories* (1981), *Interlunar* (1984) – present personae who do not remotely depend upon the wary sarcasm that is so prominent in *Power Politics* or the spatial paranoia we find in *The Circle Game*. One could quote from almost any part of these four later books to make the point. I shall simply choose one – 'Landcrab I' from *True Stories* – briefly to illustrate the point and to conclude the argument. Here is the poem:

> A lie, that we come from water.
> The truth is we were born
> from stones, dragons, the sea's
> teeth, as you testify,
> with your crust and jagged scissors.
>
> Hermit, hard socket
> for a timid eye,
> you're a soft gut scuttling
> sideways, a blue skull,
> round bone on the prowl.
> Wolf of treeroots and gravelly holes,
> a mouth on stilts,
> the husk of a small demon.
>
> Attack, voracious
> eating, and flight:
> it's a sound routine
> for staying alive on edges.

Then there's the tide, and that dance
you do for the moon
on wet sands, claws raised
to fend off your mate,
your coupling a quick
dry clatter of rocks.
For mammals
with their lobes and tubers,
scruples and warm milk
you've nothing but contempt.

Here you are, a frozen scowl
targeted in flashlight, then gone: a piece of what
we are, not all,
my stunted child, my momentary
face in the mirror,
my tiny nightmare.

                                                  (pp. 12–13)

It is easy to notice the attention to 'nature' here but I would want to talk of the shift in attention in other ways, not so much by naming the topic as by noting the way 'I' stations herself now. There is still a preponderance of first-person pronouns, but in 'Landcrab I' they bring her closer to the other, the 'you' in this case being nudged into intimacy with the speaker by virtue of the focus. This 'I' is no longer self-concerned, but drawn to something outside herself and beyond herself. The shift brings the speaker into a more representational style of language, one within which she is prepared to notice and to celebrate the concrete details of what she finds. The crab takes on a palpable presence at every turn. We feel the weight of the 'hard socket', the 'soft gut scuttling / sideways', the 'blue skull, / round bone'. The 'dry clatter' and the 'frozen scowl', the 'wet sand' and 'warm milk' – all these details construct a physical reality whose detail is resonant to the skin. It makes itself available to the eye and ear too, to the sense of a moving body. The poem appeals to the senses with a frequency and a vividness that none of the *Power Politics* poems did, brings the tangible world into our awareness in a way that those early speakers never could, never would, in their fixity on generalities and abstract summary. The senses become more primal now and bring 'I' and the reader into stronger and more intimate proximity – touch, taste, smell, movement – all those senses which earlier would have jeopardised the speakers in their fears of being touched. The speaker in 'Landcrab I' in a sense could care less, she loves to attend on what is around her.

The poem is affirming, accepting, celebratory. It rejoices in multiplicity, in mutuality, in extravagance, uncertainty. And so it offers us multiple tropes and many identities when it attempts to define the crab: soft gut, blue skull, round bone on the prowl, wolf of roots and corners, 'a mouth on stilts' (the most whimsical comparison), small demon. No one of these namings is meant to be definitive or limiting. Each represents a partial glimpse, a delighted glimpse, and seeks no assurance of understanding. A similar principle informs the run of appositives at the end: 'my stunted child, my momentary / face in the mirror, / my tiny nightmare'. This 'I' keeps adding to her list because she realises that it never can be complete or adequate and yet she rejoices in that fact, revels in the plenitude which replaces an earlier preference for asperity and scarcity. The persistence with which she speaks of 'my' crab in all its varieties is in its talk of mothering a kind of blessing, far from any act of mad possession the grammar might imply. It is far, too, from the enormity and wilfulness of the nominative case within which the first-person presented herself in *Power Politics*. The possessive case shows a reaching out of herself, a relinquishing of hold on the predicate (here the crab does all the doing), and of wanting to enter into some affirmative relationship with the external world. How much this happens we can discern, I think, in noting that the larger world, the physical world the early speakers inhabited so obliviously, or so manically, seldom mentioning its specific sensations – this world now moves from symbolic distances in the third person into the closeness of second person in the crab called 'you'. Further, the world is exempted from the provenance of irony and its scathing distance with which earlier speakers supervised things. Metaphor begins to emerge with its more expressive and perhaps less guarded basis – trope which, one could argue, in these poems seeks identity.

Another way of saying this is to note how decentred the speaker is, she who in *You Are Happy*, the book following *Power Politics*, dispersed her voice, lovingly and inventively and hilariously, to other creatures – pigs, owls, foxes, hens, crows, worms – and sang their songs. How much now, in subsequent poems, she opens to the world and invites it in. The imperatives fall away, the scoldings lie in abeyance, fears give way to love, the 'I' begins to lose its stranglehold and the 'you' becomes more prominent and honoured. The speaker's stance permits reciprocity between inside and outside, goes so far (in 'Landcrab II') as to imagine what the crab's perspective might be and to realise that, finally, she and the crab, though they are fellow creatures, are separate and unknown to one another. There is a new humility, too, in her saying that the crab is beyond her capacity to know it and to handle it in language (pp. 14–5). Simpler, more understated, more outward and confirming, these speakers constitute entirely different poems. They are different at least for Atwood, although they in certain ways are more traditional in the conventions they observe than are the earlier ones.

In laying out these distinctions I make no claims about large shifts in Atwood's own emotional or psychological economy. My argument has sought, simply, to identify through style and grammar two very different strategies which the speakers assume at different times in Atwood's poetry. Further, the argument does not find the later poems, or the earlier poems, 'better', it merely finds them different (though if I were to insert a gratuitous opinion I myself would vote for the later poems, finding them more resonant and, yes, more poignant).

Notes

1. George Bowering has recently said that the lead poem 'has worked itself free from the book it first began, then decorated. If it gets more famous it will work itself free from its author, as quotations from the Bible, Shakespeare and Pope have done' (p. 90).
2. Gloria Onley, for one, is inclined to see the speaker in *Power Politics* as 'the female prisoner of the machismo love structure that romantic love, in its modern version' (p. 22) has made so 'frustrating' and so 'mechanical' (p. 21). She intriguingly names the relationship sadomasochistic and identifies as central to the relationships enunciated in Atwood's book a 'concept of ownership or romantic "possession" resulting in exploitation by the man and idealization and obedience by the woman', who is forced into prison or victimisation (p. 34). As will soon become apparent, I hear the book quite differently being more inclined to see a state of mind (female fear) where Onley sees actual action (male aggression), and finding the protagonist or protagonists, until the beginnings of reconciliation late in the book, to be assertive to the point of command. I also take

the speaker to be complicit – caught as agent and victim – in the violence in ways which Onley, it seems to me, does not.

3. My argument here parallels one which Jean Mallinson has made in a remarkable 1985 monograph on Atwood. Whereas my analysis largely concentrates on a grammar of power, hers explores tropes and poetic kinds in Atwood. I want to note, however, her descriptions of the early Atwood personae and their rhetorical strategies, acknowledging how similar are our claims:

> The tense aesthetic of the earlier poems [up to and including *Power Politics*] moved the poet towards tropes of evasion, fragmentation, or disguise – periphrasis, synecdoche, kenning; of containment or power – the impaling epithet, the simile in oxymoronic pairs; of risk and the cancelling of risk in enjambement balanced on revisionary disclosure; of the high theatrics of hyperbole and the accumulation of elements in apposition.

> Mallinson also identifies, as do I, a shift in Atwood's personae in the later collections, a shift into 'tentative rhetoric, with its nuances of expression, its transformation of definition, argument, and imperative' and its emphasis on 'rendering, suggestion, and longing' (p. 35).

4. See, for instance, Judith McCombs's summary (see note 11).

5. *20th-Century Poetry and Poetics* and *15 Canadian Poets* × 5.

6. In his 1965 'Conclusion to a *Literary History of Canada*', for instance, Frye writes:

> It seems to me that Canadian sensibility has been profoundly disturbed, not so much by our famous problems of identity, important as that is, as by a series of paradoxes in what confronts that identity. It is less perplexed by the question 'Who am I?' than by some such riddle as 'Where is here?' (p. 220)

7. Mandel provocatively locates the Atwood protagonist, in all the early writings, within the conventions of Gothic 'in which the chief element is the threat to a maiden, a young girl, a woman' (p. 167). Judith McCombs later develops this approach, oddly with no acknowledgement of Mandel.

8. Davey later qualifies his claims when he acknowledges that the speaker 'has adopted "male" language structures' but supposes she has done so 'in order to communicate with men' without endorsing the structures (p. 43).

9. If my comments seem severe, a reader might consider what Michael Ondaatje has said about the central figure in *The Circle Game*: 'the cannibalistic speaker . . . demands to know everything of the people around her' (p. 23).

10. Linda Sandler's remarks could be mildly illustrative. *Power Politics*, she has said, is 'a book of poems which coolly dissects the foetid corpse of a love affair' (p. 6). Judith McCombs and Gloria Onley both

lay out more extensive feminist readings of Atwood's early poetry, McCombs being to my mind more persuasive of the two in her awareness of the speakers' complicities and the males' vulnerabilities. Here is part of what McCombs says about *Power Politics*:

> the Gothic sadomasochistic pair are true – so true that the book is usually read as sexist realism, women readers confirming it and men readers protesting, as Atwood has observed. But the pair are also true reversed, he victim and she heartless. And always they are characters within a third, Frankensteinian Gothic where as creator-seer she is Victor, he the hapless being.   (pp. 47–8)

It is this other and underdeveloped reading of the poetry – the protagonist as site of power – which I want to look at.

11. See Bowering's 'Atwood's Hook' for an interesting meditation on the status and meaning of these lines.

12. The placing of 'now' is instructive. Setting it not at the end of the penultimate line (a lineation which would have worked semantically), but at the beginning of the ultimate one makes a difference. If we were to read 'I don't / want to hurt / you any more now' instead of 'I don't / want to hurt / you any more', the second-last line would not bear the same firmness of promise. It would not speak so clearly or so unequivocally of the speaker's reassurance. It's: I don't want this any more, period, no ifs, ands or buts, no qualifications or reservations – just the simple assertion, brought home with the stress on 'more'. The line, ending after 'more', and not after 'more now', eliminates what would have been a limp after-thought falling away into the unstressed word.

13. Judith McCombs points out, though, that in accordance with female Gothic the imperilled hero-victim whose narratives these are seldom if ever speaks herself (p. 38).

14. One index of failed love in these poems is the bed. It figures as overturned bed (p. 6), place of occupation but not rest or love (p. 14), as deserted mattress (p. 21), as 'impartial' hospital bed and therefore site of sickness and potential cure (p. 42). In no case, at least in no case until late in the book, does the bed become site for love or passion.

15. Jean Gibbs makes a related point when she detects in *Procedures for Underground* a pattern of affirmation which emerges in the sequencing (pp. 61, 64).

References

Atwood, Margaret, *The Circle Game* (Toronto, 1966).
—— *Power Politics* (New York, 1971).
—— *True Stories* (Toronto, 1981).
—— *You Are Happy* (Toronto, 1974).
Bowering, George, 'Atwood's Hook', *Open Letter*, eighth series (Winter 1992) pp. 81–90.
Colombo, John Robert, '*Selected Poems*', *Globe and Mail*, 24 April 1976, p. 38.
Davey, Frank, *Margaret Atwood: A Feminist Poetics* (Vancouver: Talonbooks, 1984).
Frye, Northrop, 'Conclusion to a *Literary History of Canada*', in his *The Bush Garden: Essays on the Canadian Imagination* (1965; Toronto: Anansi, 1971) pp. 213–51.
Geddes, Gary, 'Now You See it . . . Now You Don't; An Appreciation of Atwood and MacEwen, Two Grand illusionists', *Books in Canada*, vol. 5, no. 7 (July 1976) pp. 4–6.
—— (ed.), *15 Canadian Poets x 5* (Toronto: Oxford University Press, 1985).
—— (ed.), *20th-century Poetry & Poetics*, 3rd edn (Toronto: Oxford University Press, 1985).
Gibbs, Jean, '*Procedures for Underground*', *Fiddlehead*, vol. 87 (Nov.–Dec. 1970) pp. 61–4.
Grace, Sherrill, *Violent Duality: A Study of Margaret Atwood* (Montreal: Vehicule, 1980).
MacCallum, Hugh, 'Letters in Canada: Poetry', *University of Toronto Quarterly*, vol. 36, no. 4 (July 1967) pp. 354–79.
Mallinson, Jean, *Margaret Atwood and Her Works* (Toronto: ECW, [1985]).
Mandel, Eli, 'Atwood Gothic', *Malahat Review*, vol. 41 (January 1977) pp. 165–74.
Marshall, Tom, 'Atwood Under and Above Water', *Malahat Review*, vol. 41 (January 1977) pp. 89–94.
McCombs, Judith, 'Atwood's Haunted Sequences: *The Circle Game, The Journals of Susanna Moodie*, and *Power Politics*', in Arnold E. Davidson and Cathy N. Davidson (eds), *The Art of Margaret Atwood: Essays in Criticism* (Toronto: Anansi, 1981) pp. 35–54.
Ondaatje, Michael, '*The Circle Game*', *Canadian Forum*, vol. 47 (April 1967) pp. 22–3.
Onley, Gloria, 'Power Politics in Bluebeard's Castle', *Canadian Literature*, vol. 60 (Spring 1974) pp. 21–42.
Sandler, Linda, 'Preface', *Malahat Review*, vol. 41 (January 1977) pp. 5–6.
York, R. A., *The Poem as Utterance* (London: Methuen, 1986).

4

Surfacing: Separation, Transition, Incorporation

DAVID WARD

I

Arnold van Gennep's classic in comparative ethnography, *Les Rites de passage*, was first published in 1909.[1] It collects accounts, more often anecdotal than scientific, of customs and societal patterns throughout the world in which the experience of change was supported, mediated, protected, magically assisted, its meaning constructed and validated, by ceremony and ritual. Van Gennep began by looking at territorial division, movements across boundaries or frontiers, from one linguistic, religious, social or political domain to another. The journey across the frontier may be shortened to the crossing of the threshold where, nevertheless, interdictions must be overcome by magico-religious sanction. Territorial divisions such as these are never simply spatial: transit from one to another will always have implications which are cultural, religious, legal, broadly speaking ideological.

Territorial transit, and the rites associated with it, merge into transitions of personal status: movements from one social, economic or occupational state of being to another: birth, initiation to adulthood, betrothal, marriage, priestly, political or other occupational function, and death. Van Gennep discerned three moments in the generalised process, which he structured by spatial metaphors of journeying and the threshold: rites of separation (*preliminal rites*), rites of transition (*liminal, or threshold rites*), and ceremonies of incorporation (*postliminal rites*).

Van Gennep and those on whom he relied for his data were, of course, selecting, structuring, and analysing according to the predispositions of their own nineteenth- and early twentieth-

94

century Europocentric ethos which differed sharply from the societies he was recording at second or third hand. His notion of frontiers was shaped profoundly by nineteenth-century Europe, with its emerging nation-states – a very specialised system of political cultures. In 1886, 24 years earlier, it had attempted to impose its own concept of 'frontier' on a reluctant Africa, with all the confusion that has entailed. Five years after the book was published the 1914–18 war raised profound questions about the system of frontier division in Europe itself.

Across the Atlantic the concept of 'frontier', whatever it may or may not have meant in indigenous societies, had acquired an almost magico-religious force of its own. Among other things, the invader defined the line in terms of possession. Until the latter part of the century, to cross the western frontier into a nation with entirely different concepts of ownership or trusteeship might be thought of as removing that frontier: to cross was simultaneously to possess and redefine, to be redefined and possessed by it. A 'frontiersman', as well as economic and political functions, accomplished a quasi-magical function. Instead of claiming ritual protection and submitting to restrictions imposed by the alien structures of the cross-border territory he declared them invalid. The frontier became the man – the 'frontiersman'. As a final validation of the process he imposed an alien culture of borders on the indigenous peoples by the enclosure in reservations, contemptuous minuscule parodies of the nation-state.

II

Surfacing is a novel which both invites and resists interpretation: its force is bound in with its indeterminacy. Much of that indetermination arises from the fact that, like much of the best contemporary writing, it occupies itself with internal frontiers – and it's worth noting that this concern is strongest where the writers, for cultural, geographical, historical or gender reasons, have a consciously oppositional stance towards the structures and centres of social, economic, political, ideological and magico-religious power. Even in societies which permit limited entry from the out-groups into the centres of power, frontiers are internalised, sensed intimately as enclosure, division, exclusion. The winning of an internal freedom, the invasion of forbidden territories of the self, may involve a kind of painful transit which cries out for ritual, magical expression. If the reversion of the narrator in *Surfacing* to a quasi-animal state is to be thought of as madness, then it may be that some kinds of madness are approaches to sanity in a society which resolutely defines its own sickness as a norm. Such experiments in alternative forms of consciousness, however painful, may be thought of as transit, in a sense which is quite close to van Gennep's. Some such deep syntax is at the heart of Doris Lessing's *Briefing for a Descent into Hell* and Bessie Head's *A Question of Power*, as it is at the heart of R. D. Laing's persuasions, but unlike these, the narrator of *Surfacing* takes, as the crucial experiment in consciousness, a transit through radical rejection of humanity.

In an interview with Graeme Gibson, Atwood begins to comment on the sentence from *Surfacing*: 'The trouble some people have being German ... I have being human' (p. 130)[2] by talking about original sin, then withdraws from that line of enquiry with 'this is too complicated to talk about' and laughter.[3] She expands this later, with an obvious determination not to seem to take herself too seriously:

> the ideal thing would be a whole human being. Now if your goal is to be whole, and you don't see the possibility of doing that and also being human, then you can try being something else ... there are great advantages in being a vegetable, you know ...[4]

The presence of frontiers is felt from the beginning of the book, in the city 'as the last or first outpost depending on which way we were going' (p. 7). With 'the disease is spreading up from the south' (p. 7) (though this in the first place refers to tree-disease) the ambiguity between territorial and internal, bodily or mental frontiers begins to develop. Then 'the signs saying GATEWAY TO THE NORTH' (p. 9) are followed quickly with a potent image of division between generations, the resentment of the unnamed narrator at her parents living long enough to change, and the serio-comic desire to freeze-frame them in an enclosure or reservation of the memory:

> I thought of them as living in some other time, going about their own concerns closed safe behind a wall as translucent as jello, mammoths frozen in a glacier. (p. 9)

– the effect is deepened by an image of real and brutal power, the abandoned rocket silo which 'looks like an innocent hill, spruce-covered, but the thick power lines running into the forest give it away' (p. 9). The narrator's frustrated sense of her failure to control the residual tyranny of parents, to isolate them behind a boundary of the mind, is echoed and given depth by this memento of the failure of the US–Canadian border to exclude alien political power. David's repeated litany of 'Bloody fascist pig Yanks' has some of the impotent resentment of the insecure trying to shake off the introjected dominance of father and mother: it parodies but doesn't exorcise the sense of subordinating force crossing borders, exerting secret power wherever it goes.

The knee-jerk response places the novel, not only in territorial and psychological space, but also in a characteristically Canadian ideological dilemma; anxiety about economic domination, anxiety about cultural pressures, lead to a concern which is more profound than David's slogans of envy. But at least equally important to the novel as production in a specific space and time are the events occurring on another continent, the conflict in Vietnam, with its profound effects on American perceptions of power, responsibility and pride: *Surfacing* was written at a time when Canadians viewed this brutal episode as an impulse to an even greater energy in searching for an independence which was border, marked by the sign that says BIENVENUE on one side and WELCOME on the other' (p. 11). It's a preoccupation with the anxiety of linguistic alienation which echoes that of *The Journals of Susanna Moodie* (1970) where 'Disembarking at Quebec' is crossing a frontier, not just into a francophone province, but into a radical questioning of the stability of self: 'I am a word / in a foreign language'[5] is a separation from familiar cultural and linguistic constructs, a preliminary moment which parallels the wry paradox of 'Now we're on my home ground, foreign territory', and later, 'Language divides us into fragments, I wanted to be whole' (p. 146) So 'This is border country' (p. 26) challenges questions about what is being left behind, what is being entered:

> Now we're on my home ground, foreign territory. My throat constricts as it learned to do when I discovered people could say words that would go into my ears meaning nothing.   (p. 11)

If home is a territory of incomprehensible language, to return home is painfully to deconstruct all the acquired meanings which protect and enable the social self – to separate and, perhaps, after a process of transition, to begin to acquire the rudiments of a new, seemingly alien, 'language', to become incorporated into a different state. Language defines states of being in a sense much more profound than the Babel-division of man. Language can dehumanise, make us what David or the narrator call 'Americans', body-snatchers from outer space:

> If you look like them and talk like them and think like them then you are them, I was saying, you speak their language, a language is everything you do. (p. 129)

But there is another level of inhuman language which guarantees, a deep structure which survives the radical instability of personality. When the narrator wakes to birdsong she finds that she has lost the capacity to understand it – but she retains sensitivity to its assertion of territorial integrity:

> They sing for the same reason trucks honk, to proclaim their territories: a rudimentary language. Linguistics, I should have studied that instead of art. (p. 41)

In the boundary country of dawn Joe, too, experiments with a pre-human language, like an animal or bird, jealous of some mind-territory, whose instincts to defend one must treat with caution:

> 'It's all right,' I said, 'I'm here,' and though he said 'Who? Who?', repeating it like an owl, he allowed me to ease him back down into the bed. I'm afraid to touch him at these times, he might mistake me for one of the enemies in his nightmare; but he's beginning to trust my voice. (p. 41)

The crossing of a linguistic border, like 'surfacing', a transit from one medium and another, is a premonition of its inversion, the entry into a pre-linguistic state, prefiguring the wordless signing of a territory, and the identity which prowls within its frontiers, like the self of dream: 'They were here though, I trust that. I saw them and they spoke to me, in the other language'. (p. 188). Jenness reports that some indigenous tribes believed that there had once been a golden age in which 'man could freely communicate with the animals, which had the same thoughts, the same emotions' as man, and could take off their animal skins when they wished, but 'tricksters or heroes transformed the world, and a chasm began to separate man and the animals'. The animals then became unable to reveal their inner identity to man, only taking off their dress in private in their homes.[6] In *Surfacing*, Atwood's complex variations never quite repeat the original Amerindian theme, but in multiple ways they indicate the inversion of that separation and transformation, or translation. At the heart of this there is the notion of a level of language largely unregarded by man, one which might be said to exist around or beneath the elaborations of a human dialect – a level which has a semiotic if not a symbolic force.

There's a knot of paradox here. Since *Pamela* there has been a strong vein of narrative, particularly crucial in woman-centred narratives, in which the act of writing is intimately related to the process of being: Pamela's and Clarissa's letters are the means by which they preserve identity and integrity under siege. In Proust, James, Virginia Woolf, Joyce, Lessing, different as they are from each other, there are conventions which, similarly, permit us to see the flow of language as the act of life – almost as the complex inner flow and movement of the body. Each of these artists also shares a sense, paradoxically confirming this, that the self may survive the breaking down of language. Atwood takes the matter further. She maps a transition in which release from language becomes a condition for the discovery of self. Language, far from being a liberating resource, becomes an instrument of control, of confinement, of deformation, and yet, paradoxically neither limitation nor liberation can be expressed except in language.

WELCOME/BIENVENUE is a border of separation, then, even though the 'I' of the book carries with it the world, the state, the language, the art, the totality of conditions that pre-exist the separation, in the form of Anna, David, Joe, and the artefact-self, the 'I' that accompanies them. It is an ethos of accumulation and incoherence, of uncommunicating words and arbitrary signs. David and Joe are making a movie, *Random Samples*:

'How can you tell what to put in if you don't already know what it's about?' I asked David when he was describing it. He gave me one of his initiate-to-novice stares. 'If you close your mind in advance like that you wreck it. What you need is flow'.   (p. 10)

David teaches Communication. If *Random Samples* is bird-song without territory, hieroglyphic without text, Anna maintains

herself and their marriage by a similar communication. It isn't even
clear that David is receiving the message she sends by her own
artifice, the cosmetic manufacture of self. It may be that the
communication is for Anna's own benefit, the illusion being the
only form of statement she can bear to make or to inhabit:

> her artificial face is the natural one . . . Anna says in a low voice,
> 'He doesn't like to see me without it,' and then, contradicting
> herself, 'He doesn't know I wear it.' . . . Maybe David is telling
> generous lies; but she blends and mutes herself so well he may
> not notice. (p. 44)

Language, movies, make-up, the mutual illusion of marriage, form
the communicating surfaces which structure and are structured by
David and Anna, structure and are structured by their society. The
magical book behind these acts of transformation is the glossy
advertisement or *Playboy* centrefold, icons manufacturing desire
and the object of desire, distorting the feminine body to the
power/possession fantasy of the phallocrat:

> a seamed and folded imitation of a magazine picture that is itself
> an imitation of a woman who is also an imitation, the original
> nowhere, hairless lobed angel in the same heaven where God is a
> circle, captive princess in someone's head. (p. 165)

The narrator's work as an illustrator is one of the ways in which
this territory of the mind claims her, though her discomfort is
patent: 'I can do that, I can imitate anything' (p. 53) though 'It isn't
my territory but I need the money' (p. 52).

'Surfacing' is not only a word for emergence; it may also mean
the making of surfaces, the occupation at the heart of the society to
which David and Anna belong. To which the 'I' of the fiction
belongs, partially, as well; though she brings to the frontier a
diversity of conscious separations, a suspension awaiting a moment
of over-determination. 'A divorce is like an amputation, you survive
but there's less of you' (p. 42); ' "Do you have a twin?" I said No.
"Are you positive," she said, "because some of your lines are
double" ' (p. 8), missing father, absent brother, dead mother,
invented husband and, as emerges later, aborted child: 'A section of
my own life, sliced off from me like a Siamese twin, my own flesh
cancelled' (p. 48).

Her residual affection for Joe is at least partly because he seems potentially to be detachable from surfaces – not the *loup-garou* but the other sort 'in some of the stories they do it the other way round, the animals are human inside and they take their fur skins off as easily as getting dressed' (p. 56) – the very same Indian stories reported by Jenness.

Her own failures as illustrator echo Joe's as a potter; it's a treasured evidence of failure to speak the language, to belong to the territory which must be left: 'Perhaps it's not only his body I like, perhaps it's his failure; that also has a kind of purity' (p. 57). Like 'madness' it might be that 'failure' in this sense is the first glimmer of a capacity to be whole. And her affection for his body seems to be that, under the surfaces, its vulnerability to the distortive machine is as great as any woman's.

III

Van Gennep's three moments, separation, transition, incorporation, are all present in *Surfacing*, broadly coinciding with the Parts One, Two and Three of the novel. Part One ends with an immersion, a separation from land and a movement into water, another kind of border and the inversion necessary for 'surfacing':

> I stand there shivering, seeing my reflection, and my feet down through it, white as fishflesh on the sand, till finally being in the air is more painful than being in the water and I bend and push myself reluctantly into the lake.   (p. 75)

But the connections are too subtle for one to see the discourse as sliced simply into three pieces of narrative cake. Part Two begins with a brief meditation on what separation does *not* mean:

> The trouble is all in the knob at the top of our bodies. I'm not against the body or the head either: only the neck, which creates the illusion that they are separate. The language is wrong, it shouldn't have different words for them.   (p. 76)

We are reminded that the separation is from linguistic habit, and from the social and cultural deformations that accompany it, from

David and Anna and Joe's world and language. The paradox is that the comfortingly familiar illusions of language have to be deconstructed from within the language itself, with all its socially constructed kits of deception:

> I was seeing poorly, translating badly, a dialect problem. I should have used my own. In the experiments they did, they found that after a certain age the mind is incapable of absorbing any language; but how could they tell the child hadn't invented one, unrecognizable to everyone but itself?   (p. 76)

The problem of whether a private language may be called a language at all is compounded by the problems of whether it can be a first and only language. 'Translation' as the conversion of a stable unit of meaning from one linguistic structure to another won't do, in any case, for the simultaneously subversive and creative process the narrator suggests. 'Translation' becomes available as a concept only if one recovers its parallel meanings: 'Translation, *O.E.D.*, 3. Transformation, alteration, change; changing or adapting to another use; renovation'. In Atwood's use of the concept of language in this novel there has always been the sub-text of language as, in a Platonic sense, the form of a society. But, in so far as it is that, it becomes the *persona* too, the social self. 'Translating', then, becomes, not a linguistic transit, but a personal one: Joe's outer body shows the capacity to slip away, revealing the naked self – a translation which will be seen as failure, if that is what your language names it. The translation of 'I' will be seen as madness, if that is what your language names it. But the process is reversible: like Einsteinian relativity an effect which depends on the place from which one sees it – it's a matter of decipherment. The translation of 'I' is simultaneously the change in 'them', and that perception is the inversion which enables the self, permits the radically unstable self to grasp the power from which it had seemed excluded by language's uncrossable frontiers:

> I'm not sure when I began to suspect the truth, about myself and about them, what I was and what they were turning into . . . but it was there in me, the evidence, only needing to be deciphered. From where I am now it seems as if I've always known, everything, time is compressed like the fist I close on my knee in the darkening bedroom, I hold inside it the clues and solutions

and the power for what I must do now.   (p. 76)

Translation becomes transition, transition becomes a deciphering. And, of course, much of Part Two is concerned with enciphering and deciphering. There are the childish scrapbooks, records of her own and her brother's educations in being conventionally constructed male and female. The images are as accumulative as David and Joe's *Random Samples*, but they do not lack a coherence, unless we see the whole of that culture – its gender rhetoric, its internalisation in the minds and lives of its victims, male and female, whatever their sexual orientation – a matter of incoherence. And that, too, is a question of decipherment, of where one is now, as relative as the recession rate of a red-shift star.

The other set of ciphers is, of course, the hieroglyphics left by the missing father. These were introduced briefly in Chapter 6, and the context of their introduction is interesting. The family had moved to its territory, the cabin enclosed on an island, surrounded by a lake, in this linguistically alien territory, to defend reason: 'isolation was to him desirable. He didn't dislike people, he merely found them irrational . . . that's what Hitler exemplified: not the triumph of evil but the failure of reason' (p. 59). It's a cabin in the woods, but not Walden, even though his aim is reported as being to recreate the life 'of the earliest ones who arrived when there was nothing but forest and no ideologies but the ones they brought with them' (p. 59). Eventually those 'earliest ones' become, not white invaders, but the indigenous peoples, with a very different approach to reality than the father's trust in reason.

Both children have been brought up in isolation, anonymity, within boundaries which define an ideal of reason, protected by exclusion in a territory which excludes the irrational, which favours 'the knob at the top of our bodies' over the rest. And yet what the sketchbooks show is children being brought up in the most banal kind of socially endorsed unreason, defining stereotypical roles as the norm. The 'I' who is so constructed cannot decipher the hieroglyphics left by her father because she is aware only of a dipolar opposition: a reason which excludes the irrational, and a set of social norms and expectations which exclude any deviation as madness. So 'he might have gone insane. Crazy, loony. Bushed, the trappers call it when you stay in the forest by yourself too long' (p. 60).

It is only in Part Two that the narrator glimpses as one of the rudiments of 'translation' the idea that there should be a way for head and body, reason and unreason to atone to each other, and blames 'the neck, which creates the illusion that they are separate'. When she looks at the drawings for a second time her unreconstructed self still can find only 'total derangement', but a hint of translation comes through: 'The drawing was something he saw, a hallucination; or it might have been himself, what he thought he was turning into' (p. 101), a cipher key which is set by with the alternative, reasonable, but empty theses of Dr Robin M. Grove. Appearance of reason displaces and destabilises the self, the transit towards incorporation of reason and unreason has faltered at the beginning. It is as if a patient of Jung, examining the *mandala* images she herself has made, refuses them as evidences of an interior territory, hieroglyphs which bring to the surface an archetypal drama of momentous significance, running with relief to the handiest rationalising explanation:

> I pressed my fingers into my eyes, hard, to make the pool of blackness ringed with violent colour. Release, red spreading back in, abrupt as pain. The secret had come clear, it had never been a secret, I'd made it one, that was easier. My eyes came open, I began to arrange.   (p. 103)

It's not quite the same as 'the stranger' in Indian territory Atwood describes in *Survival*:

> There *is* an image of the divine present in the landscape – the 'manitou' which the Indians have carved – but since the traveller is looking where he has been taught to look, up towards the sky, and since he is demanding that any revelation shall arrive in his terms – terms he has learned in Europe – he misses the real revelation which is there on the ground . . . [7]

but only in that the estrangement of the observer is in her nurturing in a continent of reason, rather than in Christian Europe.

The eye-pressing might be thought of again, as retreat from magical frontier; a line at which violence, pain, applied force are the only ways to prevent the decipherment, the translation of the text which demands translation of the self, to prevent the sight of what might be another translation: 'what he thought he was turning into'.

In 1928 C. G. Jung, writing 'On Psychic Energy', spoke of symbolic formations expressive of the 'extraordinarily important transition from the biological to the cultural attitude' with its redirection of human energies. He adduces examples from several Indian magico-symbolic practices to illustrate the process of symbol formation which goes with this transformation: *wakonda* among the Dakotas, *oki* among the Iroquois and *manitu* (or manitou) among the Algonquins. According to Jung, all concepts have the abstract meaning of magical potency or productive energy, and their emergence into symbolic discourse is accompanied by a changed teleology in the human libido.[8] With this in mind, the father's encoding of 'what he thought he was turning into' (p. 101), or indeed the decoding of ambiguous glyphs by the narrator, might be seen as evidences of their respective relationships, real or assumed, to this transforming energy. The hints continue, from the old rationality of the father, denying that people resurrect like daffodils: 'but people are not onions, as he so reasonably pointed out, they stay under' (p. 104), to the change in name and the small red x which marks the location of the drawing on the map as White Birch Lake, itself transformed: 'The printed name was different, *Lac des Verges Blanches*, the government had been translating all the English names into French ones' (p. 105) – and, as we later learn, this lake is one place where the southern tree-disease has not harmed the birches.

The outward form of the treasure hunt or the detective story, with clues scattered on maps and mysterious ciphers, covers another text: the inability to translate, the separations, the barriers, the invisible surfaces which reveal yet distort:

At some point my neck must have closed over, pond freezing or a wound, shutting me into my head ... it was like being in a vase, or the village where I could see them but not hear them because I couldn't understand what was being said. Bottles distort for the observer too: frogs in the jam jar stretched wide.   (pp. 105–6)

IV

Looking at the hieroglyphs, looking at 'I' looking at the hieroglyphs, might prompt us to go one step further in examining the linguistics, and, fused with the linguistics, the philosophy and psychology of it.

In *La Révolution du langage poetique*[9] Julia Kristeva points to what she calls the translinguistic elements in signifying practices such as art, poetry and myth. She adduces two essays in what she calls the 'interrogation of externality' in this translinguistic dimension.

Followers of Melanie Klein have attempted to restore the dimensions and operations of the Freudian unconscious to the linguistic process, and in doing so have rehabilitated the notion that the pre-Oedipal fragmented body is at work in all the subject's semiotic activities. This approach, however, has failed to account for the transition from the pre-Oedipal semiotic to the post-Oedipal symbolic and syntactic operations of language. Others, by proposing the idea of a 'subject of enunciation', have sought to account for intersubjective relationships. This school of thought sees language operating within deep categorial structures, semantic, logical and inter-communicational. In these two approaches Kristeva distinguishes two modalities, the semiotic and the symbolic, but urges that no system of signification can be exclusively the one or the other: if we reject the subject-less approach of formal linguistics, we have to account for the relationship between language and a subject who is simultaneously semiotic and symbolic in the modality of his/her production.

Kristeva adopts Plato's term *chora* to denote the primary processes which lie behind all signification, a totality which itself is non-expressive, constantly in motion under the impulsion of instinctual drives and stases, fundamentally unstable and provisional in nature. It has no position, no thesis, it does not itself signify, and yet, in tandem with the Freudian concept of the subject implicit in the proposition of an subconscious, it can be used to propose ways in which significance is constituted. Kristeva refers to Plato, giving the idea of the *chora* a distinctively Kleinian dimension, and one which gives the thesis a force in gender politics. Plato:

> calls this receptacle or *chora* nourishing and maternal, not yet unified in an ordered whole because deity is absent from it. Though deprived of unity, identity or deity, the *chora* is nevertheless subject to a regulating process [*reglementation*] which is different from that of symbolic law but nevertheless

effectuates discontinuities by temporarily articulating them and then starting over, again and again.[10]

The drives at work in the *chora* are seen as being dominated by the sensorimotor organisation, itself structured in and by the mother's body, and the subject is seen as being both generated and negated by the process of drives and stases at work within the *chora*.

Kristeva distinguishes a frontier-line between the semiotic and the symbolic, the emergence into signification (what she describes as a thetic phase) through a 'rupture, and/or boundary':

All enunciation, whether of a word or of a sentence, is thetic. It requires an identification; in other words, the subject must separate from and through his image, from and through his objects. This image and objects must first be posited in a space that becomes symbolic because it connects the two separated positions, recording them or distributing them in an open combinatorial system.[11]

There are profound ontological and epistemological difficulties in Kristeva's thesis. Like Freud's theory of the subconscious, Lacan's account of the instability of the self, like Melanie Klein's hypothesis of the role of the mother in the child's developing awareness, Kristeva's position, which owes much to all of them, cannot by its very nature be submitted to audit by experiment, cannot be proved or disproved. Like the myths of Jung or those of Plato, its persuasions may be seen as a kind of poetic fiction, and there's nothing wrong with that: there is no hard technology appropriate to a mentalist approach to consciousness or to the artefacts of consciousness in language and art. But attempt to detach the argument from the rhetorical force of its enunciation and you are in difficulty – to describe the inarticulacy which underlies and controls the articulation of that description is to construct a self-supporting edifice which creates meaning in the terms it uses to define that meaning. Naming – *'chora'*, 'thetic phase' and the like – shares something with the enunciation of words of power by adepts in magic. The networking of a technical vocabulary special to the artist gives an air of authenticity and stability to what might otherwise be a very tentative analysis.

V

Kristeva argues that the semiotic and the symbolic modalities are at work in all subjects; they are indivisible and interpenetrating. Atwood's subject objects to the language's separation of head and body: it is that, rather than the neck, which 'creates the illusion that they are separate'. Her father's old commitment to reason has marked him as a person determined to act as if he inhabited a universe of discourse entirely governed by the symbolic modality. The education of the narrator has not merely been a matter of adopting the symbolism of the advertisement, the cartoon, the magazine picture; it has also involved a closure, or more accurately, the illusion of one, one which occurs precisely at that point where Kristeva identifies the thetic boundary, leaving her in an amputated world where symbolic consciousness refuses to pay attention – or rather to recognise the formative urgency of – the semiotic *chora*: 'At some point my neck must have closed over, pond freezing or a wound, shutting me into my head.' To treat the father's hieroglyphic bequest as clues in a treasure hunt that will lead to his discovery is to treat his communication as having no other possible substance than that which belongs to symbolic discourse: to translate will be to incorporate the head and the body, to restore the rightful symbiotic relationship between the thetic sign of the father and the unordered, provisional, motile, maternal *chora*.

Until the 'ghosts' appear, the mother is not represented except by a leather jacket, hanging on a nail, vestigial, unexpected so many years after her death: 'Dead people's clothes ought to be buried with them' (p. 43) – but the jacket is eloquent of her presence, or her absence there, a kind of skin which recalls a richly resourceful space. Clothes are frequently seen as vestiges of the body in *Surfacing*, as in this miscellanea of surfaces: 'They were pegged out to dry now on the line behind the cabin, shirts, jeans, socks, Anna's coloured lingerie, our cast skins' (p. 133), but the singularity of mother's jacket, and her absence, and the fact that she is only known to us as a mother, makes her coat the memory of a containing space, a *chora*, an absent, creative source. It's a symbol, a product of the thetic break, but one which is a memento of a way of being which precedes and enfolds the symbolic.

Territorial transit is symbolic device too, nowhere more so than in the fact that the search for its deepest significance is in submersion. The natural lake itself has been submerged by damming – any rock-paintings, hieroglyphics, *signifiants*, archetypal residues, manitous, must be sought in another medium. In the pressure which fuses the metaphors, translation becomes submersion, carrying with it the danger of the known self dying.

She is looking for an Indian symbol which leads to a father, and when she finds a dead thing she thinks momentarily that it is her brother, but realises that that thought is a disguise for something else. Why does she never think that she has found or will find a mother, a manifestation of the rich, containing, Kleinian source, something communicated in the profound translinguistic dialect of the *chora*? Even in its dealings with the undifferentiated drives and stases of the maternal *chora* symbolic discourse is an ideological product, shaped by the contemporary perception of womanhood, by the insensitivity of the Davids, the self distortion of the Annas, the amputations of divorce, the mutilation of abortion.

The deep sign she sees is one of mutilation, but it's fascinating the way it mutates from a manufactured symbol, a projection of horror and fear, 'a dark oval trailing limbs. It was blurred but it had eyes, they were open, it was something I knew about' (p. 142), to a grotesque laboratory monster contained clinically within glass boundaries' in a bottle curled up, staring out at me like a cat pickled; it had huge jelly eyes and fins' (p. 143), to a perverted magico-religious object of mythical quest 'like a chalice, an evil grail', and finally to a bleak but only provisional resolution of the deep structure of separation:

> Whatever it is, part of myself or a separate creature, I killed it. It wasn't a child but it could have become one, I didn't allow it.   (p. 143)

Immediately it becomes both 'it' and self, egg and life-blood: 'I knocked it off the table, my life on the floor, glass egg and shattered blood'; that too is negated: 'That was wrong, I never saw it'; and the negation is ambiguously withdrawn: 'I stretched my hand up to it and it vanished.' What we have here is not only the panic and grief of the woman after an abortion, swinging from fear through horror to remorse to fury to guilt, but also a meeting with the undifferentiated drives, the flux of an interior world which only partially yields to the symbolic modality, and to which the symbolic, with its leaning towards categorial logic, proves inadequate:[6] 'The bottle had been logical, pure logic, remnant of the trapped and decaying animals, secreted in my head, enclosure, something to keep the death away from me' (p. 143).

Something parallel to the paradoxical Lacan/Kristeva formulation of the dialectic of identification and separation in the thetic phase is at work here:[6] 'It requires an identification; in other words, the subject must separate from and through his image, from and through his objects.'[12] But there is also the painful meeting with that undifferentiated motility which Kristeva calls the semiotic *chora*, internalisation of that maternal warmth and creativity now warped and abused through abortion, its conflictual drives all leading to the repetition of a self-negation, and its signs are charged with terror on the first acquaintance. There's a sense in which the rejected embryonic body is the suppressed bodily self consigned to a submarine area of dream or myth, or, alternatively, trapped behind boundaries of glass. This memorial of a deeper separation points to the need for what is literally incorporation, the home-coming of consciousness and imagination to identification with the body.

If the search for a father has revealed a mother in the self, a *chora*, or space, the contents of which enable her to dismantle the surfaces of logic, the 'father' who is sought has been ahead of her on that track (but by now 'father' and 'mother' are both translated by processes of identification and projection). There was no painting at White Birch Lake (that place which has been translated) because the later drawings were not copied: 'He had discovered new places, new oracles, they were things he was seeing the way I had seen, true vision; at the end, after the failure of logic' (p. 145). And for 'I', the acceptance of 'true vision', one which reveals the terrible inner consequences of that negation of self, that death within, is the final boundary, the final separation which prepares for life.

VI

Once again the conclusion of a section prefigures the next: 'they think I should be filled with death, I should be in mourning. But nothing has died, everything is alive, everything is waiting to become alive' (p. 159).

I think one should be suspicious of interpretations which seize on Christian imagery in *Surfacing*, just as one should be suspicious of the mobilisation of all the images of the natural world, herons, fish, forests, water and so forth, to discover a simple pantheistic creed. And yet both Christian and pantheistic imagery are vital to the book's economy. Just before the diving episode some of these images are rehearsed, but in a way which is askew to the Christian myth:

> The animals die that we may live, they are substitute people, hunters in the fall killing the deer, that is Christ also. And we eat them out of cans or otherwise; we are eaters of death, dead Christ-flesh resurrecting inside us, granting us life.   (p. 140)

The point about the two herons, the one a 'bluegrey cross' in the sky, the other 'hanging wrecked from the tree' is that they are, respectively, alive and dead, the living one distinct and separate, not itself a symbol, but converted into such by human magico-religious habits of language, the dead one equally converted by the human greed to assimilate alien things to its own discursive practice: 'I said "It's a heron. You can't eat them", but David wants to collect it for *Random Samples*: "We need that . . . we can put it next to the fish guts" '(p. 116).

The need to worship is there, but veneration is seen as something immensely more painful in achievement, involving an entire reconstruction of the self, and the object of veneration is seen, not as located in the immediately available symbols – cross, Christ, heron, fish, Indian hieroglyph and so forth – but in the 'places', the territory, that they mark, as in the discovery that the father's mark, x, indicates a place of power sacred to the Indians, or, following on from them, to the father. Of course the sense of 'territory' has gone far beyond geographical location. Under a symbolic assertion there's a semiotic space to be explored, which maintains any real power that symbol may have. And that exploration is one which demands a further separation. The refusal of 'the death machine' (p. 162) – whether that means the abortion table, the hunter's bullet crashing into the heron's bone and blood, or the cannibalistic ritual of the eucharist – in favour of re-entry into the life-process.

Part Three begins with rites of passage marking the approach of incorporation. The narrator seduces Joe, his human skin unzipped, leading him barefoot to the lake, where, as she takes his body into hers, 'He trembles and then I can feel my lost child surfacing' (p. 161). Then she destroys the obscenity of *Random Samples*, the records of accumulative habit, the capturing of life in mere images

– she imagines the captured images 'swimming away into the lake like tadpoles', 'hundreds of tiny naked Annas no longer bottled and shelved' (p. 166). The process of incorporation becomes a celebration of creative energies, now seen as a constant process at work both inside and outside her, in which dying and living become a generous cycle, separations and amputations resolved, transition renewed in rebirth. Incorporation becoming a mutual participation, self in other, other in self:

> energy of decay turning to growth, green fire. I remember the heron; by now it will be insects, frogs, fish, other herons. My body also changes, the creature in me, plant-animal, sends out filaments in me; I ferry it secure between death and life, I multiply. (p. 168)

'This above all, to refuse to be a victim', as many critics have noted, recalls the basic victim positions of *Survival*[13]: the basic game of Position Three is to refuse to be a victim, but, as Atwood remarks, 'experience is never this linear: you're rarely in any Position in its pure form for very long – and you may have a foot, as it were, in more than one Position at once'.[14] Whether offered as a typology of Canadian literature, Canadians or humans in general, the game Atwood plays is both amusing and revealing about Atwood's own fiction. For 'I' to aspire to Position Three is deliberately modest; in the last few chapters she straddles Three, repudiation of the role of victim; Four, to be a creative non-victim; and Five 'for mystics; I postulate it but will not explore it here, since mystics do not as a rule write books'[15] – a disclaimer that will do nicely if you like to maintain as much contact with the realist mode as possible. Another typological game Atwood plays in *Survival* is the division of Canadian fictions of Nature/Woman, Woman/Nature into the three aspects of a triple goddess Diana/Venus/Hecate. It's done lightly enough, as is everything in *Survival*, gently rejecting any pretence to an authoritative thesis, teasingly employing the pantheon of Olympia to explore presences abroad in the lakes and forests of the North. If anything, in *Surfacing* we have a premature Hecate being translated into a Venus, celebrating the creative mother-role, dedicating her body to become the fertility of Nature itself.

But this won't do. The old European gods don't change any more: they do not transform, unless the teller and the tale are both radically remade. Like *Quebec Folk Tales* they can be illustrated if, like the narrator you can say 'I can do that, I can imitate anything' (p. 53), but what happens to 'I' is, essentially, that she ceases to imitate, she begins to be (or to see). The mimetic personality, like mimetic art, finds its justification in the images the mirror returns. But the sequence of separation, transition, incorporation, demands something else. The mirror on the wall in the story of Snow White records the attempt at magical capture of another, the incorporation of others into the vengeful self. Anna's reflection in the make-up mirror is submission to the magical capture of herself by her own image, an inversion of the narcissistic constitution of a specular self in the mirror image. Something else is demanded:

> I must stop being in the mirror . . . Not to see myself but to see. I reverse the mirror toward the wall, it no longer traps me, Anna's soul closed in the gold compact, that and not the camera is what I should have broken.   (p. 75)

As Lacan has pointed out, the only animal able to recognise him/herself in the mirror is man. Lacan and, following him, Kristeva, see, in this discovery of the specular image, the root of the development of signification in the thetic stage.[16] The child must remain separate from the mirror image in order to capture it, to identify with it, and the agitation caused by this separation in the semiotic *chora* fragments the self which strives to capture, more than the representation of himself in the image unifies. This primary narcissism leads to the constitution of objects outside the semiotic *chora*, and thus to a model for the constitution of a world of objects outside the self. To reject the mirror is a quasi-suicide, as is the abandonment of language: in the narrator's idiolect a resignation from humanity only to find some other *decorum* to supervene upon the humanity imposed by the mimetics of the mirror:

> The gods, their likenesses: to see them in their true shape is fatal. While you are human; but after the transformation they could be reached. First I had to immerse myself in the other language. (p. 158)

I do not understand this, literally at least. It carries with it, perhaps, some Hebraic memories of the prohibition upon seeing Jehovah face to face, but these may be irrelevant when set next to the idea of 'transformation', and its twin in the metaphorical economy of *Surfacing*, immersion.

As with Kristeva, Freud, Klein or Jung, who also posit areas of being which are analytically unthinkable, it may be justified. For propositions about such areas to be spoken of, or illustrated, they have to be articulated metaphorically, gestured towards in a quasi-mythic structure, in which a surface of denotation covers a deeper area of inarticulate structures, a recapitulation, perhaps, of the emergence of the psyche from the looking-glass stage (whether that stage has more to do with Alice than with Jacques Lacan I can leave to the reader).

It all goes back to Plato, as so many things in the European universe of thought do. In Book X of *The Republic*, Socrates proposes the idea that there may be 'another artificer ... One who is the maker of all the works of all the other workmen, as well as all the things in the natural world.' He isn't a wizard, though:

> there are many ways in which the feat might be quickly and easily accomplished, none quicker than that of turning a mirror round and round – you would soon enough make the sun and the heavens, and the earth and yourself ... [17]

Glaucon remarks that these would be appearances only (and his observation includes what is vital to Atwood's persuasions, the implication that the self which is constituted by the mirror mode of vision is appearance too). Socrates goes on to argue that all poets are merely imitators 'who copy images of virtue and the other themes of their poetry, but have no contact with the truth'.[18]

Rejecting the mirror, Atwood's narrator declares, is 'Not to see myself but to see'. If that is so, then the essence of seeing – in Socratic terms, going beyond appearances to make contact with truth – is the meeting with unnamed presences on the island, just as the essence of an alternative way of being might be called a newly discovered language: 'I am the only one left alive on the island. They were there though, I trust that. I saw them and they spoke to me, in the other language' (p. 188).

Atwood's comments on this in an interview are interesting. She avoids discussing certain aspects of her own work, saying that it is easier for her to talk about the formal problems of writing a ghost story. Then she declares her method resembles the kind that Henry

James wrote 'in which the ghost that one sees is a fragment of one's own self which has split off'.[19] There are other ways of looking at, for instance, *The Turn of the Screw*. That tale is wrapped around an indeterminate centre, a puzzle at the heart of the act of reading itself. But *if* the interpretation of James's novella offered by Leon Edel and Edmund Wilson works, it works by assuming a destructive force in the symbolic imagination. In *Surfacing*, destruction and creativity seem bound together in a complex transformation.

Whatever she *sees* occurs between two significant Socratic gestures: 'Not to see myself but to see. I reverse the mirror so it's toward the wall, it no longer traps me' (p. 175) and 'I turn the mirror around: in it there's a creature neither animal nor human' (p. 190). In between these, while the mirror is turned away 'I see her. She is standing in front of the cabin, her hand stretched out, she is wearing her grey leather jacket' (p. 182) and:

> He is standing near the fence with his back to me . . . I say Father.
> He turns towards me and it's not my father. It is what my father saw, the thing you meet when you've stayed here too long alone. . . .
> I see now that although it isn't my father it is what my father has become. (pp. 186–7)

It's natural to ask: What does this mean? What does she *see*? Perhaps the 'what' should be replaced by 'how' – if *what* she sees, and *what* it means is a fragment of the self unmediated by Plato's mirror and by 'untranslated' language, then the modalities of vision and of meaning become the twin issues.

The modalities of vision and of meaning change in the transition mapped out in this unmirrored interval by two remarkable passages which formally signal their function as poetics of experience and understanding. Both of them indicate their distance from the conventions by irregularities in punctuation. The first dispenses entirely with the full stop:

> The animals have no need for speech, why talk when you are a word
> I lean against a tree, I am a tree leaning
> I break out again into the bright sun and crumple, head against the ground

> I am not an animal or a tree, I am the thing in which the trees
> and animals move and grow, I am a place   (p. 181)

It's a brief episode of incorporation, which is followed immediately by another separation, though this time the separation is
redefined as surfacing, as a plant breaks through in its season: 'I
have to get up, I get up. Through the ground, break surfaces, I'm
standing now; separate again' (p. 181). This serial transit, from
incorporation into separation, is immediately followed by the
vision of the 'ghosts', which resolves itself, this time, into the vision
of the woman in the grey leather jacket – a fragment of the
narrator's self, perhaps, ambiguously her mother too: 'Then as I
watch and it doesn't change I'm afraid' (p. 182). To be a tree, to be a
place of power, a place of fecundity, to see the unchanging mother
who is, ambivalently 'she' and 'it' – that experience is necessary – it
may be the recognition of manitou, but it is only tolerable as one
moment in a dialectic of stasis and change.

As the first unpunctuated passage precedes the encounter with
the ghost-mother, the second occurs just after the encounter with
'what my father has become' – the end of a process of change.
He/it is described with wolf–imagery – a kind of *loup-garou* –
which, whilst it points to a flight from human reason, also suggests
a liberating fulfilment in the life of the body: something intended in
herself by the way in which the 'I' converts the familiar image of
the father into one which is both estranged and recognised. It is a
kind of *reconnaisance* (in the complete and complex multiple senses
of acknowledgement/recognition/gratitude/foray into dangerous
territory) into the domain sketched by Jenness in his account of
Indian beliefs, where a golden age of mutual recognition between
man and animal may return.

It/he turns away from her, rejecting that phase of her being
discovered earlier in her provisional identification with *place*: 'I do
not interest it, I am part of the landscape, I could be anything, a
tree, a deer skeleton, a rock' (p. 187). That experience is followed by
the poetic evocation of flux, of process, of change. It's only at the
beginning that punctuation is suspended, as this flux emerges, the
fish emerging from the lake rather as the consciousness emerges
from its identification with the nourishing, maternal *chora* across
the thetic boundary, into protean symbol, icon, hieroglyph,
specular image, language, but eventually into an unexpected fulfilment: 'it becomes an ordinary fish again'. It is separation, transit,

process and re-entry through the synthesis and reconciliation of stasis and change, a parabola of protean changes from water to air, from body to idea, from flesh to icon, from wood to stone to spirit and then at last, completing the cycle, to body and to water again:

> From the lake a fish jumps
> An idea of a fish jumps
> A fish jumps, carved wooden fish with dots painted on the sides, no, antlered fish thing drawn in red on cliffstone, protecting spirit. It hangs in the air suspended, flesh turned to icon, he has changed again, returned to the water. How many shapes can he take.
> I watch it for an hour or so; then it drops and softens, the circles widen, it becomes an ordinary fish again.   (p. 187)

It is that moment when the experience is seen to be some kind of meeting with self which may only occur when the mirror is turned to the wall, when the consciousness is enabled to extend itself by regression into an area opened by the turning away of the mirror.

The narrator tries to place her feet in the tracks left by the transformed image of the father, and finds they are her own footprints. I suppose that this can be taken in two ways. The most simple is that she has imagined it all – they *are* just ghosts.

The other is that by reconciling being and becoming, by fitting into their footsteps, she has entered a new life. By carrying a new body (which, at the same time, is primaeval in its innocence) within *her* body she dedicates this being and becoming to an unknown future, translating a culture of abortion into one of exploration, literally *incorporating* a process of transformation:

> the time-traveller, the primaeval one who will have to learn, shape of a goldfish now in my belly, undergoing its watery changes. Word furrows potential already in its proto-brain, untravelled paths. . . . It might be the first one, the first true human; it must be born, allowed.   (p. 191)

Notes

1. Arnold van Gennep, *The Rites of Passage*, trans. Monika B. Vizedom and Gabrielle L. Caffee (London, 1960).
2. Margaret Atwood, *Surfacing* (London, 1978). All future page references are to this edition.
3. Graeme Gibson, *Eleven Canadian Novelists* (Toronto, 1973) p. 22.
4. Ibid., p. 26
5. Margaret Atwood, *Collected Poems* (New York, 1976) p. 80.
6. Diamond Jenness, *The Indians of Canada*, 7th edn (Toronto, 1977) p. 187.
7. Margaret Atwood, *Survival: A Thematic Guide to Canadian Literature* (Toronto, 1972) p. 54.
8. C. G. Jung, 'On Psychic Energy', in *The Collected Works*, trans. R. F. C. Hull, vol. 8, 2nd edn (London, 1969) pp. 61–2.
9. Julia Kristeva, *La Révolution du langage poetique* (Paris, 1974) trans. by Margaret Waller as *Revolution in Poetic Language* (New York, 1984). For convenience's sake I quote from the most widely available text, Toril Moi (ed.), *The Kristeva Reader* (London, 1986).
10. Moi (ed.), *Kristeva Reader*, p. 94.
11. Ibid., p. 98
12. Ibid.
13. Atwood, *Survival*, pp. 36–9
14. Ibid., p. 39
15. Ibid.
16. Jacques Lacan, *Écrits: A Selection*, trans. Alan Sheridan (London, 1977), particularly 'The mirror stage as formative of the function of the I as revealed in psychoanalytic experience' (pp. 1–7). See also Moi (ed.), *Kristeva Reader*, p. 100.
17. Plato, *Republic*, x, 596 d–e, trans. Jowett (Oxford, 1953).
18. Ibid., 600e–601a.
19. Gibson, *Eleven Canadian Novelists*, p. 29.

5

Margaret Atwood's
Surfacing:
Strange Familiarity
PETER QUARTERMAINE

If writing novels – and reading them – have any redeeming
social value, it's probably that they force you to imagine
what it's like to be somebody else.
Which, increasingly, is something we all need to know.[1]

Surfacing is a novel obsessively private in its narrator's focus and
overtly existential in authorial intent. The narrator's uncoiling
memory domain of childhood, marriage and abortion is contrasted
with, and finally comprehended through, an almost stereotypically
'Canadian' landscape of remote cabins, canoes and male preda-
tions. The novel offers varied yet complementary readings: personal, feminist national and political. This essay is accordingly
tentative rather than definitive in spirit.

In her critical study of Canadian literature, *Survival* (1973), Atwood
discusses the possible cultural role of the Canadian writer in providing both a mirror and a map: a mirror in which readers can find 'a
reflection of the world' in which they live; a map which may provide
'a geography of the mind'.[2] In arguing that in both respects Canada is
still largely 'an unknown territory for the people who live in it',
Atwood refers not to 'This Great Land of Ours' but to 'Canada as a
state of mind, as the space you inhabit not just with your body but
with your head. It's that kind of space in which we find ourselves
lost' (p. 18) In its linking of mental and physical responses to 'Canada'
this remark illuminates the focus and methods *Surfacing*, a novel concerned with complementary – at times contradictory – aspects of

human intercourse and with exploring mankind's place in a wider scheme of things.[3]

For Atwood, literature is both mirror and map only 'if we can learn to read it as *our* literature, as the product of who and where we have been' (pp. 18–19).[4] Just such a reading should, she argues, replace the historical tendency she sees in Canada 'to emphasize the personal and the universal but to skip the national and the cultural' (p. 15), one reason for which may be that some believe both personal and universal issues to be explorable shorn of political issues. It was for precisely this reason that the Nigerian writer Chinua Achebe argued in 1974 that the word 'universal' should be banned from literary criticism.[5] *Surfacing* is inherently concerned with issues of nationality and culture but these are embodied in specific characters and events, and in the dangerous preoccupations of the narrator who mediates our access to reality.[6]

The title of *Surfacing* suggests powerful ambiguities which the text itself explores. The confrontation of repressed fears is a shaping metaphor throughout (most literally in the disturbingly paired sequences of the narrator confronting the body of her drowned father and the fact of her own abortion) but Atwood also renders the mundanity of life with convincing, at times chilling, particularity. In this context 'surfacing' also describes that shared survival instinct which looks only rarely beyond immediate specifics; we prefer self-reflections on a calm surface to any glimpse of monsters beneath.

In poetry, in critical writing and in fiction Atwood has shown alertness to the personal and national specificity of place. As a Canadian and as a woman she defines strong images of identity which combine wry humour and a contemporary myth-making capacity informed by broad cultural awareness and sharp local observation. Evocative dimensions of *Surfacing* for any reader (especially for any Canadian) are its observation and recreation of the 'simple' intricacies of bush life. The primal lure of withdrawal to a hidden house on a small island in a remote area of Quebec is as powerful for the narrator (and for us) as it was for her father, yet she is also painfully aware of the stunted lives such places can produce; the impressions that excite her friend David – 'he thinks this is reality: a marginal economy and grizzled elderly men, it's straight out of Depression photo essays' (p. 30)[7] – are all too familiar. It was to escape a sense of isolation both imaged and compounded by the English/French language barrier (her English-speaking parents had moved to a small francophone village) that she had originally gone to the city; ironically, she returns as a confused failure, and only finds herself again through addressing her childhood environment anew with adult honesty.[8]

The economic drift from the country to the city has affected all rural peoples since the industrial revolution; in cultures subject to the post-colonial pressures of which the anglophone/francophone tensions in Canada are continuing evidence the shift from the relative self-sufficiency of land to selling one's labour in the city has special significance. Its typology images forced movements of peoples in the empire, first under slavery and later and more widely (under scarcely better conditions) of indentured labour. Such movement from rural setting and traditional culture to a metropolitan pooling of talents parallels the role London or Paris (say) long occupied, even after the formal demise of the empire, as a 'home' to which peoples migrated from former colonies in pursuit of their ambitions. For writers and artists such cities, together with latter-day imperial capitals such as New York (and Americanism is powerfully evoked and criticised in the novel) still occupy unique positions of cultural control. For this reason, as Northrop Frye argued in 1959:

> Poetry is of major importance in the culture and therefore in the history of a country . . . ; the centre of reality is wherever one happens to be, and its circumference is whatever one's imagination can make sense of.[9]

Such general cultural and historical perspectives form an available context for a reading of *Surfacing*, but its challenging re-vision of rural/pastoral aspirations denies our imagination a resting place. Equally, its function on this larger scale in no way denies its value as a Canadian novel written from a specific point of view and at a particular time. V. S. Naipaul has contended that 'all literatures are regional'; if we give due weight to the cultural and political aspects of the book then these will include not only attention to the details of local Quebec landscape but also what it might mean, symbolically, to be a Canadian.[10] Only through its accuracy as a mirror can the book also serve as a map for more demanding imaginative terrain, that Canada we inhabit 'not just with our body but with our head'.

The opening narrative in *Surfacing*, the offhand familiarity yet surgical anonymity of the narrator's voice, evokes landmarks well known in one sense (arrival brings no excitement) yet still mysterious and misleading in the complexity of the signs they offer: 'I never thought of it as a city but as the last or first outpost depending on which way we were going' (p. 7). These observations find natural expression in the perspective of a car passenger approaching old haunts in strange company, and the narrator's observation on her companions, that 'either the three of them are in the wrong place, or I am' (p. 8), confirms her emotional dis/location, despite the literal return to childhood landscapes. Her distance from the familiar (and the familial) we come to see as proof that she never really knew this place at all, despite having lived there. Her shaping voice is that of a bored travelogue soundtrack, the content relentlessly visual, devoid of analysis or comment:

> I watch the side windows as though it's a TV screen. There's nothing I can remember till we reach the border, marked by the sign that says BIENVENUE on one side and WELCOME on the other. The sign has bullet holes in it, rusting red round the edges. (p. 11)

The linguistic shifts here, the strictly logical yet apparently contradictory (two-faced) welcoming sign – to be welcome one side is to be unwelcome the other? – reinforce paired images throughout the book, where the significance of any one incident or relationship is completed by another. Yet the opening trajectory of the journey precludes such possibilities. The car heads north, and the text possesses a sharply defined north–south axis; a demolished covered bridge was 'too far north to be quaint' (p. 17). Significantly, the first specific geographical notation also mentions the narrator's father, later revealed as motive for the journey itself, but here only ambiguously 'dead or alive':

> the signs saying GATEWAY TO THE NORTH, at least four towns claim to be that. The future is in the North, that was a political slogan once; when my father heard it he said there was nothing in the North but the past and not much of that either. Wherever he is now, dead or alive and nobody knows which, he's no longer making epigrams. They have no right to get old. (p. 9)

More striking for the reader than any political slogan is the narrator's reaction to the BIENVENUE sign: 'Now we're on my home

ground, foreign territory' (p. 11). Almost at once the group is
entering the first human settlement in the book, and we have a
description whose oddly dislocated particularity gains quite other
significance (in other contexts) as the text peels away surfaces with
surprise, reticence and shrewd indirection:

> we're curving up into the tiny company town, neatly planted
> with public flowerbeds and an eighteenth-century fountain in the
> middle, stone dolphins and a cherub with part of the face
> missing. It looks like an imitation but it may be real.   (p. 12)

The many-layered private meanings (real and imagined) this
apparently public description accrues in the course of the book are
revealingly parallelled by the cliff the car passes, with its
palimpsest of election and other slogans, as the car enters French
Canada:

> VOTEZ GODET, VOTEZ OBRIEN, along with hearts and initials and
> words and advertisements, THE SALADA, BLUE MOON COTTAGES 1/2
> MILE, QUEBEC LIBRE, FUCK YOU, BUVEZ COCA COLA GLACE, JESUS SAVES,
> melanges of demands and languages, an x-ray of it would be the
> district's entire history.   (p. 15)

'Melanges' is precise; a word from one language serving another, it
confirms the growing sense throughout this opening chapter of the
impossibility of any simple, monocultural reading of terrain. The
cliff's message for the reader is partly of the Coca-Colonisation of yet
another 'unspoilt' corner of the world, but the narrator's own childhood memories deny any such idyllic vision; and it is the
many–layered complexities of the present to which she must return.
On second reading it signals (together with other indicators) the
unreliability of the narrator's accounts of places and people; no x-ray
of public manifestos offers even a glimpse of individual lives which
always remain as mysterious in reality as they can be made trivial in
depiction: 'deep caves paved with kitchen linoleum'.[11] It will be her
final achievement to see her parents' past lives in such a light.

Only with the start of the second chapter is there a glimpse beyond
the 'surfaces' upon which our attention has been concentrated. After
arrival at the (unnamed) village of their destination the narrator
impulsively leaves the others and we intuit – though little more – the
reasons for the journey of which we have become part:

They're doing me a favour, which they disguised by saying it would be fun, they like to travel. But my reason for being here embarrasses them, they don't understand it. They all disowned their parents long ago, the way you are supposed to: Joe never mentions his mother and father, Anna says hers were nothing people and David calls his The Pigs.   (p. 17)

Paul, an old family friend in this French-speaking village, has written to the narrator telling her that her father has disappeared. Taking tea with Paul and Madame the narrator recalls childhood family visits, and despite the humour of her rendering (one reason we are drawn to her), it is the lack of human communication at   all levels which shapes the narrator's present and remembered unease:

'Ow are *you*?' Madame would scream, and my, mother, after deciphering this, would say 'Fine, I am fine.' Then she would repeat the question: 'How are *you*, Madame?' But Madame would not have the answer and both, still smiling, would glance furtively out through the screen to see if the men were yet coming to rescue them.
   Meanwhile my father would be giving Paul the cabbages or the string beans he had brought from his garden and Paul would be replying with tomatoes or lettuces from his. Since their gardens had the same things in them this exchange of vegetables was purely ritual: after it had taken place we would know that the visit would be officially over.   (p. 21)

After confirming with Paul that no trace has been found of her father the narrator rejoins the others in the local bar; here, too, she sees unconscious humour, expressions of a community uncertain of its identity:

It's an imitation of other places, more southern ones, which are themselves imitations, the originals someone's distorted memory of a nineteenth-century English gentleman's shooting lodge, the kind with trophy heads and furniture made from deer antlers, Queen Victoria had a set like that. But if this is what succeeds why shouldn't they do it?   (pp. 27–8)

It is a contradictory and self-defensive trait of the narrator that while she appears as a shrewd depicter of personal and social 'surface' appearances she is evasive about her own past. Her apparent ability to place others is not balanced by any sure base of her own, and is a merely destructive trait; too late the reader sees her to be unreliable.[12] Disjunctions surface as the plot unfolds, the narrative drive of the novel (and it is compulsive reading) leading to discoveries quite different from those signalled, and in the past not the future. Revealingly, the early expectations of the narrator show that she feels herself to have returned to an uncomfortable past, from which her city life will offer an escape: 'There's no act I can perform except waiting; tomorrow Evans will ship us to the village, and after that we'll travel to the city and the present tense' (p. 51). This need to live in the reassuring present (and her determination to place her present location in the past) also inform her attitude to the father she seeks: he 'could have lived all year in the company town but he split us between two anonymities, the city and the bush', with a succession of apartments in the former and 'the most remote lake he could find' in the latter (p. 59). The narrator's perception of what her father attempted in that remote spot is revealing:

> Even the village had too many people for him, he needed an island, a place where he could recreate not the settled farm life of his own father but that of the earliest ones who arrived when there was nothing but forest and no ideologies but the ones they brought with them.   (p. 59)

Her gloss on this ambition is negative but specially relevant in view of her own refusal of human relationships – 'I tried; now I'm absolved from knowing' (p. 51) – rather than acceptance of commitments: 'When they say Freedom they never quite mean it, what they mean is freedom from interference' (p. 59).

A disturbing aspect of the 'freedom' the narrator seeks to preserve is her fear of the past, most obviously signalled by the sustained present tense of the narrative. Glimpsed memories of childhood penetrate the story (sometimes contradictory, as in the 'drowning' of her younger brother) but the reader is generally held in a narrated present at once exciting and uneasy. Memories themselves are a danger unless rigorously self-referential:

> I have to be more careful about my memories, I have to be sure they're my own and not the memories of other people telling me

what I felt ... I run quickly over my version of it, my life, checking it like an alibi; it fits, it's all there till the time I left. Then static, like a jumped track, for a moment I've lost it, wiped clean; my exact age even, I shut my eyes, what is it? To have the past but not the present, that means you're going senile. (p. 73)

The formal structure of *Surfacing* offers relief from this nightmare present in Chapters 9 to 19 inclusive, where the tense shifts to the past. This section of the book acts as a time loop of discovery, beginning significantly with the narrator's entering the lake at the end of Chapter 8 – 'I bend and push myself reluctantly into the lake' (p. 75) – and crucially leads to her making Joe impregnate her (it seems the appropriate term) in Chapter 20.[13] It is within this loop that the narrator's past slowly surfaces and assumes a shaping role in her ongoing present. Discussing contraception with Anna evokes bizarre 'memories' for the narrator of her abortion – 'they take the baby out with a fork like a pickle out of a pickle jar. After that they fill your veins up with red plastic. I saw it running down through the tube. I won't let them do that to me ever again' (p. 80) – and her refusal of Joe's marriage hopes (pp. 87–8) again brings 'memories' of the marriage/abortion (apparently the former, in mood the latter) her former husband had arranged. Her recollection of the 'cherub with part of the face missing' in the square validates this memory (p. 88).

These chapters also contain crucial shifts in the narrator's stance towards the disappearance of her father (she had been unwilling to contemplate the possibility his death). The strange drawings among his papers lead her readily to consider insanity, but realisation that he has been charting and transcribing ancient rock paintings brings also acceptance of his death:

> The secret had come clear, it had never been a secret, I'd made one, that was easier. My eyes came open, I began to arrange.
>
> I thought, I suppose I knew it from the beginning, I shouldn't have tried to find out, it's killed him. I had the proof now, indisputable, of sanity and therefore of death. (p. 103)

This linking of sanity and death is troubling; she wonders at her lack of emotion on realisation of her father's death. The image that recurs is that which opened Chapter 9, that of the separation of head – 'the knob at the top of our bodies' (p. 76) – from the rest of the human anatomy. Disturbingly, this image had originally signalled the narrator's supposed perception of 'the truth, about myself and about them' (p. 76), a 'truth' informed by a paranoid conviction of plotting which places her at risk: 'the island wasn't safe, we were trapped on it. They didn't realize it but I did, I was responsible for them. The sense of watching eyes' (p. 77). Now that the narrator has granted the death of her father it is her own death-like lack of emotional response (especially with her lover Joe) that concerns her. Looking through an old photograph album at the cabin she meditates on the form of her own death, and even how she might become aware of it:

> perhaps I would be able to tell when the change occurred by the differences in my former faces, alive up to a year, a day, then frozen.
>
> . . .
>
> No hints or facts, I didn't know when it had happened. I must have been alright then; but after that I'd allowed myself to be cut in two. . . . I was in the wrong half, detached, terminal.   (pp. 107–8)

A self-righteous attitude based on this presumed separation determines the narrator's attitude to the 'Americans' they meet hunting on the lake; when they prove to be Canadians she swiftly defends her prejudices (to herself); 'It doesn't matter what country they're from, *my head said*, they're still Americans, they're what's in store for us, what we are turning into' (p. 129, my emphasis). Such statements touch an emotive sensitive chord in Canadian–American relations, but the text questions rather than confirms stereotypical reactions. We may feel inclined to agree with the narrator that we are all 'turning into' one version of Americans, but realisation of her (and therefore our) groundless hostility towards the two canoeists denies us assent to her claimed resolution.

Atwood has described *Surfacing* as a 'ghost story', making clear her own preference for ghost stories of the Henry James type, where the ghost seen is 'a fragment of one's own self which has split off', and adding 'that to me is the most interesting kind . . . the tradition I'm working'.[14] The climactic scene in *Surfacing*, in which the narrator dives beneath a cliff and is confronted by the deeply drifting body of her father, owes much to ghost-story techniques. It acquires fine tension from the controlled emotional confusion following this grotesque final confrontation of father and daughter (she had never been back home since the abortion). Throughout the novel disturbing memories of the cruel amateur laboratory of bottled creatures her brother had kept hidden in the wood, of his near-drowning and of her own abortion, have appeared and reappeared with a cumulative emphasis on the frighteningly unnatural and parallel status of the various 'specimens' involved. The narrator's underwater encounter with her dead father is described in restrained detail, and introduced via descriptions of other (live) creatures which resemble those shapes which float before unseeing eyes. Vision here is not merely a question of seeing:

> It was wonderful that I was down so far, I watched the fish, they swam like patterns on closed eyes, my legs and arms were weightless, free-floating; I almost forgot to look for the cliff and the shape.
>
> It was there but it wasn't a painting, it wasn't on the rock. It was below me, drifting towards me from the furthest level where there was no life, a dark oval trailing limbs. It was blurred but it had eyes, they were open, it was something I knew about, a dead thing, it was dead.   (p. 142)

After surfacing desperately to the light (where a puzzled Joe now also waits for her) the narrator admits to herself for the first time the detailed and sordid facts surrounding her abortion, separating out the various elements and admitting the unreliability of her own memory. Lying physically exhausted in the bottom of the canoe she unravels the all-too-emotional 'logical' processes by which she has refashioned the past to suit the present:

> Water was dripping from me into the canoe, I lay in a puddle. I had been furious with them, I knocked it off the table, my life on the floor, glass egg and shattered blood, nothing could be done.
>
> That was wrong, I never saw it. They scraped it into a bucket and threw it wherever they throw them, it was travelling through the sewers by the time I woke, back to the sea, I stretched my hand up to it and it vanished. The bottle had been logical, pure logic, remnant of the trapped and decaying animals, secreted by my head, enclosure, something to keep the death away from me.   (p. 143)

Even the cherub with half a face is finally placed as a detail 'I put . . . in so there would be something of mine' (p. 144). Emotional self-understanding leads to recognition that her father had also gained revelation, at this site: 'true vision; at the end, after the failure of logic' (p. 145). Leaving an offering of clothes (another 'surface', barrier) at the cliff-face in gratitude for understanding granted, she becomes a fuller person: 'feeling was beginning to seep back into me, I tingled like a foot that's been asleep' (p. 146).

Public acceptance of her father's death (his body is accidentally hooked by the fishing 'Americans' – the grim weight of their catch contrasted with the significance of her underwater vision – is made harder by the fact that the news comes via Anna and David, her two hopelessly superficial companions: 'I realized it wasn't the men I hated, it was the Americans, the human beings, men and women both. They'd had their chance but they had turned against the gods, and it was time for me to choose sides' (p. 154). The ending of the eleven-chapter time loop is positive, the narrator's new-found knowledge freeing her also from the embarrassment at death which so constricts the others: 'They're avoiding me, they find me inappropriate; they think I should be filled with death, I should be in mourning. But nothing has died, everything is alive, everything is waiting to become alive' (p. 159).

The final stages of the novel are emblematic of new-found release and purpose: the exploitative and self-indulgent images on David's film, 'Random Samples' are exposed by the narrator to water and sunlight, and lost. And the narrator is able, finally, to grant her lover Joe positive status: 'he isn't an American, I can see that now; he isn't anything, he is only half-formed, and for that reason I can trust him' (p. 192). The possibility, no more, of building a future relationship is admitted.

The six closing chapters, in which the narrator slips away from her companions and ritually discards tokens of her former self, from wedding ring to items in the cabin remembered from childhood, are crucial to the intent of the novel: 'Soon they will reach the village, the car, the city; what are they saying about me now? That I was running away; but to go with them would have been running away, the truth is here' (p. 170). She affirms an elemental affinity with the natural world, prior to the hinted possibility of a renewed relationship back in the city with Joe, problematic as that may be. The writing is taut, and there are fine moments of self-realisation, as when the narrator thrills to find footprints by the cabin: 'I place my feet in them and find that they are my own' (p. 187). But overall the narrator's position skirts the melodramatic as the text abandons the deceptively documentary tone that has sustained narrative development. Lacking now the friction of relationships with others the viewpoint is eccentric, humourless, and we sense a quasi-authorial voice shaping the inner monologue we follow:

> I dress, clumsily, unfamiliar with buttons; I re-enter my own time.
> But I bring with me from the distant past five nights ago the time traveller, the primaeval one who will have to learn .... (p. 191)

Margaret Laurence's *The Stone Angel* (1964) and Joan Barfoot's *Abra* (published in the United Kingdom as *Gaining Ground*; 1978) offer Canadian comparisons for Atwood's use of lone figure and landscape in these chapters; Patrick White's early novel *The Aunt's Story* (1948) is a fine Australian example. Unlike these novels, though, the concluding emphasis here is, importantly, on return to a life of social and sexual fulfilment for the central character who 'seems wholly determined to "surface" in her full powers back into the world of culture'.[15] Moreover, Joe remains to be completely formed, and any dangerous eccentricities of the narrator's position must here be balanced against her return to the cabin, her re-clothing of herself, and her recognition that trying again with Joe will entail 'the intercession of words; and we will probably fail, sooner or later, more or less painfully' (p. 192).[16] The conclusion of the novel, though, is hopeful:

> She chooses ... a new life and a new way of seeing.... To the protagonist belongs the ultimate sanity: the knowledge that woman can descend, and return – sane, whole, victorious.[17]

Surfacing operates successfully as both mirror and map. Its sharp reflection of national mythologies in the unfoldings of the text yields a teasing combination of complex narrative and vivid regional locales. But it is also widely typical in the tenacity yet tenuousness of its bonding – between people and between people and place – and offers us maps for our own lives, troubling though these may be. The two aspects complement each other throughout; *Surfacing* indeed allows us to imagine, for better or for worse, 'what it might be like to be someone else'. Atwood's novel is a demanding achievement, both in its crafted execution and in its expectations of the reader. The most challenging aspect of that achievement is our realisation that someone, some place, else can be – if strangely – familiar.

Notes

1. Margaret Atwood, 'Writing the Male Character', 1982; reprinted in *Second Words: Selected Critical Prose* (Toronto, 1982) pp. 412–30. This remark is quoted in Coral Ann Howells's excellent study *Private and Fictional Words: Canadian Women Novelists of the 1970s and 1980s* (London: Methuen, 1987) p. 70.

2. Margaret Atwood, *Survival: A Thematic Guide to Canadian Literature* (Toronto: Anansi, 1972) pp. 15–16, 18–19.

3. Sherrill Grace, though, argues that *Survival* 'is hampered by its historical limits; it discusses works written chiefly between the 1930s and the end of the sixties, thus neglecting the nineteenth and twentieth centuries' (Sherrill Grace, *Violent Duality: A Study of Margaret Atwood* (Montreal: Vehicule Press, 1980) p. 1).

4. An excellent placing of Atwood's experiences and work in their Canada of the 1960s and 1970s is provided by Sandra Djwa's article 'The Where of Here: Margaret Atwood and a Canadian Tradition', in Arnold E. Davidson and Cathy N. Davidson (eds), *The Art of Margaret Atwood: Essays in Criticism* (Toronto: Anansi, 1981) pp. 15–34, 286–7. Djwa suggests it is almost as if Atwood 'consciously sets herself down, right in the middle of the Canadian literary landscape, and tries to orient herself by filtering Canadian experience through archetypes of her poetic sensibility' (p. 23).

5. 'I should like to see the word "universal" banned altogether from discussions of African literature until such a time as people cease to use it as a synonym for the narrow, self-serving parochialism of Europe, until their horizon extends to include all the world' (Chinua Achebe, 'Colonialist Criticism', in *Hopes and Impediments: Selected Essays, 1965–87* (Oxford: Heinemann, 1988) pp. 46–61, esp. p. 52). (This essay, based on a paper given in 1974, previously appeared in *Morning Yet on Creation Day* (London: Heinemann, 1975).

6. Because we never learn her name or, in fact, very much about her physical appearance, we must perceive her strictly through this voice, and we are as limited to her voice as she is to her point of view. . . .

   In fact, it is the voice that creates the claustrophobic atmosphere of the book from which we eventually wish to escape. (Grace, *Violent Duality*, p. 98)

7. Margaret Atwood, *Surfacing* (London: Virago, 1978). Future page references in this chapter are to this edition.

8. As Grace rightly argues (*Violent Duality*, p. 2), Atwood conceives of the self not as an individual ego, defining itself against its surroundings, but as a place or entity co-extensive with its environment.

9. Northrop Frye, *The Bush Garden: Essays on the Canadian Imagination* (Toronto: Anansi, 1971) p. 126; quoted Djwa, 'The Where of Here', p. 18.

10. The Naipaul remark is in 'Jasmine', in *The Overcrowded Barracoon and Other Stories* (1972; Harmondsworth, Middx: Penguin, 1976) pp. 24–31, esp. p. 30. On the local and the symbolic, Grace comments: 'One of the problems in *The Edible Woman* is what Atwood called the preposterousness of "symbolism in a realistic context". This is also a major stylistic, hence thematic, challenge in *Surfacing*. From the start, voice and language co-operate to produce an increasingly symbolic text' (Grace, *Violent Duality*, p. 100).

11. Alice Munro, *Lives of Girls and Women* (1971; Harmondsworth, Middx: Penguin Books, 1982) p. 249. For an extended exploration of this image see my article '"Living on the Surface": Versions of Life in Alice Munro's *Lives of Girls and Women*', *Recherches anglaises et nord-americaines*, no. xx (1987) pp. 117–26.

12. Atwood comments on her protagonist's problem: 'If you define yourself as intrinsically innocent, then you have a lot of problems, because in fact you aren't. And the thing with her is she wishes not to be human. She wishes to be not human, because being human inevitably involves being guilty, and if you define yourself as innocent, you can't accept that' (Graeme Gibson, *Eleven Canadian Novelists* (Toronto: Anansi, 1973) p. 22; quoted in Barbara Hill Rigney, *Madness and Sexual Politics in the Feminist Novel: Studies in Brontë, Woolf, Lessing and Atwood* (Madison: University of Wisconsin Press, 1978) p. 97).

13. I am grateful to my postgraduate student Kate Bowles for first alerting me to the importance of this structural device. Most commentators do not comment on this shift in tense, but Grace discusses the possibilities and the problems it poses (see Grace, *Violent Duality*, p. 100).

14. Gibson, *Eleven Canadian Novelists*, p. 29; quoted in Grace, *Violent Duality*, p. 109.

15. Annis Pratt, '*Surfacing* and the Rebirth Journey', in Davidson, *Art of Margaret Atwood*, p. 156.

16. 'This achievement, moreover, is at one and the same time a spiritual and a markedly naturalistic one, the green world and a green world lover or erotic figure making the outcome an integration of body and soul' (ibid., p. 151).

17. Rigney, *Madness and Sexual Politics*, p. 115.

6

Margaret Atwood's *Lady Oracle*: Writing against Notions of Unity

ELEONORA RAO

Do I contradict myself?
Very well then I contradict myself,
I am large, contain multitudes.
> Walt Whitman, *Song of the Open Road*, I.

Atwood's ironising of women's Gothic Romance fiction makes *Lady Oracle* a compelling and unsettling novel. Writing within and against the limits of the genre, exploiting and challenging its norms, she interrogates its stereotypes of womanhood as she explores the compensatory function of so-called escapist literature. As *Lady Oracle* reworks older fictional forms – the Gothic, the sentimental novel, the picaresque and fairy tales – it becomes the locus where a plurality of styles and traditions are revisited. Such a medley probes notions of unity in generic classification to subvert conventional hierarchies, dismantling their conventional iconographies. *Lady Oracle* also interrogates the notion of unity in terms of attitude to subjectivity and 'character'. By refracting the identity of her protagonist through a plethora of projected personae, Atwood emphasises the liberating aspects of a multiple, plural subjectivity, with the text withholding judgement on a range of issues and, by focusing on the fractured self of a polymorphic protagonist, endorses process and change. Deconstructing the homogeneous ego, *Lady Oracle* yields a gendered vision wherein the figure of woman assumes a multiplicity of roles and positions.

Atwood's narrative promotes its resistance to generic classification through an array of intertextual cross-identifications, and she has

133

playfully incorporated and intermingled novelistic typologies elsewhere. Her first novel, *The Edible Woman* (1969), reworks the standard eighteenth-century comedy plot to conclude with a role-reversal that Atwood herself has called an 'anti-comedy'.[1] *Surfacing* re-composes elements of the ghost-story as well as appropriating aspects of a Canadian literary tradition.[2] *Bodily Harm* (1981), advertised as a novel of adventure, intrigue and betrayal, also draws on the Gothic, especially in its representation of the female character as persecuted, as well as on journalism, in the style of its main character Rennie, the 'lifestyle' reporter. A diversity of styles is also a distinctive feature of *Murder in the Dark* (1983), while *The Handmaid's Tale* (1985) includes elements from folk and oral literature. Besides furnishing the subtext for the title-story in *Bluebeard's Egg* (1987), in variously revised forms fairy tales recur in Atwood's narratives.

This eclecticism is particularly striking in *Lady Oracle* where several generic strands and modes are interwoven. In a typical postmodernist operation this novel revisits the past ironically, rewriting it, quoting and parodying different kinds of writing and using popular fiction to produce a non-escapist text. Although there are significant differences between the two, the tactic is similar to Jane Austen's parody of Gothic fiction in *Northanger Abbey*, whose metafictional aspect is well known. While parodying the popular Gothic and sentimental texts of the time, *Northanger Abbey* discusses the novel form, offers a criticism of the genre, and considers the value of reading novels. *Lady Oracle* follows similar lines, and both texts can be considered as studies of fiction from within. Like *Northanger Abbey*, *Lady Oracle* focuses comically on a female protagonist who interprets her life in terms of Gothic adventures. In its reflexive and playful imitation of fictional modes, parody constitutes itself as a metalanguage, one that critically reworks original versions, often to hilarious effect.

The target texts in *Lady Oracle* announce various genres, although the novel itself does not easily belong to any particular one. The Gothic is parodied together with the Harlequin Romance, Victorian poetry, concrete poetry and the Picaresque. They are the forms of writing which the female character Joan Foster creates, and which in turn create the texture of the novel, besides contributing to its effect of heterogeneity, and enable seriousness to coexist with laughter. The comic effects of the novel stem mainly from Joan's own detachment in her ironic rethinking of her past, since a discrepancy is created between the 'self' who is telling the story and the various 'selves' represented in the narrative.

Interactions between diverse novelistic modes in *Lady Oracle* also call into question the difference between so-called 'high' and 'low' forms of art, subverting the notion of artistic hierarchies.[3] Yet at the same time, comic effects in the novel often depend on the writer's and reader's shared assumption of a hierarchy between genres. Both modes of writing, the popular Gothic and the more sophisticated poetry Joan writes, are consistently exploited. The question of hierarchy is one that is raised by the theory of genre to which *Lady Oracle* playfully contributes, for genre implies 'hierarchy of meaning'.[4] Furthermore, a genre does not constitute simply an aspect of a given work, but 'one of its principles of unity'. A genre is an 'invitation to form', 'a struggle for order'.[5]

The presence of various genres in the novel creates a network of references on which the main plot, and those embedded within it, are built. Joan Foster's own poem 'Lady Oracle' is a further example of pastiche. The characterisation of its 'dark lady', and of her unhappy power, resembles that of the queen of the fantastic kingdom in Rider Haggard's *She*, 'she who must be obeyed', as the texts of both writers read. But 'Lady Oracle' does not burn to death in the flame of the fire of Life; instead, she drowns in the river, like Tennyson's 'Lady of Shalott':

> She sits on the iron throne
> She is one and three
> The dark lady the redgold lady
> the blank lady oracle
> of blood, she who must be
> obeyed forever
> Her glass wings are gone
> She floats down the river
> singing her last song.[6]

Haggard's and Tennyson's female characters became emblematic figures in the nineteenth-century iconography of women. If She, or Ayesha, embodies a myth of ruling womanhood, the Lady of Shalott proposes a Victorian ideal of feminine self-renunciation. Elsewhere, Atwood has suggested that the ideology which permeates Haggard's texts is one where 'the only good woman is a dead woman',[7] and in *Lady Oracle* Joan's survival qualities, her fake deaths and rebirths, are set against such tragic fates. Atwood also emphasises the double nature of Ayesha. The polarities attributed to her in *She* oscillate between positive and sinister qualities, a dualism in the presentation of the female character that *Lady Oracle* problematises.

The multiplicity of styles in Atwood's text further signifies authorial freedom from any unitary or singular discourse. A unity of style conceives 'on the one hand the unity of language (in the sense of a system of general normative forms) and on the other hand the unity of an individual person realizing himself in this language'. But textual plurality, as Bakhtin argues, 'opens up the possibility of never having to define oneself in language'.[8]

Parody, however, does not constitute the exclusive mode of Atwood's novel: it is also permeated by a satire directed at radical militant politics, including the Canadian nationalism of the 1960s and early 1970s, and at the cult of 'sincerity', particularly in relation to sexuality and feeling. The novel also presents a vivid description of the anxieties and terrors of female childhood and adolescence. Joan Foster keeps her identity as Louisa K. Delacourt, author of costume Gothics, secret from the young revolutionary she eventually marries. She is ashamed to admit that she makes a living by writing popular fiction, and until the very end of the novel nothing breaks this silent deception. This reinforces Joan's self-division and highlights her duplicity, thus helping to create the character's double voice. Joan's narrative reveals a public voice that is cheerfully accepting and selflessly accommodating, and a silent one, itself double-edged, that is critical, enquiring, discontented and desiring.

The revision of Gothic Romance in *Lady Oracle* breaks down its typical representations of character, by deconstructing its stereotypes of 'villainess' and 'heroine' (woman as 'seductress' and as 'virgin'). Yet, at the same time, the novel constitutes an attempt to comprehend the reader's need for romantic fiction. In so far as *Lady Oracle* 'examines the perils of Gothic thinking', that is, of casting otherwise realistic characters in certain roles proper to the genre, as Joan does, it could be defined as an 'anti-Gothic' novel – as Atwood herself has called it[9] – in the tradition of *Northanger Abbey*. Both novels expose their heroine's tendency to apply the patterns and roles found in such fiction to their own realities; to mistake life for fiction. Indeed, Joan, like Jane Austen's heroine, interprets her life as if it were a Gothic text; which is partly why her life resembles a tale from romance. After a period of some years Joan meets Paul, her first lover, who, convinced of her unhappy situation, wants to take her away with him. She interprets his proposal in the manner of the sentimental heroine: 'was this my lost love, my rescuer?' (p. 280). In the best Gothic tradition, men are regarded by her as the embodiments of villain and rescuer. Joan asks herself: 'Was the man who untied me a rescuer or a villain? Or, an even more baffling thought: was it possible for a man to be both at once?' (p. 64). Following the same pattern, she suspects her father of having murdered his wife, another recurrent Gothic motif whereby an aura of suspicion descends on the characters involved. In *Northanger Abbey* Austen parodies such attitudes when Catherine makes a fool of herself by exposing to Henry Tinley her suspicion that his father, Captain Tinley, had locked up and perhaps murdered his wife. A further feature of the genre is to be found in Atwood's characterisation of Joan as the persecuted heroine, eternally 'on the run', although there is also something of the picaresque in Joan's adventurous flights and escapes across the Atlantic.

But Atwood and Austen enact the genre differently. *Northanger Abbey* undermines it from within so that the text creates a mocking parody of the tradition. Its criticism of Gothic writers and readers is much sharper, due perhaps to Austen's wish to educate her readers towards a more critical literary taste, although she does not deny the pleasure that can be gained from reading Gothic texts, as long as the reader takes them for what they are. Henry Tinley achieves this, in contrast to Catherine Morland who continually confuses the two. Margaret Rose points out that 'in parodies such as *Northanger Abbey* ... the clash between the worlds of fiction and reality is shown in the example of naive readers, who, because they are unable to clearly distinguish the two worlds, cannot cope with either'.[10]

But Atwood produces samples of women's popular romance in the novels that Joan Foster writes, fiction that is halfway between the historical romance of Barbara Cartland and the popular Gothic romances of Victoria Holt. Charlotte, the heroine whose adventures we follow, has all the generic characteristics of such a protagonist. With her features left vague enough to encourage a degree of reader-identification, the heroine is presented as alone in the world, poor but well-bred, naïve, simple and pure-hearted, yet also able to display determination when necessary. Charlotte's feelings towards Redmond, the hateful but always ambiguous master of the mansion where she lives, are a mixture of attraction and hate. The triangle is completed by the figure of the master's unfaithful wife, Felicia, who plays here the role of rival and villainess.

However, when Joan Foster's romance *Stalked by Love* is approaching the supposedly happy ending of the heroine Charlotte's adventures, Joan realises she cannot elaborate it any more, and refuses to obey the laws of the genre. At this point *Lady Oracle* deconstructs the kind of fiction it is parodying. Joan, tired of the heroine Charlotte's 'perfection', tries to retell the story from the perspective of the evil Felicia. After composing Felicia's version, she realises that the idea is not tenable, that 'sympathy for Felicia was out of the question, it was against the rules, it would foul up the plot completely' (p. 319). A transgression of the genre is implemented at the very moment the novel points out its norm, and one of the consequences of this defiance of limits relates to its typical characterisation of woman, always indissolubly located around the two polarities of good and evil, angel and monster. The urge to undermine and subvert such iconographies stems from a belief that the power of fiction resides – as Atwood has repeatedly stated – in its capacity to make us *see* ourselves and the world, and accordingly to modify our versions of them. But this power also implies a risk that literary conventions can come to control our perceptions and self-perceptions.

In *Lady Oracle*'s embedded text, *Stalked by Love*, Redmond's response to Felicia's sensuality is expressed as a contempt for her sexual desire:

> He had become tired of the extravagance of Felicia; of her figure that spread like crabgrass, her hair that spread like fire, her mind that spread like cancer or pubic lice. 'Contain yourself,' he'd said to her, more than once, but she couldn't contain herself, she raged over him like a plague, leaving him withered. But Charlotte now, with her stays and her particular ways, her white flannelette face, her blanched fingers ... her coolness intrigued him. (p. 319)

Atwood's comic and disturbing characterisation of Felicia here is achieved by exploiting and contrasting different styles. A conventional Gothic expression: 'hair. . . that spread like fire' (which is also an attempt at seriousness) is undermined by the description of a figure 'that spread like crabgrass'. Felicia's portrayal culminates in the unromantic and male-threatening image of her mind 'that spread like cancer or public lice'. Similarly, Charlotte's delicate and virginal appearance, 'her white flannelette face, her blanched fingers', is also undermined by an incongruous use of rhyme.

But Felicia rebels against the repression of sexuality and its denial of the body and she fights it, becoming, like Du Maurier's Rebecca, 'the wife who refuses to go mad'[11] on account of male failure to recognise her desires. This rebellion will be fatal for her. In *Stalked by Love*, as in *Rebecca*, the death of the wicked and / or mad wife is a guarantee of male authority and of masculinity itself. The problem is that there is a risk here for Charlotte since Redmond found the sexuality of Felicia, and possibly also that of his previous wives, dispensable (Charlotte will be the fourth Lady Redmond). She could therefore, in her turn, easily be accommodated to the remorseless logic of this Bluebeard.

The question of how the woman reader faces and deals with contrary versions of femininity present in popular romance – woman as virgin and woman as sensual seductress – is problematic. It has been noted that it can be strictly connected with the fear women experience of men and of their own sexuality, fears also explored in *Lady Oracle* (p. 140).[12] The overtly sexual villainess, and the 'overwhelming desire' of the hero, in sharp contrast to the passive sexuality of the heroine, are related, according to Rosalind Coward, to the way in which women have to cope with 'the repression of active female sexual choice and activity by which women's subordination is secured'. The reluctant heroine in romantic fiction may be interpreted as a magnified expression of passive sexuality, and psychoanalytic theory sees such fantasy as 'the projection of active desires by yourself on to another person, who then becomes responsible for that desire'.[13] Such a fantasy may also be explained by relating it to the way in which children outgrow infantile sexuality. But there remains in women an unconscious experience of guilt related to infantile sexuality, an inhibition towards any sexual activity for which they alone are responsible. Romantic fiction typically resolves this dilemma since its heroine does not express an active desire for sexual experience and therefore 'sexuality is safely secured in the other person'.[14]

Through its parody *Lady Oracle* contributes to a continuing revaluation of popular fiction. In the early 1970s, sharp criticism of popular romance came from such authors as Germaine Greer and Shulamith Firestone, who condemned it out of hand, showing contempt and mockery for its readers. *Lady Oracle* refuses to label such works as trash, and thus actually precedes later feminist-Marxist-orientated defences of the genre. Such defences agree that it is hardly possible to displace the pleasures of romance by appeals to reason. The ideologies of romance are seen as reflecting rather than creating the contradictions of women's experience, but while many critics now share this common ground, they offer different responses. For Tania Modleski romance enables woman to transcend, if only momentarily, their divided selves. Romance texts show, she maintains, that 'it is possible really to be taken care of and to achieve that state of self-forgetfulness promised by the ideology of love'.[15] Other feminist responses suggest that gender roles in romance are not as simple as earlier critics have supposed. The characterisation of the hero is rarely entirely negative, since in the course of the narrative he usually undergoes certain positive changes. More importantly, the heroine 'is fulfilled not through his cruelty but through his transformations'.[16] The crucial point in these novels, as in those written by Joan Foster, is the moment of collapse which causes power relations between hero and heroine to be reversed. There often occurs a momentary situation of extreme risk for the heroine (due to illness or other external evil forces) and/or for the hero. The emotional response embedded in these scenes has also been interpreted in different ways, with Rosalind Coward maintaining that this turning point appeals to infantile fantasies of winning parental love. The illness or injury of the hero, as a narrative device, allows the heroine to gain power over him, the power of a mother looking after a child. The concluding marriage, a conventional feature of these novels, despite the apparent submission of the female partner, is none the less a means by which the heroine gains the power of the mother so that, at least, 'the daughter has taken the mother's place'.[17] Janice Radway focuses differently, on the moment of collapse experienced by the heroine which turns the hero into a gentle, tender, nurturing figure, to argue that such moments act as a fulfilling of women's desire to be nurtured and mothered as in childhood.[18]

As an author of popular romance Joan Foster shares certain characteristics with her readers. She has always loved the element of romance in the films she frequently went to see with her aunt and has always had a special liking for happy endings: 'I was a sucker for ads, especially those that promised happiness' (p. 29). She needs escape as much as her audience: 'Escape literature. . . should be an escape for the writer as well as the reader' (p. 155). She is brought up by her aunt on a diet of Hollywood romance films, and this provides her with an understanding of the need for escape. She makes Arthur's dismissal of popular literature, as writing that merely 'exploits' and 'corrupts' the masses and offers 'degrading stereotypes of women as helpless and persecuted' (p. 35), look simple-minded. Commenting on Arthur's ideology and her own writing of romances, Joan observes:

> Sometimes his goddamned theories and ideologies made me puke. The truth was that I dealt in hope, I offered a vision of a better world, however preposterous. Was that so terrible? I couldn't see that it was much different from the visions Arthur and his friends offered, and it was just as realistic.   (p. 35)

In Joan's perception, Arthur fails to recognise that escapist literature has very little to do with role models and that it 'works at the level of sensibility'.[19] Escape into fantasy, however unreal and recognised as such by its readers, provides enjoyable feelings which are needed by those women 'who had got married too young, who had babies too early, who wanted princes and castles and ended up with cramped apartments and grudging husbands' (p. 95).

Like female readers of romance, Joan's women acquaintances conceive of themselves or the heroine as the objects of need; they require the love and desire of a strong male who is at the same time also capable of being kind, sensitive and concerned for their pleasure. As Joan puts it:

> The other wives, too, wanted their husband to live up to their own fantasy lives.... They wanted their men to be strong, lustful, passionate and exciting, with hard rapacious mouths, but also tender and worshipful. They wanted men in mysterious cloaks who would rescue them from balconies, but also they wanted meaningful in-depth relationships and total openness . . . They wanted multiple orgasms, they wanted the earth to move, but they also wanted help with the dishes.   (p. 216)

Lady Oracle attempts to understand how women, constantly bombarded with promises of 'ideals', are to cope with the fact that those ideals do not actually exist. Romance as 'wish fulfilment' for women offers compensation for all the pleasures of romantic love that, despite being so frequently offered by the media and the advertising industry, are as constantly denied. Despite the fact that women readers know that the promises of romance cannot be kept, 'many women return to romance for its promises. Promises of love, security and power'.[20]

In Atwood's treatment it is Joan Foster's own writing that allows her to explore a plural subjectivity and it is her writing that will enable her to *live through* this division, this split. In *Stalked by Love* the maze in the castle acquires an alternative significance: the descent in the maze is also a 'descent into the underworld',[21] which suggests the labyrinth of the psyche. The scene provides a confrontation in which subjectivity alters and is altered by aspects of itself confronted for the first time. The women Felicia finds in the labyrinth are her husband's previous wives, undoubtedly resembling aspects of Joan's past selves; conventional stereotypes of femininity into which she has hitherto been slotted:

> A stone bench ran along one side, and on it were seated four women. Two of them looked a lot like her, with red hair and green eyes and small white teeth. The third was middle aged, dressed in a strange garment that ended half way up her calves, with a ratty piece of fur around her neck. The last was enormously fat. She was wearing a pair of pink tights and a short skirt covered with spangles. From her head sprouted two antennae, like a butterfly's, and a pair of obviously false wings was pinned to her back.   (p. 341)

Confronting images of her past and present selves, Joan comes to terms with her own self-division, with the 'otherness' within herself, since this time she does not suppress one in favour of another. Instead, she realises that she has to accept her multiple, numerous selves. Art here transforms life as Joan now resolves to face reality.

The different stylistic levels of the text, especially in the fictional narratives Joan creates, become a sign of contradictory tendencies that co-exist within the character. They show contrasting world-views and systems of belief, thereby proposing the self as a site of antithetical positions and conflicts. Popular art, then, does not simply or merely reproduce ways and means proper to the dominant discourse, but acts as a locus of conflict where a double movement between acceptance and dissent can be continually discerned.[22] Subjectivity is the site for this oscillation, and the double movement is embodied by Joan herself. Her humanist self, in constant search for reassurance and unity, resents 'this other place where everything changed and shifted' (p. 284). It does not accept being 'closed out from that impossible white paradise where love was final as death' (p. 284). Her drive to write romance fiction responds to this longing for certitude and unity, mirroring a need for that 'feeling of release when everything turned out right and I could scatter joy like rice all over my characters and dismiss them into bliss' (p. 320). The fiction she writes represents her need to conceal the existence of those conflicts which appear in her collection of poetry, 'Lady Oracle'. Advertised as a struggle between the sexes, the title-poem's cryptic story of the unhappy queen and her knight encodes her 'need to explore' an antihumanist self seemingly aware of the endless process of transformation.

In *Lady Oracle* the notion of a coherent, unified self is rejected along with the concept of life as fixed and static. It is through Joan's crisis and subsequent rebirths that she becomes other than she was. Her bodily transformation from overweight girl to slim attractive woman – to the extent that Arthur does not recognise her in a photograph taken at the time of her adolescence – suggests a notion of being as becoming, and opens up the possibilities of another order, of a completely different world that Joan pursues. 'I wanted to have more than one life' (p. 141). She 'dies' as Joan Foster in the Toronto harbour, only to be born anew in Italy where she 'celebrate[s] the birth of [her] new personality' (p. 184), after cutting and dyeing her red, waist-length hair. As a consequence, death also loses its tragic overtones to suggest instead metamorphosis, an idea that has always fascinated Atwood.[23] These concepts of self and body challenge all notions of stability and permanence. Self and body are thus positioned outside hierarchies, since 'a hierarchy can determine only that which represents stable, immovable, and unchangeable being, not free becoming'.[24]

. . .

Nevertheless, *Lady Oracle* shares with the Gothic some of its basic assumptions. The vision that informs the Gothic is one which does not attempt to solve any of the contradictions and conflicts of this world, one that does not offer absolute truth, one that lacks 'faith in organic notions of wholeness'.[25] Subjective, relativistic positions are emphasised especially through the multiplicity of narrative lines. The use of suspense and doubt renders it difficult to draw a clear line between fantasy and reality. Gothic fables developed round 'those points of vision and obsession where the individual blurs into his own fantasies'. As a result they 'questioned the boundaries on which individual identity depends',[26] and these elements are present in *Lady Oracle*'s denial of the classical unities of space, time and character. The novel's 'plot within a plot' also interrupts the chronology of the main narrative, creating different temporal levels, while its web of intertextual references proposes alternative temporal dimensions. In order to decode parody, the addressee has to transcend the boundaries of the text and explore her/his competence within the corpus of writing that exists before it. During this operation, which requires a time measurable in fractions, the reader engages in a dialogue with the text, as he/she partakes in this game of intertextual quotation, where the reader's time becomes the time of her/his 'encyclopaedic competence'.[27]

Unity of character is subverted by the novel's polyhedric protagonist. The self is represented as being an unstable entity: it doubles and multiplies through the different identities assumed simultaneously by Joan Foster and/or Louisa K. Delacourt as well as through the spectrum of her projected personae. The self becomes – as Atwood herself states – 'a place where things happen', or where experience intersects. Relevant to this is Joan's comment, ' "You must learn to control yourself" she said kindly . . . She didn't know what a lot of territory this covered' (p. 58). Joan's own identity is dispersed in a multitude of projected personae ranging from film stars to heroines of fairy tales. Atwood brings into the text 'voices' and 'characters' from a range of different kinds of writing and these intertextual references relate also to the theme of sexual politics in the novel. They show Atwood's concern with how cinema and fairy tales, for example, construct female subjectivity and female desire and how they function for the female spectator. There is Joan Delacourt, the adolescent overweight girl, behind whom appears the shadow of Joan Crawford – the Hollywood actress she was named after.

As a girl, Joan feels an intense empathy with the unhappy heroine of the Hollywood film *The Red Shoes*, acted by Moira Shearer. Joan identifies strongly with the dilemma of this professional red-haired dancer, with her lovely costume and red satin shoes, who faces a drastic choice between career and marriage, and who consequently commits suicide.[28] Dancing as a language of the body becomes then a sign of sexual desire or, in turn, of a repressed sexuality which takes the form of female sacrifice. The liberating and subversive significance of dancing is also emphasised by Atwood's reference to the Hans Andersen's fairy tales 'The Red Shoes' and 'The Little Mermaid'. Recurringly Andersen's stories present images of mutilation and death which caught Atwood's poetic imagination. It is death above all that awaits Andersen's heroine whenever she attempts to deviate from or rebel against her prescribed role as passive, selfless giver.

In 'The Red Shoes' the girl's desire to dance – seen in the story as a manifestation of selfishness – becomes a means of both enjoyment and punishment. It is Andersen's Little Mermaid – another of Joan's projected personae – who finally manages to dance beautifully in front of her beloved Prince. But in order to become human, to have legs and feet, she has to sacrifice her voice. Once she is deprived of that, she fails to conquer the Prince's love, which for the Little Mermaid would also have meant the acquisition of an immortal soul. Failure for her will mean death, and her dancing is therefore her last tribute to an impossible dream. Later in life Joan, in an attempt to dance for no one but herself, figuratively *becomes* the dancer with the red shoes. She discovers her feet red with her own blood, from having danced on cut glass, 'The real red shoes, the feet punished for dancing' (p. 335).

Joan also projects herself on to her own heroines: there is more than one correspondence between Joan and Felicia,[29] while affinities as well as differences exist between her and Charlotte. Joan's persecuted heroines, eternally 'on the run', are but another version of her own persecutions (by her mother and by men) and flights. But she is not merely a 'victim': she is also a 'survivor' who by shifting roles and positions manages to survive physically and psychically. This may be the symbolic meaning of her identification with the trapeze artist and contortionist. A liberating aspect seems attached to such identifications, since they signify flexibility and adaptability. Another example of Joan's identifications is to be found in her close resemblance not only to Tennyson's 'Lady of Shalott', but also to the various Pre-Raphaelite paintings that the Lady in the poem inspired at the time. One such evocation, of a painting by John William Waterhouse which shows the Lady casting off in the barge for Camelot, occurs after Joan has been reading the news report of her death: 'There I was, on the bottom of the death barge where I'd once longed to be, my name on the prow, winding my way down the river' (p. 313). Although Joan the narrator encompasses all these identities within herself, it is not possible to limit her to any of them. Like the trapeze artist of her daydream, she oscillates between them, she 'floats', as Joan herself calls her strategy of coping with her plurality: 'if there's one thing I knew how to do it was float' (p. 303). She has a strange sense of being carried away 'like the Little Mermaid in the Andersen fairy tale ... Perhaps ... I had no soul, I just drifted around, singing vaguely' (p. 216). The plurality and juxtaposition of different styles in the novel appears then to find a correspondence in the scattered identifications of its character.

'*It is always best to be oneself*' reads a fortune cookie message which Joan interprets as a warning and rebuke, yet her impatient question, 'But which one, which one?' (p. 231) is left unresolved. In Atwood's collection of poetry *The Circle Game*, where a recurring imagery of entrapment and duality is haunted by Gothic overtones, the question of identity is posed in a similar way. In 'A Place: Fragments', identity becomes synonymous with 'largeness' and 'confusion', an entity which appears unpredictable and diffuse:

> something not lost or hidden
> but just not found yet
> that informs, holds together
> this confusion, this largeness
> and dissolving:
>
> not above or behind
> or within it, but one
> with it: an
>
> identity:
> something too huge and simple
> for us to see.[30]

This notion of identity parallels Atwood's characterisation of Joan as possessing a contradictory and plural subjectivity. It also parallels some developments in recent psychoanalytic theory which conceive of the subject as a product of an unconscious always in process, and therefore always unanalysable, uncharacterisable ('something too huge and simple for us to see').[31]

If Joan then does reveal a quixotic and capricious aspect, her inclination to live partly in a fantasy romance world acquires the positive significance of a strategic defensive and survival device. Open, direct confrontation with reality, though necessary, can be very dangerous: witness the fate of Tennyson's Lady of Shalott. Various references to the poem in *Lady Oracle* emphasise this fact. Confined in her tower where she weaves and sings, the Lady can look at reality only through a mirror, and she copies in her web the reflections of the outside world. Metaphors of the perceiving mind and the creative consciousness, the mirror and the web signify the problematic relationships between art and life, testing and challenging the solipsistic tendencies of the individual imagination. The Lady's bower represents safety, and the mirror acts also as a protection from life. But it cracks when she looks down to Camelot and leaves her place in the tower to reach out for the knight, only to drown in the river. 'The Lady of Shalott' thus effectively creates a tension between conflicting desires to face reality and to shun it. But it does so without providing an answer to the questions it poses, and similar contradictions are found in Joan; although in *Lady Oracle* there seems to be a more gloomy suggestion about the possibility of coping with reality: 'You could stay in the tower for years, – weaving away, looking in the mirror, but one glance out the window at real life and that was that. The curse, the doom' (p. 313).

Joan's stories represent for her a way of enjoying fantasy and reality in close conjunction, something which Arthur could not possibly have accepted. But for Joan it is not an *either/or*, it is an *and*, as she herself observes:

> As long as I could spend a certain amount of time each week as Louisa, I was all right, I was patient and forbearing, warm, a sympathetic listener. But if I was cut off, if I couldn't work on my current Costume Gothic, I would become mean and irritable, drink too much and start to cry.   (p. 213)

She requires both dimensions, and later realises that she could not possibly live with the 'Royal Porcupine', since she would not have the coexistence of fantasy and reality that she needs. 'For him reality and fantasy were the same time, which meant that for him there was no reality. But for me it would mean there was no fantasy and therefore no escape' (p. 270). Since one excludes the other, the opposition truth/fantasy is discarded. Instead we have seen how one term of the antithesis can be inherent within the other. Rachel Du Plessis calls it the 'both/and vision':

> A both/and vision born of shifts, contraries, negation, contradictions; linked to personal vulnerability and need.... Structurally such a writing might say different things, not settle on one, which is final. This is not a condition of 'not choosing', since choice exists always in what to represent and in the rhythms of presentation.[32]

The deconstructive attitude which woman adopts towards the either/or dualism is related to her marginal position within the dominant discourse. Woman's position on the margin of the symbolic order means that she may be regarded by patriarchy as the borderline or limit of that order:

> From a phallocentric point of view women will then come to represent the necessary frontier between man and chaos; but because of their very marginality they will also always seem to recede into and merge with the chaos of the outside. Women seen as the limit of the symbolic order will in other worlds share in the disconcerting properties of *all* frontiers: they will be neither inside nor outside, neither known or unknown.[33]

As insider–outsider, woman inhabits simultaneously two dimensions as does the speaker in one of Atwood's poems: 'I exist in two places, / here and where you are'.[34] Having a 'double consciousness' could imply, as Du Plessis suggests, a 'double understanding'. We find therefore a predilection for simultaneity and coexistence, which according to Dorothy Richardson's happy intuition, seems to be a 'unique gift of the feminine psyche': 'Its power to do what the shapely mentalities of men appear incapable of doing for themselves, to act as a focus for divergent points of view ... The characteristic ... of being all over the place and in all camps at once.'[35] Simultaneity as a typical property of woman has been emphasised by the Luce Irigaray, for whom woman belongs to an altogether different economy, which does not rely on an either/or model.[36] Another economy which 'diverts the linearity of a project . . . explodes the polarization of desire on only one pleasure . . . disconcerts fidelity to only one discourse.'[37]

There appears in the novel an attempt to explore different forms of subjectivity according to gender. Male characterisation seems still confined to that divided subjectivity, typical of Gothic and modern sensibility, which is a locus, a dwelling of polarities.[38] If not entirely coherent and unified, none the less it appears less radically open to change and far more inflexible and dogmatic. Arthur in his attempt to try 'new paths' in his life, his going through different phases, undergoes certain changes. These changes occur, though less dramatically than those in Joan's life.[39] Besides, in Atwood's characterisation of the male figure the presence of a key self set against the splintered identity of Joan can still be felt. Joan's partners remain two dimensional, in contrast to her own many-sided identity. That is how Joan comments on the difference existing between them: 'for Arthur there were true paths, several of them perhaps, but only one at a time. For me there were no paths at all. Thickets, ditches, ponds, labyrinths, morasses, but no paths' (p. 169).

Despite the fact that the psychic multiplicity which Joan possesses starts as a kind of strategy for survival, it finds receptive soil, since she later welcomes all the possibilities that such a subjectivity opens up:

> But not twin even, for I was more than double, I was triple, multiple, and now I could see that there was more than one life to come, there were many. The Royal Porcupine had opened a time space door to the fifth dimension, cleverly disguised as freight elevator, and one of my selves plunged recklessly through. (p. 246)

Notes

1. G. Gibson, 'Interview with Margaret Atwood', in *Eleven Canadian Writers* (Toronto, 1973).
2. The novel presents many of the recurring features of Canadian literature Atwood had traced in *Survival*. Here, though, they are used in a rather different way, since the author works within the tradition but only to suggest a way out of it. As she writes in *Survival*: 'A tradition doesn't necessarily exist to bury you: it can also be used as material for new departures' (Toronto, 1972), p. 246.
3. L. Fielder, 'The Death and Rebirths of the Novel'; 'Response: American Fiction' , *Salmagundi*, vol. 50–1 (1980) pp. 142–52; 153–71.
4. F. Sharpshott, 'The Last Word in Criticism', *Transactions of the Royal Society of Canada* (1982), pp. 117–28.
5. C. Guillen, *Literature as a System* (Princetown, N. J., 1971) pp. 386; 12. A reading of the novel in terms of only one genre, such as the Picaresque (L. Freibert, 'The Artist as Picaro', *Canadian Literature*, vol. 92 (Spring 1982) pp. 23–33), does not account for the implications of the contamination within genres that is present in *Lady Oracle*. Undoubtedly, certain elements of the Picaresque do appear in the novel, the most evident being that of the artist as a trickster, but on the whole the novel defies generic classifications (C. Guillen, 'Toward a Definition of the Picaresque', in Guillen, *Literature as a System*, pp. 71–106).
6. Margaret Atwood, *Lady Oracle* (London, 1982) p. 226. Further references to this edition are given in the text.
7. M. Atwood, 'Superwoman Drawn and Quartered: the Early form of *She*' (1965), in *Second Words* (Toronto, 1982) pp. 35–54, esp. p. 54.
8. M. Bakhtin, *The Dialogic Imagination*, trans. C. Emerson and M. Holquist (London, 1981) pp. 315, 364.
9. M. Atwood, interview with J. Struthers, *Essays in Canadian Writing*, vol. 6 (Spring 1977) pp. 18–27, esp. p. 19
10. M. Rose, *Parody/Metafiction* (London, 1979) p. 72.
11. A. Light, 'Returning to Manderley – Romance Fiction, Female Sexuality and Class', *Feminist Review*, vol. 16 (Summer 1984) pp. 7–25.
12. J. Batsler, 'Pulp in the Pink', *Spare Rib*, no. 109 (1981) pp. 51–5.
13. Rosalind Coward, *Female Desire* (London, 1984) p. 194.
14. Ibid., p. 195. Rosalind Coward sees evidence of this in the feeling of guilt that accompanies onanistic practice in women. The activity is in fact reminiscent of an infantile kind of pleasure, which differs from the 'approved', heterosexual act. For this reason it is experienced as wrong, somehow not quite right.
15. T. Modleski, *Loving with a Vengeance: Mass-produced Fantasies for Women* (Handen, Conn., 1982) p. 37.
16. A. Jones, 'Mills & Boon Meets Feminism', in J. Radford (ed.), *The Progress of Romance: The Politics of Popular Fiction* (London, 1986) pp. 195–220, esp. p. 200.
17. Coward, *Female Desire*, p. 196.

18. Janice Radway, *Reading the Romance* (London, 1984).
19. R. Dyer, 'Entertainment and Utopia', in R. Altman (ed.), *Genre: The Musical, A Reader* (London, 1981) pp. 175–89, esp. p. 177.
20. Coward, *Female Desire*, p. 13.
21. Batsler, 'Pulp in the Pink', p. 53.
22. L. Sandler, 'Interview with Margaret Atwood', *Malahat Review*, vol. 61 (January 1977) pp. 7–26, esp. p. 16.
23. Stuart Hall, 'Notes on Deconstructing the Popular', in R. Samuel (ed.), *People's History and Socialist Theory* (London, 1981) pp. 227–40.
24. Concepts of transformation and metamorphosis inform Atwood's poetic vision, and are a recurrent concern in her poetry, where life appears a 'constant process of reformation . . . Nothing is destroyed in Atwood's universe: it simply assumes another space, another form' (J. Forster, 'The Poetry of Margaret Atwood', *Canadian Literature*, vol. 74 (autumn 1977) pp. 5–20, esp. pp. 6, 8.
25. Michael Bakhtin, *Rabelais and his World*, trans. M. Iswolsky (Bloomington, Ind., 1984) p. 215.
26. R. Jackson, *Fantasy: The Literature of Subversion* (London, 1981), p. 198.
27. D. Punter, *The Literature of Terror* (London, 1980) p. 73.
28. Quoted by S. Grace, *Violent Duality: A Study of Margaret Atwood* (Montreal, 1980) p. 76.
29. Atwood's comment on the film in *Second Words* (p. 224) shows how she regards it as a cultural precept for a generation of young girls, who 'were taken to see it as a special treat for their birthday parties . . . The message was clear. You could not have both your artistic career and the love of a good man as well, and if you tried, you would end up committing suicide.'
30. Margaret Atwood, 'A Place: Fragments', in *The Circle Game* (Toronto, 1966) p. 76.
31. Beside Felicia's glamorous red hair, the identification is stretched to an extreme point when in one of the final scenes of *Stalked by Love* (one among Joan's various attempts to conclude the novel) Felicia emerges from the water invoking Joan's husband's name, Arthur (p. 323). Also when Felicia enters the maze, the villain appears for a moment to resemble Arthur (p. 343).
32. R. B. du Plessis, 'For the Etruscans', in E. Showalter (ed.), *The New Feminist Criticism* (London, 1985) pp. 271–91, esp. p. 276.
33. T. Moi, *Sexuality/Textual Politics: Feminist Literary Criticism* (London, 1985) p. 167.
34. Margaret Atwood, *You Are Happy* (Toronto, 1974) p. 43.
35. Quoted in Du Plessis, 'For the Etruscans', p. 276.
36. The starting point in Irigaray's argument is an equation between women's psychology and women's 'morphology' (Gr. *morphe*, 'form'). Contrary to male sexuality, which is monolithical and unified, female sex is not *one* since in itself it is 'composed of two lips . . . Thus within herself she is already two – but not divisible into ones.' Besides it is woman's *jouissance* which is in itself different, diffuse, since she does not have to choose between different pleasures, her sexuality is inclusive, multiple, always plural (Luce

Irigaray, *This Sex Which is Not One*, trans. C. Porter (New York, 1985) p. 20.

37. Ibid., p. 22.
38. 'Every man I'd ever been involved with, I realized, had had two selves: my father, healer and killer; the man in the tweed coat, my rescuer and possibly also a pervert; the Royal Porcupine and his double Chuck Brewer; even Paul, who I'd always believed had a sinister other life I couldn't penetrate. Why should Arthur be the only exception?' (p. 292).
39. 'Once I'd thought of Arthur as single minded, single-hearted, single-bodied; I, by contrast, was a sorry assemblage of lies and alibis, each complete in itself but rendering the others worthless. But I soon discovered there were as many of Arthur as there were of me. The difference was that I was simultaneous, whereas Arthur was a sequence' (p. 211).

7

Hope against Hopelessness: Margaret Atwood's *Life Before Man*

JANICE KULYK KEEFER

These are the only words I have, I'm stuck with them, stuck in them. (That image of the tar sands, old tableau in the Royal Ontario Museum . . . how persistent it is. Will I break free, or will I be sucked down, fossilized, a sabre-toothed tiger or lumbering brontosaurus who ventured out too far? Words ripple at my feet, black, sluggish, lethal. Let me try once more . . . before I starve or drown . . . . It's only a tableau after all, it's only a metaphor. See, I can speak, I am not trapped, and you on your part can understand. So we will go ahead as if there were no problem about language.)

Margaret Atwood, 'Giving Birth' (*DG*, p. 229)[1]

But as we all know, especially if we have read more than a little of Margaret Atwood's poetry or prose, there *is* a problem about language. Inherently duplicitous, seductively manipulable, it is still, however, the only medium the writer has with which to tell the truth – even if that truth be that there is no one, stable, universal truth to tell.[2] As the narrator of 'Giving Birth' suggests, language is acutely paradoxical, both trapping us in and releasing us from whatever 'tar sands' into which we've chanced to stumble. Literary language demands from both writer and reader a curious mix of naïvety and complicity. In one sense, we cannot help but write or read a text 'as if' language were utterly tractable and transparent, and the fictive world created by language were a mirror held up to the world outside the book. And yet from literature we demand a richer,

153

heightened, stronger use of language than we're accustomed to find in daily life; and we want the fictive world that language creates to be meaningful and coherent in ways that our own world can never be. And finally, we want both judgement and absolution from the novels we read. We understand that fiction can show us things about ourselves, our world and our condition therein to which we'd previously been blind; and yet we also know that if the text tells us things we do not wish or cannot bear to hear, we can dismiss it: after all, it's 'just a book', something made and, by corollary, made up.

Margaret Atwood is a writer whose work shows her to be acutely aware of the paradoxical nature of language and the problematics of novel-writing. Yet not only is she extraordinarily prolific, she is also phenomenally popular. Only a fraction of her readership is accounted for by cognoscenti who, versed in the precepts of postmodernist literary theory,[3] demand that literature be overtly self-reflexive and insistently intertextual, that it subvert the supposed norms of such established aesthetic modes as realism, for example. For the most part, Atwood writes for and is read by the educated but not academic reader, the kind of person whose Janus-faced approach to fiction I have described in the preceding paragraph. This is not to say that Atwood does not, as Linda Hutcheon argues, 'us[e] and abus[e] the conventions of both novelistic language and narrative in her fiction to question any naïve notions of both modernist formalism (art is autonomous artifice) and realist transparency (art is a reflection of the world)'.[4] But it is to say that, as must any writer who wishes to live off as well as by fiction, Atwood must attract as wide as possible a readership, and this she does by letting her readers have their cake and eat it too. A novel such as *The Handmaid's Tale* is a perfect case in point, giving us both Ofred's predominantly transparent-realist narrative and an epilogue which is, among other things, a large and succulent bone thrown to the postmodernist watchdog.

Atwood's novels, for the most part, make admirably adroit use of all the tricks of the trade to entice and entertain the largest possible number of readers, while presenting them with a complex and challenging vision of the reality she shares with them. The exception to this rule – and a highly peculiar exception at that – is *Life Before Man*, a work which conspicuously lacks the comic structure and caricatural edge of *The Edible Woman* and *Lady Oracle*, the mythopoeic power of *Surfacing* and *Cat's Eye*, the overt political focus, exotic locales and suspenseful plots of *Bodily Harm* and *The*

Handmaid's Tale. *Life Before Man* is concerned with the private lives of a very few lower-middle-class urbanites: deracinated, isolated, miserably pressured by the mundane. The terrain of this novel's fictive world is irremediably flat, dun-coloured, harshly-lit; the weather foul, and tolerable accommodation near-impossible to find. The novel has little plot to speak of, portrays remarkably unempathetic characters, and offers a vision of human possibility that is constricted in the extreme. And yet *Life Before Man* has proved popular with the common reader: by July 1989 the low-priced paperback version had gone into its seventh printing.

What is the explanation for the enthusiastic reception of a novel that puts one more in mind of the world-view of *Malone Dies* than of *Lake Wobegon Days*? Perhaps it is that readers recognise, in *Life Before Man, a tour de force*. Using a minimum of novelistic tools and materials, Atwood has created a convincing fictive world whose authenticity derives both from a compulsive detailing of surface reality and from a stark consistency of vision. One can offer the hypothesis that thousands of North American readers opened this novel and, finding in its pages a mirror of their own inert, constricted and bewildering lives, were 'sucked in' as surely as brontosauri into tar sands. Can we assume that most readers gave to *Life Before Man* the kind of assent which a reviewer for the *Spectator* did to *Dancing Girls*?: 'Everything Margaret Atwood says in this book is overwhelmingly true ... You're sure to recognize yourself somewhere.'[5] It is a sobering thought, given the appallingly limited possibilities for even a minimal degree of contentment with life, love and work which Atwood concedes to her characters.

Yet if *Life Before Man* displays the degree zero of 'the way we live now' it is not because the novelist, like her characters, cannot 'imagine what else to do' (*LBM*, p. 123). She has taken for her subject matter the near-terminal impoverishment of the human, and therefore moral, imagination as applied to contemporary urban life, and she has attempted to situate this impoverishment in its proper, devastating context. In 1976 Atwood explained that, for her, writing was in part 'an exploration of where in reality I live' (*SW*, p. 112). *Life Before Man* maps out a significant portion of that reality; in it Atwood returns to the setting of her first novel, downtown Toronto, but strips it of all typology except for the Museum, which functions as a 'collectio[n] of memories ... a giant brain'[6] – suggesting a gigantic version of what *Surfacing* decries: the 'knob' artificially separated from the rest of the body, and the deathly constriction it creates (*S*, p. 76). There are no lakes to be submerged in or reborn from in *Life Before Man*; the closed circle, or rather oval, of Queen's Park is the closest we come to wilderness, and even that Atwoodian *locus classicus*, the ravine, whose depth, darkness and solitude offer dramatic possibilities for destruction or salvation, appears only peripherally.[7] No magical transformations take place in this novel, and the token rituals and ceremonies which occur – Hallowe'en, Remembrance Day, Christmas – are ironically displaced to the point of insignificance. The only extraordinary event – Chris's suicide – takes place before the novel opens, and whatever plot the novel can be said to possess consists of the perturbations and repercussions caused by this suicide in the lives of five other people: Chris's ex-lover, Elizabeth, her husband Nate, Lesje, with whom Nate's fallen in love, and the minor characters Martha (Nate's ex-mistress) and William (Lesje's 'partner' – one hesitates to call anyone likened to a slab of Philadelphia cream cheese a 'lover': *LBM*, p. 196).

In giving us a minute account of the frustrated interactions of these characters, Atwood produces an anatomy not so much of melancholy as of joyless endurance, controlled despair and active paralysis. In its mimetic accuracy, its emphatic minimalism of tone and technique, and its masterly deployment of language – those 'black, sluggish, lethal words' with which Atwood manages to play crack the whip – *Life Before Man* is one of Atwood's most accomplished fictive structures. And yet it is one of her least typical texts, one whose 'formula' she has never yet repeated. It is widely seen as a turning point for Atwood, a form of 'clearing the ground' for the more political novels which were to be raised on the site it exposed. What I shall attempt in this essay is an examination of this site and the techniques which expose it to view, and of the paradoxical response which this novel elicits: the pleasure and pain of recognition, and the hope and hopelessness which such recognition engenders.

What is the characteristic literary mode in which *Life Before Man* is written? The question is an important one, since our response to the novel will be governed by the expectations it raises. In an interview conducted between the publication of *Lady Oracle* and

Life Before Man, Atwood insists that she writes not satire but 'realism verging on caricature', and declares: 'I try to select characters who are outgrowths of their society. But my writing is closer to caricature than to satire – distortion rather than scathing attack – and as I say, it's largely realism.'[8] 'Largely realism' may be an adequate portrayal of her first and third novels, if hardly of her second, but how does it suit her fourth? One critic has described *Life Before Man* as Atwood's 'first attempt at social and domestic realism unmediated by satire, comedy or symbolism'.[9] I would suggest that, due to this lack of mediation, (countered by a prodigal attention to the details of surface reality), Atwood achieves not realism, but a minimalist form of naturalism. Linda Hutcheon has argued that, in correct postmodernist fashion, Atwood uses the conventions of the realist novel to 'self-consciously mil[k] realism for all its power, even while parodying and subverting its conventions'.[10] The question that remains to be asked of *Life Before Man*, then, is this: why did Atwood deprive us of the eventful plots and the kind of characters – vulnerable, flawed, yet capable of growth, change, and fruitful interaction – which one finds in such traditional realist fiction as *Anna Karenina* or *Middlemarch*? Garcia Marquez may, as Robert Kroetsch suggests, 'ni[p] at the heels of realism and mak[e] the old cow dance',[11] but what Atwood does in *Life Before Man* is closer to flogging a horse she has deliberately starved to death. Before we address the question of why she does so, we should acknowledge the rigour and assiduity with which she goes about restricting her novelistic options.

To say that *Life Before Man* is a deliberately restrictive and reductive work is not to deny that it introduces certain formal innovations into Atwood's *oeuvre*. With regard to narrative technique, for example, we can point to Atwood's adoption of multiple consciousness, male as well as female, to register overlapping and often contradictory perceptions of a rigidly controlled number of phenomena. (We might also remark that this is an innovation she has not decided to exploit in her later works of fiction.) And yet such is the general atmosphere of this novel that polyphony is subsumed into monotone: Lesje, Nate and Elizabeth may be quite different people, from a variety of backgrounds, and they may possess contrasting preoccupations and expectations, but they are hardly done 'in different voices'. What the reader hears, regardless of the occasional slip into first person narration by Elizabeth, is not the voice of individual characters, but that of their common predicament, as transcribed by a disinterested authorial observer.

Atwood's approach to character in *Life Before Man* gives us pause as well. She has often stated her belief that character should be understood not as ego but rather as a site or through which things happen.[12] The problem for the characters in this novel is that most of these sites resemble vacant lots fitted with detour signs. It is almost as though Atwood had selected a number of 'typical'[13] characters and set them up in a controlled experiment in which all possibilities for random interaction and fortuitous interventions by outside influences have been eliminated. So incestuous is this control group that Elizabeth revenges herself on Lesje for Nate's defection by sleeping with Lesje's partner, William; to further enmesh the group's members, she arranges for Nate's ex-mistress Martha to meet Lesje in the cafeteria of the museum where Elizabeth herself works. One cannot imagine how the circle could be closed tighter. There is no escape or relief through either friends or family: Lesje's parents are stick-figures, hermetically sealed-off from the realities of their daughter's life: Nate's mother is unapproachable in her concerted selflessness, and the one 'outside' intervention by Elizabeth's wicked witch of an Auntie Muriel is both fruitless and unconvincing. Lesje's acquaintance Marianne is hardly a confidante (she is a vestigial form of the predatory friend found in other novels: Ainsley in *The Edible Woman*; Jocasta in *Bodily Harm*; Cordelia in *Cat's Eye*), and for Elizabeth there is no companion remotely like Aunt Lou in *Lady Oracle*, Moira in *The Handmaid's Tale*, or even Lora in *Bodily Harm*. As for Nate, the only contact he seems to have with anyone other than wife or mistress is with Elizabeth's volatile and violent lover, Chris.

Atwood's cast of characters is remarkable for its refusal to provide us with anyone to whom we can connect our own sense of self or situation. We may, of course, be involved in disastrous love affairs, find our working lives meaningless and our family lives bewildering, but it is difficult to want to put ourselves in such scuffed, narrow and repellent shoes as those which Nate, Elizabeth and Lesje are made to wear. It is not, of course, necessary to 'identify with' a novel's characters, but towards them we should manifest what Kundera, in the opening pages of *The Unbearable Lightness of Being*, calls 'co-feeling', signifying 'the maximal capacity of affective imagination, the art of emotional telepathy'.[14] This proves difficult for readers of *Life Before Man*, partly because, apart from Chris, the characters all use or submit to codes of civility and decorum in order to anaesthetise themselves from their violently disordered pasts or appallingly etiolated presents. Emotional telepathy is rather hard to achieve with characters deliberately kept at so many removes from their own emotions.[15]

There is, for example, an extreme degree of stress and strain but never pathos in Elizabeth's predicament. However deplorable, even shocking, we may find her hard-luck childhood, Elizabeth repels us by her practiced manipulation of others, her deliberate removal of all but the shell of herself from her children, husband and lover, and by her rigid rage for order and control. (She elicits from the reader the same kind of grudging acknowledgement of strength and staying power one might extend to a Margaret Thatcher.) Lesje's fundamental detachment from what most of us would consider as ordinary life, and her preference for fossils over human beings make her resemble a creature from a species different from our own. Even her 'refugee' condition – the result of her being the product of a racially and religiously mixed marriage – does not particularly recommend her to the reader's sympathies, and this is largely because, though we are given carefully researched facts about Lesje's ethnic background, they never really quicken into 'felt' life.

As for the lapsed lawyer-turned-toymaker, Nate,[16] it is hard for the reader not to feel for him the same 'slight contempt' Elizabeth manifests towards his goodness (*LBM*, p. 242). Both *homme moyen sensuel* and ethical man, Nate stumbles through life with conscience and desire, like undone shoelaces round his feet, constantly tripping him up and preventing him from ever taking any direct, unambiguous or immediate action. He is disillusioned about everything, most of all himself, and his love affair with Lesje is largely the product of mistaken identity – though she can never be what he thinks she represents, she remains for most of the novel addicted to his false image of her. Perhaps the most damning thing that can be said about Lesje is that she is capable of falling in love with Nate. Perhaps the problem with Nate is that he is so over-schematised, so elaborately 'typical', that he can't help emerging on the page as the tin man and sawdust-stuffed doll he perceives himself to be.

What Atwood achieves with her choice of characters is thus a species of *Verfremdungseffekt*. Her decision in *Life Before Man* largely to forgo the first-person narration employed in most of her other novels heightens this alienation device. By giving us three different perceptions and interpretations of the same snail's-paced 'event', Atwood means to prevent us from sympathising with or trusting any one point of view. We have only one character's word against another's to go by; whatever Elizabeth tells us is immediately qualified by what Nate thinks, which is further qualified by Lesje's reflections. Though the narrative contains a degree of dialogue, remembered or direct, the bulk of the novel consists of descriptions of day-to-day motions rather than actions, and of what might be called 'think-overs': hypotheses, deliberations, carefully selected as opposed to random memories. Typically, the native hue of resolution is sicklied o'er; uncertainties and qualifications continually erode or dilute most of the characters' perceptions and responses, as for example in this rumination by Lesje about the pink-cheeked, would-be-rapist, William: 'It isn't the violence but the betrayal of the innocent surface that is so painful; though possibly there was no innocence, possibly she made it up' (*LBM*, p. 179). Ironically, what increases the passivity, not to say paralysis, of the protagonists of this novel is the fact that any fixed or given reality has succumbed to the flux of ambiguity. No one can know anything for certain; any one action can be interpreted in conflicting ways.

The radical ambiguity and uncertainty pervading day-to-day life in *Life Before Man* has a paradoxical effect: the novel seems much more monochromatic and constricted because of it. The disturbing *Handmaid's Tale*, with its punning title and parodic/satiric afterword is far more open and ludic in its effects. Overt wordplay in *Life Before Man* is fairly leaden: for example, Elizabeth's turning 'Armadillo' into 'Armoured dildo' (*LBM*, p. 3). Even the dominant use of the present tense fails to vitalise the text. In Atwood's short story 'The Sunrise', the chief character enjoys what is called 'the freedom of the present tense': while out walking, 'she feels as if her feet are not on cement at all but on ice. The blade of the skate floats, she knows, on a thin film of water, which it melts by pressure and which freezes behind it' (*BE*, pp. 234–5). Yet instead of giving Nate, Lesje or Elizabeth a liberating 'sliding edge', Atwood's use of the present tense traps them in the ramifying limitations of immediate perception.

Yet it is in the region of plot that Atwood restricts herself most severely in this novel. 'People will do anything rather than admit that their lives have no meaning. No use, that is. No plot' (*HT*, p. 227), or so Ofred informs us in *The Handmaid's Tale*. Yet this is just what Nate, Elizabeth and Lesje do admit in the course of this novel. It was in order to give his existence the semblance of a plot that Chris blew off his head with a shotgun: 'he wanted to be an event, and he'd been one' (*LBM*, p. 269). Instead of having *Life Before Man* begin six months or a year before 29 October 1976 and building up to the crisis of Chris's suicide, Atwood makes a whole novel out of a *dénouement*. Those who survive Chris accept the fact that their response to his death and its consequences will eventually compose not a plot, but simply a past, the past being 'the sediment from [negligible] acts, billions, trillions of them' (*LBM*, p. 284). What the reader is offered as an alternative to plot – the unfolding of significant events over time – is the near-random turning over of calendar pages.

What happens in the novel? Basically, Elizabeth 'gets over' Chris's suicide; Nate leaves Martha and takes up with Lesje; Lesje leaves William and sets up house for Nate; Elizabeth and Nate divorce, Nate stops making handcrafted toys and goes back to practising law, part-time; Auntie Muriel dies, Lesje decides to have a baby, and Elizabeth sees it through. There is no sense of flourish or even finale to the closing chapters of the novel: as several commentators have remarked, there is no particular reason for *Life Before Man* to end where it does.[17] Not only is there no happy ending to this novel – there isn't even a determinate ending. Things will simply drift on and on and on: more peanut butter sandwiches will be made and more fossilised teeth catalogued; at least one more child will be born, and Nate will keep running round and round the oval track of Queen's Park.

For the most part, critics have been respectful of *Life Before Man*, confining themselves to close readings of a text bottom-heavy with 'solidity of specification', and to thoughtful analyses of the motifs and meanings of the constricted fictive world Atwood so painstakingly creates. But certain critics, mindful of Atwood's insistence that we must not merely observe or even interpret constructs but judge them as well, go so far as to evaluate the novel. Sherrill Grace, for example concludes that in this work

Atwood has dropped the romance conventions of her previous novels ... in order to capture the empty inconclusiveness of

modern marriage and urban existence. She does so with
remarkable success, but unfortunately, the subject is one that is
already overexploited and more tedious than terrifying. . . . [T]he
artist withdraws behind realist conventions, appearing only as
the hand that chooses a title, the self-important dates that head
each section, and the prefacing quotes. Through these selected
glimpses of her presence, Atwood implies not only that we are
trapped in our mundanity, but that history, science and art
cannot redeem us, offer alternatives or even shape the dull
routine of our lives.[18]

Grace's objections to the sense of tedium and entrapment the
novel evokes and her contention that both language and character
in *Life Before Man* lack depth and passion[19] can, of course, be
countered on mimetic or naturalistic grounds. For only by a
deliberate restriction of her range of vision, technical skills and
linguistic powers can the author produce a convincing presentation
of actual as opposed to ideal reality. The question remains,
however: was this 'remarkably successful' book on an overexploited subject worth writing – and reading – in the first place?
Linda Hutcheon would respond with a resounding yes. She views
Life Before Man as a cautionary tale on the dangers of 'retreating into
a fantasy world to escape the "real" and its dangers'. Hutcheon
even finds a process of redemption at work in the novel: 'Like the
narrator of both *Surfacing* and *Bodily Harm*, Lesje in *Life Before Man*
finally renounces at once the passivity that permits victimization
and also the evasion offered by fantasy, and opts for life and
responsibility.'[20] Hutcheon would, of course, be quick to point out
that the action Lesje takes is paradoxical and problematic (those
very qualities by which Hutcheon defines the nature and project of
postmodern fiction). She would no doubt cite the novel as a
paradigm of the postmodernist urge 'to trouble, to question, to
make both problematic and provisional any . . . desire for order or
truth through the powers of the human imagination'.[21] This is
certainly an accurate description of the effect of *Life Before Man* on
the reader, for this novel exposes not only the fictive nature of
order, control and civility in human relationships, but also the way
in which such concepts are used by the powerful against the weak,
or merely uncertain. In this way *Life Before Man* is very much a
political novel, as Hutcheon insists,[22] a logical predecessor to *Bodily
Harm*.

Thus for Sherill Grace *Life Before Man* is a paradoxically successful failure, both a turning point in and an odd text out in Atwood's *oeuvre*; for Hutcheon it is a necessary, worthy and foreseeable development of the Atwood canon. An impressive number of ordinary readers have bought what is an admittedly grim novel on contemporary mores, and the majority of reviewers have found this book enlightening as well as entertaining. Is this due to Atwood's sheer verbal skills, her sardonically amusing, even addictive way with words? Do readers of this novel see in its pages, not a despairing reflection of their own hampered and stymied lives, but simply an astute account of the luckless loves of a trio of singularly unattractive people – specimens for whom one has no more real co-feeling than does the entomologist for the insect wriggling on his pin? What really 'holds' us in this novel?

Before attempting an answer to these questions, we might ask ourselves how Atwood herself would judge *Life Before Man* in terms of her stated views on the nature and function of the novelist's art. Though, as Linda Hutcheon has argued, Atwood's work can be taken as typically postmodernist in its interrogation of established social, philosophical and aesthetic 'truths', and in its concern with the process as well as the product of writing, the bulk of Atwood's statements regarding her vocation are orientated quite otherwise. They have, in fact, a distinctly traditional – dare one say even nineteenth-century? – ring. Atwood declares, for example, that writing is not self-expression but evocation of external reality as interpreted and judged by the writer (*SW*, p. 348); in addresses delivered the year preceding and the year following the publication of *Life Before Man* (1979) she insists upon the moral nature of novel-writing. In 'The Curse of Eve – Or; What I Learned in School' (1978) she poses a question George Eliot might have asked:

> *What are novels for?* ... [A]re they supposed to delight or instruct, or not, and if so, is there ever a conflict between what we find delightful and what we find instructive? Should a novel be ... about how one ought to live one's life, how one can live one's life (usually more limited), or how most people live their lives? Should it tell us something about our society? Can it avoid doing this? (*SW*, p. 217)

(The question reads almost like a conceptual précis of *Life Before Man*.) In 'An End to Audience' (1980) Atwood declares that fiction writing is the guardian of the moral and ethical sense of the community ... [F]iction is one of the few forms left through which we may examine our society not in its particular but in its typical aspects; through which we can see ourselves and the ways in which we behave towards each other, through which we can see others and judge them and ourselves. (*SW*, p. 346)

And she goes on to give a definition of writing which is influenced more by her engagement with such human rights organisations as Amnesty International than by any commitment to the ethos of postmodernism. Writing, she declares, is the giving of a voice to the silenced or mute, a form of 'sooth-saying [and] ... truth-telling. It is a naming of the world ... a witnessing.... The writer *bears witness*.... The world exists; the writer testifies. She cannot deny anything human' (*SW*, pp. 348–9).

And yet it is not enough, Atwood suggests, for writers merely to tell the terrible or tedious truths of how we live and how things are, truths most readers would rather forget about. The writer's other fundamental duty as Dr Minnow reminds the 'fallen writer', Rennie Wilford in *Bodily Harm*, is to 'imagine things being different' (*BH*, p. 229), to envision alternatives to the morally intolerable reality we've created, to bring something different and, one hopes, better into being. This use of imagination is a profoundly moral act, in which power *over* is transformed into power *to* – the power to salvage, to change, to create. The power, for example, that Rennie feels in her hands as she tries to coax the viciously beaten Lora back to life at the end of *Bodily Harm*; the power which informs the resistance movement in *The Handmaid's Tale*; the power Elaine Risley assumes in acknowledging her own complicity in acts of torture and victimisation in *Cat's Eye*.

The exploration of the possibilities which exist for the development of this kind of moral imagination has been one of the most important aspects of Atwood's practice as a novelist. One can say that – with one important exception – there has been a steady development in her protagonists of the capacity to feel with others, to see through their eyes, and to imagine things differently, as a consequence. Compared to Marian MacAlpin in *The Edible Woman*, whose only autonomous imaginative act is to rid herself of a predatory suitor and, like a serpent biting its own tail, to eat an iconic image of her 'feminized' self; compared to Joan Foster, who has the imaginative power to devise ingenious escapes from threatening realities only to find herself fleeing from one impossible maze into another, characters like Rennie, Ofred and Elaine become fully moral beings, to the best of their abilities and limitations. Yet the same can hardly be said for the protagonists of *Life Before Man*. Marian MacAlpin may run around in circles, Joan Foster may wander forever in a labyrinth of her own devising, but for the bulk – and the most convincing part – of *Life Before Man*, Nate and Elizabeth are almost incapable of movement at all, remaining interlocked and paralysed.

Even Lesje, whose preference for life in the Mesozoic era demonstrates some sort of ability to think beyond the 'given', is suspect. Lesje is an ironic counter to the narrator of *Surfacing*; her salvation lies not in embracing flux and organic process but in classifying rock and bone. Her dream of bringing the dinosaurs back to life, making the badlands moisten and flower, is a regressive fantasy rather than an act of creative imagination. As she finally admits, the Mesozoic is only another name for something that doesn't exist, a place to which you can never go, rather like the vegetable paradise Elizabeth wistfully admires in the Chinese propaganda posters on display in the museum. Lesje's attempt to direct her fantasies of revivification forwards instead of backwards by conceiving a child rather than attempting to resurrect a camptosaur, is hardly redemptive. Because the child is conceived in a spirit of vengefulness rather than love, she envisions it developing not as 'the first true human' (*S*, p. 191), as does the narrator of *Surfacing*, but as 'a throwback, a reptile, a mutant of some kind with scales and a little horn on the snout' (*LBM*, p. 270).

If it is Atwood's avowed intention as a novelist not only to show us how we live our lives, but also to envision the ways in which we should or could live them, why does she fail in the latter regard in *Life Before Man*? 'I don't know how I should live. I don't know how anyone should live. All I know is how I do live', the novel begins. At its end life continues to be intolerable, the characters remain incapable of either ending or changing their lives, and alternatives are seen as either interchangeable with original conditions, or else, as in the case of the propaganda-poster vision of China, unattainable. The source of this stasis, I would argue, lies deeper than the atrophy of the moral and ethical sense which Atwood so convincingly anatomises in the greater part of this novel. It is, in essence, metaphysical, and it is to foreground this perception and its ramifications that Atwood adopts the minimalist-naturalist mode and can provide no convincing alternatives or real possibilities for change among her characters.

What Atwood exposes to view in this novel, is the utter and indifferent emptiness of the heavens. Two related, recurring motifs in this sparsely imaged novel are Kayo's porcelain bowls, holding 'their own beautifully shaped absence' (*LBM*, p. 16) and the black holes which, as Elizabeth learns at the Planetarium, 'are stars collapsed to a density so great that no light can escape from them. They suck energy in instead of giving it out. If you fell into a black hole, you would disappear forever; though to anyone watching, you would appear to have been frozen for eternity on the black hole's event horizon' (*LBM*, p. 67). Both Lesje and Elizabeth envision themselves so falling – into the indifferent dark of outer space or the nullity of the grave (*LBM*, pp. 67, 114, 118, 277). Atwood attempts a moral extension of this metaphysical blackness by having Lesje picture the enmity between herself and Elizabeth as a 'secret area of darkness like a tumor or the black vortex at the center of a target' (*LBM*, p. 285).[23]

Atwood's darkest novel illuminates the fact that life *during* man – human life, that is – has no special status or significance in metaphysical terms, that human intentions and desires are marginal at best, their destructive effects completely out of proportion to their random cause. Acknowledgement of this has different effects upon the characters. Nate, for example, is stranded in more ways than one by his perception that '[t]he world exists apart from him. . . . It follows that his body is an object in space and that someday he will die' (*LBM*, p. 255). Lesje, on the other hand, knowing that 'all the molecular materials now present in the earth and its atmosphere were present at the creation of the earth itself', is consoled to perceive that she is not an immutable object, but only a molecular pattern capable of dissolution (*LBM*, p. 153). And yet it is Lesje, not Nate, who has a go at slashing her wrists. Towards the end of the novel, pregnant and solitary as usual, she contemplates her place in the evolutionary scheme: 'Fishes, Amphibians, Therapsids, Thecodonts, Archosaurs, Pterosaurs, Birds, Mammals, and Man, a mere dot. And herself another, and within her another, which will exfoliate in its turn. . . . Or not' (*LBM*, p. 284). It is a view of human possibility which can be juxtaposed with that adopted by Nate's mother, who regularly consults a map of the world on which she has pasted red stars to mark those places where power politics are most bloodily at work. Between Lesje's poster of the tree of evolution, and Nate's mother's blood-dimmed map, the metaphysical and moral/ethical dimensions of Atwood's universe are drawn. For all that human lives are meaningless and peripheral in any cosmic scheme of things, for all that our evolutionary success story cannot hold a candle to that of the dinosaurs, we have proved ourselves, none the less, to be atrociously adept at maiming, torturing and murdering one another.

In *Life Before Man* Atwood's grim metaphysic emerges with a prominence unprecedented in her other fiction, largely because there are no structural diversions or symbolic devices to mediate it. For the most part, Atwood's novels give us glimpses not of the intractable heavens but of the mess we have made of our life on earth. The redemptive wilderness in *Surfacing*, for example, is shown to be threatened by the 'human disease'[24] (*S*, pp. 129-30) – those capacities for barbarism, vandalism and destruction innate in human beings, children and adults alike. In *Life Before Man* the wilderness exists only in that never-never land of prehistory – the fictive Mesozoic. What Atwood's novel makes clear is that far from representing some heroic mammalian advance upon the dinosaurs, human beings are in fact a frighteningly inferior species – Lesje even muses that man may have been invented by viruses 'to give them a convenient place to live' (*LBM*, p. 21). Towards the end of the novel, Lesje's 'theoretical opinion that man is a danger to the universe, a mischievous ape, spiteful, destructive, malevolent' (*LBM*, p. 270) is confirmed by her own inability to act in a morally responsible way. This moral failure has implications far beyond the difficulties it creates between Nate and Lesje. Taken to its logical extreme, it augurs ill for our very fate as a species.

And Atwood does insist on this extremity of interpretation. We are headed, her novel posits, for the same fate as the dinosaurs, sooner rather than later, and thanks not to some cosmic cataclysm but to our own steady efforts. The two scientifically trained characters in the novel, Lesje and William, share an 'interest in extinction. She confines it to dinosaurs. William applies it to everything' (*LBM*, p. 111). A specialist in 'environmental engineering' or sewage disposal, as Lesje prefers to refer to it, William fights for the survival of the human race by preventing people from 'drowning in their own shit' (*LBM*, p. 19). William, rosy-faced and squeaky-clean, is, of course, a joke. The joke is, however, his 'optimism, his belief that every catastrophe is merely a problem looking for a brilliant solution' (*LBM*, p. 19). William's announcements of the various disasters facing the planet, his thesis that it is the cockroaches that will inherit the earth, are forerunners of the chorus of equally dire predictions voiced by Elaine's scientist father and brother in *Cat's Eye*. The difference is that *they* are disinterested pessimists, and that there is no longer any joke to be made.

In her 'bleaker moments', Lesje doesn't know whether she cares if the human race survives. 'The dinosaurs didn't survive and it wasn't the end of the world .... Nature will think up something else. Or not as the case may be' (*LBM* p.19). 'Or not' marks a grim advance on the narrator's desire in *Surfacing*, for 'a machine that could make [human beings] vanish ... evaporate them without disturbing anything else, that way there would be more room for the animals, they would be rescued' (*S*, p. 154). Ten years on from the publication of *Life Before Man*, the end of the world, sooner rather than later, seems an increasingly likely possibility. Yet even in the hypothetical form which this possibility takes in *Life Before Man* it has an enormous influence, a sort of pernicious trickle-down effect, on the lives of Atwood's characters.

If extinction is a kind of metaphysical bell-jar roofing-in the protagonists of *Life Before Man*, then death would seem to permeate the trapped air they breathe. Chris commits a rather spectacular form of suicide, one meant to call attention to the mind-body split so characteristic of his autocratic lover, Elizabeth, who contemplates killing herself in turn (*LBM*, p. 78). Nate's former mistress, Martha, pretends to have swallowed a cabinetful of sleeping pills and anti-depressants; Lesje goes as far as grabbing a knife to slash her wrists; Nate's mother confesses that she'd been strongly tempted to commit suicide after her husband had been killed in the war. (For Lesje, pregnancy, and for Mrs Schoenhof, good works, turn out to be acceptable alternatives to self-slaughter.) Then there is a whole background of deaths which figure in the novel, the quasi-suicidal deaths of Elizabeth's alcoholic mother and of her disturbed sister, Caroline; of Nate's father (from hepatitis) during the war; of Lesje's Aunt Rachel who perished in a Nazi camp; of both of Lesje's grandmothers. The death from cancer of Elizabeth's malevolent Aunt Muriel is a complement to the suicide of Elizabeth's equally demonic lover, with which the novel begins.

I have stressed the darkness of the vision which informs *Life Before Man*, the bearing witness to such realities as the deaths of individuals, and the possible extinction of the human species, not to accuse Atwood of unwarranted negativity, but in order to point out the major flaw of this scrupulously fashioned novel. This flaw is not, I repeat, that Atwood has shown the world to be 'too dark altogether', but that, having revealed how desperate our 'given' condition is and the mess we have gone on to make of life under the sway of black holes and tar pits, Atwood feels compelled, in the last 40 pages or so of her novel, to cheer things up. Lesje, reflecting on her relations with Nate, wishes they both could be different. 'Not very different, a little would do ... All she wants is a miracle, because anything else is hopeless' (*LBM*, p. 249). Seven pages later the miracles begin: Elizabeth effects a reconciliation of sorts with her dying aunt; Nate reappraises his mother's idealism in such a way that his own capacity to attempt the ethical life is restored; Lesje abandons her child's garden of dinosaurs and enters 'an adult world where choices had consequences, significant, irreversible' (*LBM*, p. 203). Even the perennial loser, Martha, announces her intention to stop being an underpaid and overworked legal secretary and become a lawyer herself. The effect, for this reader at least, is dubious; given what has come before, the final section of *Life Before Man* is too light altogether. Revelations and shifts in self-perception come too fast and thick. As if in recognition of this unconvincing provision of better-things-to-come, Atwood follows up the literally touching deathbed scene with Auntie Muriel, Lesje's speedy maturation in the Gallery of Vertebrate Evolution and Nate's mother's liberating confession to her son with a final chapter which reveals the primacy of our desire to believe what we want, over our ability to acknowledge what we have. Lesje may have finally conceded that the site of her fantasies, the Mesozoic, is a place you can never go to, because it never existed. But in the novel's last line Elizabeth longs to be in a paradise she knows all too well can never exist. This awareness that our only feasible escape from, or alternative to, painful reality is through conscious make-believe is far more persuasive and moving, given the context of the novel, than a last-minute swerve in the direction of a happy, or at least tolerable, ending.

Why did Atwood go against the conceptual grain of her narrative in the last few chapters of *Life Before Man*? Perhaps because of an awareness that she'd failed to live up to the novelist's moral code, as she envisaged it; perhaps because of the insistently schematic nature of her imagination.[25] As Linda Hutcheon has observed, 'in all of Atwood's fiction, death and its associations of stasis are played off against life and process'.[26] And as Sherill Grace argues in

Violent Dualities, Atwood persistently 'emphasizes the need for affirming our experience through acceptance of our duality', and to recognise 'elements which ... transcend [negativity] – the collective hero, the halting but authentic break-throughs made by characters who are almost hopelessly trapped, the moments of affirmation that neither deny the negative ground nor succumb to it'.[27] And yet *Life Before Man*, by refusing to affirm or deny or succumb but seeking merely to expose and bear witness, succeeds against great odds in gripping the reader's attention and in imposing itself as a forceful work of the creative imagination. The pity is that the power of the novel is vitiated, in its last chapters, by a deviation from the norm the novelist has laboured to establish. Instead of fidelity to her vision and the aesthetic she has adapted to articulate it, Atwood produces fidelity to schema and intention instead.

Atwood, who has defined herself primarily as a storyteller, informs us that 'Story-telling at its most drastic is the story of the disaster which is the world' (*SW*, p. 350). This disaster is presented comically in her first and third novels which only narrowly escape turning into tragedies or, rather, disasters. The heroine of *The Edible Woman* is not dissimilar to the heroine of *The Bell Jar*, and Joan Foster, escape artist nonpareil, achieves only a risky and hypothetical integration of her multiple selves by the end of *Lady Oracle*. Both these works make us recall the definition of humour as concealed pain. In *Life Before Man* Atwood shows how 'the disaster that is the world' is both a metaphysical *donnée* and a human construct.[28]

Atwood has suggested that those who find her vision to be a perversely negative one should leaf through a few Amnesty International bulletins. Certainly, her profound concern with the violence of sexual politics, and with environmental devastation as well as the proliferating number of torture academies and silenced prisoners of conscience has led her to adopt a stance which I would call stoic pessimism *vis-à-vis* reality; pessimism, because, as we have seen, the metaphysic which informs Atwood's vision is dark indeed; stoic because the corollary to a grim metaphysics, for Atwood as well as Joseph Conrad, is human solidarity, an obligation for people to act responsibly towards one another, so as to make it possible for us to go on living at all. Paradoxically, the adoption of stoic pessimism, which is perhaps our most hopeful possible response to our condition, can only be authentic when we realise just how hopelessly inevitable is our progression into the tar sands, under the light of a dying star. This is what *Life Before Man* so effectively reveals to us. Yet, since some readers are bound to demur, pointing out that Atwood has described herself as an optimist and that I have downplayed the positive and life-affirming possibilities set forth by the novel, let me make one last defence of my position.

Life Before Man begins with a paragraph that echoes Atwood's question in 'The Curse of Eve' regarding the purpose of novels. 'I don't know how I should live', Elizabeth Schoenhof exclaims. At the end of the novel, Elizabeth contemplates an exhibit of artwork from communist China which shows her, all too clearly, not how people actually do live, but how harmoniously, prettily and unproblematically they might live were they not in fact human beings, but eggplants and tomatoes. Were Elizabeth to pick up a novel in the course of this novel – and it is noteworthy that neither Elizabeth, Lesje or Nate ever seem to read works of literary fiction – were she to pick up *Life Before Man*, for example, what would she discover about how to live?

According to some Atwood specialists, Elizabeth would learn that she should live by acknowledging her own multiplicity, by acknowledging both order and flux, and by allowing that which is rigid/construct/product to submit to that which is fluid/organism/ process. Yet Elizabeth's rejoinder might very well be that when one's obliged to build one's house over an abyss, rigidity is preferable to flux. There are dangers in surrendering to certain kinds and forms of fluid, as the deaths of her alcoholic mother and bathtub-drownee sister amply illustrate. And when the same specialists point to the redeeming creativity and moral res- ponsibility involved in the act of giving birth, Elizabeth might counter that raising children is another matter altogether.[29] In *Life Before Man*, Nate and Elizabeth, though they genuinely love their children, can't help using them as threats or excuses in their negotiations with one another and with Lesje. There is, in fact, an unnatural calm and politeness about the parent–child relations in this novel; Chris's suicide and the threat it poses to the shell of the Schoenhof's marriage erects a glass panel between parents and children similar to the window that walls-off newborns in a hospital nursery (*LBM*, p. 4). Atwood is careful to show the subtle narcissism that flavours these exemplary parents' concerns for their children. Nate's fear of losing Janet and Nancy is expressive, we are told, of his fears about his own eventual death (*LBM*, p. 150). Elizabeth's anxiety for the children's safety underscores her private apprehension of how dangerous and uncontrollable a place the world outside her own four walls can be.

What the author of *Life Before Man* holds out to us is not assurances, however hedged, but paradox. Elizabeth longs to be in paradise almost because it does not exist; Nate preserves the vestiges of the ethical life by defending the guilty; Lesje, that living contradiction, a pregnant paleontologist, 'may have done a wise thing for a stupid reason' in conceiving a child without her lover's knowledge or consent (*LBM*, p. 286). These paradoxes do not solace or divert us – rather, they force us to acknowledge the intolerable reality which inspires them, a reality in which we are all implicated. Where else is there to build a house, Elizabeth asks, but over an abyss? And isn't the birth of a child the most paradoxical and ambiguous event possible according to the Atwoodian view of things? A baby is not only an emblem of a new beginning, another chance to 'imagine things differently', but also another contribution to the human disease which, as *Cat's Eye* makes clear, has reached epic proportions.[30]

Paradox of this kind is one of the most disturbing ways to reach one's readers. By writing *Life Before Man*, by pulling *in* all the stops which would otherwise divert and console us, by holding up the mirror to life that is meaningless, menaced and long – life as the novelist's vision compels her to see it, not life the way we'd prefer it to look, *Life Before Man* possesses 'the profoundly moral purpose' and effect that Sherill Grace finds in a volume of poetry such as *Power Politics*: 'to shock us with recognition'. 'But what', Grace asks, 'do we do if we accept Atwood's mirror of ourselves? What does one do with the truth?' Basically, one holds on: 'beyond truth/tenacity'.[31]

In an essay written a year after the publication of *Life Before Man*, Atwood appears to answer the question of why she wrote this novel as she did:

> When you're a fiction writer, you're confronted every day with the question that confronted, among others, George Eliot and Dostoevsky: what kind of a world shall you describe for your readers? The one you can see around you, or the better one you can imagine? If only the latter, you'll be unrealistic; if only the former, despairing. But it is by the better world we can imagine

that we judge the world we have. If we cease to judge this world, we may find ourselves, very quickly, in one which is infinitely worse. (*SW*, p. 333)

Life Before Man is informed precisely by this sense of judgement. Readers will derive as much pleasure from Atwood's acuity and wit, her impressive marshalling of language and evocative detail, as pain from her exposure of how we live now, and why. Though there is despair, there is also something quite different, something to which it is important to call attention, as Atwood did in an interview conducted some eight years after the publication of *Life Before Man*. Asked by Geoff Hancock whether she had an 'optimistic sense of resolution' and whether there was 'hope in art ... [i]n the bigger sense of comedy as life affirmation', Atwood's response was characteristically double-edged. Having declared herself so much of an optimist that she included the epilogue in *The Handmaid's Tale* to show that 'the Fifth Reich did not last forever', having insisted 'I *do* feel hope', she goes on to give hope an aesthetic interpretation. 'Hope comes from the fact that people create, that they find it worthwhile to create. Not just from the nature of what is created'. The 'well-doneness' or excellence of a work of art arouses in her a pleasure that is akin to hopefulness. At its best, she argues, literary art gives to the reader '[a] revelation of the full range of our human response to the world – this is what it means to be human, on earth. That seems to be what "hope" is about in relation to art. Nothing so simple as "happy endings"'.[32]

By skilfully and unstintingly showing us 'what it means to be human, on earth' in *Life Before Man*, Atwood gives authentic substance to the hope she continues to voice in her fiction:

Words ripple at my feet, black, sluggish, lethal. Let me try once more ... before I starve or drown.

Notes

1. The following abbreviations will be used throughout this essay:

BE   *Bluebeard's Egg* (1983; rpt. Toronto: Seal, 1984)
BH   *Bodily Harm* (1981; rpt. Toronto: Seal, 1982)
DG   *Dancing Girls and Other Stories* (1977; rpt. Toronto: Seal, 1988)

HT   *The Handmaid's Tale* (Toronto: McClelland & Stewart, 1985)

LBM *Life Before Man* (1979; rpt. Toronto: Seal, 1989)

S   *Surfacing* (Toronto: McClelland & Stewart, 1972)

SW   *Second Words: Selected Critical Prose* (Toronto: Anansi, 1982).

2. As Atwood says of Audrey Thomas, 'Her finest stories not only demonstrate language, they are about language: the impossibility, and the necessity, of using it for true communication' (*SW*, p. 270).

3. In an interview with Geoff Hancock in *Canadian Writers at Work* (Toronto: Oxford University Press, 1987), Atwood appears to find marginally amusing but ultimately insignificant the efforts of literary theoreticians to fit her work to their precepts.

4. Linda Hutcheon, *The Canadian Postmodern: A Study of Contemporary English-Canadian Fiction* (Toronto: Oxford University Press, 1988) pp. 10–11.

5. Quoted inside the 1988 Seal edition of *Dancing Girls*.

6. Geoff Hancock, *Canadian Writers at Work: Interviews with Geoff Hancock* (Toronto: Oxford University Press, 1987) p. 285.

7. Elizabeth, standing on a bridge over a ravine, throws the scraps of fur she has begged off Chris's successor at the museum, in order to perform a kind of burial rite.

8. Quoted by Sherrill Grace, *Violent Duality: A Study of Margaret Atwood*, ed. Ken Norris (Montreal: Véhicule, 1980) p. 90.

9. Ibid., p. 135.

10. Hutcheon, *The Canadian Postmodern*, p. 20.

11. Ibid., p. 21.

12. See Grace, *Violent Duality*, p. 80: 'Atwood's contention that the self is a place, not an ego ... rules out the portrayal of character in the Jamesian or Faulknerian sense; nowhere yet has Atwood given us a rounded personality, a firm sense of the self, such as I find in Laurence's Morag Gunn.'

13. Though Atwood has argued in her critical writing that the novelist's characters are not simply mirrors of his or her own deepest self, but rather, are created as 'typical' representatives of the novelist's perceived social context, the reader may legitimately ask how typical a character so rigidly controlled as a Lesje, Nate, or Elizabeth can be.

14. *The Unbearable Lightness of Being*, trans. Michael Henry Heim (New York: Harper & Row, 1984) p. 20.

15. Characters in this novel are often described as having a sheet of glass between them and other people or the objects of their perception. The Museum in which Elizabeth and Lesje work is, of course, a storehouse of exhibits in glass cases.

16. It is, of course, significant that Atwood chose a man as one of her major characters, instead of relegating the male sex to peripheral or secondary roles. The context for her creation of Nate emerges in 'Writing the Male Character' (1982) in which she states that she expected denunciations from feminists for having created such

unlikeable characters as Elizabeth and Auntie Muriel. 'By the time the book appeared', however, 'even feminist critics ... were willing to admit that women too might have blemishes, and that universal sisterhood, though desirable, had not yet been fully instituted upon this earth. Nevertheless, women have traditionally been harder on women's image issues in connection with books by women than men have. Maybe it's time to do away with judgement by role-model and bring back The Human Condition, this time acknowledging that there may in fact be more than one of them' (*SW*, p. 422).

17. '*Life Before Man* has a final page, but no conclusion, no finality, no anagnorisis. Elizabeth, Nate and Lesje will simply go on, unable to feel and unaware that they are already museum pieces, gray dinosaurs. The lesson from pre-history is that history repeats itself, and "what defeats us, as always, is / the repetition" ' (Grace, *Violent Duality*, p. 138).

18. Ibid., pp. 137–8.

19. Ibid., p. 137.

20. Hutcheon, *Canadian Postmodern*, p. 152.

21. Ibid., p. 2.

22. Hutcheon argues that Lesje, through the 'creative act' of her pregnancy accepts moral, and by extension political responsibility for the creation of life. Her reproductive act is thus analogous to the novelist's act of creation (ibid., p. 152).

23. It is interesting that supernovas and black holes, rather than starry constellations, predominate in the imagery of *Life Before Man*. At the planetarium, the stars are shorn of all mythological and biblical resonance, becoming mere mechanical projections on a painted dome; to Nate, stars are the bright red stickers with which his mother covers her map of global atrocities.

24. The narrator of *Surfacing*, speculating on the origin of evil, dismisses America as a possibility, and settles on humanity, pure and simple. She admits that the trouble some people have in being German, she has in being human (*S*, pp. 129–30). Her virus theory of human evil is transformed into the graffiti Rennie refers to in *Bodily Harm*: 'Life is just another sexually transmitted disease' (*BH*, p. 201).

25. Frank Davey's reservations, stated in *Margaret Atwood: A Feminist Poetics* (Vancouver: Talon, 1984) are relevant here:

> The didactic tone that characterizes much of Atwood's writing, its overt sense of deliberate patterning and organization ... often seems inimical to her endorsement of irrational energies. Most of Atwood's fiction, in particular, seems written at least in part to render a commentary on contemporary society – in Atwood's own words, 'to examine our society'; a character, she tells us, 'fulfills ... a function' in a novel. In this rationalist use of fiction the irrational properties of language, its unpredictable, undefinable and magical qualities, remain uninvoked'; a certain predictability of image, symbol and structure is unavoidably created.   (p. 165)

In this context, Davey cites Carolyn Forché's 1978 review of *Selected Poems* in *The New York Times Book Review*: 'It is lamentable that her voice so often indulges itself, meandering through these narratives with a stridency and submission to intention that preclude any power of language itself to issue its mysteries ... [R]eading these poems is like following the maps she so much wishes destroyed' (Davey, *Margaret Atwood*, p. 165)

26. Hutcheon, *Canadian Postmodern*, p. 151.
27. Grace, *Violent Duality*, p. 3.
28. In terms of the compounding of human misery, none of us is innocent, none of us is exempt, as Atwood's other novels also show us. Thus, for example, mortality may be the bottom line of the human condition, but as *Cat's Eye* reminds us in passing, it is we who have created 'the killing industry' – that is, perpetual warfare – and made it the mainstay of the global economy.
29. Were she well read in Atwood she could, of course, point out how seldom are pregnancy, childbirth and the nurturing of small children presented in a positive light. In this novel, as in all her others, the notion of 'having babies' is fraught with difficulties and dangers, not to mention disgust. The pregnant Clara in *The Edible Woman* reminds Marian of a tuberous growth; Rennie declares 'I didn't want to have a family or be anyone's mother, ever' (*BH*, p. 58). Nate is hardly more affirmative at the birth of his daughter, imagining that Elizabeth and the baby have died during the birth, envisioning a baby 'the color of suet' (*LBM*, p. 148) and describing Elizabeth after childbirth as 'depleted' (*LBM*, p. 148).
30. Whereas the narrator of *Surfacing* accuses her lover and abortionist of turning her into both killer and corpse – 'They had planted death in me like a seed' (*S*, p. 144) – there is at least a wilderness to which she can turn in order to effect a magical transformation, an immersion into the fluid processes of the natural world. In *Cat's Eye*, however, not only most human relationships but the world itself is poisoned – there is no green world to redeem us. Elaine's genial scientist-father and -brother provide a kind of doomsday chorus in the novel, reiterating that human beings are bringing about their own extinction and, what's worse, ensuring that when we go down, we take our planet with us, 'I live in his nightmare, no less real for being invisible', Elaine confesses, 'You can still breathe the air, but for how long?' (*CE*, p. 418). 'Eventually there's nothing you can put into your mouth without tasting the death in it' (*CE*, p. 425). The poison and the death, Atwood makes clear, are human products, not divine afflictions.
31. Grace, *Violent Duality*, p. 63.
32. Hancock, *Canadian Writers at Work*, pp. 284, 287.

8

Versions of History:
The Handmaid's Tale and its Dedicatees

MARK EVANS

The Handmaid's Tale is dedicated to two people, Mary Webster and Perry Miller, and since Margaret Atwood frequently keeps her dedications to such simple anonymities as 'For J.', the significance of this act of naming should not be overlooked. In a talk called 'Witches' given in New England, Atwood has this to say about Mary Webster:

> I did feel ... that it was appropriate to talk of witches here in New England, for obvious reasons, but also because this is the land of my ancestors, and one of my ancestors was a witch. Her name was Mary Webster, she lived in Connecticut, and she was hanged for 'causing an old man to become extremely valetudinarious'. Luckily, they had not yet invented the drop: in those days they just sort of strung you up. When they cut Mary Webster down the next day, she was, to everyone's surprise, not dead. Because of the law of double jeopardy, under which you could not be executed twice for the same offence, Mary Webster went free. I expect that if everyone thought she had occult powers before the hanging, they were even more convinced of it afterwards. She is my favourite ancestor, more dear to my heart even than the privateers and the massacred French Protestants, and if there's one thing I hope I've inherited from her, it's her neck.[1]

What becomes interesting about this story in the light of the novel's dedication is that, like many a family legend, different sources relate different versions of Mary Webster's life, and what happened to her. The quotation referred to by Atwood is taken from Cotton Mather's *Memorable Providences, Relating to Witchcrafts and Possessions,* and there is ample evidence to suggest that Atwood would have encountered Mather's writings during her period of study and residence at Harvard in the early 1960s. But one point can immediately be corrected: Mather locates the story in the town of Hadley, which is in Massachusetts, not Connecticut.

> Among those judgements of God, which are a great Deep, I suppose few are more unfathomable than this, That pious and holy men suffer sometimes by the force of horrid Witchcrafts, and hellish Witches are permitted to break through the Hedge which our Heavenly Father has made about them that seek Him. I suppose the Instances of this direful thing are Seldom, but that they are not Never we can produce very dismal Testimony. One, and that no less Recent than Awful, I shall now offer: and the Reader of it will thereby learn, I hope, to work out his own Salvation with Fear and Trembling.
>
> *Sect. I* Mr. Phillip Smith, aged about Fifty years, a Son of eminently virtuous Parents, a Deacon of the Church at Hadley, a Member of our General Court, an Associate in their County Court, a Select-man for the affairs of the Town, and Lieutenant in the Troop, and, which crowns all, a man for Devotion and Gravity, and all that was Honest, exceeding exemplary; Such a man in the Winter of the Year 1684 was murdered with an hideous Witchcraft, which filled all those parts with a just astonishment. This was the manner of the Murder.
>
> *Sect. II* He was concerned about relieving the Indigencies of a wretched woman in the Town; who being dissatisfied at some of his just cares about her, expressed her self unto him in such a manner, that he declared himself apprehensive of receiving mischief at her hands; he said, he doubted she would attempt his Hurt.
>
> *Sect. III* About the beginning of January he began to be very Valetudinarious, labouring under those that seemed Ischiadick pains. As his Illness increased on him, so his Goodness increased in him; ... Such Assurance had he of the Divine Love unto him, that in Raptures he would cry out, "Lord, stay thy hand, it is enough, it is more than thy frail servant can bear!" But in the midst of these things he uttered still an hard suspicion That the ill woman who had threatned him, had made impressions on him.
>
> ...

Sect. VII. In his distresses he exclaimed very much upon the Woman aforementioned, naming her, and some others, and saying, 'Do you not see them; There, There, they stand'.

. . .

Sect. IX. Some that were about him, being almost at their wits end, by beholding the greatness and the strangeness of his Calamities, did three or four times in one Night, go and give Disturbance to the Woman that we have spoken of: all the while they were doing of it, the good man was at ease, and slept as a weary man; and these were all the times they perceived him to take any sleep at all.

. . .

Section XV. Mr. Smith dyes. The Jury that viewed the Corpse found a swelling on one Breast, Which rendered it like a Womans. His Privities were wounded or burned. On his back, besides bruises, there were several pricks, or holes, as if done with Awls or Pins.

. . .

Upon the whole, it appeared unquestionable that Witchcraft had brought a period unto the life of so good a man.[2]

The 'ill woman' referred to here is assuredly Mary Webster: the only bone of contention lies in the date given by Cotton Mather, as other sources of evidence indicate he must be out by a year or two. In the contemporaneous *Records of the Court of Assistants of the Colony of the Massachusetts Bay*, it can be read that on the 22 May 1683 Mary Webster was 'sent downe upon suspition of witchcraft & Comitted to prison in order to hir tryall'.[3] This subsequently took place before the Court of Assistants in Boston on 4 September that year, when:

Mary Webster wife to Wm Webster of Hley having binn presented for suspition of witchcraft by a Grand Jury in Boston 22th of may last & left to further tryall was now called and brought to the barr and was Indicted by the name of Mary Webster wife to Wm Webster for that shee not having the feare of God before hir eyes & being Instigated by the divil had entered into covenant & had familiarity with him in the shape of a warreneage & had hir Imps sucking hir & teats or marks found in hir secret parts as in & by severall testimjes may Appeare Contrary to the peace of our Soveraigne Lord the king his Crowne & dignity the lawes of God & this jurisdiction to wch

Indictment making no exception & evidences in the case were read Comitted to the Jury and are on file the Jury brought in hir virdict they found hir not guilty.[4]

For Cotton Mather, sexual organs are considered, perhaps inevitably given the general constitution of this puritanical society, as instruments of witchcraft, though the 'warreneage' referred to is that more traditional prop, the black cat. There are further pieces of information that fill out this story, and return us more closely to Margaret Atwood's family narrative. According to Samuel Drake's *Annals of Witchcraft*[5], Mary Webster was a swineherd, or 'hog-reeve'. And in a history of the town of Hadley which Carol F. Karlsen cites in her book *The Devil in the Shape of a Woman*, the following unfortunate events occurred after the trial:

> The acquittal of impoverished Mary Webster of Hadley in 1683 aroused an even more vindictive response from several young men of the Massachusetts town. After she returned from the Boston jail, they 'dragged her out of the house ... hung her up until she was near dead, let her down, rolled her sometime in the snow, and at last buried her in it, and there left her'.

Apparently, the community considered these reprisals justified: there is no evidence of any action taken against Mary Webster's attackers.[6] It would seem, then, that Mary Webster indeed survived her hanging, but not, alas, for very long. But what is interesting is the way in which this part of the story, apparently unknown to her descendant Margaret Atwood, should echo the account of the dispensation of mob justice in the section of the novel called 'Salvaging' (a hint of Cotton Mather's 'Salvation' there, perhaps), where a man presumed guilty of the rape of a fertile woman is handed over to the otherwise powerless Handmaids to be torn apart by them in a form of licensed reprisal, of ritualised victimisation. If the story of Mary Webster reveals a sorry side of early American history, it soon becomes clear that Perry Miller, the novel's other dedicatee, refocuses and deepens our interest in the conduct of this society, and how it relates to the futuristic world of *The Handmaid's Tale*.

In her lecture on 'Canadian–American Relations', also delivered in the United States, Atwood talks about some of the critical reaction when *Survival* was published. 'Canadian critics felt it owed much to the noxious influence of Northrop Frye, under whom I'd studied up there, but they overlooked the noxious influence of Perry Miller, under whom I studied down here' (*SW*, p. 385). She goes on to remark that this book represents the point where 'the revolutionary seed planted at Harvard many years before burst into full flower' (*SW*, p. 385), this seed being the notion Perry Miller helped instill in her that the study of any written material, whether it be diaries (such as those of Cotton Mather) or other occasional and ephemeral writings, was a necessary component in the attempt to recover the pattern and nature of the way the United States had developed from its inception. She realised, as she says, that she could ask the same question about the mindset of both these neighbouring societies:

> If old American laundry lists were of interest at Harvard, why should not old Canadian laundry lists be of interest in Toronto, where they so blatantly weren't?   (*SW*, p. 385)

It is, however, clear that her period of study with Perry Miller enlightened her as to the more grotesque aspects of the religious imagination in New England under its 'founding fathers', and that this information resurfaces in the ideological hierarchy propounded and examined in a novel written over 20 years later. Moreover, her study at Harvard coincided with a contemporary historical crisis, which must have helped sharpen her perceptions of American society and politics: the Cuban missile crisis of 1962. Of this period she comments:

> wondering whether the human condition was about to become rapidly obsolete, it was possible to look back through three hundred years of boring documents and see the road that had led us to this nasty impasse. The founding fathers had wanted their society to be a theocratic utopia, a city upon a hill, to be a model and a shining example to all nations. The split between the dream and the reality is an old one and it has not gone away. (*SW*, p. 385)

Through Perry Miller, Atwood would have become acquainted with his historian's *modus operandi*, and further light will be shed on her treatment of history and narrative through an examination of what constituted his methods and approach. Writing about him in their collection of essays entitled *Puritan New England*, Alden T. Vaughan and Francis J. Bremer declare:

Miller's explanations of early New England thought are not easy reading; he recognized the complexity of seventeenth-century religious ideology and respected its intellectual integrity. He attempted to reconstruct the New England mind, therefore, without reducing it to simplistic formulas or facile explanations ... What we know of the Puritan mind still depends heavily on Miller's analysis, augmented here and there by more recent scholarship.[7]

We should now consider more closely the nature and purpose of these connections between the real and imaginary histories of past, present and future. Cotton Mather provides us with one starting point, for it is he who invests biblical phraseology with a particular resonance when, during the course of a piece produced in memory of a deceased 'Gentlewoman', he makes mention of the women of New England as: 'Those *Handmaids of the Lord*, who tho' they ly very much Conceal'd from the World, and may be called *The Hidden Ones*, yet have no little share in the *Beauty* and the *Defence* of the Land'.[8] Cotton Mather here employs a typically patriarchal sleight-of-hand, emphasising woman's importance, but at the same time advocating their self-effacement and effective subordination. This is a device that will be repeated in Atwood's fictional world.

One difference between the society of the novel and that of Puritan New England appears at first sight absolute. For in the novel it is the lack of women with functioning ovaries which turns those who are capable of reproduction into a commodity controlled and exchanged by the men, and some women, who run this society. In colonial New England, however, the birth-rate was very high, although matched by a correspondingly high rate of infant mortality, and remained so until large-scale urbanisation brought on by the Industrial Revolution caused it to start to fall. But the experiences of childbirth depicted in both historical sources and the fictional text do display another aspect of the interaction between history and technology, between the dream and the reality of possible versions of society. For it seems that the laws of supply and demand have always played a role in reproduction. Catherine M. Scholten in her book *Childbearing in American Society: 1650–1850* notes that wet-nursing was common at this period, and that as a consequence: 'Breast-milk, judges one historian of colonial paediatrics, was the most frequently advertised commodity in American newspapers.'[9] Discussing the associations of pregnancy and childrearing in a book called *A Search For Power*,

whose subtitle is *The 'Weaker Sex' in Seventeenth-century New England,*
Lyle Koehler writes:

> Of course, childbirth was associated with age-old, biblically
> ordained risks and difficulties. John Oliver's *Present for Teeming
> Women*, the standard pregnancy guide in England and America,
> directed women to prepare diligently before their delivery for
> their own possible death. If they did not do so, Oliver warned,
> God would deliver them 'in anger not in favour', making death
> even more probable. Mather considered severe delivery pains a
> divine sign that a woman needed to cleanse her soul.[10]

In a footnote to this last sentence we are referred to a verse from
Genesis (3: 16) which Atwood employs in the course of the novel:
'Once they drugged women, induced labour, cut them open, sewed
them up. No more. No anaesthetics, even. Aunt Elizabeth said it
was better for the baby, but also: I will greatly multiply thy sorrow
and thy conception; in sorrow thou shalt bring forth children.'[11]
There are further significant similarities between the procedures of
childbirth in Atwood's fiction, and what can be gleaned from the
available historical documentation. Here is her description of the
entourage of attendant women during labour: 'There's a crowd of
them, everyone in this district is supposed to be here. There must
be twenty-five, thirty' (*HT*, p. 127). This practice is one for which
Laurel Thatcher Ulrich provides historical confirmation:

> Labor and delivery were central events not only for the mother
> and baby but for the community of women. Depositions in an
> Essex County case of 1657 reported a dozen women present at a
> Gloucester birth ... But Sarah Smith, the wife of the first minister
> of Portland, Maine may have set the record for neighbourly
> participation in birth. According to family tradition, all of the
> married women living in the tiny settlement of Falmouth Neck in
> June of 1731 were present when she gave birth to her second son.[12]

With so many people gathered under one roof, refreshments
naturally play a prominent part, and in the novel we are shown the
Commander's Wives downstairs drinking freely while Warren's
'expectant' wife hovers about with an uneasy smile, and upstairs
the Handmaids are offered grape juice and food. Scenes similar to
this were enacted in the New England of history: 'For many

women, the first stage of labor probably took on something of the character of a party. One of the mother's responsibilities was to provide refreshment for her attendants. The very names *groaning beer* and *groaning cakes* suggest that at least some of this food was consumed during labor itself.'[13] Both sets of expectant women are encouraged to walk round as much as possible during these early stages, and so assisted by their attendants. As the labour proceeds, Atwood describes a 'Birthing Stool', designed like a double-seated throne, with one seat raised above and behind the other, within which the Commander's wife: 'sits on the seat behind and above Janine, so that Janine is framed by her: her skinny legs come down on either side, like the arms of an eccentric chair' (*HT*, p. 135). This is an echo of the procedures of Puritan New England, where 'A mother might give birth held in another woman's lap or leaning against her attendants as she squatted on the low, open-seated "midwife's stool" .'[14]

The safe delivery of the infant is not, however, the end of the story in either society. In *The Handmaid's Tale*, the world has been so contaminated by man-made pollutants that the narrative voice finds herself wondering:

> What will Ofwarren give birth to? A baby, as we all hope? Or something else, an Unbaby, with a pinhead or a snout like a dog's, or two bodies, or a hole in its heart or no arms, or webbed hands and feet? ... To go through all that and give birth to a shredder: it wasn't a fine thought. (*HT*, p. 122)

This passage can be set alongside an unpleasantly detailed description of a stillbirth made by John Winthrop (the man who uttered the famous phrase as referred to above by Atwood, 'for we must consider that we shall be as a City upon a Hill, the eyes of all people are upon us'):

> It was a woman child, stillborn, about two months before the just time, having life a few hours before; it came hiplings till she turned it; it had a face, but no head, and the ears stood upon the shoulders and were like an ape's; it had no forehead, but over the eyes four horns, hard and sharp; two of them were above one inch long, the other two shorter; the eyes standing out, and the mouth also; the nose hooked upward; ... behind, between the shoulders, it had two mouths, and in each of them a piece of red

flesh sticking out; it had arms and legs as other children; but, instead of toes, it had on each foot three claws, like a young fowl, with sharp talons.[15]

John Winthrop makes it very clear elsewhere as to his opinions on the role of women within his theocratic Utopia, informing one woman during her trial that: 'We do not mean to discourse with those of your sex ... We are your judges, and not you ours, and we must compel you to it.' Not surprisingly, comparable methods are used in both societies to ensure a high level of societal compliance with religious proscription. 'Eyes' and 'Guardians' and 'Angels' are employed in the novel to check on each and everybody, in much the same way as in Puritan New England the 'Select-men' were directed by the Deputies of each town to observe carefully the doings of each family, rewarding and encouraging those whose diligence and obedience made them pillars of the community, and disciplining those who failed to bring their behaviour up to scratch.

The 'Aunts' of the novel are given a title that appears to be reassuringly familiar, but here too can be shown an inheritance of centuries of domination and oppression. We can read this much in one of the few diaries by a woman to have survived from the seventeenth century in New England, written by a young girl called Hetty Shepard. So we learn that on her fifteenth birthday she faced censure by her aunt on account of wearing a 'fresh kirtle and wimple, though it be not the Lord's Day ... my Aunt Lydia coming in did chide me and say that to pay attention to a birthday was putting myself with the world's people'[16] This kirtle was a dress, and the wimple a head-covering not dissimilar to those the Handmaids are compelled to wear in the novel. Hetty's aunt believes not only in restraining her youthful urges, but in also making her believe that her own thoughts and wishes are generally inferior, and properly deserving of subordination to those of others in her society, so that as Lyle Koehler recounts:

In February 1677, Hetty considered it unjust that her uncle had been voted into the first (most prestigious) seat in the meeting-house, but her aunt only into the third seat. After she expressed that concern to her aunt, the latter 'bade me consider the judgement of the Elders and the tithing-man as above mine own'. And so Hetty did. Hetty Shepard's brief diary indicates that the women in her extended family helped create feelings of guilt over her desire for some merriment, a pretty dress, and independent thought. She took to heart the words of her female elders.[17]

The Handmaids experience a re-education that mirrors, historically, the way in which their Puritan forebears were brought up, so that just as they find themselves being renamed to be the personal possessions of their Commander, in an equivalent way the daughters of New England were given names that, as Koehler puts it: 'providentially reminded them of their feminine destiny: Silence, Fear, Patience, Prudence, Mindwell, Comfort, Hopestill and Be Fruitful'.[18] Their upbringing was marked by plenty of 'freedoms from', being taught to avoid the blandishments of vanity brought on by combs, mirrors and fancy clothes, and encouraged to read no lust-inducing material, only the Bible.

There is also an established historical basis for the novel's episode where Offred's child is removed from her on no grounds other than ideology and force. For, as Koehler records: 'Town selectmen periodically checked upon families to make sure children were taught religious principles at home. If, in the selectmen's judgement, a child was not receiving proper religious training, said child might be taken away from his or her parents and placed with a more holy family.'[19]

If both these societies, the historical and the fictional, share certain significant features as to their ideology and ordering, we should now examine the general import of these resemblances for the relationship between individual, family and broader society in this theoretical future modelled upon an actual past. A contemporary of Winthrop, James Fitch, observed: 'Such as families are, such at last the Church and Commonwealth must be.'[20] And this indicates how these matters were perceived in Puritan thought to be inextricably entwined. John Winthrop's own expressed notions of how best to run society display few tendencies to deviate from the authoritarian towards anything more humane. In his essay 'Errand into the Wilderness', Perry Miller gives a reading of John Winthrop's *A Modell of Christian Charity*, a particularly ironically named volume, and one which expresses Winthrop's vision of the ideal society. Miller writes:

There was no doubt whatsoever as to what Winthrop meant by a due form of ecclesiastical government: he meant the pure Biblical polity set forth in full detail by the New Testament, that method would settle down to calling Congregational, but which for Winthrop was no denominational peculiarity but the very essence of organized Christianity. What a due form of civil government meant, therefore, became crystal clear: a political regime, possessing power, which would consider its main function to be the setting up, the protecting and preserving of this form of polity. This due form would have, at the very beginning of its list of responsibilities, the duty of suppressing heresy, of subduing or somehow getting rid of dissenters – of being, in short, deliberately, vigorously, and consistently intolerant.... What it set out to do was the sufficient reason for its setting out.[21]

This picture of a society where the 'errand' of the society proves to be its own full and sufficient reward is, I feel, particularly reminiscent of the role allotted Offred in the novel, whereby her function as a provider of children is determined by the nature of the Republic of Gilead (as laid down by men like her 'Commander') to be her be-all and end-all outside of which she has no life, and where a safe birth, like the 'prosperity' Winthrop fondly imagines will be generated by the working of his state is seen as being not a consequence of her labour but rather an achievement that belongs to the rest of society, a self-bestowed sign of divine approval from which she is excluded.

In her interview with Linda Sandler, Margaret Atwood makes a comparison between the American and Canadian systems of government, saying 'America is a tragic country because it has great democratic ideals and rigid social machinery ... Our constitution promises "peace, order and good government" – and that's quite different from "life, liberty and the pursuit of happiness".'[22] It is clear which actual version of society seems to Atwood preferable. Yet there is a sense, in her choice of adjective to describe 'America', that her preference is based on a combination of pragmatic sense and felt history. And it is this combination which is reflected in her choice of dedicatees for *The Handmaid's Tale*: Perry Miller, who elucidated as best he could these founding fathers' ideological baggage and religious machinery, and Mary Webster, whose life story, however told, is a familiar tale of persecution, escape and death.

Notes

1. Margaret Atwood, *Second Words* (Toronto: Anansi Press, 1982) pp. 330–1. Hereafter cited as *SW*, with page references given parenthetically.
2. Cotton Mather, 'Memorable Providences . . . ', in George Lincoln Burr (ed.), *Narratives of the Witchcraft Cases* (New York: Charles Scribner's Sons, 1914) pp. 131–4.
3. *Records of the Court of Assistants of the Colony of the Massachusetts Bay 1630–1692* (Boston, Mass., 1901; reprinted New York: AMS Press, 1973) p. 229.
4. Ibid., p. 233.
5. Samuel G. Drake, *Annals of Witchcraft in New England, and Elsewhere in the United States* (New York: W. E. Woodward, 1869) p. 117.
6. Carol F. Karlsen, *The Devil in the Shape of a Woman* (New York: W. W. Norton, 1987) p. 30.
7. Alden T. Vaughan and Francis J. Bremer (eds), *Puritan New England* (New York: St Martin's Press, 1977) p. 43.
8. Cotton Mather, *El-Shaddai: A Brief Essay Produced by the Death of That Virtuous Gentlewoman, Mrs Katharin Willard* (Boston, Mass., 1725) p. 31.
9. Catherine M. Scholten, *Childbearing in American Society: 1650–1850* (New York: New York University Press, 1985) p. 62.
10. Lyle Koehler, *A Search for Power* (Urbana: University of Illinois Press, 1980) p. 34.
11. Margaret Atwood, *The Handmaid's Tale* (London: Jonathan Cape, 1986) p. 124. Hereafter cited as *HT*, with page numbers given parenthetically.
12. Laurel Thatcher Ulrich, *Good Wives* (New York: Alfred A. Knopf, 1982) p. 126.
13. Ibid., p. 128.
14. Ibid.
15. From David E. Stannard, *The Puritan Way of Death* (Oxford: Oxford University Press, 1977) pp. 89–90.
16. Koehler, *Search for Power*, p. 59.
17. Ibid., p. 60.
18. Ibid., p. 29.
19. Ibid., p. 14.
20. Ibid., p. 22.
21. Perry Miller, 'Errand into the Wilderness', *William and Mary Quarterly*, for the Associates of the John Carter Brown Library, Williamsburg (January 1953) p. 5.
22. Linda Sandler, 'Interview with Margaret Atwood', *Malahat Review*, vol. 61 (January 1977) p. 27.

9

Gender as Genre: Atwood's Autobiographical 'I'

SHERRILL GRACE

The self that would reside at the centre of the text is decentred – and often is absent altogether – in women's autobiographical texts. The very requirements of the genre are put into question by the limits of gender.[1]

To initiate a discussion of Atwood's autobiography is not to invite gossip about the Canadian woman called Margaret Atwood who happens to be a writer of poetry and fiction; it is not to talk about a real life at all. It is *not* – because Atwood's autobiographical 'I' is always a fiction, a creation and a discourse. It is *not* – because Atwood's autobiographical 'I' has little directly to do with 'Margaret Atwood', but a great deal to do with the practices of writing and of autobiography. There is a sense, in fact, in which much of Atwood's work could be described as autobiography from the earliest poems in *The Circle Game* (1966), through novels like *The Edible Woman* (1969) and *Life Before Man* (1979), to recent stories and poems.[2] And her work has often been read, much to her chagrin, as about herself. To conflate the 'I' or Subject of her writing with the real woman, however, is not only to misread but to miss the point.

In the discussion that follows, I shall not attempt to consider all her work but to focus instead on three of her novels which I think are of particular interest in this connection: *Lady Oracle* (1976), *The Handmaid's Tale* (1985) and *Cat's Eye* (1988).[3] Before I turn to the novels, however, I want to examine the concept and the genre of autobiography, to consider, at least briefly, what is meant by the term and how it is or can be written. To say, with received opinion,

189

that an autobiography is a self-authored life-story is to beg the question, for what, after all, is the Self and how can it be authored (or written)? Where do I begin the story of my life and why? Where do I end? Is it the Self that gives meaning to a Life, or is it the Life, viewed in retrospect, that imbues a Self with meaning and value? Either way, why write about it, why write it?

If, as Bruce Mazlish has argued, autobiography is a 'consciously shaped literary reproduction', then it must have rules, generic models, underlying principles and assumptions, and a function.[4] Moreover, as a 'literary production' there can be no formal distinction between the so-called real-life story and the fictional autobiography, which may in part explain why some readers insist upon seeing Atwood in all her female characters. Certainly, autobiography has had many practitioners and some influential theoreticians whose work has isolated at least two distinct models for autobiographical writing – the male and the female.[5] Until fairly recently, the male model described by Georges Gusdorf has been assumed to be *the* universal, definitive one, the yardstick against which one can measure success or failure in the genre. Feminist scholars, however, have begun to point out that because autobiography is inextricably caught up with notions of selfhood and identity which are gender-specific and socially conditioned (as they are also by class, race and other factors), Gusdorf's concept of autobiography largely excludes autobiographical writing by women.[6] Gender, they argue, conditions genre. Ignoring this connection between gender and genre has meant that woman's writing has often been dismissed as merely personal, private, restricted to the categories of diary, journal and letter, and therefore as irrelevant and lacking importance. Their fiction, moreover, is often criticised for being a blurred mixture of novel and autobiography, their characters insufficiently realised, objectified and universal. Serious novels, then, like serious autobiographies, are written by men.

Rather than rehearse the rights and wrongs of this gendered categorisation of genre, it is more important to isolate those qualities (identified by Gusdorf and others) as characteristic of autobiography. First, an autobiography is self-conscious, deliberate and authoritative. The Subject (I) is central, self-centred, and its own Object (he). Perhaps most important, this 'I' is individualistic, asserting its separateness from others, its distinct boundaries and unique qualities. Through careful delineation of genealogy, the location of origins and the plotting of destiny, this autobiographical

'I' enforces (writes, creates) an image of unified identity; it denies *différance*, fragmentation, gaps, otherness. Discourse (symbolic language and narrative structure) becomes a defence against the unconscious which, if allowed semiotic expression, would most certainly disrupt the conscious ordering of things and expose the teleological Self as an illusion, a game, a fraud. The very seamlessness of the deliberate reconstruction through/in time of the traditional autobiography functions to buttress a largely white, Western, middle-class, male concept of identity and to confirm and re-present a sense of power and authority.

When the Object of the Subject writing autobiographically is a she, the assumptions and codes of the genre shift dramatically. To begin with, the Self is not as easily posited as an individual, if to be individual must mean to be separate, discrete, bounded, distinct from the Object of its own discourse as well as from all others. Even when the female Self resists the constraints of contexts, relatedness, connection and collective identity, these remain the familiar parameters of her existence and are, what is more, potentially empowering. The female model for autobiography, like the female concept of identity, stresses interdependence, community, multiplicity and a capacity for identification *with* rather than *against*. Fixed categories and distinctions tend to break down; private and public blurr, as do Subject and Object, and it is not always easy – or useful – to say that this text is a novel, that an autobiography, let alone a fictional autobiography. Something happens, too, to the notion of a teleological Self, authoritative, conscious, centred, developing inexorably towards its public goal, which, in turn, affects the causal, unidirectional, climactic plotting familiar from male autobiography. The female autobiographical 'I' is more like a process than a product, and its discourse is more likely to be iterative, cyclical, incremental and unresolved, even a mystery.

Despite their important differences, *Lady Oracle*, *The Handmaid's Tale* and *Cat's Eye* all explore, test and redefine our gendered concept of identity and the practice of autobiography. In each, Atwood questions the human desire for origins and our construction of genealogies, in an individual woman's attempt to tell her life-story. Joan flounders comically through *Lady Oracle*, multiple, disorganised, unfinished (unfinishable), only to acknowledge that she will *never* 'be a very tidy person' (*LO*, p. 345). Offred, in *The Handmaid's Tale*, faces a more extreme, if omnipresent, challenge: how to have a female Selfhood at all when every discourse (be it genealogy, theology, biography) has been appropriated by the ruling patriarchy? *Cat's Eye* returns to the question once more, and while it may not be Atwood's last word on the subject, it does provide what is to date her most profound, satisfying and, in a sense, 'complete' rendering of the autobiographical 'I' as a female Subject.

> I fabricated my life, time after time: the truth was not convincing
>
> (*Lady Oracle*, p. 150)

Joan Delacourt Foster is Atwood's funniest, messiest, least predictable character. The more we try to pin her down, the more determined is she to escape. Joan typifies the character as escape artist, and she represents, from the first pages of her story (and the earliest years of her 'life', a familiar human desire, not so much for origins as for an escape from and a denial of them; in/from the beginning she hopes for 'magic transformations' (*LO*, p. 46). We would be mistaken, however, to take her entirely at her word and dismiss her as nothing but a fictional romp, an image of woman as air-head with beautiful red hair and small white teeth, an incorrigible child who stubbornly refuses to improve herself, to 'learn some lesson from all this, as [her] mother would have said' (p. 345). Joan's story is a delightful parody with some sharp satiric edges, and as with all parodies and satires there is both an obvious target to be parodied and an implicit alternative to the values being satirised. There is, indeed, something to be learned from all of this.

The object of Atwood's parody is the traditional autobiography. Joan, after all, is telling us her story, or to be more precise, she is telling her story – *a story* – to the Canadian reporter who has come to her Terremoto hideaway with the hope of telling her story for her, the very reporter whom she has bashed over the head with a Cinzano bottle. This reporter, of course, is our surrogate, the listener/reader within the text who (unlike the readers of *Lady Oracle*, surely) must be knocked unconscious before he is capable of *hearing* what is said. Perhaps it is this lingering concussion that accounts for the apparent disorder of Joan's story, because all the usual plot ingredients of autobiography are present. Joan has reached a mid-life crisis point which forces her consciously to reconstruct and attempt to make sense of her life thus far. To do this she goes back to her origins and traces her genealogy, she recounts key, formative childhood experiences, recalls her sexual initiation and subsequent adventures with men, and spends a great deal of time describing (and inscribing) her work. The resulting narrative, however, refuses to meet our autobiographical expectations: no clear, purposeful picture of a teleological Self emerges from the discourse of this text. But this is the point where it is wise to remember the reporter's fate and to reconsider the text as we have it.

Joan's genealogy is shrouded in mystery. For reasons the child cannot understand, her mother does not approve of her and perhaps never wanted her, and her father is a largely absent, indefinable presence – like God. And yet, her mother haunts her adult life, triggering feelings of guilt, anxiety and self-doubt, while simultaneously (and psychologically this is the point) mirroring her own duplicitous, multiple state. Early in her story, Joan recalls watching her mother put on her make-up before her triple mirror. This childhood act of passive watching is then transformed into a recurring dream in which the adult Joan realises ('something I'd always known', p. 67) that her mother is a monster with three heads and a 'curious double mouth' (p. 68). Although she never explicitly links her Self with this image of the mother (a point I shall return to), she does acknowledge, over and over, that she too is a 'duplicitous monster' (p. 95). The link can be made by the reporter, by us: her mother is the Other-Self, the Self as Other.

Several of her childhood experiences are significant, if not clearly formative. The 'daffodil man' in the ravine becomes a touchstone for the puzzle of reality which seems radically uncertain, contingent and unstable to the child. People, she is forced to conclude, can be both good *and* bad; life is not a clear choice of either/or but a sorry mixture of both/and. Her ballet lessons and her debut as a mothball under Miss Flegg's sinister influence focus attention upon Joan's longing for transformation (from fat, clumsy youngster into slim nymphet), upon her need for escape from the repressive authority figures scripting her life and defining her in their terms, and upon her instinctive ability to use her condition as the vehicle for rebellion and self-assertion. Aunt Lou, a figure diametrically opposite to her mother, becomes the inspiration and the model, not so much for an alternative life, as for a *modus vivendi*, an alias, a second self that allows her a certain freedom, a measure of real and imagined transformation.

In ways too numerous to be traced here, the three women in Joan's life – her mother, her aunt and Miss Flegg – all contribute to the complex, composite, multiple 'I' revealed through her narrative. The men in her life, however, have very different roles. From the shadowy figures of her father and the 'daffodil man' to Paul (the Polish Count), Arthur (the bourgeois enthusiast) and Chuck ('The Royal Porcupine'), Joan's men are objects of desire, custodians of something she wants, not something she is. From each of these males she takes something she needs – experience and a literary genre from Paul, security and normalcy from Arthur, fantasy and abandon from Chuck. Around each of them she constructs a story, an aspect or layer of her Self. 'I wanted to have more than one life' (p. 141), she comments, while recognising that others do too. 'The difference' between herself and Arthur, however, is 'that [she is] simultaneous, whereas Arthur [is] a sequence' (p. 211). And it is this simultaneity that creates the problem, that leads to her final (at least, as far as *Lady Oracle* goes) extravagant escape. As Joan gradually comes to see, she did not begin her 'double life' with 'The Royal Porcupine' (p. 246), or for that matter with Miss Flegg, or with her costume Gothics, or with Arthur. In a radical sense she has 'always been double' (p. 246), always been a simultaneously layered Subject.

The consequences of this simultaneous, layered, multiple identity for the discourse and the text of autobiography are profound and striking. Joan has several voices (like her three-headed double-mouthed mother) all trying to talk at once in a story that disrupts linear sequence to circle back on itself, rushes off in one direction only to digress into another, and contains at least one fiction ('Stalked by Love') within what seems to be the primary autobiographical text. Reading *Lady Oracle* is like entering a labyrinth, so it should come as no surprise that Joan finally provides us with that mirror image, that *mise en abîme*, of her text.

When Joan speaks as the woman telling her story to the reporter she has a characteristic voice, one comprised of rhetorical questions, apologies, self-justifying outbursts and a series of grotesque, incongruous similes: she describes the readers for whom she writes her costume Gothics as having lives that have 'collapsed like soufflés in a high wind' (p. 34); she herself has a 'dormant past' that bursts into life 'like a virus meeting an exhausted throat' (p. 229). When she is narrating her costume Gothics or creating the thoughts and dialogue of her long-suffering heroines, she speaks in romantic clichés, using a pastiche of historical terms and a breathless rush of short sentences held together with predictable adjectives: 'tempestuous', 'rapacious', 'helpless'. Her poetry is a mixture of Kahlil Gibran, Rod McKuen and Leonard Cohen (p. 225). To the image of Joan as the fat lady in pink tights or as an escape artist, we must add that of ventriloquist.

Joan is also, of course, the heroine of her own story, a life-story with a perverse structure all its own. Earlier I touched upon the fact that Joan does not establish explanatory links between events or experiences. She does not, for example, explicitly connect her mother's monstrous multiplicity with her own. Cause and effect are either subverted or merely implied. Instead of assuming or imposing a logical, linear pattern that would order and explain her existence, Joan searches out various clues, explores intriguing moments, spins new versions, fresh interpretations of events already described and, when the pressure to tell, to face the facts (such as they are), becomes too great, she jumps sideways, without warning, into a secondary narrative, an alternative fiction. If we are to follow her at all, we must do so by imitating her method, responding to and gathering up the tell-tale images of mothballs, wings and mirrors, remembering the feelings, dreams and memories, relinquishing our conditioned desire for a developing narrative with a beginning, middle and end in order to enter the narrative labyrinth of Joan's text – for Atwood has provided us with this structural image of her novel, and when we enter it at the end we should realise that this is where we have been all along. This image of the labyrinth is both the key to the structure of the text and a gameplan for reading it. According to *Lady Oracle*, autobiography is a labyrinth in which we must follow an elusive 'I' through the complex, multiple layers of her being.[7]

I am a refugee from the past ... I go over the customs and habits of being ... I try to regain those distant pathways.

The Handmaid's Tale, p. 239

Offred in Atwood's *The Handmaid's Tale* is faced with what is surely the most radical, fundamental, existential challenge. Her problem is not how to survive in the theocratic dictatorship of Gilead, but how to *be* – as a human being, as a woman. As she observes of Janine, a sister handmaid: 'people will do anything rather than admit that their lives have no meaning. No use, that is. No plot' (*HT*, p. 227). Story, in other words, is crucial to our lives; life-stories give our lives meaning and confirm our being, even when they refuse to conform to the accepted pattern. What Offred sets before us in this autobiography is her desperate struggle to reconstruct her being across an all but unbridgeable, violent severing of time before and after the imposition of Gilead. To do this she must insist upon her own script in a world where her voice has been erased and her role in life rescripted for her by others, where her meaning, use and plot are totally controlled by other interests and forces. Gilead denies Offred, indeed all women, any Subjecthood at all, thereby reducing her to the status of Object, natural resource, a pair of 'viable ovaries'.

To combat this enforced state of suspended animation, of nothingness and utter passivity, Offred calls upon two resources of her own from the time before: memory and language, the twin powers that make us human. With these tools she is able to recollect all the traditional elements of autobiography from the time before and to weave them into a discourse that includes the present. At one point or another we learn about her genealogy, key childhood experiences, her marriage and her work. There are, however, two autobiographical touchstones that, more than any other, facilitate her attempt to bridge the abyss between past and present, to establish relationship and, from there, a plot. The first of these is community (which includes genealogy), the second is the game of Scrabble. Despite the extreme measures taken by the state to deny all biological links between mother and child and to appropriate that nexus of power and identity to the father, Offred remembers her mother and daughter and her friend, Moira, continuously. Indeed, she remembers them, understands and cherishes them, more than she did before because now, in her dismembered present, she recognises instinctively their importance to her life, their parts in her story. Mother, daughter and friend become foci for historical meaning and personal context; they are the vital signs of her own continuity in time. The scrabble games which Offred plays with her Commander serve several purposes. On one level, they remind us of the fact that we were and still are a games-playing species: *homo ludens*. Not even Gilead can change that. On another level, the Scrabble games remind us of the constant games we play with language and, thus, of the power and potential freedom of words.

Of the many striking symbols and image patterns in this novel, Scrabble seems to me to be the most important, the key in a sense to the entire autobiography. Offred uses it as a mirror for herself, as a way of *hearing* her own voice in an otherwise engulfing, enforced silence. Atwood uses it, I would suggest, as an image of the text, as a *mise en abîme*, in which one can see this autobiographical 'tale' as a Scrabble board on which we must also play. If we have trouble with the plotting of the narrative or the structure of the text, we can think of it as a Scrabble board which grows (one step, one letter, one word at a time) in a seemingly haphazard manner in several directions at once around the invented, constructed centre: OFFRED. And the combinations and permutations of that single word, that arbitrary combination of letters, are – if you stop to play with it – many.

Because I see it as so important, I should like to pursue this Scrabble analogy a little further. As a mirror for the self, or as an answering machine that allows Offred to hear her own voice and that of another (in a world where mirrors and dialogue are, as she tells, denied her), Scrabble becomes a vivid image of what is necessary to human beings and what is repressed, withheld (it cannot be absolutely destroyed) in Gilead: communication. However, in order to communicate we must have access to our own voice, discourse, story which, as Bakhtin tells us, can only take shape in dialogue, dialogistically.[8] Gilead, of course, is the ultimate monologistic authoritarian discourse that permits no other voice to speak, and this silence/silencing is the chief source of Offred's pain and dislocation.

Her need to speak, to tell, however, is matched by her need to have someone to speak to:

> But if it's a story, even in my head, I must be telling it to someone. You don't tell a story only to yourself. There's always someone else.
>
> Even when there is no one.
>
> A story is like a letter. *Dear You*, I'll say. Just *you*, without a name. . . . who knows what the chances are out there, of survival, yours? I will say *you, you*, like an old love song. *You* can mean more than one.
>
> *You* can mean thousands.   (*HT*, pp. 49–50)

And this is where we come in; we sit opposite her at the Scrabble board, listening, hearing, acknowledging, contributing the letters, the words,the sounds that, in combination with hers, make dialogue, story, the Scrabble of autobiography.

Atwood has always insisted that our existence in language is dialogic, double-voiced, and here in *The Handmaid's Tale* she warns us just how much we stand to lose by opting for the seductive, reductive simplicity of a monologic either/or.[9] Her skill in conveying this message can be measured in the subtle and ironic way she creates the autobiographical 'I' of this discourse by imaging, thematising and constructing positions for us. We can play the game the way the Commander does. Or we can play the game the way that learned historian, Professor James Darcy Pieixoto, does. Or we can construct our own role, filling in the spaces on the board of life as we go along.

Offred's scrabble board, of course, takes on a shape and structure all its own. The historical and ontological rupture represented by Gilead forces Offred to create a new autobiographical form, one that may seem sprawling, plotless and formless if one insists upon autobiography as a linear, causal, teleological genre. There is, however, a form to this story, one that alternates, irregularly, between past and present, dream and waking, 'Night' and day. There is a pattern that emerges from the repetition of image and event, a pattern of accumulated details and a mounting intensity of feeling as one event after another – from shopping trips and regulation copulation to public rituals like birthing and salvaging – increase the claustrophobia, violence, and dehumanisation of existence without seeming to lead anywhere. Like what Tzvetan Todorov describes as the centripetal structure of mystery stories,[10] the pattern here is vertical instead of horizontal; rather than moving across time, progressing from one event to the next, we are led deeper and deeper into a situation that was there from the beginning until, hopefully, we understand it – understand that Gilead is a distorted mirror image of this world, that Offred's inconclusive, fragmented story reveals the unconscious gaps and teleological illusions of traditional autobiography.

What we will not find in Offred's story, however much we feel we understand it, is a conclusion. Offred's inability or refusal to conclude can have several explanations, of course, but on the level of genre Atwood has, I think, made an important point. Endings are things that happen; conclusions are things we make. And lives, like scrabble games, grow, spread in many directions simultaneously, connect in retraceable but unpredictable ways, then end.

Autobiography, if it is to be true to life, will do the same. By creating a character whose life and story provide extreme examples of that plotless inconclusiveness, she forces us to experience that autobiographical 'I'.

Atwood's culminating irony and most generically subversive gesture is to give us the conclusion we long for in the 'Historical Notes on The Handmaid's Tale'. Like Janine, Professor Pieixoto 'will do anything rather than admit' that life, his life and his life's work, have no meaning, no use, no plot. What he does, of course, is to explain, order, interpret and conclude. He provides us with a scholarly genealogy, a historical context and a generic formula for the 30 tapes comprising Offred's tale, but these confirm his own credentials rather than illuminating what we have just read. The *presence* of her voice is appropriated, then erased, by his. His joking, sexist language, his punctilious search for evidence about the Commanders and the State, his impatience with the personal, private bias of the female autobiographer, his authoritarian, condescending discourse, hold up to ridicule the entire edifice of traditional, patriarchal scholarship. What is perhaps more to the point, his blindness and his rage for order are appalling. To be told that we know little about the woman called Offred (p. 317) and that 'many gaps remain' (p. 322) should jolt us into questioning the validity and authority of all those discourses that insist upon a single truth, a predetermined genre, a seamless narrative and a conclusion. *The Handmaid's Tale* is a disturbing story not only, or even primarily, because of its dystopic vision so uncannily rooted in contemporary North American reality, but also because it challenges and subverts traditional ideas of genre and received concepts of the Self. If we have played our game of scrabble thoughtfully, we shall not be able to dismiss the autobiographical 'I' as easily as the Professor.

I look into it, and see my life entire.

Cat's Eye, p. 398

Where *Lady Oracle* comically deconstructs the traditional idea of autobiography and *The Handmaid's Tale* questions the very nature and possibility of autobiography, *Cat's Eye* recapitulates many of the strategies employed by the autobiographical 'I' in those earlier texts, and shapes them into a new, complex and deeply satisfying image of the female self. Like *Lady Oracle* with its labyrinth and *The Handmaid's Tale* with its Scrabble board, this novel also carries within it its autobiographical *mise en abîme*; when Elaine Risley finds and looks into the cat's eye marble towards the end of her story, she sees her 'life entire', and none of the other images for the self in this novel quite captures the sense of harmonious completion-in-multiplicity as well as the marble. Though it may not represent Atwood's final conclusions on the subject of autobiography, this image and this text do provide a consolidation and resolution of the questions raised by her use of the autobiographical 'I' and, thus, a basis for my concluding remarks.

Cat's Eye is a self-portrait of the artist as child, young woman and mature painter. Elaine Risley has returned to the city where she grew up to attend the first retrospective exhibition of her paintings, and as she waits for the show to open and then suffers through the opening itself, she remembers and revisits her past. Through her conscious reconstruction of this past, and the often painful recollecting of what she has forgotten, she creates a verbal equivalent of her canvases, of one canvas in particular – 'Unified Field Theory' (*CE*, p. 408) – which is an autobiography, a self-portrait.

Before I consider this painting, however, I should like to look at the structure of this text and at the speaker's voice. From the opening lines, the voice of this speaker is clear, determined and assertive. Moreover, she commands our attention when she states that 'Time is not a line but a dimension' (p. 3); then, dissatisfied with her brother's explanation, goes on to provide her own, one that the narrative we are about to look into will demonstrate:

> I began then to think of time as having shape, something you could see, like a series of liquid transparencies, one laid on top of another. You don't look back along time but down through it, like water. Sometimes this comes to the surface, sometimes that, sometimes nothing. Nothing goes away.   (*CE*, p. 3)

Where Joan Foster lapses into questions and apologies, and Offred stammers in a speech fragmented, uncertain of itself, or vitiated by programmed rhetoric, Elaine's voice is, by comparison, confident and reflective, calm even when remembering moments of confusion and pain. 'I know I have the will to do these things. I intend to do them' (p. 194), she tells us and herself at the moment of rejecting her so-called girlfriends. 'I am going to be a painter'

(p. 255), she states at another turning point. If the structure of this narrative does not follow the accepted pattern for autobiography it is not because the Subject lacks an identity or a story.

Although the overall narrative moves forward through time from a point in the past up to the fictional present and the story is bounded by the knowledge of a speaker looking back on a series of events only she can know well, the events themselves are not organised in either a causal or a progressive order. Instead, events are presented in discrete fragments surrounded by intense emotion, partial memories and vivid images. One key example will illustrate Atwood's method throughout. When Cordelia and the others abandon Elaine in the ravine, the child has what can only be described as a vision of the Virgin Mary and it is this vision which inspires her to climb out and which strengthens her resistance against her tormentors (pp. 186–94). How this can be and what the lady in the vision means to Elaine, however, are never explained. Instead, she jumps ahead in time to a trip to Mexico where she finds her own 'Virgin of lost things, one who restored what was lost' (p. 198). Immediately after this remembered event, she jumps back to her childhood again and to events she has forgotten she forgot. The Virgin will surface again later, but she will never be explained as a cause or a link; she will never be invoked to provide a reason, a purpose or a meaning. Nothing in Elaine's past leads into or explains her present and her future, because her past co-exists in her present. What the Virgin restores is a conscious awareness of what she already has or is, of what she has forgotten.

Just as events are not laid out causally here, so they do not build to a decisive climax, some point from which Elaine can look back and say that everything culminates in and is made sense of by this event, this achievement, this *now*. The opening of her retrospective seems the most likely teleological moment, except that Atwood appears almost to have used it parodically, paradoxically to subvert that function. The *vernissage* is a non-event in the autobiographical story; it is almost completely lost sight of beneath the layers of narrative and recollected time. By the time we see her canvases we already know them for the autobiographical constructions they are. The real autobiography goes on around them, and it carries Elaine back once more (though surely not for the last time) into the ever-present ravine of childhood. What she sees there is Cordelia, her soul-mate, *doppelgänger* and Other. In this moment of vision, so reminiscent of a similar moment in *Surfacing*, what she remembers is a forgotten layer of her Self.[11]

And yet Elaine's paintings should not be dismissed as mere gestures. 'Unified Field Theory', the last one Elaine describes for us, replicates the novel *Cat's Eye* and provides us with an alternate image of the autobiographical 'I'. As might be expected of this woman's autobiography, it is 'a vertical oblong' (p. 408) which must be read in layers. The bottom third depicts a night sky with stars and galaxies which are also stones and roots. The top third is filled with 'the sky after sunset; at the top of it is the lower half of the moon' (p. 408). The central figure of the painting is the 'Virgin of Lost Things' and 'at the level of her heart', the pictorial centre of the composition, she holds a large cat's eye marble. In the painting, all things are interconnected, contained, and joined by the repeated curves of the night sky, the bridge, the moon and the marble. The image of the Self portrayed in this painting remains enigmatic and mysterious, but the mystery nevertheless exists in a unified field of time–space where nothing is lost and everything connects.

Unless a reader is as obtuse as Professor Pieixoto, it would be difficult to deny that a strong sense of the autobiographical 'I' emerges in Atwood's work. At the same time as that Subject speaks with increasing confidence and authority, it is one that recognises and accepts its own multiplicity, its indissoluable connections with others and the unfinished, inexplicable ground of its being. The generic form that Atwood develops to inscribe this gendered Self is one that denies logical categories and teleological order and presents instead a cyclical, iterative, layered narrative that invites exploration rather than arrival, one that reveals gaps instead of disguising them in a seamless narrative. And just when we come to an ending and think we can draw conclusions, the narrative circles back once more and that unforgetable voice tells us that once the portraits have been painted or the stories told, we still have not grasped the Self because 'Whatever energy they have come out of me. I'm what's left over' (*CE*, p. 409).

Notes

1. Shari Benstock (ed.), *The Private Self: Theory and Practice of Women's Autobiographical Writings* (Chapel Hill: North Carolina University Press, 1980) p. 20.
2. Atwood's novels are all written, in whole or in part, in the first person. Her poetry also uses a first-person voice, sometimes with the characteristics of dramatic monologue, sometimes with a more lyric or meditative quality. This 'I', the Subject in her work, is what I am calling here the autobiographical 'I', but this is only one limited attempt to discuss a central aspect of her *oeuvre* which needs further attention.
3. I have used the following first editions of her novels, and all references, using the abbreviations indicated here, are included in the text: *Lady Oracle* (*LO*) (Toronto: McClelland and Stewart, 1976), *The Handmaid's Tale* (*HT*) (Toronto: McClelland and Stewart, 1985), and *Cat's Eye* (*CE*) (Toronto: McClelland and Stewart, 1988).
4. Bruce Mazlish, 'Autobiography and Psychoanalysis: Between Truth and Self-deception', *Encounter*, vol. 35 (October 1970) p. 36.
5. The following consideration of autobiography owes much to the essays in Benstock (ed.), *The Private Self*, and to recent feminist studies of the theatre.
6. See Susan Stanford Friedman's thoughtful discussion of the Gusdorf model and its limitations in 'Women's Autobiographical Selves: Theory and Practice', in Benstock (ed.), *The Private Self*, pp. 34–62.
7. When we do reach the centre of *Lady Oracle's* labyrinth, the maze in 'Stalked by Love' (pp. 431–43), it should come as no surprise to discover four women seated there. These four represent Joan's multiple identity, the layers of her Self.
8. Mikhail Bakhtin's concepts of dialogic and monologic discourse are clearly set forth in *Problems of Dostoevsky's Poetics*, ed. and trans. Caryl Emerson (Minneapolis: University of Minneapolis Press, 1984) pp. 181–204.
9. I made an earlier study of this feature of Atwood's work in 'Margaret Atwood and the Poetics of Duplicity', in A. E. Davidson and C. N. Davidson, *The Art of Margaret Atwood: Essays in Criticism* (Toronto: Anansi Press, 1981) pp. 55–68.
10. Tzvetan Todorov, *The Poetics of Prose*, trans. Richard Howard (Ithaca, N.Y.: Cornell University Press, 1979) pp. 135–7.
11. I am thinking of that moment towards the end of the novel when the narrator turns to see 'the thing you meet when you've stayed here [in the wilderness] too long alone' and then finds that the footprints by the fence where 'the thing' was standing are, in fact, her own (*Surfacing* (New York: Simon and Schuster, 1972) pp. 216–17).

10

Cat's Eye: Elaine Risley's Retrospective Art

CORAL HOWELLS

> What's the difference between vision and a vision? The former relates to something it's assumed you've seen, the latter to something it's assumed you haven't. Language is not always dependable either.[1]

This passage from Margaret Atwood's prose poem with its questioning of the reliability of modes of visual perception and of language might serve as preface to *Cat's Eye*, her autobiographical fiction which is itself a challenge to life-writing, that ambiguous literary genre which Shirley Neuman claims lacks any generic unity and which Paul De Man asserts is no genre at all.[2] Incidentally, the hybrid form of the prose poem would seem to prefigure the transgressive form of the novel itself, with its combined discourses of fiction and autobiography, painting and science, in its attempts to represent the subject of/in the text. Arguably we could read *Cat's Eye* as Atwood's own retrospective glance back at the imaginative territory of her earlier fictions,[3] but I do not want to pursue that exploration here. Instead, I shall focus on *Cat's Eye* as Atwood's version of life-writing in the feminine, where her middle-aged protagonist Elaine Risley struggles to define herself as a subject through figuring out her life-story in different versions. Who is she? And what is the significance of the *Cat's Eye* of the title? Elaine is a painter; the story is littered with references to her pictures and culminates in her first retrospective exhibition in Toronto. It is her return to her home town for this exhibition which provides the stimulus for her curiously doubled narrative with its 'discursive' memoir version and its 'figural' version presented through her paintings.[4] Indeed, it is this double figuration of the self, projected through the relationship between the discursive and the figural as forms of autobiography, that is the site of my inquiry. I shall pay particular attention to Elaine's paintings and the retrospective exhibition in order to highlight Atwood's distinctive contribution to the problematical construction of female subjectivity in fiction.[5]

The retrospective exhibition positioned at the end of the novel (or almost) might be taken as Elaine's final statement, a *summa* of all the elements of her life already contained in the narrative. The exhibition is presented as a chronicle, with its brief views of earlier paintings and detailed descriptions of five late paintings (the last one with the promising title 'Unified Field Theory'), together with a few less-than-helpful interpretations from the catalogue supplemented by/contradicted by Elaine's comments. As readers we have the advantage over the compiler of the catalogue because we already know the private references which are coded into the paintings, whereas she does not. What we also know (if we remember back 318 pages) is that this retrospective statement is not an authoritative one, for Elaine has left the arrangement of the paintings to the gallery's director (p. 87). Her own position at the opening is that of a visitor:

> I walk slowly around the gallery, sipping at my glass of wine, permitting myself to look at the show, for the first time really. What is here, and what is not.   (p. 404)[6]

Actually the exhibition has the same kind of provisionality as *The Handmaid's Tale*, where Offred's narrative transcribed from her tapes is presented as the editor's version rather than as her own. In both cases, the recording subject remains elusive; she cannot be defined by the statements made on her behalf. Yet *a* retrospective exhibition (not the one described at the end) is the informing principle of the novel, for it has already been constructed on the Contents page, where the chapter titles are all given the names of paintings mentioned in the text. (That is, all except for the first one, 'Iron Lung', which Elaine cannot paint because she is still inside it for as long as she lives, 'being breathed' by time.) Throughout the narrative, individual paintings offer a disruptive commentary figuring events from a different angle to the memoir, so that it is only appropriate that they should be collected and shown in a gallery named 'Sub-Versions'. The doubled retrospective device[7] creates a complex patterning where painted surfaces present a riddling version of the truth. These visual artefacts (always of course mediated through/invented by language) represent the relation between 'vision' and 'a vision' (what it's assumed you've seen and what it's assumed you haven't), where socially accepted codes of seeing are challenged by the eye of the artist. As Elaine looks through the lens of her Cat's Eye, her Third Eye, 'the single eye that sees more than anyone else looking' (p. 327), she sees more because she sees differently.

However, for all her insight Elaine remains a slippery subject, difficult to get into focus. Even now at the age of nearly 50 she is a 'blur' to herself when she looks in the mirror:

> Even when I've got the distance adjusted, I vary. I am transitional; some days I look like a worn-out thirty-five, others like a sprightly fifty. So much depends on the light, and the way you squint. (p. 5)

And again, 'There is never only one, of anyone' (p. 6). It is surely significant that the first and only complete picture of her face is the photograph on the poster near the gallery where her exhibition is to be held: 'The name is mine and so is the face, more or less. It's the photo I sent to gallery. Except that now I have a moustache' (p. 20). Her view of her own face 'defaced' is surrounded by images of multiple identities, disguises ('I could be a businesswoman . . . a bank manager . . . a housewife, a tourist, someone window-shopping'; p. 19), and by a reference to her double, Cordelia – all of which underline Elaine's indeterminacy and multiplicity as a subject.

In order to 'read' Elaine's autobiography we could not do better than turn to the theoretical essay by Paul De Man, 'Autobiography as De-facement', which would seem to be signalled by the grotesque visual self-image on the poster. Atwood's project in this novel bears a fascinating resemblance to De Man's deconstructive critique:

> Are we so certain that autobiography depends on reference, as a photograph depends on its subject or a (realistic) picture on its model? We assume that life *produces* the autobiography as an act produces its consequences, but can we not suggest, with equal justice, that the autobiographical project may itself produce and determine the life and that whatever the writer *does* is in fact

governed by the technical demands of self-portraiture and thus determined, in all its aspects, by the resources of his [her] medium?[8]

This construction of subjecthood would seem to be confirmed by Elaine's response to the poster, which may be, as she says, a feeling of wonder, but which also may be read as a self-reflexive comment on her autobiography: 'A public face, a face worth defacing. This is an accomplishment. I have made something of myself, something or other, after all' (p. 20). Elaine's confrontation with her own face defaced, like her return to Toronto, constitutes that 'specular moment' which De Man identifies as the autobiographical impulse with its sudden alignment between present and past selves that opens up multiple possibilities for 'mutual reflexive substitution', displacements and doublings. These are for him the 'defacements' endemic to the autobiographical project, which 'deals with the giving and taking away of faces, with face and deface, *figure*, figuration and disfiguration'.[9]

Cat's Eye would seem to provide the perfect exemplars of such 'defacements' – wittily in the comic-book story of the two sisters 'a pretty one and one who has a burn covering half her face' who comes back from the dead to 'get into the pretty one's body' (p. 211); and more seriously, in Elaine's portrait of Cordelia which is called 'Half a Face' (p. 227). It is Cordelia, her childhood companion and tormentor, for whom Elaine searches incessantly on her return to Toronto, Cordelia who belongs to that city which 'still has power; like a mirror that shows you only the ruined half of your face ' (p. 410). Lacking, her dark double trapped in an earlier period of time, Elaine remains unfixed, incomplete: 'We are like the twins in old fables, each of whom has been given half a key' (p. 411). Cordelia as the absent Other would also confirm De Man's theory of autobiography as a double project of self-representation, moving towards self-restoration at the same moment as it marks otherness and deprivation: 'Autobiography deprives and disfigures to the precise extent that it restores'.[10]

Returning for a moment to an earlier stage of De Man's critique, I should like to highlight his question about figures and figuration:

Does the referent determine the figure, or is it the other way round: is the illusion of reference not a correlation of the structure of the figure, that is to say no longer clearly and simply a referent at all but something more akin to a fiction, which then, however, in its own turn, acquires a degree of referential productivity?[11]

The notion that it is the mode of figuration which produces the referent is crucial to Atwood's subject-constructing project where two modes of figuration are used. While Elaine's discursive narrative remains incomplete (she is still looking at the end for what is lost in the past), her paintings offer a different figuration, acting as a kind of corrective to the distortions and suppressions of memory and offering the possibility of theoretical solutions. Not that autobiography can ever attain completeness:

> The interest of autobiography, then, is not that it reveals reliable self-knowledge – it does not – but that it demonstrates in a striking way the impossibility of closure and totalization (that is the impossibility of coming into being) of all textual systems made up of tropological substitutions.[12]

Though De Man's discussion focuses exclusively on linguistic signifiers here, and Elaine's autobiography offers the variant of (verbalised) visual images, the result is the same. As seeing eye or discursive recorder, she tells her own private history, fragments of Cordelia's story, her brother Stephen's story, the stories of her parents and of Josef, Jon and Ben the men in her life, and the story of Mrs Smeath. She also presents a historical documentary account of Toronto in the 1940s and 1950s from the perspective of an English-speaking Canadian girl, together with a cultural critique of feminism in Canada in the 1970s and 1980s. Arguably, Elaine succeeds in establishing her position as a speaking/painting subject, but she herself always exceeds her carefully constructed parameters of vision: 'I'm what's left over' (p. 409).

Atwood's novel adds one important dimension to De Man's theory of autobiography, and that is the dimension of time. Curiously, he neglects this, possibly because he is more interested in the opposition between life and death implied by life-writing, but Atwood does not. As she said in her *Cat's Eye* discussion at the National Theatre, London, in April 1989, 'The thing I sweated over in that novel was Time', for Elaine's story covers a period of nearly 50 years from the early 1940s to the late 1980s. This is a 'space–time' novel (a phrase with precise scientific connotations here) where the

narrator tries to establish her position by using the three spatial co-
ordinates plus the temporal co-ordinate, only to discover that back
in Toronto, though her space might be defined, she is living in at
least two time dimensions at once as she remembers the past:
'There are, apparently, a great many more dimensions than four'
(p. 331). Here Elaine transcribes the words of her dead brother
Stephen, who grows up to become a theoretical physicist and is
later killed by terrorists in an aircraft hijack incident. As so often
happens in life-writing, her story is also a memorial to the dead.
The narrative begins with a speculation on time: 'Time is not a line
but a dimension, like the dimensions of space . . . It was my brother
Stephen who told me that' (p. 3). It is filled with echoes of Stephen's
voice in allusions to his theories about space–time, curved space,
the expanding universe, light, black holes, string theory and the
uncertainty principle.[13] In significant ways Stephen's scientific
enthusiasms have shaped Elaine's imagination, so that her
paintings and his theories come to occupy the same area of speculation on the mysterious laws which govern the universe. They are
both engaged in trying to reconstruct the past, he through physics
and mathematics and she through memory and imaginative vision.
His discourse from theoretical physics provides the conceptual
framework for her paintings, for Elaine is 'painting time': 'These
pictures of her, like everything else, are drenched in time' (p. 151),
and finally at the retrospective, 'I walk the room, surrounded by
the time I've made' (p. 409). Recording her brother's death, she
recalls his anecdote about identical twins and the high-speed
rocket, part of his youthful disquisitions on the theory of relativity
and its effect on the behaviour of time:

> What I thought about then was the space twin, the one who went
> on an interplanetary journey and returned in a week to find his
> brother ten years older.
> Now I will get older I thought. And he will not.   (p. 219)

Perhaps the most important single memorial to her brother's
influence is her last painting, 'Unified Field Theory', to which I
shall return in my discussion of the retrospective exhibition.

We should remember that Elaine trained not as a painter but as a
biologist, like her father, producing slide drawings of planaria
worms that looked like 'stained glass windows under the
microscope' (p. 247), and that her instructor Dr Banerji appears in

one of her late paintings dressed like a magus holding a round object figured with bright pink objects ('They are in fact spruce budworm eggs in section: but I would not expect anyone but a biologist to recognise them'; p. 406). The boundaries between science and art are dissolved here in what might be seen as an act of gendered transgression, where Elaine's paintings and drawings show one way in which a woman deals with the master discourse of science, transforming it through another medium or 'another mode of figuration'.[14]

Whether as a trainee biologist or a painter, or as the sister of a budding astronomer, Elaine's primary activity is 'seeing'. Eyes are important, but so are microscopes and telescopes, and so are lenses, with their ability to magnify and to focus more powerfully than the naked eye. It is in this context that we might consider the significance of the Cat's Eye of the title. Certainly the cat's eye marble exists as a referential object in the text, introduced first in the childhood games in the schoolyard with 'puries, bowlies, and cat's eyes' ('my favourites'; p. 62), where it is strongly associated with her brother's superior skill.[15] It recurs many times in an almost casual way, as something to be fingered in Elaine's pocket as a secret defence against her tormentors when she is nine years old (p. 141); later, as something she has grown out of, like her red plastic purse (p. 203); and later still, as an object to be rediscovered among the debris in the cellar:

> The red plastic purse is split at the sides, where the sewing is. I pick it up, push at it to make it go back into shape. Something rattles. I open it and take out my blue cat's eye . . . I look into it, and see my life entire. (p. 398)

Suddenly the cat's eye marble is transformed into the lens of imaginative vision, becoming that Third Eye[16] through which 'each brick, each leaf of each tree, your own body, will be glowing from within, lit up, so bright you can hardly look. You will reach out in any direction and you will touch the light itself' (p. 12).

But is it a sudden transformation? Hardly that, for the cat's eye marble has always had a duplicitous existence: 'The cat's eyes really are like eyes, but not the eyes of cats. They're the eyes of something that isn't known but exists anyway . . . like the eyes of aliens from a distant planet. My favourite one is blue' (p. 62). Invested by the nine-year-old girl with supernatural powers to protect her, it becomes for her a talismanic object and the sign of her own difference: 'She doesn't know what power this cat's eye has to protect me. Sometimes when I have it with me I can see the way it sees . . . I am alive in my eyes only' (p. 141).

Cat's eyes, planets and stars swirl together in Elaine's power dream, when the cat's eye enters her body:

> It's falling down out of the sky, straight towards my head, brilliant and glassy. It hits me, passes right into me, but without hurting, except that it's cold. The cold wakes me up. My blankets are on the floor. (p. 145)

It functions as the nexus for all those contradictory feelings of fear and longing, love, hatred and resistance that she feels towards Cordelia, Grace Smeath and Carol Campbell 'in that endless time when Cordelia had power over me' (p. 113). Indeed, it is already functioning beyond her consciousness as her Third Eye when, deserted by her friends and lying in the snow in the dark, she has her vision of the Virgin Mary, 'Our Lady of Perpetual Help', floating over the footbridge in the Toronto ravine. Elaine's reassumption of her own independence after this agony is marked by the sign of the cat's eye: 'I am indifferent to them. There's something hard in me, crystalline, a kernel of glass. I cross the street and continue along, eating my licorice' (p. 193). Much later Elaine will recognise it as the sign of the artist's powers of vision, and it will appear again and again in her paintings as her signature (the pier glass, the globe, the cat's eye marble). She will use it to figure curved space where 'Nothing goes away'.

The cat's eyes disappears entirely from her discursive memoir narrative of her adolescence and early adulthood in a complex process of repression:

> I've forgotten things, I've forgotten that I've forgotten them . . . I find these references to bad times vaguely threatening, vaguely insulting: I am not the sort of girl who has bad times. (p. 201)

However, in the double mode of figuration employed in this novel, the discontinuous narrative constructed by Elaine's paintings tells a different story about Elaine as subject. She may feel like 'nothing' but a 'seeing eye', though her paintings display an excess of signification that goes beyond the discursive narrative produced by her conscious mind. They are truly 'sub-versions', uncovering that highly complex network of conflicting energies, conscious and unconscious, which make up the human 'subject' in its psychoanalytical definition.[17] The presence of the cat's eye is signalled in Elaine's fascination with the effects of glass when she is studying the history of visual styles, and a little drama of substitution is played out for the reader (though not for her) in her particular concern with the pier-glass in Van Eyck's picture 'The Arnolfini Marriage', where the 'round mirror is like an eye' (p. 327). The cat's eye is there, multiplied, in some of her early still lifes, though scarcely visible; 'far back, in the dense tangle of the glossy leaves, are the eyes of cats' (p. 337). Arguably, it is through that alien lens that Elaine paints her savage exposures of Mrs Smeath: 'One picture of Mrs Smeath leads to another. She multiplies on the wall like bacteria, standing, sitting, flying, with clothes, without clothes, following me around with her many eyes' (p. 388). This is a form of revenge that her conscious mind fails to understand, either at the time of painting or when her pictures are attacked by the ink-throwing woman at the feminist art show in Toronto: 'It is still a mystery to me, why I hate her so much' (p. 352). The answer hovers in the reader's mind as the words of Atwood's prose poem whisper, 'The third eye can be merciless, especially when wounded'.[18]

What is never explained in either the discursive or the figural narrative are Elaine's moments of revelation: her childhood vision of the Virgin Mary or that moment when she looks through the lens of the cat's eye marble and sees her 'life entire' (p. 398). Yet these are perhaps the crucial moments which determine her life as an artist and they both figure together in her final painting, where the Virgin Mary holds 'an oversized cat's eye marble, with a blue centre' (p. 408). ('[V]ision . . . a vision: something it's assumed you've seen . . . something it's assumed you haven't.') Through the logic of the image Elaine's paintings present 'a vision' as 'vision', so that as we follow the verbal descriptions of the paintings, reading changes to gazing. We 'see' through Elaine's mediating eye which dissolves the boundaries between the visionary and the visible.

The retrospective exhibition occurs in the chapter, 'Unified Field Theory', which, with its echoes of Stephen's lecture, 'The First Picoseconds and the Quest for a Unified Field Theory: Some Minor Speculations' (p. 331), places it in a relational context and also signals its function in this autobiographical narrative. Within the perameters of theoretical physics Elaine traces her figural interpretation of her life-story, which offers a significantly different series of projections from her discursive memoir. By way of explanation for such differences, we might consider briefly Norman Bryson's emphasis on the double nature of painting, which he calls 'the divided loyalty of the image'.[19] This seems a useful analogy to describe the fissure within Elaine's remembering process, between her conscious mind's discursive narrative and the figural narrative of her imagination. From physics comes the definition of a 'field':

> In physics a field can only be perceived by inference from the relationships of the particles it contains; the existence of the field is, however, entirely separate from that of the particles; though it may be detected through them, it is not defined by them.[20]

Unified Field Theory itself (the attempt to formulate a comprehensive theory of the laws that govern the universe) belongs to the discourse of theoretical physics; to a non-physicist like Elaine, her brother's lecture sounds as close to metaphysics as to physics.[21] At the end of it, after his speculation on picoseconds, space–time and matter–energy, Stephen does, however, give her a sentence which is crucial to her project of self-representation: 'But there is something that must have existed before. That something is the theoretical framework, the parameters within which the laws of energy must operate' (p. 332). It is this relationship between the cosmic and the humanly particular that Elaine figures in her paintings, none of which offer a totalised representation of her 'self', though maybe that 'self' is the 'field' that might be inferred from the constructions of her pictures.

At the retrospective, we are invited to 'read' the pictures in sequence as we are led by Elaine past the 'early things' and the 'middle period' (all of which we have already 'seen'), to her five most recent paintings which she has never shown before. These are described in detail, and we realise first that these paintings have a double significance as representations. There is a personal rationale behind the collocation of images in each picture which Elaine interprets for us, for these are plain statements in her own private narrative of crises, revelations and memories. However, as the wickedly satirical extracts from the catalogue commentary suggest, they also have a public life as paintings in an exhibition, available to the viewer's interpretation, so that plain statements become riddles provoking other people's narrative solutions: 'I can no longer control these paintings or tell them what to mean. Whatever energy they have came out of me. I'm what's left over' (p. 409).

The second thing we notice is that these late paintings share a common structural feature: they all introduce further dimensions of meaning into the figural image by their pier-glass motifs or their triptych designs, which initiate shifts in perspective. A host of possible meanings are generated through different spatial patternings, different time dimensions, executed in different painterly techniques. As each painting contains several styles of representation, so the referentiality of any single image is undercut. These multiplicities are quite simply illustrated in Elaine's self portrait, 'Cat's Eye' ('There is never only one, of anyone', and anyway her portrait, like the one she painted of Cordelia, is only 'Half a Face'), while more complex representations of space–time and vision are developed in 'Unified Field Theory'. The structural feature of the convex lens also highlights artifice, for these paintings reveal themselves as constructions/reconstructions, where realistic images are used to map a psychic landscape in Elaine's project of painting time.

It is important in the double mode of figuration of this novel to note that the paintings effect quite significant revisions in Elaine's retrospective narrative, for they encode insights that she herself only later realises when she looks at the paintings. Now she reads the Mrs Smeath paintings differently, understanding at last not only 'Why I hated her so much' but also how vengeful she was, and how her earlier self lacked the compassionate recognition which she had actually painted into Mrs Smeath's eyes:

> It's the eyes I look at now. I used to think these were self-righteous eyes, piggy and smug inside their wire frames; and they are. But they are also defeated eyes, uncertain and melancholy, heavy with unloved duty. The eyes of someone for whom God was a sadistic old man; the eyes of a small-town threadbare decency. Mrs Smeath was a transplant to the city, from somewhere a lot smaller. A displaced person; as I was. (p. 405)

This process of moving from the blindness of consciousness to the insight of imaginative seeing occurs in Elaine's reading of all her late paintings, with her questioning of the reliability of memory in 'Picoseconds', her awareness of mutual limits of understanding in 'Three Muses', her ignorance of her brother's last moments in 'One

Wing', and her recognition of what her childhood torments were and how they were crucial to the development of her artistic powers.

It is the last painting, 'Unified Field Theory', which effects the most significant revision of all in its effort at synthesis. Elaine's figuration of her vision of the Virgin Mary holding the cat's eye marble and floating above the bridge of her childhood traumas combines with her brother's cosmic imagery ('Star upon star, red, blue, yellow and white, swirling nebulae, galaxy upon galaxy'). This representation of the night sky could also be read as a black hole under the ground, as the secret place of her brother's buried treasure, or as 'the land of the dead people', one of the many terrors of her childhood. Here the figural presents oppositions as co-existing on the same plane: the past and the present, 'a vision' and 'vision', the sacred and the profane, science and art, the universal and the particular. This is Elaine's attempt to present her 'life entire' in an impersonal vision of wholeness, painting the forces which govern the laws of her being. All this is carefully spelled out by Elaine (there is no comment from the catalogue this time) and as readers we probably believe her interpretation because it gathers up so many anecdotes from her memoir text, offering a possible site for accommodating the Virgin Mary vision. The meanings also work forwards as well as backwards to enhance Elaine's discursive narrative when she will record her last 'vision' of Cordelia, in language which sets up parallels and echoes with the account of the first vision. However, the painting might also work another way, to problematise further her memoir narrative by highlighting its gaps and omissions. In a universe where 'Nothing goes away' (p. 3), 'What have I forgotten?' (p. 334) always remains an open question.

Of course, the last painting like the retrospective, like the memoir, offers only a theoretical framework for the definition of Elaine's self, providing an illusion of completeness which is dispelled by the final chapter entitled 'Bridge', where the narrative takes up once again the quest for Cordelia and Elaine's registration of lack and loss. Our view of Elaine herself remains partial and provisional; though we have learned to see through her eyes, we have only ever seen half her face or her face 'defaced'. Apparently the human subject is as mysterious as the universe: 'The universe is hard to pin down; it changes when you look at it, as if it resists being known' (p. 388).

In this version of life-writing in the feminine with its double project for constructing female subjectivity through the discursive and the figural modes, the emphasis on displacements, doublings and 'defacements' underlines the inherent instability of the narrating subject at the same time as it 'undoes the model [of autobiography as a genre] as soon as it is established'.[22] Though we may be persuaded that Elaine succeeds in locating her distinctive 'position' as a subject in her figural constructions of space-time, the discursive narrative as a 'textual system made up of tropological substitutions'[23] will always register some incompleteness in the construction of 'subjecthood', a lack that is confirmed at the thematic level by Elaine's failure to find Cordelia:

> This is what I miss, Cordelia: not something that's gone, but something that will never happen. Two old women giggling over their tea.   (p. 421)

Through the multiple modes of narrative representation Elaine, like Offred or Cordelia, 'slips from our grasp and flees'. By telling the reader so much, Atwood has paradoxically exposed the limits of autobiography and its artifice of reconstruction. The best Elaine Risley or Margaret Atwood can offer is a Unified Field Theory from which inferences about the subject may be made, but the subject herself is always outside, in excess, beyond the figurations of language. The 'I' remains behind the 'eye'. At the end, Elaine recedes back into her seeing eye, voided of personality, as her narrative dissolves into light:

> Now it's full night, clear, moonless and filled with stars, which are not eternal as was once thought, which are not where we think they are. If they were sounds, they would be echoes, of something that happened millions of years ago: a word made of numbers. Echoes of light, shining out of the midst of nothing.
>
> It's old light, and there's not much of it. But it's enough to see by.   (p. 421)[24]

Notes

1. Margaret Atwood, 'Instructions for the Third Eye', in *Murder in the Dark* (Toronto: Coach House, 1983) pp. 61–2.
2. Shirley Neuman, 'Life-Writing', in W. H. New (ed.), *Literary History of Canada: Canadian Literature in English*, vol. 4, 2nd edn (Toronto: University of Toronto Press, 1990) pp. 333–70; Paul De Man, 'Autobiography as De-facement', *MLN*, vol. 94 (1979) pp. 931–55. See also K. P. Stich (ed.), *Reflections: Autobiography and Canadian Literature* (Ottawa: University of Ottawa Press, 1988).
3. This point has already been made by Constance Rooke in 'Interpreting *The Handmaid's Tale*: Offred's Name and the Arnolfini Marriage', in *Fear of the Open Heart: Essays on Contemporary Writing* (Toronto: Coach House, 1989) pp. 175–96.
4. In its use of paintings *Cat's Eye* focuses on a similar area of inquiry to Norman Bryson, *Word and Image: French Painting of the Ancien Régime* (Cambridge: Cambridge University Press, 1981). His discussions about writing and painting have suggested important directions for my inquiry into Atwood's novel.
5. Sharon R. Wilson has commented on Atwood's involvement with the visual arts, discussing photographic images and some early watercolours: 'Camera Images in Margaret Atwood's Novels', in B. Mendez-Egle (ed.), *Margaret Atwood: Reflection and Reality* (Texas: Pan American University Press, 1987) pp. 29–57; and 'Sexual Politics in Margaret Atwood's Visual Art', in K. Van Spanckeren and J. Garden Castro (eds), *Margaret Atwood: Vision and Forms* (Carbondale: Southern Illinois University Press, 1988) pp. 205–14.
6. Margaret Atwood, *Cat's Eye* (Toronto: McClelland & Stewart, 1988). All page references will be to this edition.
7. There is a third mini-retrospective as well, when Elaine at her mother's house after her father's death finds the cat's eye marble in her old red plastic purse (p. 398).
8. De Man, 'Autobiography as De-facement', p. 920.
9. Ibid., p. 926.
10. Ibid., p. 930.
11. Ibid., p. 920.
12. Ibid., p. 922.
13. For definitions of these terms, see Stephen Hawking, *A Brief History of Time* (London: Bantam, 1988), a book to which Atwood draws attention in her Acknowledgements.
14. See Lola Lemire Tostevin's interview with Christopher Dewdney, *Poetry Canada Review*, vol. 3 (1989) pp. 1–3, 29.
15. In my thinking about the way that objects work in texts, I am indebted to Simone Vauthier's exemplary essay, 'Images in Stones, Images in Words', in C. Nicholson (ed.), *Critical Approaches to the Fiction of Margaret Laurence* (London: Macmillan, 1990) pp. 46–70.
16. Atwood, 'Instructions for the Third Eye', p. 62.
17. For a brief discussion of subjectivity, see Toril Moi, *Sexual/Textual Politics* (London: Methuen, 1985) pp. 9–11.

18. Atwood, 'Instructions for the Third Eye', p. 62.
19. Bryson, *Word and Image*, p. 13: 'A sign is always divided into two areas, one which declares its loyalty to the text outside the image, and another which asserts the autonomy of the image: a ratio of the sign which is as important a fact of art history as any of its discoveries about the individual styles that form variables within this overall sign-format – the typical sign-format of painting in the West.'
20. Dennis Lee's definition, quoted by Helen Tiffin, 'Post-Colonial Literature and Counter-Discourse', *Kunapipi*, vol. 9, no. 3 (1987) pp. 17–34.
21. For a glimpse into this territory, see Hawking, *A Brief History of Time*, pp. 155–69.
22. De Man, 'Autobiography as De-facement', p. 922.
23. Ibid.
24. Elaine's final words echo Stephen's (p. 104); see also Hawking, *A Brief History of Time*, p. 28.

11

Gender and Narrative Perspective in Margaret Atwood's Stories

DIETER MEINDL

Let me sketch my conception of narrative perspective first (cf. Meindl, pp. 14–30). It hinges upon the distinction between what I call the authorial and figural frame of reference in narrative discourse. This distinction governs a system of narrative privileges and limitations. The figural frame of reference features a first-person narrator or, in third-person narrative, a centre-of-consciousness figure. These narrator or reflector figures have no direct access to the minds of other characters, whose thoughts cannot be simply stated. Thus, narrative perspective is limited in quantitative terms. On the other hand, the attitude and views of a narrator or reflector figure are only conditionally valid. They can occupy the whole range of human modes: reliability, error, deception of self or others, and so on. In qualitative terms, narrative perspective is thus unlimited. Conversely, in the authorial frame of reference of third-person narrative, the minds of the fictional characters are open to inspection. A character's thought can be simply stated. Quantitatively speaking, narrative perspective is thus unlimited. On the other hand, authorial attitude is not equivalent to a narrating figure or subject with potentially subjective views. Authorial attitude has authority for the reader or, what amounts to the same thing, if the reader rejects this authority, he is not interpreting but criticising the text, whereas the reader's interpretation of figural narrative (for example, first-person narrative) often presupposes the rejection of the narrative perspective conveyed. Hence, in qualitative terms, narrative perspective in the authorial frame of reference is inescapably reliable or, to put it differently, limited in not commanding the whole range of human modes.

Margaret Atwood's short story collections, *Dancing Girls* (1977) and *Bluebeard's Egg* (1983), contain 26 stories. Twelve of them are in the first person; invariably the 'I' is a woman. In 11 of the 14 remaining stories using third-person narrative a female centre of consciousness is employed. As all 26 stories are keyed to the figural frame of reference (none of them centrally occupying the authorial frame of reference), the female narrative perspectives conveyed are qualitatively unlimited, that is, potentially unreliable or censurable. These female perspectives tend to be concerned with a man or group of men – to the extent that the outward view of a male provided by the female point-of-view character constitutes her mind or inner world. This structure is made explicit in 'Bluebeard's Egg', which treats of a wife's fixation upon her husband: 'In her inner world is Ed, like a doll within a Russian wooden doll, and in Ed is Ed's inner world, which she can't get at' (*BE*, p. 133). The Atwoodian prototypical story is a dual or polar affair in being both woman-derived and man-focused. Its structure enables it to function both as a criticism and a reflection of an androcentric world. This type of story is gender-based in the sense that gender, 'the social construction of sexual difference' (Miller, p. xi), plays a structurally constitutive role in it.[1]

In a first cluster of stories, the female focalisers display their particular personality through their failure to communicate with the focal figures, men. 'The Man from Mars', in *Dancing Girls*, is exemplary in this respect. It is the grotesque story of a bulky Canadian upper-class girl pursued by a tiny, seedy Asiatic student. Christine absolutely refuses to get to know the meekly obstinate man, who insists on calling her his friend. Only after his deportation does she develop a romantic interest in him and recognises that he must have been Vietnamese. Musing about the destiny of such an unmartial person in a war-torn country, she reflects: 'He would be something nondescript ... Perhaps he had become an interpreter' (*DG*, p. 37). Her view of him as an interpreter ironically underscores the theme of non-communication.

Similarly, in 'Dancing Girls', the vaguely Arab student in the furnished room next door remains a mystery to a Canadian student: 'Ann sympathized with his loneliness, but she did not wish to become involved in it, implicated by it. She had enough trouble dealing with her own' (*DG*, p. 218). In 'Rape Fantasies', the narrator, Estelle, tells about her and her office colleagues' conversations about rape – conversations which inevitably turn into stories about imagined funny or sentimental encounters with men who prove to be patient listeners. It is easy to miss the point of the story: Estelle monologises in front of a male stranger in a bar. This narrative situation may be a set-up for a rape. In 'The Grave of the Famous Poet', a couple is engaged in a literary pilgrimage. The woman is not narrating for an imagined audience, but rather registering and reflecting: 'In the last few days he's become not more familiar to me as he should have but more alien' (*DG*, p. 84). She feels they have come to the place and to the point they have 'because dead people are more real to him than living ones' (p. 85). After their relationship has foundered completely, we see her arranging shells in a square in the sand: 'Inside I plant the flints, upright in tidy rows, like teeth, like flowers' (p. 92). The image suggests her allure and at the same time her insistence on her defenses.

In ' The Sin Eater', in *Bluebeard's Egg*, a woman is confronted with the death of her cynically wise psychiatrist: 'Here it is, finally, the shape of my bereavement: Joseph is no longer around to be told. There is no one left in my life who is there only to be told' (p. 217). Joseph, however, refused to function as a human dumping ground comparable to the Sin Eater of Welsh folk religion, whose job it was to eat a meal placed on a coffin and thus remove the dead person's sins. Joseph told stories himself, stories with a tendency to become parables, as the woman notes. In the straightforwardness of its moral, ' The Sin Eater', an interior monologue in the present tense, is parabolical itself. As a parable, this story of a woman and her psychiatrist would be about reciprocity denied. Significantly, the woman has a dream in which Joseph fails to persuade her to eat a plateful of cookies, his sins.

The stories dealt with so far could be called fables or parables of non-communication. Margaret Atwood implements the quantitative limitations of figural narrative perspective, in which the inner world of the other is fundamentally inaccessible. In these stories, the other person is indeed an alien, a stranger talked to by a woman in a singles bar, an estranged lover, or a psychiatrist whose function is conceived as a communicational one-way street, of whom his client says: 'I don't *have* to like him' (p. 216).

Two stories told from a man's point of view can also be adduced here. 'Polarities', in *Dancing Girls*, uses as its centre of consciousness an American teaching at a Canadian university who refrains from committing himself in his relationship with a Canadian female colleague. It is only when she is institutionalised as a schizophrenic, when her mind is doubly inaccessible, that she becomes the object of his desire. 'Spring Song of the Frogs', in *Bluebeard's Egg*, deals with a middle-aged man's fiascoes in what he experiences as an era of slenderising, flesh-denying women. Generally speaking, in Margaret Atwood's stories of non-communication, men and women define each other by mutually constricting and rejecting each other. The point-of-view characters, mostly women, are trapped in their inner worlds. This treatment of alienation and depersonalisation, more salient in *Dancing Girls* than in *Bluebeard's Egg*, gives a typically modernist ring to these gender-based stories.

In turning to another group of stories, we realise that often the alternative to non-communication is victimisation. 'The Resplendent Quetzal', in *Dancing Girls*, depicts a middle-aged couple during a vacation in Mexico. Edward and Sarah have been victimising each other since the child who prompted their marriage was still-born. Narrative perspective alternates between him and her as reflector figures. We learn from her that she is scornful of his boyish enthusiasm. He is exasperated by her placidity and deviousness. The story closes with a symbolic note of hope that the couple may have a new start, as Sarah, who is secretly on the pill, throws a plaster Christ-child figure into an Aztec sacrificial well dedicated to the god of fertility.

Marital relations definitely improve in another story of Latin American travel, 'The Scarlet Ibis', which ends on a good wife's retrospective note: 'She was glad she had never said anything, forced any issues' (*BE*, p. 179).

'Hair Jewellery', in *Dancing Girls*, is told, with humour and insight, by a retrospective first-person narrator. The remembrance is of her bohemian graduate student days, when her romantic attachment to a drop-out male graduate student foundered on his cynicism. Meeting many years later at an academic conference, each is disappointed that the other has a successful professional and family life. Pleased with how things have turned out for her, the narrator nevertheless regrets the exorcism of the irrational element from her life.

All three stories employ the conventional narrative past tense and offer hope for three marriages. Figural perspectives appear reliable and result in more or less commendable conduct. With the next five stories, keyed to the present tense, we move into Margaret Atwood's particular narrative territory.

'Under Glass' presents a registering 'I' who knows her partner, sees through him, as it were. She comes to him, eager for domesticity. He is just after a one-night stand with another woman. In her mind, she apostrophises him as a 'self-propelling prick with a tiny brain attached to it like a termite's' (*DG*, p. 74). The reader is likely to endorse this grotesque portrait. But why can she not bring herself to leave him? *Survival*, Margaret Atwood's guide to Canadian literature, distinguishes between four victim positions: position no. 1 consists in denying the fact that one is a victim; no. 2 is believing oneself incapable of changing the situation in which one is victimised; no. 3 is repudiation of the victim role; no. 4 is being a creative non-victim. The woman in 'Under Glass' occupies victim position no. 2: she knows she is a victim, but deems herself helpless for reasons of love, sex, biological determinism. The persistent night animal and plant imagery in the story strikes the reader as symbolic of her craving for a mindless, psychically painless state.

In 'Lives of the Poets' there is Julia, a promising writer with writer's block, suffering from a psychosomatic nose-bleed before one of the public readings which she detests, though by doing them she supports herself and her partner, the painter Bernie. She calls him long-distance: '"Hi." A woman's voice, Marika, she knew who it would be' (*DG*, p. 208). This hints at the fact that Julia has been closing her eyes to Bernie's philanderings: victim position no. 1. There is also ground for thinking that she will accept her victim status: 'maybe I'm wrong, I'll never know. Beautiful' (*DG*, p. 209). But then there erupts 'this rage that has been going on for a long time, energy, words swarming behind her eyes like angry bees' (p. 209). At the end, there is rebellion against her victim role and even, as the image of the word 'swarm' suggests, a hope of renewed creativity.

In the remaining stories in *Bluebeard's Egg* we notice a formal development, a narrative mode classifiable as free indirect discourse in the present tense with authorial overtones. Consider this passage in the well-known story 'Bluebeard's Egg':

Sometimes Sally worries that she's a nothing, the way Marylynn was before she got a divorce and a job. But Sally isn't a nothing; therefore, she doesn't need a divorce to stop being one. And she's always had a job of some sort; in fact she has one now. Luckily Ed has no objection; he doesn't have much of an objection to anything she does.   (*BE*, p. 122)

The first sentence strikes one as a somewhat ironic authorial statement of Sally's ideas of herself. The ironic tone is maintained by the use of 'Sally', rather than 'she', at the beginning of the second sentence. Yet, with increasing clarity, the passage slips into free indirect discourse in the present tense, becomes an illustration of Sally's thought processes which, but for the retention of third-person usage in 'she', would be interior monologue. The overlay of authorial irony in 'Bluebeard's Egg' suggests that Sally's approach to her marriage is a self-protective delusion, that her trust in the stupidity of her husband – a successful heart surgeon who is extremely attractive to women – places her in victim position no. 1. In terms of the fairy-tale meta-text in the story, Sally shuns Bluebeard's secret room (cf. Wilson, p. 392).

In 'Uglypuss', Joel, a political street-drama activist, and his long-time partner Becka have split up. On the night she calls, asking him for a talk, he promises to be there but goes out and picks up another woman. When he comes home he finds that Becka has vandalised his apartment and abducted his cat. A note advises him to look for Uglypuss in an ash-can. Narrative perspective is tied to Joel's consciousness during two-thirds of the story. This enables the reader to realise that he really is the heel she thinks he is. The last part of the story reveals that Becka acted out of desperation over her loneliness: 'She doesn't want to be angry; she wants to be comforted. She wants a truce' (*BE*, p. 90). Figural perspective acquires the authorial overtone of reliable comment.

An authorially coloured figural narrative perspective is also used in two stories about independent women. Alma, in 'The Salt Garden', is content to be on intimate terms with both her husband, who has moved in with a girl friend, and her married lover: 'This is how Alma feels: removed from time. Time presupposes a future. Sometimes she experiences this state as apathy, other times as exhilaration. She can do what she likes. But what does she like?' (*BE*, p. 191). Alma lives under the sway of death, death brought close to her both in her fantasies of nuclear holocaust and her physical blackouts. She appears static, without preferences. Why move when every move leads to the last stillness? In 'The Sunrise', the painter Yvonne is engaged in living serenely, in what she thinks of as 'the freedom of the present tense, this sliding edge' (p. 235). Conscious of death, but in control of it, she draws sustenance from the sunrise, which she watches every morning. Soliciting men in the street, she acquires models, sometimes a lover. An encounter with a rocker provides a creative impetus, but also fills her with existential doubt: 'Though if art sucks and everything is only art, what has she done with her life?' (*BE*, p. 237). Grappling with such problems, narrative perspective verges on the authorial frame of reference.

Certain tendencies seem to crystallise in Margaret Atwood's stories. Half the stories – two-thirds in *Bluebeard's Egg* – employ the present tense. The penchant for the present tense, in combination with either first-person interior monologue or, increasingly, centre-of-consciousness technique with authorial overtones, asserts itself. It corresponds to the two-fold goal of these gender-based stories: to render the immediacy of experience of the female point-of-view characters and to endow them with representative, parabolical significance. The decreasing emphasis on the theme of non-communication corresponds to a lessening interest in exploiting the quantitative limitation of the figural frame of reference, in which the mind of the other person cannot be finally gauged. The female focalisers, though sometimes deluded or censurable on account of passivity, tend to become remarkably perceptive and accurate. Particularly in the last two stories discussed, approximation to the qualitative limitation of the authorial frame of reference is used to endorse women's perspectives. All this appears ultimately expressive of a paradoxical goal which male writers have always unthinkingly treated as their domain: gender-based universality of meaning. In this, Margaret Atwood's short fiction parallels a tendency in feminist or gender-orientated literary criticism which stresses woman not as the object but as the subject of enquiry. Myra Jehlen states:

> rather than appending their findings to the existing literature, [the majority of feminist scholars] generate a new one altogether in which women are not just another focus but the centre of an investigation whose categories and terms are derived from the world of female experience. They respond to the Archimedean dilemma by creating an alternative context, a sort of female enclave apart from the universe of masculinist assumptions.

Most 'women's studies' have taken this approach and stressed the global, structural character of their separate issues. (Jehlen, p. 70)

There are two stories left which do not quite fit any of the categories established but which shed further light on Margaret Atwood's development in the short story genre. 'The War in the Bathroom', dating from 1964, is the earliest story in *Dancing Girls* and placed at its beginning. It is a veritable *tour de force*, consisting of seven notebook entries in which a first-person narrator describes a woman's first week in her new furnished room. The reader soon realises that the first-person narrator and the woman are the same person, that the 'I' represents the superego of the woman. A little incident, related by the 'I' as having occurred when the woman moved in, sets the tone: 'A man came along and offered to help her, rather a pleasant-looking man, but I have told her never to accept help from strangers' (*DG*, p. 1). Here, principle overrides spontaneous sympathy. The 'I' also deprives the woman of creature comforts, rewards good behaviour, insists on cleanliness, generally deals with her in the imperative mode. Ironically, this rational superego is shown as deranged. The title of the story refers to the 'I's paranoiac belief that the janitor of the house, an old man who conducts his morning toilet every day from 9 to 9.30 in the common bathroom behind the thin partition of the 'I's room, purposely makes unpleasant noises. The story ends with the 'I' taking a bath on Sunday from 9 a.m. onward, causing the old man to wait, then to run and fall on the stairs. The 'I' suppresses the woman's impulse to come to his aid. The story also contains a *mise en abîme*, a symbolic concentration or convergence of its configuration of meaning. One of the occupants of the house, called by the 'I' the woman with the two voices, turns out to be two women: a sharp-voiced invalid old lady carried by a thick, dim-witted female. The whole story presumably ridicules rationalism, somewhat in the spirit of the 1960s. It derides the maniacally proper and self-centred 'I' imposed on a 'She'. Inasmuch as it treats this superego as the internalisation of parental and social rules sanctioned by our patriarchal system it is but another male-versus-female story. Yet, as a skit on the Freudian scheme of the psyche, it implicitly subscribes to that scheme. In terms of gender, this experimental story apparently still accepts the traditional alignment of the male/female dichotomy with the rational and irrational compartments of the psyche, a thought pattern which has come under feminist attack. To cite Myra Jehlen once more: 'assumptions such as the one that makes intuition and reason opposite terms parallel to female and male may have axiomatic force in our culture, but they are precisely what feminists need to question' (Jehlen, p. 69).

In a recent study of contemporary English Canadian fiction, Margaret Atwood is treated as a postmodern writer (Hutcheon, pp. 138–60). This strikes me as problematic. In view of her concern for the individual (individual woman, that is), her meticulous craft, which has led her to explore modes of presenting consciousness and the possibilities of the present tense, and her penchant for myth (cf. Wilson) and symbolism (cf. Davey), Margaret Atwood is, for all practical purposes, a writer in the modernist tradition, at least in her short fiction. In one of her stories, though, we have a definite approach toward the postmodern regime.

'Loulou; or,The Domestic Life of the Language', in *Bluebeard's Egg*, uses the present tense with authorial overtones, in accordance with the author's more recent manner. The centre of consciousness is Loulou, an expert potter, around whom sundry male writers revolve, some of them her consecutive husbands or lovers. Her rebellion against the definitions forced upon her by the writers takes the shape of a seduction of a very different man, her accountant – with inconclusive results, as it turns out: 'What, underneath it all, is Loulou really like? How can she tell? Maybe she is what the poets say she is, after all; maybe she has only their word, their words, for herself' (*BE*, p. 65). In modernism, language along with reason and convention, tends to be a barrier before experience and truth, a surface over existential depth. Or, as one critic puts it: 'Along with some of her contemporaries, Atwood sees every act of intellection as distancing from a more primary world' (Brown, p. 41). Typically, in 'Giving Birth', the protagonist experiences 'finally ... the disappearance of all language' (*DG*, p. 241). Words are apt to misrepresent profound experience and a person's identity. Loulou reacts modernistically, as it were, in her irritation with the poets calling her 'geomorphic', 'chthonic', 'telluric' – their gender-based labels for her, which make her run to the dictionary. At the end, however, she is at a loss for a different mode of viewing herself. She senses that she only has words for herself, that cultural notions of the feminine are inevitably inscribed by, and in, language. In the final analysis, the thematics of language of this story conforms to the particular self-reflexivity or self-referentiality of postmodern literature. The text suggests the primacy of language as man's – and woman's – epistemological determinant, as the matrix of reality. In concert with such thinkers as language philosopher Ludwig Wittgenstein, the postmoderns have abandoned the notion of states of affairs (*Sachverhalte*) which exist independent of language, the idea of preverbal existential depths. This view of the primacy of language in the construction of reality has led to a levelling – often playfully authorial – of the distinction between fact and fiction and to a great emancipation of fabulation in North American literature (see Meindl, pp. 223fo).

It is such a vision that Margaret Atwood entertains in 'Loulou' – perhaps also in 'The Sunrise', where Yvonne meditates upon the theme that 'everything is only art', and, possibly, in the title, the first and last stories of *Bluebeard's Egg*, which emphasise the constant fictionalising we engage in as human beings (cf. Godard). In the over-all perspective, however, Margaret Atwood's short stories display a gender-based rather than a language-based conception of reality.

Note

1.   Not all 26 stories conform to this particular pattern, although gender issues impinge on all of them. In 'Giving Birth', the concluding story of *Dancing Girls*, the 'I' is a mother and author who writes a story about a woman's giving birth, a profoundly enriching experience involving an irreproachably helpful male partner. Treatment of gender yields a positive picture, perhaps not unrelated to the fact that the story carries an autobiographical imprint. In an analogous fashion, in *Bluebeard's Egg*, which is dedicated to Margaret Atwood's parents, the opening story, 'Significant Moments in the Life of My Mother', and the concluding story, 'Unearthing Suite', cast parental figures as life-affirming agents. In the same volume, 'Hurricane Hazel' and 'Betty' also feature cherished mother figures, although the daughter status of the narrator is not central. In both stories, the pangs and pains of growing up influence the narrative perspective, which focuses on gender issues: adolescent love in 'Hurricane Hazel', husband-worship in 'Betty'. 'Training' deals with a maladjusted upper-class boy's stint as a counsellor in a crippled children's camp and his attachment to a paraplegic nine-year-old girl. Two stories can be seen as deviating from the rest. For whereas, in general, the author portrays a more or less mundane environment,

'When it Happens' and 'A Travel Piece', placed next to each other in *Dancing Girls*, extend into nightmarish, dystopian fantasy. This leaves 18 stories for closer inspection.

Sources

Atwood, Margaret, *Dancing Girls and Other Stories*, Bantam Seal Book (Toronto: McClelland & Steward-Bantam, 1978).

——, *Bluebeard's Egg*, Bantam Seal Book (Toronto: McClelland Steward-Bantam, 1984).

Brown, Russell M., 'Atwood's Sacred Wells', *Essays on Canadian Writing*, no. 17 (1980) pp. 5–43.

Davey, Frank, 'Alternate Stories: the Short Fiction of Audrey Thomas and Margaret Atwood', *Canadian Literature*, no. 109 (1986) pp. 5–16.

Godard, Barbara, 'Palimpsest: Margaret Atwood's *Bluebeard's Egg*', *RANAM*, no. 20 (1987) pp. 51–60.

Hutcheon, Linda, *The Canadian Postmodern: A Study of Contemporary English-Canadian Fiction* (Toronto: Oxford University Press, 1988).

Jehlen, Myra, 'Archimedes and the Paradox of Feminist Criticism', in Elizabeth and Emily K. Abel (eds), *The 'Signs' Reader: Women, Gender and Scholarship* (Chicago, Ill: University of Chicago Press, 1983) pp. 69–75.

Meindl, Dieter, *Der amerikanische Roman zwischen Naturalismus und Postmoderne (1930–1960): Eine Entwicklungsstudie auf diskurstheoretischer Grundlage* (Munich: Fink, 1983).

Miller, Nancy K. 'Preface', in Nancy K. Miller (ed), *The Poetics of Gender* (New York: Columbia University Press, 1986) pp. xi–xv.

Wilson, Sharon R., 'Bluebeard's Forbidden Room: Gender Images in Margaret Atwood's Visual and Literary Art', *American Review of Canadian Literature*, vol. 26 (1986) pp. 385–97.

12

'Yet I Speak, Yet I Exist': Affirmation of the Subject in Atwood's Short Stories

ISABEL CARRERA SUAREZ

Margaret Atwood's creative world, as has repeatedly been noted, possesses a coherence which spreads across genres, its motifs and structures recurring in different texts, whether fiction, poetry or essay. In a study published in 1983 Sherill E. Grace attempts to describe this coherence by defining Atwood's system with reference to four elements: duality, nature, self and language.[1] While all four are found to some extent in any volume of Atwood's, it is the latter two that seem to dictate the literary function of nature and duality, and to constitute the key to the author's literary world. A reading of the three volumes of short stories published so far, *Dancing Girls* (1977), *Bluebeard's Egg* (1983) and *Wilderness Tips* (1991),[2] allows, by means of the cumulative effect of the genre, some insight into the recurrences and changes in the treatment of the self and its representation in language. Such a reading shows a gradual amplification of the subject, a self which survives (and communicates) against all theoretical odds, against fragmentation, gaps and deconstructions. This affirmation of the subject and of language is suggested in selected stories of *Dancing Girls* and asserted in the subsequent volumes.

Considered together, the three collections of stories waver between confirming and contradicting Atwood's statement that authors do not 'grow' or 'develop', but rather do something which is closer to 'a theme with variations'.[3] Perhaps 'growth', with its proximity to 'growing up' (or, in Atwood's own simile, radishes) is the wrong metaphor to apply to the progression of her work. In the essay quoted, she goes on to affirm that 'writers' universes may become more elaborate, but they do not become essentially different', and this is true of her collections of stories and their treatment of the subject. However, while the latter does not become *essentially* different from one collection to another, it is the concept of the subject, together with its relationship to language, that marks the evolution (if not growth or development) in the universe of Atwood's short fiction. There is a shift in emphasis from the individual, soul-searching subject of *Dancing Girls* to a wider extended subject, begun in the family 'we' of *Bluebeard's Egg* and expanded further, as in a widening ripple, in *Wilderness Tips*. The relation of this subject to language also experiences a shift, as a rather deterministic view of the limitations of language gives way to a more pragmatic critique of its use as instrument of power, modified by a belief in the possibility of appropriation and transformation of words.

Nine of the 16 stories in *Dancing Girls* (including 'The War in the Bathroom' and 'Rape Fantasies'),[4] are narrated in the first person; a significant number when compared with the later collections: four in *Bluebeard's Egg*, one in *Wilderness Tips*. The voice in all these stories is female and predominantly young. This young female subject perceives itself as struggling against an Other who, more often than not is a *he* and a sexual partner, but can also be her own unacknowledged self or, more widely, the world. In several of the stories the main syntactical opposition is I/he, a metonymy for the main conflict in the text ('Under Glass', 'The Grave of the Famous Poet', 'Lives of the Poets', 'The Sin Eater'). In others, the same opposition appears in the form of I/you, the *you* referring again to a sexual partner ('Hair Jewellery', 'Rape Fantasies'). The struggle is rarely limited to this opposition, however, and most of the protagonists are engaged in a battle with their own unacknowledged or repressed selves, or the selves they have left behind, having 'shed identities like snake-skins' ('Hair Jewellery'). Their split personalities are described in detail, as in the schizoid pains of the woman in 'Under Glass', or conveyed by the narrative technique, as in 'The War in the Bathroom', where the two narrative voices, in the first and third persons, are revealed as having only one owner. A similar grammatical and thematic predominance can be found in the rest of the stories in the collection; in most, the dialectics of she/he are central, and reveal a hidden structure of a female subject defining itself mainly against a male antagonist, and/or struggling to accept supposedly unacceptable aspects of her own personality.

This recurrent pattern, however, is broken totally or partially in certain stories within the collection, notably in 'Betty' and 'Giving Birth', where the antagonists are multiple and female, and in 'Polarities', where the binary opposition he/she is secondary to the more crucial struggle by Louise to reconcile her fragmented selves, or the fragments out of which she has attempted to create her personality.

While containing a 'he' (Fred), and an opposition of I/she (sister), 'Betty' centres on the mirror image of the character who gives name to the story. A retrospective narration, it shows the choices made in the development of the self, and those left behind. It presents an adult first-person narrator who, while telling the story of her childhood neighbour Betty (a devoted, obliging wife, eventually abandoned by her husband, Fred), analyses her own past motives for seeing this woman as her double, and her later arrival at the ability to choose a different role-model. The young narrator feels that Betty's marital failure, and subsequent death, is the doom of 'nice' girls like herself, as opposed to that of 'vivacious' girls like her sister, whom Fred had clearly preferred. A romanticised version of Betty's death recedes into the background when the narrator decides to reject her as a model: 'People change, though . . . As I passed beyond the age of melodrama I came to see that if I did not want to be Betty, I would have to be someone else. . . . People stopped calling me a nice girl and started calling me a clever one, and after a while I enjoyed this' (*DG*, p. 50). This story offers one of Atwood's most optimistic endings, in the possibilities it leaves open for change, for the construction of the self, or rebirth. The narrator, faced with two opposed role-models, has been able to discard both and adopt her own, escaping her victim position.

As a counterpoint, 'Polarities' shows the main character, Louise, trying and failing to bring her self to life. Her personality seems to suffer multiple splits, suggested by the fissures detected in her brisk, practical manner (her poetry, the fuzzy slippers, the frilly underwear) and also represented, after her internment, in her invention of a schizophrenic parentage for herself (mother a French Protestant, father an English Catholic; mother an Italian opera singer, father a Nazi general). Her friend Morrison, focaliser of the story, provides a crucial image when he observes that her house has the strange effect of separate rooms, whose decoration is copied from acquaintances' houses: 'Poor Louise had been trying to construct herself out of the other people she had met' (*DG*, p. 70).

Her growing mental unbalance, reflected in her plans to form a circle which would hold the world together, does not prevent her seeing Morrison's own unreconciled duality more clearly than anyone else: 'He needs to be completed, he refuses to admit his body is part of his mind' (p. 69). Louise tries to create a circle and contain the polarities, to be 'all-inclusive' (p. 55), but her practice of *excluding* things from this circle seems to lie at the root of the theoretical failure of her system. In her metaphor, as in her own personality, she fragments instead of embracing, and the story remains one of failure of the self.

Throughout the collection, the treatment of the subject is closely linked to its definition in language. Characters are represented, or misrepresented, by the language applied to them. In some cases, they are labelled by others: Christine, in 'The Man from Mars' (*DG*), is in turn 'ordinary' (as seen by her parents), 'plain' (by her sisters) or an 'honorary person' (as defined by men, who cannot fit her into the female categories of cock-teaser, cold fish, easy lay or snarky bitch). This self she temporarily escapes from through the fantasies awakened by her persecution by a 'person from another culture'. In other stories characters invent their own personality through words: 'the word she had chosen for herself some time ago was "comely"' ('The Resplendent Quetzal', *DG*, p. 145), and split identities find their expression in duality of language, as does the writer in 'Lives of the Poets' (*DG*), who must choose between her 'nice' persona, represented by her gentle poems, and her repressed rage, with its 'bloody' language.

Characters in these early stories struggle with language, with a need to speak or make themselves understood. While the healing nature of speech is shown in 'The Sin Eater', most of the stories in *Dancing Girls* underline the inadequacies of the word as a means of communication: 'We've talked too much or not enough: for what we have to say to each other there's no language, we've tried them all' ('The Grave of the Famous Poet', *DG*, p. 93). 'My hands function, exchanging round silver discs for oblong paper [buying a ticket]. That this can be done, that everyone knows what it means, there may be a chance. If we could do that: I would give him a pebble, a flower, he would understand, he would translate exactly' (*DG*, pp. 86–7). The woman in 'Under Glass' thus wishes for comprehension through other gestures, or for the chimera of perfect interpretation. A theoretical argument is provided by Joseph, the psychiatrist of 'The Sin Eater', who has a phobia about telephones because 'most of the message in any act of communication [is] non-verbal' (*DG*, p. 216). And non-verbal communication is, in fact, the distinctive trait of some of Atwood's 'inarticulate' characters, such as the eponymous Betty and Loulou, who transmit thought or feeling through gestures; but significantly, this characteristic renders them the powerless element of the binomy which they form with their partners (Fred/Betty, the poets/Loulou).

I have elsewhere discussed Atwood's short stories, together with Doris Lessing's, as an example of the subversive strategies in women's writing, and the move away from a concentration on the traps of language into a more hopeful acceptance of the possibility of change in linguistic practices.[5] This attitude has run parallel with an evolution in linguistic and literary theory, towards the rejection of notions of fixed meanings and of linguistic determinism (present in early structuralism, including feminist critics such as Dale Spender, and also in Lacanian theory) in favour of the idea of *construction* of meaning, and the subsequent responsibility of users in transforming the language. Linking in with current philosophical and psychological theories, but with a more pragmatic focus, feminist Deborah Cameron defends an integrational theory,[6] in which external factors (social, psychological, familial) are taken into account, and earlier linguistic theories are abandoned in favour of communicative concepts such as those defined by Roy Harris or Trevor Pateman. The latter's *radical discourse* explores an active discourse that subverts, instead of reproducing, the established social institutions. Imperfect communication is thus accepted as the natural consequence of the indeterminacy of linguistic signs, but the focus is put on precisely this indeterminacy, which allows for multiplicity of meaning, for change and thus for subversion. Freed from the belief that we are controlled by our language, we can begin to assume control of it ourselves.

'Giving Birth', the final story in *Dancing Girls*, is the first to suggest such an attitude to language. One of the most complex and original of Atwood's early stories, it splits into three women, a trinity who protagonise the act and word of 'giving birth', and emerge as a remarkably solid subject at the end of the process. 'Giving Birth' is an explicit commentary on the difficulties of verbal communication and a practical example of the link between language and subject in Atwood's writing. Beginning with a long commentary on the phrase 'giving birth' and such related terms as *delivering*, the narrator mediates on their inadequacy and the need to rename the act. While she refuses to rename it herself, she is determined, nevertheless, to speak:

> These are the only words I have, I'm stuck with them, stuck in them. (That image of the tar sands, old tableau in the Royal Ontario Museum, how persistent it is. Will I break free, or will I be sucked down, fossilized, a sabre-toothed tiger or lumbering brontosaurus who ventured out too far? Words ripple at my feet, black, sluggish, lethal. Let me try once more, before the sun gets me, before I starve or drown, while I can. It's only a tableau after all, it's only a metaphor. See, I can speak, I am not trapped, and you on your part can understand. So we will go ahead as if there were no problem about language.) (*DG*, p. 226)

It is worth noting there that the distinction between metaphor and reality, which will recur in later work, functions as an antidote for inaction, allowing communication, and therefore the story, to take place.

Thus the subject begins to be defined in language, the three women who make it up (the narrator, Jeanie and her unnamed alter ego) being differentiated by their attitudes to words: Jeanie, in her articulateness and obsession with reading manuals, her alter ego in her wordless existence, the narrator as a writer, self-consciously bring her past self back to life in the story, and naming that self Jeanie. These three selves, and the concepts of language and the subject, are brought together again in the description of the pain at the culminating moment of giving birth: 'When there is no pain she feels nothing, when there is pain she feels nothing because there is no *she*. This, finally, is the disappearance of language' (p. 237). The statement reinforces the argument used elsewhere in the story that events of the body, such as giving birth or orgasm, may be impossible to describe in words. It also unites the three subjects in a common disappearance: the inarticulate *other*, for whom the *words* 'giving birth' don't exist, the articulate Jeanie, who loses the power of speech, and the narrator, who admits her difficulty in putting this event into words. All three go through the experience, a reality untranslatable into language, but whose existence is affirmed to the point of superseding the concepts of subject and of speech: rather than a reduction of the subject to text, there is a reduction of both, text and subject, to the event. After the birth, the final lines express the new order: 'in the days that follow

Jeanie herself becomes drifted over with new words, her hair slowly darkens, she ceases to be what she was and is replaced, gradually by someone else' (p. 240), and 'it was to me, after all, that the birth was given, Jeanie gave it, I am the result' (p. 239). Both statements emphasis the notion of the subject as *process*, every stage the result of previous (multiple) *others*. Such a conception of the self will be crucial in later stories, and particularly in the third collection, *Wilderness Tips*.

Bluebeard's Egg, published six years after *Dancing Girls*, lifts the emphasis from the l/he pair, and explores a first extension of the self into family grounds. If we ascribe 'Betty' and 'The Sin Eater' to the first collection or period, there is a substantial change in narrative technique, since only four stories ('Significant Moments in the Life of my Mother', 'Hurricane Hazel', 'In Search of the Rattlesnake Plantain' and 'Unearthing Suite') are narrated in the first person; furthermore, the 'I' that these stories present, again female, could more accurately be described as a family 'we', being defined mainly by its relationship to the parents. Rather than a self by opposition, we face a self by addition, an 'I' not in struggle with its other, but accepting its extension into the family circle, with its influences and limitations.

'Significant Moments in the Life of my Mother', the opening and perhaps key story in the collection, blends in its narrative technique the point of view of the mother (who tells stories about herself and her family) with that of the daughter and ultimately leaves the reader to complete the portrait by adding her own. It is not, as the title may suggest, a story about the narrator's mother, for it clearly shows the narrator in the act of reconstructing her own past and present, analysing herself as a result of her childhood as recreated in the older woman's narration. The stories told by them both show the gap between daughter and mother, but just as obviously show their continuity, thus offering a portrait of daughter with mother (or m/other). The self becomes an entity whose borders are undefined, a subject, as Barbara Godard has pointed out,[7] with the blurred ego boundaries described by Nancy Chodorow for women's subjectivity. The continuity of the mother–daughter dyad is shown not only in their connection through story-telling itself (a rich motif in the collection), but also in the parallel stores about their lives (haircuts as rites of passage, dodging as tactics) and in their respective constructions of each other through narration.

'Unearthing Suite', which closes the collection, insists on the idea of self as process/result, with the narrator 'unearthing', among other things, her own past and the origins of her dual tendency to slothfulness (the father) and order (the mother), made tangible in the two rooms of her house, one chaotic, one neatly designed and kept. She also traces back her tendency to inertia (as a reaction to a childhood training in movement) and, more crucially, her 'translation of the world into words' (p. 271), the beginnings of her writing. 'Hurricane Hazel', for its part, makes patent the family identity that others, neighbours and friends, attribute to the narrator in her adolescent years, and some of its uncomfortable consequences. The family context and its intricacies are also explored, more incidentally, in 'In Search of the Rattlesnake Plantain'.

Other stories in the collection link with those in the previous book, and instances of suppressed selves recur. The most significant feature for our purposes, however, lies in the treatment of the first-person narrative, the pluralisation of the subject through its extension to the family circle (and hence, given the characteristics of the parents described, to nature). It hardly seems coincidental that the opening line in 'Unearthing Suite' is the suggestive 'My parents have something to tell me' (p. 263).

Questions of language in *Bluebeard's Egg* are mainly treated with reference to power and gender politics, both of which are closely related to the definition of the subject through language. 'Significant Moments' and 'Unearthing Suite' characterise the parents through their speech, and expose their generation's conventional division between 'feminine' and 'masculine' territories: 'To let the men's world slip over verbally into the ladies' would reveal you as a mannerless boor, but to carry the ladies' world over into the men's brands you a prig and even a pansy' (*BE*, p. 21). Men therefore swear, but not in front of women, while women reserve certain stories for female company only, stories of 'romantic betrayals, unwanted pregnancies, illnesses of various horrible kinds, marital infidelities, mental breakdowns, tragic suicides, unpleasant lingering deaths' (p. 21), stories which men, it is argued, are not equipped to bear or understand. The difference in language amounts to a difference of worlds, it is both consequence and cause of the social order; an order which, the daughter-narrator suggests, is changing, as her own linguistic universe reflects.

The mother of 'Significant Moments' is defined entirely though her language, shown in her story-telling. Other characters in the collection are reflected in their letters: Buddy's peculiar punctuation, ponderous compliments, blue splotchy ball-point; the brother's funny, vulgar, illustrated letters to his sister followed by factual ones to the mother ('Hurricane Hazel'). But most persistently, we find descriptions of the power of language and its use or misuse. The narrator in 'Hurricane Hazel' learns of its effects through her brother, who very effectively ridicules the advertisements of remedies for teenage problems, and through Buddy's standard (though naïve) attempt to pin her down by giving her a bracelet with his name (his 'identity' bracelet).

Linguistic disadvantage constitutes the conflict *per se* in 'Loulou; or, The Domestic Life of the Language', also collected in *Bluebeard's Egg*. It tells the story of the unbalanced relationship between a group of over-articulate poets and 'earthy' Loulou, whose mismatched name and personality embody, in the poets' opinion, the 'gap between the signifier and the signified'. The gap, in another of Atwood's ironic symbioses with theory, becomes the central motif of the story. Loulou supports a group of poets under her roof, materially with her earnings as a potter, morally with the healing power of her sexual and motherly love. Despite their constant teasing and play on her ignorance of words, she has an intuitive understanding of their motivations and abuses, and sees the trap of the role she has been cast in, that of nourishing earth-mother. While the poets wonder what there is 'in the space between Loulou and her name', she asks herself a far more relevant question: What is there between Loulou and the poets' construction of her? The question becomes more pressing after she seeks out an accountant and seduces him in his office: 'he is other, he is another. She too could be other. But which other? What, underneath it all, is Loulou really like? How can she tell? Maybe she is what the poets say she is, after all; maybe she has only their word, their words, for herself' (p. 80). The story ends unresolved, an ambiguous mixture of affirmation of Loulou, of her understanding by non-verbal means, her refusal to be defined ('nobody invented her, thank you very much'; p. 80), and of resignation towards her trap. The ending, in which she decides that being 'like Loulou', as the poets require, is not so bad after all, seems a capitulation to the power of their words, but concludes, perhaps, that it is simply too late: she lacks the confidence (or the language) to explore further, and the hope for change remains only a thwarted possibility.

The story, however, also reads as a warning against false (and convenient) metaphors posing as reality. Loulou's insistence that her name is 'just a name' tries to counteract the effects of the poets' confusion between her personality and her name, their misuse of its relationship as metaphor; we are reminded of the narrator in 'Significant Moments', checking herself after trying to interpret one of her mother's stories: 'There is, however, a difference between symbolism and anecdote. Listening to my mother, I sometimes remember this' (p. 27).

The treatment of the self and of language in Atwood's latest collection of stories, *Wilderness Tips*, once more is not radically different from that of previous books, though there is a feeling that the main characters continue from a point where *Bluebeard* stopped. They are one stage further in age (some have grown-up children, even grandchildren), and most of them look back to their formative years, whether in childhood or, more frequently, in the early years of adulthood and of their careers. The focalisation is still mainly female, though at times shared or relinquished ('True Trash' alternates Joanne and Donny; Richard is the focaliser who constructs Selena in 'Isis in Darkness'). The male characters are studied in some detail, their role often going well beyond that of the antagonist. But the most pervasive presence in the collection is that of the passing of time, with the changes produced in the individual and the collective self. Almost without exception, we face a subject and its history, a history which takes place during the past few decades, and of which the present person is the result.

Several of the texts explicitly remark on the changes brought about by specific decades, mainly the 1960s, 1970s and 1980s ('Hairball', 'Isis in Darkness', 'The Age of Lead', 'Hack Wednesday', 'The Bog Man'); others go further back in time or, at the other end, reach the beginning of the 1990s. In 'Isis in Darkness' the 'zero years' of three decades serve as a structuring element for the plot. There is a feeling of the importance of the *Zeitgeist*, which is perhaps most clearly represented in 'Isis', where Richard moves from a youth of being 'good with words', interested in their abstract meanings, towards becoming the archaeologist of the past, searching for significance in its events, which he will translate into words. The collection as a whole produces the effect of the subject expanding further, the self seen in a context which encompasses more than the family and the present circumstances. The immediacy of the first-person narration is abandoned almost entirely (the exception is 'Weight'), seemingly in favour of a more distant, but also more knowledgeable and always retrospective, third-person narrator.

This collection presents an interesting new version of 'we' (or 'they') as a syntactical and psychological subject: that of the double subject formed by two characters who, while being each other's alter ego, share a complicity amounting to spiritual twinhood: Richard and Selena in 'Isis', Molly and the narrator in 'Weight', Lois and Lucy in 'Death by Landscape'. The relationship between these characters is closer to the idea of the lost possibilities of the self (as in 'Hair Jewellery'; *DG*) than to the opposed antagonist of the earlier I/he stories. They compose a self by addition rather than by opposition; the split is not the source of battles but of inclusion of opposites into one consciousness.

In many respects, the collection *Wilderness Tips* is, as Atwood would have it, a more elaborate variation on previous themes, a step further in diverse explorations. Elements such as duality reappear under a slightly different treatment; five of the ten stories contain the double subject mentioned above, a 'twin' of the main character who, rather than function merely by opposition, has been incorporated, to become an integral part of her/his self. This twin is poignantly symbolised in 'Hairball', where Katherine's strange ovarian cyst, surgically removed, kept on the mantelpiece in formaldehyde and referred to as 'Hairball', turns out to be her 'undeveloped twin' (*WT*, p. 54), the possibility of a self that she has not allowed to grow, but which crops up to remind her of the fact. In a similar way, Selena ('Isis in Darkness') has continued the artistic career which Richard has traded for the shelter of an income, but which he has always pined for, however romantically. She is always part of his own self and, ultimately, in putting together her pieces (writing her biography), he becomes part of her life too.

It is Selena's death, however, that triggers off Richard's conscious involvement, and death also plays a prominent role in the other three 'twin' stories. While *Dancing Girls* presented death as desire, as Gothic presence, in *Wilderness Tips* it has become a reality or a justified fear. Vincent's death, in 'The Age of Lead', breaks up the hopeful world which he and Jane had inhabited in the past, a perfectly synchronised pair, united from adolescence by their mockery of obsolete values and clichéd language. 'Death by Landscape' and 'Weight' offer a main character whose present self is explained by the death of a close friend, an alter ego. In the first case, Lucy disappears mysteriously, leaving her friend Lois suspected of pushing her off a cliff; in her mature age, a grandmother living alone, Lois sees Lucy in the landscape paintings she has collected compulsively, and remembers going through life 'as if she was living not one life but two: her own, and another, shadowy life that hovered around her and would not let itself be realized – the life of what would have happened if Lucy had not stepped sideways, and disappeared from time' (*WT*, p. 128). This carefully constructed story emphasises the effect of an accident on someone's life, but the depiction of Lucy as the alter ego of Lois, and their past naming in the plural 'Lois and Lucy' is equally important and points towards unrealised possibilities of the psyche.

'Weight', for its part, presents another pair of close female friends who make different choices in life, and later come together in the survivor's unique self. Like Vincent and Jane, the narrator and Molly have shared not only a view of the world, but a language game: the invention of absurd definitions for the abusive terms used of women. Molly becomes militant in the defence of women, marries, has children; the narrator remains single, pursues a successful career; Molly leads 'the life I [the narrator] might have led, if it hadn't been for caution and a certain fastidiousness' (*WT*, p. 189). When Molly is murdered by her husband, her friend begins a personal campaign to raise funds for a shelter for battered women, to be called Molly's Place. Conducted in her own terms (including blackmailing of ex-lovers), it nevertheless continues Molly's commitment, with the narrator becoming again, as in the times of law school, 'Molly and I', a composite subject, the result of her friend's life and death.

The preoccupation with the subject as result is, of course, concomitant with the retrospective form of most of the narratives. In this collection, the examination of lost possibilities, whether by choice or sheer chance, predominates over schizophrenic division; there is a quieter acceptance of the latter, reflected in Julie's discovery ('The Bog Man') that one of the first axioms of Logic, 'A thing cannot be both self and non-self at the same time' (*WT*, p. 98), is not so clear-cut in terms of personality.

Characters in this collection also continue to be defined, or to define themselves, through language as such. The prime example is the manipulation of names: Katherine, in 'Hairball', successfully becomes Kathy, Kath and Kat, in accordance with time, place and the image she wants to project of herself. Her lover, Ger, had also been Gerald in his conventional past, before she transformed him into a successful man. The change of names is a structural element in the story: towards the end, Katherine dismisses Gerald by calling him by his full name; she signs her own merely *K*, and in the last line, having faced the truth about herself and taken a drastic decision, feels 'temporarily without a name' (p. 56). Selena, in 'Isis in Darkness', has also chosen this new name for herself, her previous one being the common Marjorie (dangerously close to 'Mary Jo', name of the narrator's wife). When Selena loses faith in poetry, she also denies her chosen name.

As in earlier collections, certain adjectives define a character: the deceived wife in 'The Bog Man' will always have the upper hand because she is 'homely'; Molly dies because she is a 'toad-kisser', a 'fixer'; that is, for her belief that she can transform men. She also significantly uses the term *cynicism* for what the narrator calls *compromise*. Ronette, the naïve, desired waitress in 'True Trash' is defined by the sexist language that judges her for being sexually active; like Loulou, she is 'stuck with other people's adjectives' (*WT*, p. 77). Like Betty and Loulou, she fails to articulate her thought or feeling in words, and offers her body instead.

No story in this collection is free from self-conscious questioning of specific words, from the exposure of 'the gap between the signifier and the signified'. This gap, however, no longer seems unbridgeable. It is a reality to be dealt with and even taken advantage of. While the socio-linguistic powerlessness of characters like Ronette is given full credit, the attitude to language allows a more playful response than previous volumes, shown particularly in 'The Age of Lead' and 'Weight'. This attitude is often united to an acute awareness of the uses to which language is put, the power of abusive labels and the symbolic power of words. Molly and her friend invent new meanings of terms such as *strident, shrill, hysteria, pushy*, in a playful subversion of their power against women. Clichés are mocked not only by Jane and Vincent in 'The Age of Lead' but also in 'Wilderness Tips', as signs of the mentality behind language. But overall, the deterministic view of language as an unavoidable and paralysing trap is absent from the collection, as are the instances of violent struggle; in their place, a more pragmatic view of communication, and the subversive power of word-play, show a belief in an active participation in the creation of language, and in the potential for transformation also contained in words.

Seen together, the three collections of stories form a continuum in the two aspects of the subject and its representation in language. The subject, always complex, moves from the struggle with itself and the other towards an inclusion of opposites and an extension into its context. The self as process/result/place, only suggested in the earlier stories, is stressed in the last collection. A similar evolution can be observed in the reflections on the use of language: the earlier characters struggle, feel trapped or doomed; the later stories, without losing sight of inadequacies or abuses, take a more pragmatic approach and assume, however tentatively, control of speech.

Thus language and the subject evolve together in Atwood's stories, towards a more inclusive, but also more pragmatic conception. For it would be mistaken to equate the author's perception of the subject with the deconstructionist view of its fictionality, its reduction to words. Without doubt Atwood makes use of the insights of contemporary theory, as has been evident in our analysis. She deconstructs the traditional subject and its language, fragments it and represents the self by reducing it *symbolically* to language – but 'symbolically' is, as her texts repeatedly warn us, as far as we can go in the equation of both elements. For nowhere in her texts does Atwood give evidence of the conversion of the subject into a fiction, nowhere is it equated with its construction in words, nor does fragmentation suppose a negation of the subject. Rather, while pointing out the importance, the motivation, and the consequences of the various constructions of a self (*Bluebeard's Egg*), her stories suggest the existence of a hidden, perhaps intangible but experiential self, which either survives fragmentation, de/construction and language problems ('Betty', 'Giving Birth'), or perishes through madness ('Polarities'). In later stories the division is less clear-cut, the self emerging neither triumphant nor wholly deconstructed, but the result of a previous process, a turning point or a temporary stage in an evolution which is left open.

The notion of the subject in Atwood's texts, therefore, is closest to Ihab Hassan's theory:[8] a kind of 'common-sense' belief in the experiential self, as perceived by the subject from childhood to old age, despite (or by means of) the multiple transformations of a lifetime.

It is possible, of course, to find resonances of almost any current theory in Atwood's work, as her awareness of academic debate often finds reflection in her writing, albeit in her own terms (I do not think it entirely coincidental, for example, that in Foucaultian times archaeology is such a prominent symbol in *Wilderness Tips*). I should like to sketch, however, the proximity between some of the arguments and metaphors used by Hassan and Atwood.

'The self may rest on no ontological rock', Hassan declares, 'yet as a functional concept, as a historical construct, as a habit of existence, above all, as an experienced or existential reality, it serves us all even as we deny it theoretically. The self represents something to us, even when we select some aspect of it to act.' His essay reviews the theories (philosophical, psychological, political) which in the twentieth century have contributed to defining the self as a fictional construct; but despite these, Hassan maintains the survival of the subject, argues for the metaphors of 'accident, invention, pattern, process, or mutation' to describe it, and answers French deconstructionists and Hillis Miller's nihilism by exposing the 'intellectualistic fallacy ... that logic invariably grounds practice'.[9] Refusing the equation of self or identity with unity or coherence, he claims that current theories have only served to change our perception of the subject, but not to deny its existence.

There is much in these descriptions which is immediately relevant to Atwood's writing, and which ties in with feminist debates. Experienced reality, revalued by some feminisms, is pervasive in Atwood's stories, and her work has a strong 'realistic' component blended in with its theoretical complexity: it is not surprising, then, that the duality experience/abstract representation should be present in her conception of the subject. As to the metaphors of *accident, invention, pattern, process* and *mutation*, they all apply, as we have seen, to the treatment of fictional selves by the author, while the fallacies of logic are also exposed in her work, notably in the direct reference in 'The Bog Man' (*WT*, p. 98).

Against deconstructive theories of the subject, Hassan poses those of psychologists of identity, and specifically those of Norman Holland and Sharon R. Kaufman.[10] Holland "limns a model of human identity composed of theme and variations, much like a sonata, much like any work of art. The self maintains an intense, if unnamed awareness of itself through great changes, from infancy to death'.[11] The parallel with Atwood's' concept of an author's creation, quoted at the beginning of this essay, speaks for itself, and allows for an extension of her metaphor to her conception of the subject.

An equally interesting coincidence is found in the metaphor used to describe Kaufman's definition of the 'ageless self'. Having quoted her as saying that 'I have found that in the expression of the ageless self, individuals not only symbolically preserve and integrate meaningful components of their past, but they also use these symbols as frameworks for understanding and being in the present',[12] Hassan defends this apparently 'naïve' insight as containing the crucial concept of an 'inhabited self', an expression with strong resonances of Atwood's metaphor of a 'habitable interior' in 'Polarities'. This 'habitable interior' (quoted from Margaret Avison) is the comfortable identity, the reconciled self that neither Louise nor Morrison have achieved.

Atwood's multiple, ever-expanding and contextualised subject is an example of Hassan's 'survivor self' (434), a self redefined by contemporary theory, rather than reduced to a textual fiction. Writing in the same issue of *Contemporary Literature* which features Hassan's essay, Eugene Goodheart reinforces Hassan's approach by insisting that the experiential self is a natural fact, without which 'we would go crazy, suffering a radical sense of fragmentation, discontinuity and emptiness',[14] and that the coherent or repressed selves are not necessarily the true selves. The contrast between texts such as 'Polarities' and 'Giving Birth' seems to exemplify this: in the first, Louise, lacking a sense of self, suffers tragic fragmentation and final madness; 'Giving Birth', however, shows a subject indeed redefined by contemporary theory, who survives, emerging from the experience of the multiple, mutating selves as a solid entity, capable of finding meaning in her past and awaiting a future. The narrating subject perceives herself in wider terms than language: the repressed self, the transforming power of events, her representation in language, are all integrated into the final result, a new, presumably temporary, but *solid*, self. The subject becomes language, inasmuch as words are the raw material of narration, and, again, in the metaphor which language constitutes for representing the self (Jeanie becomes drifted over with new words; in pain, both *she* and language disappear). But language, like the tar sands, is 'only a metaphor' in the stories, a metaphor of the self.

The fallacy of the textual self as superseding the experiential self is described by Goodheart in the conclusion to his essay in the following terms: 'The danger posed by writing is the temptation it offers to life to imitate writing – that is, to imitate the adventurous incoherence of the self that is possible only in writing.'[15] The statement compares with Morrison's analysis of Louise's madness: 'she's taken as real what the rest of us pretend is only metaphorical' (p. 69). The moral joins other warnings pointed out earlier, warnings against excessive theorising of events, against reducing people to metaphors, or trapping subjects in language.

The 'survivor self', the pragmatic vision, is then, though not without struggle, the protagonist of Atwood's work, whether as presence or as suggested option. Equally surviving, after its own struggle, is the 'common sense' communicative experience of language. From tentative explorations into the exclusion of women from language (whether viewed from structuralist-deterministic positions, or as Lacanian exclusion from the symbolic), there is a movement towards a pragmatic analysis of social facts (Ronnette, Loulou) and an acceptance of imperfect communication through language, a language which can and must be transformed; the embryo of this attitude is contained in the early statement of intention in 'Giving Birth': 'we will go ahead as if there were no problem about language'.

Margaret Atwood's combination of pragmatic and textual elements, of which the treatment of the subject is an example, undoubtedly constitutes one of the keys to her success for readers and is largely responsible for the controversy over her ascription to postmodernism, within whose boundaries certain practices seem to situate her. Poststructuralist notions and deconstruction have, like other theoretical concepts, influenced Atwood's writing; but from the evidence of her stories, they seem to constitute a tool for more inclusive analysis or representation, rather than a view of the world. From Atwood's careful process of redefinition, both language and the subject emerge affirmed.

Notes

1. Sherrill E. Grace, 'Articulating the "Space Between": Atwood's Untold Stories and Fresh Beginnings', in *Margaret Atwood: Language, Text and System* (Vancouver: University of British Columbia Press, 1983) pp. 1–16.
2. All references in the text are to the British editions, except in the stories 'The War in the Bathroom' and 'Rape Fantasies' (*Dancing Girls and Other Stories* (Toronto: McClelland & Stewart, 1977)); *Dancing Girls* (London: Virago, 1984); *Bluebeard's Egg* (London: Jonathan Cape, 1987); *Wilderness Tips* (London: Bloomsbury, 1991). The following abbreviations will be used in the text: *DG*, *BE* and *WT*.
3. Margaret Atwood, 'Valgardsonland', *Essays on Canadian Writing*, vol. 16 (Fall-Winter 1979–80) p. 188. Grace quotes this as support for her own argument, 'Articulating the "Space Between" '.
4. *Dancing Girls* has a slightly different selection in the Canadian and British editions; the former includes 'The War in the Bathroom' and 'Rape Fantasies', excluded in Britain, while the latter includes 'Betty' and 'The Sin Eater', which were to appear in Canada in the later collection, *Bluebeard's Egg*. For purposes of our generalisations, we shall treat all four stories as part of the first volume, though keeping in mind that 'Betty' and 'The Sin Eater' lie between the two books, and can be seen as transitional.
5. I. Carrera Suarez, 'Metalinguistic Features in Short Fiction, by Lessing and Atwood: From Sign and Subversion to Symbol and Deconstruction', in J. Bardolph (ed.), *Short Fiction in the New Literatures in English* (Nice: Faculté des Lettres, 1988) pp. 159–64.
6. Deborah Cameron, *Feminism and Linguistics* (London: Macmillan, 1985).
7. Barbara Godard, 'My (m)Other, My Self: Strategies for Subversion in Atwood and Herbert', *Essays on Canadian Writing*, vol. 26 (1983) pp. 13–44. Godard discusses the importance of Chodorow's theory of female identity with relation to Atwood's novels (Nancy Chodorow, *The Reproduction of Mothering* (Berkeley, Cal.: University of California Press, 1978).
8. Ihab Hassan, 'Quest for the Subject: the Self in Literature', *Contemporary Literature*, vol. 29(3) (1988) pp. 420–37.
9. Ibid., pp. 422, 425, 429.
10. Norman Holland, *The I* (New Haven, Conn.: Yale University Press, 1985); Sharon R. Kaufman, *The Ageless Self: Sources of Meaning in Late Life* (Madison, Wis.: University of Wisconsin Press, 1986).
11. Holland, *The I*, p. 432.
12. Kaufman, *Ageless Self*, p. 433.
13. Hassan, 'Quest for a Subject', p. 434.
14. Eugene Goodheart, 'Writing and the Unmaking of the Self', *Contemporary Literature*, vol. 29(3) (1988) pp. 438–53.
15. Ibid., p. 453.

13

Interpreting and Misinterpreting 'Bluebeard's Egg': A Cautionary Tale

W. J. KEITH

This chapter takes its origin from a specific incident. Some months ago I was asked in the course of my academic duties to read an unpublished essay that offered a strictly feminist reading of four short stories by Margaret Atwood. I was especially interested in the treatment of 'Bluebeard's Egg' because the interpretation turned out to be radically different from what I had remembered of the story; on checking the text I discovered that the reading was based on highly selective evidence and could not be reconciled with a careful response to the subtleties of the narrative. Such an experience is not, in itself, uncommon, but the particular example seems to me important as a peculiarly contemporary phenomenon. This circumstance provides an unusually clear instance of what can happen if one begins from a theoretical position and imposes it upon a work of art to which it is not suited. The example therefore deserves more detailed attention. I shall begin with a brief summary of the essay's argument and an explanation of why it seemed to me inadequate. I shall then go on to offer what I hope will be a more satisfactory response to the challenge of the text.

The paper began by asserting that Atwood's was a subversive art, concerned with the overturning of the accepted myths of a 'patriarchal' society. In such a society, the writer continued, women are inevitably alienated. The purpose of the essay was to show how

Atwood documented this alienation in the female protagonists of 'Bluebeard's Egg' and three other stories. The argument is , of course, to all intents and purposes circular: the result is implicit in (even guaranteed by) the terms of the original – I believe, questionable – assertion. In introductory remarks, much was made of the psychological patterns said to distinguish female from male. The underworld, I read, is an emotional world associated with the feminine but is feared and misunderstood by men, and so remains for the most part a feminine domain. Fair enough. I would not pick any quarrel with that formulation. A difficulty came, however, a few pages later when details of the opening of the story were being examined.

'Bluebeard's Egg' begins with Sally, the protagonist, looking out of her kitchen window at the garden lot that 'sweeps downwards, into the ravine; it's a wilderness there (*Bluebeard's Egg*, p. 133).[1] She wanted 'to have a kind of terrace . . . , but Edward [her husband] says he likes it the way it is' (p. 133). Sally, however, is disturbed by drunks who, she claims, live in the ravine and occasionally wander over the broken-down defence 'to emerge squinting like moles into the light of Sally's well-kept back lawn' (p. 133). The critic referred to this passage, but drew attention only to the suggestion of male dominance ('Edward says he likes it the way it is'). No mention was made of the surely significant fact that, in this case, it is the woman who fears the ravine and that the supposedly feminine domain is specifically described as inhabited by men. (Ravines, it should be noted, are used in this virtually archetypal sense throughout Atwood's fictional writing, from *The Edible Woman* through *Lady Oracle* to *Cat's Eye*, and this symbolism is clearly insisted upon here as the drunks 'emerge . . . into the light'. Oddly enough, two pages later, the critic went on to quote Frank Davey[2] on the language of the male formal garden, without apparently noticing that in 'Bluebeard's Egg', we are concerned with a *female* formal garden (Sally's 'terrace', 'well-kept backlawn'). What we must surely deduce from all this is that Atwood does *not* work in terms of these simple dichotomies. 'Bluebeard's Egg' would seem to challenge rather than to uphold the kind of interpretation that the commentator tried to force upon it. One might even go so far as to suggest that, major writer as she is, Atwood uses her subversive art to deconstruct the inadequate clichés of certain kinds of feminist theory.

A similar instance occurred a few pages further on. Here the critic made the acceptable, indeed perceptive, observation that in this story Atwood often encloses her characters' true feelings in parentheses. Several instances of such parentheses were quoted, all designed to back up the paper's feminist thesis. Again, fair enough. But here is an example, that wasn't quoted:

> Why did she choose [Ed] (or, to be precise, as she tries to be with herself and sometimes is even out loud, *hunt him down*), when it's clear to everyone she had other options?   (*BE*, p. 135; Atwood's emphasis)

The implications of this passage are interesting. The title (and, so far, only the title) has alerted us to read Sally's situation in terms of the original Bluebeard story, which is, of course, a 'patriarchal' fairy tale with a vengeance. Yet there is surely something odd about a potential Bluebeard story in which the woman hunts down the wizard instead of vice versa! The critic presumably ignored this example of parenthetical usage because it didn't fit the essay's thesis; I would argue, however, that it is important for the very reason that it undercuts the thesis. Atwood is indeed being 'subversive', but not in the way the critic thought; on the contrary, Atwood is careful to *balance* the insight derived from these parenthetical passages, to *complicate* the meaning of her story so that it cannot be read as a simple tract, feminist or otherwise.

I have written enough, I think, to cast doubt on the adequacy of the interpretation of 'Bluebeard's Egg' that was proposed. Let me now offer an alternative reading, which will concentrate on the actual use of the traditional fairy tale within Atwood's story (a central topic about which the critic had virtually nothing to say). As I have already indicated, the title provides an initial clue, though Bluebeard is not otherwise mentioned until two-thirds of the way through the narrative. Careful readers, however, will be put on their guard by the title, and will begin to draw certain conclusions. Within a few paragraphs a very different 'fairy tale' reference occurs. Ed, we are told, is 'a child of luck, a third son who ... manages to make it through the forest with all its witches and traps and pitfalls and end up with the princess, who is Sally, of course' (pp. 134–5). On the other hand, a reference soon follows to 'Ed's two previous wives' (p. 136) that neatly fits the Bluebeard story. Ed, however, seems an unlikely candidate for a modern Bluebeard. He is presented as stupid, easy-going, apparently considerate, a bit pompous and (when his profession as 'heart man'

(p. 139) is concerned) earnestly serious. At the opening of the story there is no evidence that he is a woman-chaser; on the contrary, women chase him – they 'corner him on sofas, trap him in bay-windows at cocktail parties' (p. 139). If he has a secret room, it is not in their house but in the hospital, the room where a new X-ray facility is located; moreover, Sally pursuades him with little difficulty to take her into it – there is nothing forbidden about it.

It is possible, none the less, to entertain some doubts about Ed. Can he really be as stupid as Sally paints him? Indeed, Sally herself sometimes 'sees his stupidity as wilfulness, a stubborn determination to shut things out. His obtuseness is a wall, within which he can go about his business' (p. 135). He professes not to know 'what happened with [his earlier] marriages, what went wrong' (p. 136), which causes Sally to wonder – in a reference which again recalls fairy tale – whether 'she isn't the true bride after all, but the false one' (p. 136). And the X-ray room, however different from the traditional forbidden chamber in the 'house in the forest' (p. 157), still conceals a hint of Bluebeard: '[I]t was clearly a dangerous place. It was like a massage parlour, only for women. Put a batch of women in there with Ed and they would never want to come out' (p. 147).

Apart from the title, as I have said, any specific reference to Bluebeard is delayed until comparatively late. Eventually we learn that Sally has been taking a night-course entitled 'Forms of Narrative Fiction' (p. 154). After exploring 'The Epic' by reading *'The Odyssey* (selected passages, in translation, with a plot summary of the rest)' (p.154) – Atwood's subversive art, again – and poking around in Joyce's *Ulysses* in order to suggest Toronto equivalents for the Dublin locales, they go on to discuss 'The Ballad' and are now studying 'Folk Tales and the Oral Tradition' (p. 155). The instructor introduces them to orally transmitted stories and sets them an exercise in which, after listening to a story, they must 'write a five-page transposition, set in the present and cast in the realistic mode' (p. 156). The tale chosen (Atwood reproduces the Grimm version in her text) is the story of Bluebeard. Above all, they are not allowed to use the Universal Narrator, which they have already exploited: 'This time they had to choose a point of view' (p. 156).

That last sentence is, I would submit, the crucial statement in Atwood's story, one that causes us to reconsider all that we have been told in the story so far. If point of view is central to Sally's assignment, it is also central to 'Bluebeard's Egg'. We now realise, if we hadn't noticed before, that Atwood is employing limited third-person narration. An authorial voice is invoked, but everything is seen from Sally's viewpoint and consciousness. Moreover, it is now clear that everything we have so far been told has come from the perspective of a Sally who has, throughout the action of the story, had this point-of-view assignment on her mind. (We learn a little later that she first received the assignment 'a full two weeks ago' (p. 158).) If we have speculated about the application of the Bluebeard story to Ed, it may be only because Sally is herself superimposing the story upon the pattern of Ed's life. This is a variant of the characteristic satiric trap that Atwood introduces into so many of her fictions. The whole story, we now see, is about 'point of view'. Once we have assimilated the full implications of this insight, we have to reconsider and reassess all that we have been told.

If we return to the opening of the story with Sally's possible bias in mind, the identification of Ed as Bluebeard begins to look decidedly doubtful. This is our first sight of him: 'He's puttering around the rock garden now; some of the rocks stick out too far and are in danger of grazing the side of Sally's Peugeot, on its way to the garage, and he's moving them around' (p. 134). In other words, he is considerately making things easier for his wife. (The description of the car 'on its way to the garage', as if self-propelled, is a brilliant stroke. It can be interpreted either as Ed's polite refusal to acknowledge Sally's poor driving or Sally's own reluctance to admit this fact.) A few lines earlier, when she has been trying to imagine Ed at high school, she observed: 'Girls would have had crushes on him, he would have been unconscious of it; things like that don't change' (pp. 133–4). Hardly a Bluebeard characteristic! The implication, surely, is that Sally's attempt to interpret him as Bluebeard conflicts hopelessly with the evidence.

A little later in our rereading, we shall be struck by the extent to which Sally sees Ed and her relationship with him in specifically literary terms. In the third paragraph, she associates him with A. A. Milne's Winnie the Pooh: '*My darling Edward*, she thinks. *Edward Bear, of little brain. How I love you*' (p. 134). Soon afterwards, she switches to detective fiction:

she was spoiled when young by reading too many Agatha Christie murder mysteries, of the kind in which the clever and

witty heroine passes over the equally clever and witty first-lead
male, who's helped solve the crime, in order to marry the second-
lead male, the stupid one, the one who would have been arrested
and condemned and executed if it hadn't been for her cleverness.
Maybe this is how she sees Ed .... (p. 135)

Maybe. But if so, this is again a very different Ed from the one who
is offered as a stand-in for Bluebeard – not to mention the
interesting association of Ed with a character who is wrongly
suspected of a crime. It may also be significant that the first
reference to 'Ed's two previous wives' (p. 136), with its Bluebeard
implications, occurs within a few lines of the passage just quoted,
as if to point up an incongruity.

A children's book, a murder mystery, and now a fairy tale. Sally
responds more fully to these than to the abridged and translated
Odyssey or the brief dip into *Ulysses*. However, these two classic
texts may now set up some interesting though complicating
reverberations. Homer's hero is a womaniser who eventually
returns to an archetypally faithful wife; in Joyce, however,
positions are reversed – not only is Molly Bloom unfaithful to
Leopold, but Leopold knows it. 'Bluebeard's Egg' is clearly a
complex, postmodernist narrative that both flaunts its artifice and
depends upon an elaborate intertextuality.

It is evident that 'Bluebeard's Egg' has to be read very warily
indeed, and at this point it may be worthwhile considering the
section about Sally's job – a section that doesn't immediately further
the basic plot. Of her current job we read: 'Luckily Ed has no
objection; he doesn't have much of an objection to anything she does'
(p.140). In other words, he is *not* a male chauvinist who interferes
with his wife's freedom of action. We are presumably intended to
regard this as the opposite of Bluebeard's giving his wives orders as
to what they must and must not do. The job in question, second-in-
command to the incompetent male editor of a business magazine
who does none of the work but receives all the official credit, enables
Atwood to make fun of various business attitudes. But even these
details are double-edged. Sally's boss was a failure in management
but 'couldn't be fired because his wife was related to the chairman
of the board' (p. 141). This is (one must assume, deliberately)
ambiguous: perhaps the chairman is protecting one of his own sex;
but it is equally possible that the editor's wife is exerting indirect but
effective female pressure on her male relative. Two paragraphs later,

Atwood makes reference to a perennial 'sexist' controversy: do a
female employee's duties include making coffee for her male boss?
Atwood's detail is incisive: 'she stops short of behaving like a
secretary: she doesn't bring him coffee. They both have a secretary
who does that anyway' (p. 142). The undermining force of that last
sentence contains an almost Swiftian intensity. Clearly, Atwood
cannot be easily pigeonholed in any clear-cut feminist category.

We need to be fully aware of all these complexities of
interpretation before we approach the tricky final pages of the
story. The immediate emphasis, once the Bluebeard story has been
told, is upon Sally's efforts to produce 'her present-day realistic
version' (p. 158). And her first response is to reject precisely those
versions which, as careful readers, we have been testing: 'The great
temptation is to cast herself in the role of the cunning heroine, but
again it's too predictable. And Ed certainly isn't the wizard; he's
nowhere near sinister enough' (p. 158). But then she decides that
'the intriguing thing about the story, the thing she should fasten
on, is the egg', and from there it's a short step first to 'the brilliant
idea of writing the story from the point of view of the egg' and then
to the parenthetical realisation: '(Ed isn't the Bluebeard: Ed is the
egg)' (p. 159). Clever; perhaps too clever – on Sally's part, not
Atwood's. In the fairy tale 'the wizard met his come-uppance'
(p. 158); in 'Bluebeard's Egg' it appears to be Sally herself. At her
party, imaginative as ever, she decides that one of the guests,
Walter Morly, is paying far too much attention to her friend
Marylynn for Sally's comfort. She therefore directs her to show Ed
the antique she has just bought. Marylynn is quick to read her
motive: ' "Don't worry," she says, "I won't rape Dr Morly" '
(p. 162). But soon afterwards Sally sees Marylynn and Ed together
and convinces herself that Ed had his hand on Marylynn's thigh.

Is Ed a candidate for the role of Bluebeard after all? The feminist
critic assumed this, but Atwood is not so clear-cut. A few minutes
later, Sally begins to doubt the evidence of her own senses: 'Now
she isn't sure whether she really saw what she thought she saw'
(p. 164). As in *Lady Oracle*, the world of creative fantasy and that of
real life have become thoroughly snagged. Ed may be guilty, but if
we think back we shall remember how, in the past, Sally has
continually fantasised about Ed and other women. I have already
shown how she imagines girls having crushes on him when he was
a schoolboy, and have commented on her readiness to notice
women cornering him on sofas. Earlier in the day she has teased

him about women' "hiding in the forsythia" ' (p. 148), though she is aware that 'she's made them up' (p. 149). The possibilities of interpretation are now manifold. Perhaps he has been having an affair with Marylynn all along; perhaps Sally is imagining it all; perhaps, with her perpetual teasing, she has actually put the idea into his head; perhaps she is projecting the Bluebeard story on to a very different reality without being aware of it. Later, in the kitchen, Ed makes a general reference to the cleaning-woman as if he doesn't remember her name. Sally, now suspicious, is bothered by this in a way she had never been before, yet it could well be a sign that he doesn't notice – is not interested in – other women. Yet as soon as she begins to interpret, to imagine other versions and other points of view, all seems ambiguous.

And inevitably the story itself ends on a note of ambiguity. After the party, Ed goes to bed while Sally roams the house like a ghostly visitant. When she eventually goes upstairs, we are told that Ed 'is breathing deeply as if asleep. *As if*' (p. 165; Atwood's emphasis). The critic took this at face value, assuming that Ed, having transferred his attention to Marylynn, is feigning sleep in order to avoid his marital obligations, but the italicised phrase draws attention to the ambiguity of the point of view. Once Sally doubts, anything can become 'as if'. We are trapped with her in her limited perspective. The story ends with Sally in a state between sleep and waking, imagining first her own heart in black and white, as on Ed's X-ray screen, and then the egg, pulsing, alive and in colour. The two images are either opposite or complementary. Her heart is 'cold and white and inert' – as hearts should not be; the egg, previously associated with Ed, is 'glowing softly as though there's something red and hot inside it. It's almost pulsing' (p. 166). Each manifests the basic qualities of the other.

The story ends enigmatically on a question – 'what will come out of it?' (p. 166) – but we have already been informed that an egg is a symbol with numerous possible meanings. It can be 'a fertility symbol, or a necessary object in African spells, or something the world hatched out of' (p. 159). Or, in this story, it may be 'a symbol of virginity' (p. 159). And if 'Ed is the egg', what then? If the story closes on a puzzling vision of the egg, this is because Sally has chosen to interpret the story from the egg's point of view and finds that the possibilities are endless. Atwood's story is called 'Bluebeard's Egg' and *is* Bluebeard's egg – an object with a multiplicity of possible interpretations.

The above reading lays no claims to comprehensiveness. I have inevitably stressed some aspects of the story and passed over others. But I would submit that it is reasonably faithful to the tone that Atwood establishes and the general narrative movement of the story. In emphasising the centrality of interpretation rather than advocating *one* interpretation, it at least avoids a blinkered narrowness. Others may well draw attention to further subtleties and refinements, but I see no reason why my reading should not be regarded as an acceptable foundation for further literary-critical discussion.

I must return now, however, to the writer of the unpublished essay. The difference between my reading and hers is that mine arises out of what the story actually says while hers forced the story into a preconceived and distorting pattern. What happened, I suspect, is that, having accepted the ideological attitudes of feminist criticism, the critic jumped to the unjustified conclusion that, because Atwood is a writer interested in feminist issues, she *must* accept this viewpoint and that, as a result, her stories *must* be compatible with the theory. The critic therefore searched 'Bluebeard's Egg' for any evidence that seemed to fit the theoretical imperative and failed to notice the numerous details that conflicted with it.

I write all this not just to cast doubt on one extreme application of feminist theory but to register a warning against excessive reliance on *any* theory. Art, to put the matter bluntly, is larger than theory. If the two conflict, then it is the theory that must be adapted or discarded. The critic came to grief because she had become bemused by theory and assigned to it an authority that it could not sustain. There is, when we come to think of it, something absurd in supposing that a work of art of any complexity can be adequately discussed by attempting to demonstrate that it conforms to some general and independent principle. Unfortunately, of course, it is much more difficult to formulate the unique qualities of an individual work than to force it into a pre-existent mould. A full reading requires response to tone, nuance and the numerous stylistic effects that, however neglected in some quarters, remain the stuff of literature.

This, then, is a cautionary tale. I have written it, not to show up the errors of an inexperienced commentator, but rather to take a convenient opportunity to draw attention to the dangers that beset all literary critics. We need to approach literature not with made-to-measure theory but with a flexible, verbally sensitive critical practice that attempts, tentatively, humbly, sometimes painfully, to develop a tradition of close and accurate reading. Such a reading should highlight literary complexities instead of obscuring them. Above all, we must encourage our students – and ourselves – to recognise what is there on the page rather than to read simpler and perhaps inappropriate notions into works that have so much more to offer. I must end, however, with a sincere acknowledgment. The writer of the unpublished essay persuaded me that 'Bluebeard's Egg' is a supremely effective work of art by goading me into challenging her reading. This is an important way in which the discipline of criticism proceeds. Her essay provoked me into a deeper realisation of the complexity and artistry of Atwood's story – and for that I am grateful.

Notes

1. All references to *Bluebeard's Egg* are to the first edition (Toronto: McCelland and Stewart, 1983).
2. Frank Davey, *Margaret Atwood: A Feminist Poetics* (Vancouver: Talon Books, 1984).

Index